VOGUE
HISTORY OF 20TH CENTURY
FASHION

JANE MULVAGH

WITH A FOREWORD BY
VALERIE D. MENDES

VIKING

For my parents

VIKING

Published by the Penguin Group
27 Wrights Lane, London W8 5TZ, England
Viking Penguin Inc., 40 West 23rd Street, New York, New York 10010, USA
Penguin Books Australia Ltd, Ringwood, Victoria, Australia
Penguin Books Canada Ltd, 2801 John Street, Markham, Ontario, Canada L3R 1B4
Penguin Books (NZ) Ltd, 182–190 Wairau Road, Auckland 10, New Zealand

Penguin Books Ltd, Registered Offices: Harmondsworth, Middlesex, England

First published 1988
1 3 5 7 9 10 8 6 4 2

Designed by Paul Bowden

Filmset in Vogue Didot and Bodoni Roman

Printed in Great Britain by Butler & Tanner Ltd
Frome and London

A CIP catalogue record for this book is available from the British Library

Library of Congress Catalog Card Number: 88–50528

ISBN 0–670–80172–0

CONTENTS

FOREWORD

Today, perhaps as never before, there is a widespread interest not only in current fashions but also in the styles of the near past. Clothes of our own century retain a peculiar mystique and exert an inevitable fascination, nurtured by recent publications and exhibitions as well as by accurately dressed period films, television series and histories of the art of fashionable dress. Assembled here is an incomparable array of photographs and illustrations from *Vogue*, which since its inception has been of central importance to the world of fashion as both a recorder and an innovator. Consulting early issues of *Vogue* is a rewarding experience; turning the glossy pages printed with images indicating the new directions in which fashion is moving gives particular satisfaction. The much thumbed leaves reveal that innumerable readers consult the magazine for reliable and detailed information about stylish clothes, their makers and their owners. Historians of twentieth-century fashionable dress – indeed, recorders of all aspects of modes and manners – find *Vogue* essential to their work. It is rare to see a modern text exploring that maddening phenomenon – fashion – which does not borrow quotations, references or illustrations from this rich fund, which minutely details the vicissitudes of fashion over a long and fluctuating period.

As well as being an invaluable factual source for students of fashion history, *Vogue* is equally important to budding fashion designers. If they reject the slavish copying that has led to certain spiritless 'retro' movements, they will discover that this volume contains visual suggestions that they could use as starting-points for their own creations.

Museum curators responsible for collections of twentieth-century dress find that *Vogue* is an indispensable ally. Clothes of obvious distinction but lacking labels or documentation are frequently acquired for posterity and have to be identified. 'Is it in *Vogue*?' is one of the first questions to be asked and, if it is, the attribution problem is speedily resolved. In museum collections most outfits of the not so distant past lack their original accessories. For display purposes these are vital to create the correct 'total look'. Fortunately *Vogue*, with its long history of accurate fashion reportage in the form of lively, up-to-the-minute copy, illustrations and photographs, depicts and describes the elegant woman from head to toe, providing a complete guide that can be followed in selecting the right finishing touches.

Jane Mulvagh has meticulously combed through all editions of *Vogue*, painstakingly selecting images to give a balanced view of national stylistic characteristics in addition to an overall picture of fashion's internationalism. The detailed year-by-year surveys chart tiny seasonal changes alongside revolutionary breakthroughs. Trend-setting developments, which became instant headline news, are featured in company with a multitude of other less well-known creations that are essential to complete the *Vogue* fashion story. Compelling photographs of accessories and looks sum up an era, a year or just a moment – long, slender umbrellas of the Fifties, silver space-age boots of 1966 and mud-plastered hair of 1983. This wide-ranging compendium will save many hours of research by serving as an instant and reliable reference, enabling readers to grasp quickly the general flavour of a period or to obtain facts about the materials and construction of a particular ensemble. Refreshingly, the accompanying text sometimes challenges long-held beliefs, and occasionally the author steps out of her *Vogue* shoes and draws attention to the rare moments when the magazine has failed to spot the emergence of a new talent or movement. Interviews with countless famous designers throw new light on their own work and the way in which they perceive their art. Emphasis is upon the twentieth-century evolution of fashionable clothes, but along the way the curious will learn much about the designers, craftspeople, models, photographers, illustrators, journalists and fashion pundits who inhabit and motivate this rich and complex world.

In 1909 Condé Nast bought a modest American society magazine, which he promptly revamped to lay the foundations for the valuable record of international fashionable dress and life that *Vogue* rapidly became. By 1910 it had fresh style, vitality and direction – powerful forces that, though adapted to suit the ever-changing times, have never been allowed to desert the magazine. In addition to this publishing milestone, 1909 also marked the sartorial watershed when truly modern elements became discernible in women's dress. Trailing gowns, rigidly corseted curves and associated froth of the early 1900s were banished in favour of clothes that appeared more practical. Ironically, many suffragettes advanced the cause of women while they dressed in elegant costumes that made few concessions to comfort and movement, though in Paris Paul Poiret loudly championed the freer, vertical, high-waisted look, claiming to have released women from the bondage of their corsets. Far-reaching changes had begun: what better time to start the *Vogue History of 20th Century Fashion?*

by Valerie D. Mendes
Curator of The Collection of Dress,
Victoria and Albert Museum, London

1909-1918

The skirt was longer than ever, and within her narrow bell of drapery woman still glided footless, as though on castors. The breasts, it was true, had been pushed up a bit, the redundant posterior pulled in. But the general shape of the clothed body was still strangely improbable. A crab shelled in whalebone. And this huge plumed hat of 1911 was simply a French funeral of the first class. How could any man in his senses have been attracted by so profoundly anti-aphrodisiac an appearance? And yet ... at the sight of that feathered crab on wheels, his heart had beaten faster.

Aldous Huxley, *Eyeless in Gaza*

Portrait of a fashionably dressed Edwardian woman, 'that feathered crab on wheels', by François Flameng.

What one Vogue *artist thought of the 1909 mode.*

The Edwardians in *Vogue*, the leisured élite, were dressed in clothes that hampered movement and were decorative rather than functional. Their lives were almost exclusively domestic, and social life was private, time-consuming and precisely ordered, in terms of both etiquette and dress. Having little else to do, women were preoccupied with the minutiae of clothing and its upkeep. The ability to be fashionable was a sign of social status; clothes were consequently given the utmost consideration and investment.

The stately and curvaceous figure was the delight of the Edwardians; youthful slenderness was not considered erotic until after the First World War. Artifice and conspicuous consumption characterized the mode. 'Fantastic, elaborate, shaped as nature never made her, the fashionable Edwardian lady is infinitely beguiling in the aplomb and serenity with which she carries off the daunting elaboration of her toilette', wrote Elizabeth Ewing in her *History of Twentieth-century Fashion* (1974). Marital status determined dress. Coming out at eighteen, a young woman was simply dressed in virginal white; at a society dance she would wear a modest family ring and string of pearls. Within a couple of years she was expected to rise to the rank of wife, and only then would she wear prominent jewels and be allowed the privilege of colour in her dress.

The Edwardian woman consequently aspired to maturity, to a full shape, and was bolstered and encased in many layers, underpinned by an S-shape corset, which was introduced in 1900. Sonia Keppel, Edward VII's illegitimate daughter, recalls the sight of her nanny dressing every morning;

once she had laced herself tightly into her stays, 'there followed the camouflage of her petticoat, concealing the pulling on of her knickers; more whalebone, more starch, clamping down a vast bosom; the fastening of sharp buckles and a brooch, like the riveting of armour. With each controlling layer the pink folds were packed back into their shell until only I, as an eyewitness, knew of the vulnerability beneath her crustaceous facade.' Jean Cocteau commented with exasperation on the effect: 'To undress one of these ladies was obviously a complicated enterprise that had to be planned well in advance, like moving a house.'

The actress Cécile Sorel.

The ritual of dress was impossible without a large and highly trained staff of servants to launder and sew the clothes, to dress their mistresses and do their hair, which was piled up over 'rats', or pads that added body to a coiffure. A sartorial chameleon, the Edwardian lady would change her appearance five or more times a day, wearing a boudoir gown while taking breakfast, a tailored suit for shopping, a serge skirt and blouse if remaining at home, a dress for luncheon and a more formal gown or suit in the afternoon for receiving a guest or calling for tea. During the early evening she wore a tea gown; then for dinner she changed again into formal evening wear – a gown invariably decorated with elaborate lace fichus and beadwork, worn with a headdress, fan, lavish jewellery and gloves. Special outfits were needed if a woman wished to participate in sporting events, go motoring, or attend specific social occasions such as weddings, the races or a function at court.

Paris was visited twice a year to order the season's wardrobe. The palatial couture houses were set in the most exclusive area of the city: the magnificent Place Vendôme and along the Rue de la Paix, close to César Ritz's famous hotel. Couturiers provided their clients with a constant personal service, for which they were handsomely paid. Any customer was encouraged, be she music-hall star, aristocrat, actress or courtesan, as long as she honoured her bills. The *demi-mondaines* and actresses tended to wear the most creative expressions of the mode, for, unhampered by conservative court ethics or notions of refinement, they dared to parade the latest extravagances. The drawing-room dramas of the Paris theatre mirrored society and were looked to for fashion guidance, so actresses collaborated with couturiers to manipulate the mode. Celebrities like Réjane, Cécile Sorel and Eleonora Duse dressed at the great Paris houses of Paquin, Worth, Redfern and Doucet.

A client would be greeted on the grand steps of the couture house by her personal *vendeuse* or the couturier himself, depending on her status. Attended by liveried doormen she was escorted up to one of the high-ceilinged reception rooms on the first floor, which were typically adorned with frescos, elaborate mouldings and gilt mirrors, and furnished with spindly gold chairs and brocade sofas. Glass show-cases displayed the latest trinkets for her amusement. The *vendeuse*, appointed to her client by the couturier or his right-hand woman, the *directrice*, guided the customer through the season's collection, modelled on house mannequins. The chief fitter would then be called upon to drape and pin the chosen materials on the client and at least three fittings would follow. The gown was made up by the *première main qualifiée* assisted by the *deuxième main qualifiée* and a young *arpette* – as a junior apprentice, the lowest rank in a house, she carried lengths of material and learnt to sew hems and linings.

The official body of the French couture industry was (and still is) the Chambre Syndicale de la Couture Parisienne, originally founded in 1868 as a craftsmen's guild. Membership required adherence to stringent rules,

Smart fashions at the Chantilly races, including the characteristic large, festooned hats, 1909.

models had to be made up in a house's own workrooms and created exclusively for that establishment by full-time staff. Designs could be bought in from freelance designers but they had to be on the house's permanent payroll. (These regulations were gradually relaxed as time passed.) A similar organization, the Chambre Syndicale des Paruriers, grouped the manufacturers of accessories such as belts, buttons, hats, umbrellas and shoe ornaments.

The creations of the couture industry were 'trade secrets', hence couturiers co-operated, for mutual protection, in organizing 'collections' or 'open days' to display their work (established in 1896). These August and February dates were fixed and the general public was never admitted. Some firms specialized in selling copies from the great houses, for the rewards were high. In 1913 the Chambre Syndicale outlawed copying. Wary couturiers carefully watched their personnel to ensure that details of designs were not sold to smaller houses behind their back. If found guilty, the culprit and the buyers of the stolen information could be sentenced to a term of imprisonment for theft. However, this vigilance was difficult to maintain and offenders were only sporadically caught.

Efficient copying companies sprang up in America, largely as a result of the coverage of the Paris collections in trade papers and magazines such as *Vogue*. As a result, many couturiers, led by Poiret, wanted to stop sketches of their gowns appearing in the fashion magazines. In 1914 Condé Nast, Edna Woolman Chase (the editor of *Vogue*) and Philippe Ortiz (the magazine's European representative) arranged a meeting with Poiret and on 14 June Le Syndicat de Défense de la Grande Couture Française was formed. The association sought to 'bring to an end the counterfeiting of labels and the illicit use of their names, thereby protecting the American public and honest importers from the false representations made by unscrupulous merchants and manufacturers'. The couturiers could not prevent small dressmakers from making one-off copies of their designs, but they could stop labels being attached to mass-produced copies of their collections.

Worth and Paquin were considered the most exclusive couturiers, but Paul Poiret was the most influential new designer of the pre-First World

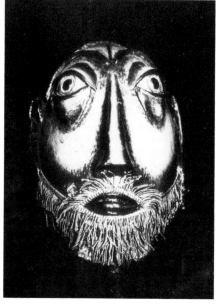

Mask of Paul Poiret by Marie Wassiliev.

The S-bend corset from The Royal Worcester Adjusto Corset Company, 1909.

War period. Born of humble origins in Les Halles in Paris, he showed a precocious interest in clothes; having sold some sketches, he was taken on by Doucet, who allowed him to create a cape for Réjane in the play *Zaza*. Réjane was so pleased with the cloak that Doucet allowed Poiret to make a dress for Sarah Bernhardt in 1900.

Under Réjane's patronage Poiret opened his own house in 1903, with only eight employees, in the non-couture district of Opéra. Poiret approached fashion like show business, seeking to shock society with theatrical styles. Having witnessed the capriciousness and domination of the great customers he was determined to master them: 'What I saw there made me convinced that one must dominate women, unless one wishes to be delivered to them, body and soul.'

Fashion rebels against the static; it is always in flux. The layers of lingerie, corsetry, lace, fichus and overskirts, and the glorification of mature womanhood that characterized Edwardian dress appeared ridiculous and dated to the young. A reaction was inevitable. 'All fashion ends in excess,' Poiret reminded the fashionable public. Edwardian dress ended as a tortured S-bend shape imposed on women's figures, which reached its extreme in 1906. Since the late nineteenth century the uncomfortable exaggeration of women's clothes had prompted many, from the Rational Dress Society to the Pre-Raphaelites and the medical profession, to criticize tightly laced corsets as being detrimental to health, freedom of movement and aesthetics. Few high-society women adopted rational dress – garments disparagingly referred to as 'robes' rather than dresses – for it was regarded as cranky and Bohemian. It took high fashion itself to promote a change, prompted not by ideals of liberty and health but simply by a desire to break the old moulds.

In 1908 Poiret revived the Empire line – its narrow, figure-revealing silhouette contrasting with the tortured S-bend shape. Poiret's wife, Denise, was unfashionably tall and slim. She prompted Poiret to favour this new unornamented straight line, which seemed almost barbaric in its simplicity. 'I like the plain gown . . . just touching the outline of the figure and throwing shadow and light over the moving form. In a *fourreau* of supple satin the plastic form of the modern woman is disclosed in its undulating sveltness,

Pre-Raphaelite dress depicted by Augustus John.

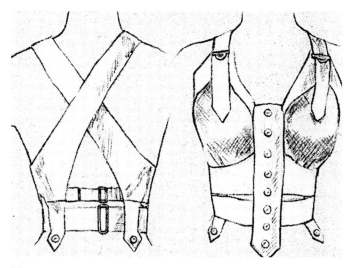

The supposedly healthier Reform Bodice, designed to fit over the corset, to compress the diaphragm by means of a double buckle and webbing adjustment at the back.

Denise Poiret in her husband's design, a grey velvet street suit, 1913.

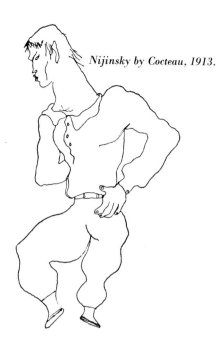

Nijinsky by Cocteau, 1913.

Raoul Dufy's black and white textile design.

Marcel Duchamp's Cubist painting, Nude Descending a Staircase.

in its indolent grace.' For most Edwardians the corset was a moral as well as a physical requirement. In 1903 Isadora Duncan, the American dancer, had outraged society by performing without a corset or stockings. It was considered indecent to reveal the natural and unrestrained lines of the body. Women were supposed to be decoratively gift-wrapped. Poiret reacted by offering simpler clothes. 'I waged war on the corset, I liberated the abdomen,' he claimed. He did not, in fact, abandon the corset, but altered its shape, extending it almost to the knees and removing the tight restrictions from the waist. He simply shifted the restriction further down the body. The waist was no longer nipped in to fainting point, but the hips and thighs were now held rigid, so that sitting became extremely uncomfortable. Many women actually padded their waists out to make them almost as wide as the hips. The lowering of the top of the new corset necessitated a brassière (the seventeenth-century French term was not used in England until 1911). The brassière had been introduced in the 1880s but was now more generally adopted.

Poiret was a rebel. He despised the pale, 'sweet pea' Edwardian hues and used brilliant, violent colours instead. The traditional black or white stockings were outmoded by brightly coloured ones, which complemented the shorter hemline and the vividness of contemporary styles. The 1905 exhibition of the Fauve artists Matisse, Vlaminck and Derain, exotica from Russia and the East following an exhibition at the Salon d'Automne in 1906, and the opening of Sergei Diaghilev's Ballets Russes in 1909 with *Cleopatra* and *Schéhérazade* in 1910 led to an explosion of colour: purple, deep orange, reds and deep greens. The dramatic sets, new dances and ethnic themes gave fashion a direction. Poiret's exotic windows displayed Oriental fans and highly coloured and embroidered clothing against deep purple or vermilion backgrounds – a collage of novelty, which sometimes took fashion to the-atrical and often laughable limits. Much of Poiret's experimentation with lavish, Eastern-style materials was done in conjunction with the textile house Bianchini-Férier, using Raoul Dufy's designs. (Poiret also com-missioned leading artists such as George Lepape and Paul Iribe to illustrate the catalogues to his collections.)

Another fruitful but less publicized source of inspiration for Poiret was the Wiener Werkstätte, an art and crafts school established in Vienna in 1903, based on the ideas of William Morris and Charles Rennie Mackintosh. The fashion students designed very simple clothes based on rational-dress theories. Artistic impulse was concentrated on decorative detail and textiles, rather than silhouette, making use of, for example, appliqué work, embroid-ery and batik printing. The influence of Gustav Klimt and Léon Bakst was clearly evident in their work. Poiret visited the school in 1911 and was impressed by the textiles, buying many examples to use in his collections. On his return to Paris he set up the Ecole Martine, inspired by the Wiener Werkstätte, gathering together thirteen-year-old working-class girls who showed artistic talent. Their natural spontaneity was encouraged and strict, formal tuition avoided. Poiret used many of their designs as textile patterns.

From 1909 Cubism, like Fauvism, inspired designers, especially the Orphic Cubism of Robert Delaunay and the work of Picabia and Léger. Delaunay's wife Sonia was a leading exponent of Orphic Cubism, which Apollinaire described as 'the art of painting new structures out of elements that have not been borrowed from the visual sphere', and applied it to textiles.

When Poiret's hobble skirt appeared in 1910 he announced, 'I have freed the bust from its prison, but I have put chains on the legs'. Legs were so tightly encased that a hobble strap or garter was worn to keep the ankles together. Only tiny steps were possible and some believed that this Japanese style of walking was very feminine. It was reported that several street cars in New York actually had steps adjusted so that women could board. The style was considered outrageous. It was condemned by the Pope and some priests in France refused to give women wearing hobbles the sacrament of absolution.

The Church also censored women for discarding their modest layers of undergarments, and for wearing skimpy skirts and the décolleté walking gown, which exposed the chest and revealed the stockings. Since 1908 and the *directoire* gown, the trend had been to discard one garment after another. Layers of petticoats could not be worn under slender skirts, which drew attention to the thighs, and even dress linings were gradually removed, until the unlined dress reigned supreme. There was even a mode for going hatless. Dress manufacturers and retailers no longer wondered what women were going to wear next; the question was what would women cease to wear next? The narrow, unlined skirt and the court gown pruned of its train reduced the demand for dress material, causing obvious concern to textile companies.

Mariano Fortuny was an artist and textile designer rather than a couturier, who experimented with the simplicity of classicism in dress from 1907. He worked in his Venetian home, Palazzo Orfei, surrounded by the extensive family collection of antique textiles. He dismissed high fashion as a constant and worthless search for novelty and sought to free the body from restricting clothes. Classical Greek and medieval dress, the English Aesthetic movement, orientalism, and Renaissance and Venetian art, notably the paintings of Carpaccio, Tintoretto and Bellini, all inspired his work. The bronze Delphic charioteer statue, the korai sculpture of the sixth century B C, and the Ionic chiton led to his creation of the Delphos dress, which was patented in 1909. It was utterly simple, hanging loosely in fine pleats from the shoulders, just skimming the body. Fortuny added Venetian glass or painted wooden beads to the edges of his dresses not only for decorative effect but also to weigh down the light silk against the body (Chanel later used gilt chains in the hems of jackets in a similar way). As well as having an immutable beauty, Fortuny's Delphos dress was very practical, as it was stored rolled up to keep the tight pleats and did not have to be ironed. Seventy years later these dresses have maintained their pleating and colours and are very collectable.

The Knossos scarf was another creation of Fortuny. It was a veil printed with motifs from Cycladic art, which was draped around his dresses and capes.

Fortuny's work inspired a great following amongst aesthetes and society figures such as Lady Diana Cooper and the actress Eleonora Duse. He was a friend of Marcel Proust and his work figures prominently in *Remembrance of Things Past*: 'The Fortuny gown which Albertine was wearing that evening seemed to me the tempting phantom of that invisible Venice. It was covered with Arab ornamentation, like the Venetian palaces hidden like sultan's wives behind a screen of pierced stone ... the oriental birds that symbolize alternately life and death were repeated in the shimmering fabric, of an intense blue which, as my eyes drew nearer, turned into malleable gold by those same transmutations, which before an advancing gondola, change into gleaming metal of azure of the Grand Canal. And the sleeves were lined with a cherry pink which is so peculiarly Venetian that it is called Tiepolo pink.'

An Edwardian woman attempting to board a tram.

Eleanora Duse, 'the greatest tragedienne of her age', according to Vogue.

Redfern seated in his atelier directing the building of a new gown, 1911.

Mrs Henry Payne Whitney, the New York hostess, in a lampshade dress.

Fortuny's student, Maria Monaci Gallenga, was to carry on Fortuny's influence using many of his materials to create her distinctive chemise dresses. Later in the century Mary McFadden in America and Patricia Lester in London were to revive the style of Fortuny's pleated dresses.

Many couture houses were run by women, including Mme Paquin, Marguerite Wagner and Madeleine Chéruit, who all started as house mannequins, the Callot Soeurs, Jenny, Lanvin and Lucile (Lady Duff Gordon). Lucile, one of the first Englishwomen to be recognized internationally as a dress designer, was a colourful character. Through a combination of talent, blatant self-promotion and speedy copies of the prevailing Paris line, she claimed to determine fashion, successfully exporting from her London-based salon and later opening in Paris and New York. She was one of the first couturiers to give her gowns amusing titles (such as 'Give me your heart' and 'Gowns of emotion') and take them on international and provincial tours.

Despite the establishment of fashion houses in London, since the days of Charles Frederick Worth Paris had attracted many of the greatest fashion talents from England, including Redfern and later Molyneux. The couturiers in Paris were innovative, developed fashion as an artform and organized themselves with great professionalism. Consequently the patronage of the French houses grew to enormous proportions, as did their international importance both in terms of dress aesthetics and big business. The London houses lacked both the professionally organized approach and the creative flair to challenge the Paris collections, although they were acclaimed for their tailoring. Most fashionable women ordered ballgowns and afternoon toilettes from French houses but bought their tailored morning suits, matching blouses and sporting ensembles from English houses such as Creed, Redfern, Amy Linker, O'Rossen (originally a gentleman's tailor) or Reville & Rossiter. Shoes were also made by hand, the most fashionable cobblers being Gillet and Hellstern in Paris and Lobb in London.

Increased trans-Atlantic travel whetted American appetites for Parisian fashions. As the era of the great liners dawned, the voyage itself became a social occasion. Women bought trunk-loads of clothing for the journey to parade on deck. At night they donned the most extravagant dinner gowns and jewels or Lucile-inspired tango frocks.

French women had access to the changing details of current fashion throughout the season. Americans did not. The Parisienne bought her autumn wardrobe in late October, while the American buyer ordered from the collection shown in August. Consequently American women were always frustrated in their attempts to appear precisely à la mode.

American couture did not exist before the First World War. There were some firms in the big cities, such as Stein and Blaine, who copied European fashion, but in high society French labels were *de rigueur*. However, after the outbreak of war America was isolated from this fashion source and imports of French garments fell by half. *Vogue* responded by organizing the first fashion show featuring the work of American designers. Under the patronage of Mrs Henry Payne Whitney it travelled round America.

Before the war, in both America and Europe women who could not afford couture prices either were dressed by a private dressmaker or bought the limited range of Parisian-inspired gowns available in department stores or smaller houses. Italian fashion houses such as Fabiani, set up in 1909, bought French patterns or toiles to copy or reinterpret for the home market. Similar establishments were set up in London, Paris, Vienna and Berlin.

With the advent of the motorcar it became easier for women to go up to town and buy clothes from metropolitan tailors and department stores. The department store was to become the major outlet for ready-made fashion for most women as the century progressed, its main patron being the middle class. The first department stores had been founded in Britain at the end of the eighteenth century, for example Browns of Chester in 1780 and Dickens & Smith (later Jones) in 1790. In America Gimbel, a travelling salesman, set up a store in 1842 in Alabama, while Lord & Taylor was founded in 1826 as a dry-goods store. Many department stores began trading as either grocers, such as Fortnum & Mason and Harrods, or drapers. In 1909 Gordon Selfridge built the first purpose-built department store, stocking a range of fashion and household goods.

The actress Miss Dorothy Lane, photographed on the London stage in a leather chauffeur's outfit, 1918.

In vivid contrast to the traditional draper's, where goods were hidden away in brown cardboard boxes, department-store customers were invited to browse amongst glamorous tableaux, which gave maximum display. Gimmicks were used to entertain the customers: free gifts, attractive display cases, eye-catching offers, cardboard cut-outs and lightshows. Stores competed with each other in the provision of amenities such as tea rooms, restaurants, cloakrooms and after-sales service.

Trade journals such as the *Drapers' Organiser and Dry Goods Journal* emphasized the need for a professional approach to sales promotion and sales expertise was encouraged by department stores. Trainees at Lewis's in England, for example, were told to 'read the fashion magazines and study adverts ... You must cultivate a sense of good taste' (Asa Briggs, *Friends of the People*, 1956).

Department stores sold dress lengths, which customers could either take to their dressmaker or have made to measure in the store's fitting rooms. They also offered semi-finished gowns, with skirts left open at the back and bodices that had to be personally fitted. In order to keep their workrooms busy, some stores began to manufacture simple ready-made garments such as mantles, aprons, blouses and cloaks. However, the frills and furbelows of women's gowns and the constant vagaries of the mode conspired against any attempts at standardization or mass-production. Hence until the 1920s only menswear was mass-produced.

Large-scale, factory-based mechanization was first introduced in America, where the clothing industry was far more advanced and the middle-class market much larger than in Europe. The Singer sewing machine had been invented in America in 1851, but although used at home, it was not applied on a significant commercial scale until the turn of the century. A button-holing machine was developed by the Reece Machinery Company in England in 1914, but during the war was only used for uniforms. Bulk cutting had been mastered but pieces were then sent to sweat-shops where the garments were made up by hand. Such low piece rates were paid to these workers, mostly women, that public concern in Britain provoked parliamentary investigation; the report of the select committee appeared in 1907 and led to three Trade Board Acts, which controlled piece rates and time worked and thus hastened the change-over to factory production.

Lunchtime in the canteen of a French factory, 1918.

Pre-war society was conservative and couturiers were tinkering with freedom to achieve superficial and daring effects rather than challenging the social basis of women's incarceration, as symbolized by corsetry. Women's 'place in the home' was sanctioned by *Vogue*; the magazine was critical of the suffragettes' antics and was unsympathetic to their ideas of liberty. Few

The man-tailored suit, a stalwart of war dressing, by Kenneth Durward, 1918.

A pre-war exercise class.

Miss Audrey Osborne posing as a Red Cross nurse at the Red Cross Benefit, Bellport, Long Island, 1918.

women participated actively in sports and those that did take an interest remained spectators or dabblers rather than players because of the physical restrictions of their clothes. Many, however, were enchanted with the new craze for motoring, which inevitably demanded a full and varied wardrobe, and entire shops were devoted to motoring attire. *Vogue* maintained that a lady required two coats for motoring round Europe: one woollen or tweed, which was semi-lined and could double-up as a steamer coat, and another for warmer weather, of sand-coloured pongee, tussore or gold cloth.

Gabrielle 'Coco' Chanel considered the complicated and formal graces of Edwardian dress absurd and effected a change in personal style that was soon to be admired and emulated. Eager to set herself apart from the 'cocotte' and enjoy the same physical freedom as the men she accompanied, she dressed in comfortable, masculine-inspired sports clothing. Wearing an untrimmed boater or bowler, tweed overcoat, straight serge skirt and white school-girl blouse or cardigan she stood out from the crowd. Her friend Paul Morand commented, 'Chanel had only to appear in order to make the whole pre-war mode fade away, causing Worth and Paquin to wither and die.' She turned elegance on its head, she made the over-decorated appear ridiculous by highlighting the charm of the tomboy. Many admired the charmingly simple hats she sold in a small boutique in Deauville in 1913. The shop was financed by her dashing lover Boy Capel and specialized in simple suits, jumpers, jersey bathing suits and her famous *marinière* blouse.

The First World War thrust Chanel's functional ideals into the limelight as simplicity became characteristic of wartime clothing. As governments were forced to utilize the hitherto unrecognized talents of women, their clothing necessarily evolved to suit a new purpose. The wartime silhouette was far easier to move in than the ankle-binding, long, narrow or draped skirts of previous seasons. *Punch* quipped that women could be seen in the parks learning how to walk again. The variety of garments available was reduced and fewer lavish evening gowns were now created. Those that were made were destined for the American market, where social life was largely unaffected. In Paris evening dress was banned in the principal theatres, and in London one West End theatre put up a notice saying 'Evening dress optional but unfashionable'.

Many garments offered by sports houses came to be worn for everyday work by women, such as the close-fitting hood attached to the coat collar, which could be unbuttoned and pocketed, the heavy, rubberized raincoat originally intended for riding, soft woollen underwear and the oilskin waistcoat with woollen-lined sleeves, which was light to wear. Pockets were now adopted on a wide scale for women's attire. One American hosiery manufacturer even offered garters with flap pockets – a safe place for money and jewellery. Hitherto fashionable garments had few pockets; it was considered more ladylike to have a pouch on a string or a small handbag, as ladies of leisure had little to carry. Purchases were put on account and delivered and society ladies did not wear make-up, resorting only to *papier poudre*, paper embedded with light powder, which was applied in private to disguise a sheen on the complexion.

As women became preoccupied with war work it became quite acceptable to wear the same ensemble right through the day and even during the evening with the addition of appropriate accessories. However some ladies attempted to carry on social life as though nothing had happened. *Vogue*, fulfilling its role as a society magazine, reflected this: alongside earnest articles on charity and voluntary work and reports from the front, there were articles on the 'hardships' suffered by the leisured classes, such as petrol rationing, which had curtailed the fun of 'joy riding'.

'Philanthropy is fashionable,' announced *Vogue*. America joined the war in 1917 but American women had begun their volunteer work three years previously. 'The result is that today, when this country has entered the war … the government may count upon groups of women trained to a degree of proficiency in their particular relief work.' The magazine encouraged the work of voluntary organizations and described the efforts of the Junior War Relief run by Mrs Lambert, Mrs Herbert Satterlee's knitting circle for the navy, and even such charmingly naive and misplaced ideas as Mrs Chester B. Duryea's requests for fans for the soldiers in the trenches, who were suffering from the intense summer heat. (She was inundated with more than 15,000 fans.)

V for Victory propaganda poster.

By the end of 1916 social life in Europe had become what *Vogue* described as Bohemian. Youth entertained war-weary soldiers in public bars, hotels and night clubs. Parties to 'give the boys a good time' were held nightly, but seldom in the big private houses, since many had been requisitioned as hospitals or army bases, and many had lost their staff, who preferred working in munitions factories. Social barriers had been broken down at the front and in hospital and could hardly be re-erected on leave. Society ladies were now seen in restaurants, whereas before the war only the *demi-mondaine* would have frequented such establishments, with the notable exception of the Ritz.

The war led to an important expansion of *Vogue* magazine. European women could not get copies because of shipping restrictions and Condé Nast decided to launch a British edition in the autumn of 1916. Eye-witness accounts were published about the work of the First Aid Nursing Yeomanry (FANYs) and the Voluntary Aid Detachment (VADs), unpaid, dedicated women working in primitive hospital huts. In one centre there had only been one surgeon and two FANYs. 'For twenty-four hours they all worked, up to the knees in blood, amputating, tying up, bandaging, without rest or relief.' Moving convoys of wounded throughout the enormous Calais district was done entirely by women. Feminine idiosyncrasies were noticed amidst the horror. There was not a woman's office, for example, without a vase of flowers or chintz curtains.

'FANYs', First Aid Nursing Yeomanry of Britain, who ran the first-aid nursing stations in France, 1917.

As the months dragged on, British *Vogue* attempted to comfort the war widow, the lonely wife and all who wanted the war to end. With the ending of hostilities on 11 November 1918, New York and London society became obsessed with amusing the returning soldier; according to *Vogue* New York became 'a three-ring circus for the boy from the west or from Europe'.

By the end of the war fashion had broken away from the tradition of full-length skirts, as hemlines now varied according to the activity and the time of day. Though many women chose to live and dress in a style similar to that prevailing before the war, for those who wanted to lead a more active life, unrestrained by dress, the barriers had been breached. Fewer clothes were worn as women discarded some of the many layers of lingerie, decorative fichus, cumbersome millinery and accessories that had weighed them down. This simplification of dress also enhanced the progress of cleanliness. The young, slender girl had become the fashionable ideal and awareness of the body underneath garments had become both acceptable and fashionable.

1909

By 1909 the artificial S-bend figure that had characterized the opening years of the decade had been modified into a straighter line at the instigation of couturiers such as Poiret, Vionnet and Béchoff-David. American fashion remained relatively unchanged, as this alteration was incorporated more slowly there. The process of narrowing began in 1908, when Parisian couturiers decided to remove the layers of petticoats and underskirts. The new corset, introduced in 1909, was worn with a chemise or camisole and extended from just under the bust to the lower thigh, creating a more tubular effect. A slender-hipped figure was now considered the fashionable ideal.

This narrow line coincided with a revival of the French *directoire* style (1795–9), an exaggerated interpretation of classical Roman and Greek dress, characterized by a long straight skirt, sometimes split, a very low décolleté, small tight sleeves and a high waistline. The new narrow line was considered more youthful. Contemporaries thought it the simplest shape possible, yet it made women walk with a waddle and dancing was impossible. Numerous dresses had the skirt fullness pulled in at the knees by button-back tabs, coiling draperies or bands of a contrasting material tied in bows.

The elaborate decorative devices and filmy layers of earlier Edwardian fashion were rejected in favour of simplicity of line, which was emphasized by the close cut and exotic, dramatic fabrics. In more elaborate cases drapery was added, falling in thick folds under the arm to the wrist, over an undergown with long, tight sleeves in a contrasting colour. Some skirts were slashed open in front or behind to show a contrasting material beneath, which heralded the daring pantaloons of 1910.

The one-piece dress, usually ungirdled, was fashionable for the afternoon. It was cut to fall flat to the hips, with a shirred or pleated skirt. The

1. Redfern's bright-green mousseline tabard dress with jabot drapery over each hip. 2. Martial et Armand's pink mousseline-de-soie afternoon gown, embroidered with pink floss and trimmed with pink satin ribbon. 3. Ney's white-work lingerie gown trimmed with a wide Bordeaux-red satin girdle. 4. Khaki-coloured foulard dress, polka-dotted in black, with a low waistline. 5. Left: black crêpe-de-Chine mourning frock banded in crêpe. Right: black Arab silk street gown trimmed with crêpe and a tucked chiffon yoke.

sleeves were straight and unfitted. Emphasis this year was concentrated on the midriff, with trailing back pieces and bead work.

In the spring the Louis XV mode – brocade and satin gowns with panniered hips and long, oval-shaped décolletés – was revived. A return to the crinolines of the 1850s was also toyed with, but

with little success, for the slender silhouette was now high fashion.

Evening gowns flaunted low, scooped necklines and had short, draped sleeves. The waist remained high and drapery fell in controlled swirls about the ankles, thereby elongating the line. The most popular colours were black and white, often spangled with jet, and pink was a

6   7   8

6. Left: *Callot's stone-coloured silk coat with red revers.* Right: *Béchoff-David's cream pongee coat with Delft-blue linen revers, black satin collar and tie and straw hat.*   7. *Kenyon's striped, frosted-green silk raincoat, with rubberized satin collar and cuffs and pockets.*   8. Left: *Persian lamb coat, set with white fox and matching hat band.* Right: *caracul coat with fox border, cuffs and revers.*

smart summer choice; alternatives were green and white and pink and white. The latest evening ensemble was the combination of tunic and undergown, which was becoming *de rigueur.* The tunic was heavily embroidered and sequinned. The grander the toilette, the more embroidered and beaded motifs, lace and bands of beads it would have. These adornments were often detachable and could be worn on a veil or a low décolleté.

Gradually prints became bolder; polka dots and other geometric designs began to appear on day dresses. Materials were soft; even taffeta felt as soft as satin, unless it was used for stiff petticoats. Lace and pearls were so fashionable that even practical garments such as shirts were decorated with them. Shirts had wide sloping shoulders and many had heavily tucked bodices or lace jabots. Some summer lingerie gowns were made of lace and were worn over silvery gauze underdresses. *Déshabillés,* or boudoir gowns, retained all the elaborate grandeur of the fashions of previous years, in contrast to the prevailing taste for greater simplicity in outer wear.

Oddly, in the early spring it became fashionable to wear thin, transparent black or white mousseline dresses, with heavy furs piled on top. Fur was important for cravats, muffs and to trim suits, evening gowns and wraps. Seal, caracul (Persian lamb), lynx and fox, a popular afternoon choice, were the most fashionable furs. *Vogue* commented that those who could not afford furs might shiver in inadequate clothing this spring.

The fashionable coat was straight and narrow and had an unmarked waistline; a semi-fitted coat was worn for more formal occasions. Sleeves were long and close-fitting, and button-back tails and revers were fashionable details. The duster, a rain coat originally introduced for motoring, was simply tailored in sand or natural-coloured silk serge, with a small collar, small, turned-back revers and a low or unmarked waistline. Long-waisted silk and pongee coats prevailed for the summer, with shorter skirts that avoided puddles and mud. Buttons were frequently the only ornamentation on both coats and suits for more practical wear. Corduroy was used for winter coats and country suits.

The house of Fabiani opened in Rome this year, offering copies of Paris-inspired gowns.

9   10   11

9. *Drécoll's mousseline-de-soie déshabillé.*   10. *Hickson's white linen tennis dress trimmed with black soutache braid.*   11. *Hynard and Meeham's white linen shirt with bands of Irish lace set into tucks.*

12. Stern Brothers' pink-net evening garniture embroidered in pink and gold. 13. Ney's black mousseline-de-soie tunic with silver embroidery and appliquéd Irish lace over clinging white satin and matching Grecian headband. 14. Buzenet's robe of ochre Alençon lace and underdress of rose mousseline de soie. The corsage and lower skirt are embroidered with jet and silver threads. 15. Buzenet's black-net evening gown is narrowly tucked, jet-adorned and clasped along the sleeves with brilliants.

1910

1. Three American dresses. Left: oyster-grey dress with a draped chiffon bodice and black chiffon looped belt. Centre: a triple-flounced dark-blue skirt, worn with a short-sleeved crêpe blouse. Right: sage-green chiffon dress and a belt of black moiré.

This spring the controversial hobble, or tube skirt, introduced by Poiret, became high fashion. Worn with a hobble garter – a strip of material that tied the ankles together allowing no more than a three- or four-inch step – the skirt was christened by the French newspapers; a sketch of a hobbled horse and a woman in the fashionable skirt had the caption '*Pauvre cheval, pauvre femme*'. Formal skirts were only twelve inches wide below the knees, so that hopping became the only means of crossing a room. Walking skirts, in contrast, became shorter and fuller, giving ease of movement.

Lucile (Lady Duff Gordon) arrived in New York this spring to promote her couture range. Her sister, the novelist Elinor Glyn, commented to *Vogue* on how well turned out the women were, particularly those in morning suits. The Americans favoured simple, clean-cut tailoring, without elaborate decoration, and skirts that were 4 or 5 inches from the ground – slightly shorter than in Europe. London tailors designed stout, practical, somewhat masculine suits, whereas French suits lacked clarity of line and tended to be over-trimmed. Poiret embellished even the most practical attire with a dashing trim this year. Both Paquin and Redfern decorated their tailored suits with small, flat buttons and Béchoff-David's suit skirts

were fastened at the back with buttons, for at least twelve inches.

Homespun, a coarse wool material, which was hard-wearing and easily cleaned, was now available in a variety of colours and was widely used for walking costumes, or *trotteurs*, and morning suits. Alternative choices were rough serge, unfinished worsteds and fine check or pin-stripe woollens. French serge was a

smart option for a winter daytime dress. Many dresses had straight, lower-calf-length skirts fitted into a deep satin yoke, with sometimes an additional layer of material falling from the yoke. Casual summer frocks were styled along very simple lines with collarless necklines and short sleeves, invariably in pongee, linen, batiste, foulard or habutai silk, in black and white, lavender or pale green.

2. *Three French natural-waisted outfits. Left: vert-de-gris linen gown trimmed with bands of black mercerized braid, Valenciennes lace and passe-menterie braid buttons. Centre: Gobelin-blue cotton dress, veiled with printed zephyr. Right: cotton voile and cashmere dress finished with silk bands. 3. Béchoff-David's pale-blue satin gown, with a three-quarter-length black-chiffon tunic banded at the hem with black lynx. Black velvet trims the belt, cuffs and yoke. 4. Theatre bonnet in dull-silver lace trimmed with cascading poppies. 5. Chéruit's simple black satin-and-chiffon dress trimmed with broad bands of black jet in geometric designs. 6. Poiret's cuirass of shining gold tissue illustrates the new narrow, moulded line. 7. Lucile's evening tunic with decorated corsage, worn with a composition of draped and lacy underskirts.*

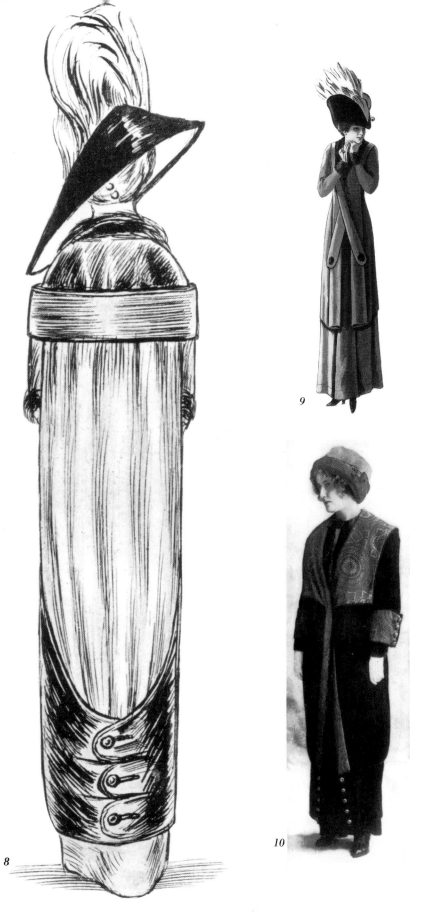

8

9

10

8. *Francis's wrap with a close-fitting cape collar.* 9. *Three-piece walking suit trimmed with skunk. The jacket has top-stitched bands crossing the front and is fastened with large fur buttons. The full skirt has a placket, which slopes to the left, and a bicorne finishes the outfit.* 10. *Poiret's walking suit in velvet and multi-coloured brocade.*

However, the heads, tails and paws of animals, which in earlier years were eagerly slung over many a fashionable shoulder, were now rejected.

The tunic line dominated evening wear. Its simplicity was set off by elaborate beadwork in glass, wood, mother-of-pearl and jet, and by ornate head-dresses. Turbans, Grecian bandeaux and aigrettes were sumptuously trimmed to draw attention to the head. The most fashionable evening look continued to draw on elements from the Middle Ages or Ancient Greece. Worth showed clothes with a medieval influence, with pleats falling from a close-fitting hip yoke. Many skirts fell from just above the natural waistline and had ornament-trimmed silk or velvet cord belts.

Black and white and a new colour combination, mauve satin veiled in coral chiffon organza, were the most popular colours. As forecast last year, French designers, notably Drécoll, styled gowns on Victorian fashions, but they did not take off – the slim silhouette prevailed. Straight tunic lines were now extended to day clothes in Paris, where extreme simplicity of line was considered both youthful and attractive. England and America were slower to adopt the new tunic mode, retaining the more curvaceous lines of recent seasons.

In France the half-length straight tunic with an underskirt was very fashionable for day and evening wear and was to be found particularly at Chéruit and Béchoff-David. The tunic or the skirt underneath was decorated below the knee with plain, self-fabric bands, beadwork or fur, according to the formality of the gown. Transparent tunics in black lace or chiffon revealed the pattern, sheen or colour of the dress underneath. The most magical were made in Persian-patterned chiffon, which was also much used this year for soft *bretelles* – ornamental braces – and as a lining for summer evening wraps. Many materials, like Persian-patterned foulard, were available in dull blue, burnt orange, olive green and faded lavender.

Decorative devices were concentrated on the belt. For more formal occasions a matching nine-tenths-length coat was worn.

The most beautiful and rare furs, worn only by the wealthy – sable, ermine, chinchilla and seal – were now styled more coquettishly. The demand for the more common furs had made them so expensive that they too had become luxuries. Opossum, racoon, squirrel, moleskin and other less expensive furs had to be used instead for trimming sporting clothes and town wear.

1911

Hemlines now returned to just two inches above the ground. The hem width of skirts designed for the average figure did not exceed two and a half yards, allowing just enough fullness to walk. No international couturier successfully challenged this Paris-influenced line.

The sensation of the spring was the *jupe-culotte*, introduced by Poiret, Bourniche and Margaine Lacroix. It consisted of either pantaloons worn under a draped and split overskirt, or a full skirt tailored into trousers at the hem. A compromise version was the bifurcated train – a train that was split into two like a fish tail – which could be worn either loose or whipped between the legs to the front to create a pantaloon effect.

Worth, a conservative couturier, was appalled by the *jupe-culotte*, which he considered 'vulgar, ugly and wicked ... The world has gone mad. No one talks

1. Two autumn suits from Francis (left) and Paquin (right), trimmed with contrasting braid. 2. Tailored grey gown with a postillion highlighted with four black buttons and contrast banding on the skirt to simulate a side-split. 3. Martial et Armand's tailored suit in reversible serge. The plain grey overskirt is split up the back to show the black-and-white plaid underskirt. The sleeves are half chiffon, half plaid.

19

4. Poiret's jupe-culottes *in gingham with satin banding.*
5. Margaine Lacroix's black-and-white striped voile dress; the bodice is veiled in green chiffon. 6. The black satin and lace day gown trails a bifurcated train.
7. Poiret's frock in dark-blue, Persian-patterned foulard with a deep black satin hem and an Empire waistline. It is worn with a Poiret signature, the turban.

of art, literature or public affairs. All conversation concentrates itself on this most detestable garment ... I shall not endorse it, Madame, but if they demand it, they must have it!' Worth also hated the Poiret-inspired turbans and close-fitting head-dresses that women insisted on wearing to the theatre and dances, because they covered their beautiful, feminine hair.

Conservative, formal evening gowns had softly looped folds and panniers, but the latter were flattened and lowered to suit the contemporary mode for a closer-fitting, less exaggerated line. The waistline was high, and decorative details were concentrated on the corsage, the skirt being straight and unadorned. In some cases, particularly at Lanvin, Chéruit and Drécoll, the ankle was daringly revealed through side slits or draperies. The latest décolleté was a deep V, sometimes inset with a contrasting material.

Persian materials woven with a pattern continued to be used for evening gowns, in bright Ballets Russes colours – blue and purple, red and purple and burnt orange – particularly by Poiret.

Ornate silver and velvet brocades were chosen for sheath gowns with fine lace or tulle overdresses, worn with luxurious furs or brocades lined and edged with fur, particularly Russian sable, royal ermine and white fox.

Soft, neutral tints prevailed for house, street and general daytime wear, gaiety being confined to trimmings and linings, although Poiret used the same vivid colours and rich materials for day as well as evening wear. Most of the embroidery and detailing on coats and dresses for the autumn were based on Egyptian or Oriental designs, although Victorian upholstery trimmings – silk fringes, ruffles, bead-and-ball fringes – were popular for all types of clothes.

Midsummer suits were made from striped silks and worn with little boleros or long-tailed *directoire* coats in plain silks, while velvet and satin were used this autumn for street toilettes and soft, thick, light woollens for winter *tailleurs*. Autumn suits were fairly elaborate. Drécoll concentrated on charming costumes reminiscent of mid-nineteenth-century styles. Many jacket-backs were pleated, belted at the waist and lengthened in a square postillion with a tiny puffed edge. Derived from the livery of the postillion, this bodice shape extended below the waistline at the back. Double-faced serge was greatly in demand for stouter tailored costumes, in grey and green, grey and purple or black with kingfisher blue. The contrasting colour showed on the lapels, which might also be embroidered, and Paquin experimented with the single-sided rever.

Coats this year could be full length or as short as a jacket, either wrapped tightly about the body or voluminously full. Many were cut with a rounded lower edge at the front, in the style of a gentleman's morning coat. Sleeve novelty preoccupied some couturiers this autumn. Even an ordinary coat sleeve was close-fitting from the elbow to the wrist and picked out by a line of buttons or a fringe.

Fashionable blouses varied from the low-necked and collarless to the high, straight choker, which fitted tightly about the neck and might be boned. The latest suit blouse had a gracefully draped fichu, which added detail under a simple bolero jacket.

The house of Premet opened in Paris with Mme Grès as an employee.

8. Satin and lace evening gown with draped and bifurcated train.   9. Lanvin's white chiffon and satin dancing frock dotted with pink chiffon roses, with an olive-green-satin tunic.   10. Worth's evening toilette: fringed tunic in black velvet with bands of white satin studded with jet and glass beads.   11. Leopardskin motoring coat with a skunk shawl collar and matching muff.   12. Worth's long, straight evening wrap.   13. Drécoll's brocaded white velvet dinner gown, edged with dark fur.

1912

A fashion war broke out between two prominent couturiers, Paquin and Callot, in the autumn: would the slim or the full silhouette prevail? For some time fabric manufacturers, moralizers, ministers and matrons had all demanded fuller skirts, for a variety of reasons. They now rallied behind Paquin, whose full silhouette was revealed on 16 August. His skirts were sufficiently wide to permit free movement, with full godets, shirred waists and voluminous, complicated draperies attached to an underskirt. The following day Callot replied to the challenge, showing skirts that were slimmer and briefer than ever before. They were slit at the back to make it possible to walk in them. In some cases these skirts were draped, but the drapery was very close and figure-revealing. *Vogue* sat on the fence.

Jackets accompanying the fuller silhouette were cut away sharply at the front and extended well below the knees at the back, in a *directoire* style. The narrow skirt was worn with a short, neat jacket, which barely reached the hips, or a waist-length bolero. Some wraps or coats were full and draped, with big stand-up collars. The latest long-line

1. Evening wrap with a black satin skirt, flesh-coloured chiffon top and white chiffon hood trimmed with ruffled black net.   2. The front and back of a raglan motoring coat in cedar-green and white double-faced cloth with a chiffon bonnet.

2

1

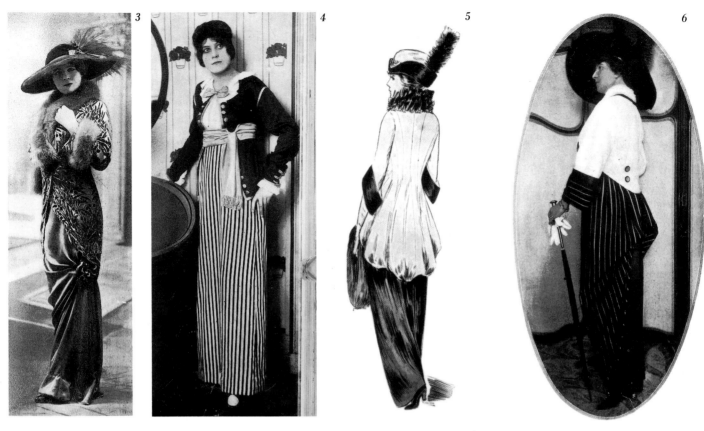

3. *Afternoon suit: a steel-grey charmeuse skirt, the drapery caught into a rosette at one side, and a brocaded velvet jacket trimmed with blue fox.*
4. *The utterly straight line, accentuated by vertical stripes on the skirt.* 5. *Straight black satin skirt and waisted grey satin jacket, which is caught at the hem to create a pannier effect.* 6. *Martial et Armand's butterfly-wing dress in black-and-white striped ratine, worn with a narrow pleated black satin underskirt and a white Eton jacket.* 7. *Doucet's straight skirt of white figured terry cloth with a crocheted trimming, and a white net blouse girdled with black satin.* 8. *Buzenet's lingerie frock with a close-fitting black satin underskirt and a draped pannier tunic of white lace.*
9. *Black Cavalier hat with green, red and brown ostrich plumes. The golden-brown crêpe-de-Chine muff and neckpiece are banded with racoon.*

11

10. *Jean's purple velvet wrap embroidered over the shoulders in oriental colours.* 11. *Lanvin's Greek-influenced slender sheath trimmed with braid.*
12. *Fortuny's 'Tangara' tea gown: a pleated silk gown under a gold-stencilled coat edged with wooden beads.*

12

coats, however, were cut in a vast circle hanging from the shoulders, with a flat collar which was short and round at the front and fell to the waist at the back. On some models the circular line was gathered into a deep round yoke trimmed with a ruche. An alternative to these voluminous wraps was the long, straight sack coat. The enthusiasm for drapery even extended to some fur coats, but only short-haired, flexible pelts such as ermine, moleskin, chinchilla and seal-skin were suitable.

Redfern's narrow evening dresses were split up the back rather than at the side or the front, revealing the ankle and foot, and consequently focusing attention on decorative hosiery and slippers. Premet added interest to the back of his gowns with Japanese sashes with long full ends, and short, narrow, pointed trains. Evening sheaths were daringly revealing, with a low décolleté cut square at the front and in a V at the back; the lower section of the skirt was either in a transparent material or slit to the knee.

An alternative to the slinky, draped and sheath mode was revived for spring and summer: the pannier gown, which was shorter and draped in every possible manner, even along the shoulders and sleeves, had been introduced by Chéruit, but Lucile, Doucet and Beer now showed versions of it. Panniers normally added bulk to the hips, but in some cases they were used to create a mock bustle at the back of the gown. Cut in rich brocade and satin, the pannier gown had a tight-fitting bodice and a low, simple neckline. The deep décolleté was not modestly filled in with lace or tulle as in previous years.

Callot's novel version of the bustle was the butterfly-wing back. The material of the skirt was drawn tightly around the figure and then folded to form a big pleat or panel at the back. Rather than being stitched in at the belt so as to form a flat pleat, it was made to stand out like a butterfly.

Fortuny's original designs received great support from the more eclectic fashionable élite at this time. His unfinished tunics, robes and kimonos were bought by couturiers and usually stencilled along the borders and trimmed with hand-made beads, lace and fur; some modified them, making them into gowns or coats à la mode.

1913

The 'minaret' or 'lampshade' silhouette, introduced by Poiret, was the most important fashion development this year. It was originally designed by him for the ballet *Les Minarets*, but was soon incorporated into mainstream fashion. It evolved from the panniered tunic and narrow underskirt, but the contrast between these two shapes was exaggerated.

Both couturiers and textile designers attempted to keep pace with contemporary art, notably Cubism, which inspired fabric prints based on architectural and geometric motifs. Cubism provided an alternative to the Oriental theme, though the latter still prevailed, influencing both fabrics and the shape of clothes: loose, kimono sleeves, mandarin coats, obi sashes and straight Chinese skirts cut with only one seam. The latter was possible because broad-loom ratine was now manufactured.

Poiret and Lanvin were responsible for an important change in taste from the richly Oriental and draped to the starkly simple, geometrically decorated mode – a forward-looking development in twentieth-century fashion. Poiret used Cubist-inspired materials and believed that line was all-important. 'I find my gowns satisfying only when all the details of which they are composed disappear in a general harmony of the whole. For this reason they may seem disappointing to the ignorant. What pleases this class is richness, redundance of ornaments and a minutiae of execution, and the latest pretentiousness and theatricality.' This was an unexpected view from Poiret, whose taste for the theatrical and the ornate reasserted itself during the war and was responsible for his failure.

At Drécoll the mannequins were very tightly corseted so that the curve of the bust was more prominent and the waistline exaggerated. The pannier mode continued, but this spring the fullness was pushed to the front. The waistline was not settled; its position varied from house to house and from season to

1. *Poiret's fur-trimmed 'Minaret' gown.* 2. *Poiret's straight silver tunic with sleeves and underskirt of Mandarin-blue velvet, worn by his wife and muse, Denise.* 3. *Paquin's orange satin foundation, heavily embroidered blue muslin overskirt, and tunic, bodice and long slashed train of gold-encrusted blue oriental crêpe.*

4. *Paquin's pagoda-shaped suit with Louis XV waistcoat, cut-away skirt and plumed tricorne.* 5. *Nardi's black-and-white wool riding coat and matching breeches.* 6. *Poiret's short white skirt, straight green jacket, Russian-style, leather boots and white hat.* 7. *Bergdorf Goodman's tennis costume: green ratine jacket with green-and-white batiste collar and cuffs and a linen skirt, worn with rubber-heeled buckskin shoes and a straw hat.* 8. *Leon Bakst's blue-and-white outfit for Paquin. The large artist's beret ends in a tasselled point.*

9. Loose tunic with kimono sleeves and obi sash worn with a fur stole at Longchamps in mid-summer. 10. The Weiner Werkstätte's ruby crêpe-de-Chine dress with a hand-blocked white sash and whitehat with a blood-red cockade. 11. Bernard's red-and-white printed dress. 12. Premet's costume with draped peplum and paisley-patterned chiffon skirt in clear pastels. 13. Chinchilla evening wrap with foxcollar. 14. Poiret's raglan-sleeved motoring coat in heavy mahogany silk, with peacock-green bindings. 15. Paquin's military-style travelling cape.

9

10

11   12

13

14   15

season. At Premet it was raised to below the bust, while Chéruit and Paquin favoured the normal waistline, with full, shirred skirts. There were no straight or pleated skirts in Chéruit's spring collection; she was preoccupied with drapery and only showed split skirts for the evening.

One-piece tub frocks challenged the pre-eminence of linen suits for casual, summer morning wear. These dresses were made in the plainest, most comfortable styles, of ratine, crêpe, mercerized lawn or linen. The tub frock was also becoming acceptable for more formal occasions, for luncheons and afternoon wear. More elaborate versions were made in a combination of plain and figured voiles, with trimmings of thread and shadow laces. Many of these dresses were cut with revers, to simulate coats, and the open neckline was filled with a tucker. The ruched, stand-up collar was very fashionable; an alternative was the Medici collar seen at Martial et Armand.

One extraordinary idiosyncrasy this year was the vogue for heavy fur trimmings in mid-summer. Even fine voile and lace blouses were edged with pelts, and full-length fur wraps were worn over light summer dresses, particularly at race meetings.

Lucile introduced a new silhouette this autumn: the tango dress, named after the fashionable new dance. Her collection was aptly presented at a *thé dansant*, with tea, music and dancing. The line was fairly slender, with moderately flounced skirts and knee-length tunics. One extraordinary accessory was the dyed wig, worn in red, green or blue by her models.

The fashionable coat fluctuated between the tight and wrapped, and the loose and draped. Fur was still the luxury choice for winter wraps, but rich brocades were more fashionable.

There were some indications that the formalities of dress were being relaxed: *Vogue* sanctioned white clothes for mourning wear for the first time, although it was not acceptable to combine black and white, or to compromise with shades of oyster or cream; simple, masculine-inspired dress had begun to be adopted for women's sportswear – for example, riding breeches were offered for those women who now rode astride; and Chanel opened her boutique in Deauville this year, offering sports clothing as day wear.

1914

1

2

3

4

There were three fashionable silhouettes for the early spring: the straight line, the puff skirt, which was wide through the hips and narrowed to a tight hem, and the short, wide line. Eighteen months earlier Premet had shown the shortest skirts in Paris – as much as 8 inches from the ground – but women had initially objected to them. This year, by mid-spring the most fashionable were wearing the ankle-length, wide skirt, which was now thought to be less outrageous than the provocative long split skirt.

As the skirt widened, the bodice narrowed and tightened. Women were to remain corseted from the waist to just above the knee and wear a brassière. The couturiers agreed on one issue: the décolleté could sink no lower, for reasons of decency. Taffeta was considered a high-fashion fabric for the summer. It was thick and rich, but just soft enough to muffle the swish that had reputedly exasperated those who had worn it in the past. Chéruit and Premet were the chief promoters of this material, which was worked into ruches, bustles and choux on dresses. Plaid silk was an alternative to plain taffeta for spring costumes.

The outbreak of the First World War had a profound long-term effect on fashion. France was called to arms on 1 August, a few days before the presentation of the autumn collections. Despite this, Callot, Chéruit, Drécoll, Premet, Lanvin, Jeanne Hallée and Bernard managed to stage their shows between 9 and 15 August, establishing the autumn silhouette. The movement towards wider skirts begun in the spring was more appropriate for wartime: busy women could not have coped with long, hobbled or draped skirts. Skirts were now widened with godets or side or box pleats, which fell flat over the hips. The long jacket tended to replace the short, and peplums or tails were still cut to flare and ripple from the waist over the top of the skirt, as they had done over the previous year's pannier skirts. The minaret line was adopted for long coats for the autumn rather than for dresses, and was popular in America.

However, after hostilities began the need to safeguard the financial operation of the fashion industry became more important than the details of the silhouette. The Chambre Syndicale de la Couture Parisienne outlined ways of dealing with the situation: gowns should

1. Left: Poiret's violet taffeta dress girdled in amber velvet with a circular lace cape, and a spirally draped skirt. Right: Bernard's blue taffeta 'Minaret' gown tapering to an ankle-binding hem. 2. The straightest waistline in Paris from Poiret. 3. Steine and Blane's tailored dress of white broadcloth – an unconstricting, simple line. 4. Poiret's high-waisted, ungirdled skirt in green-and-white check with large hip pockets. 5. Simple French tricot cardigan. 6. Buzenet's winter suit with military details. 7. Chéruit's tan-and-orange plaid suit with a shirred apron. 8. Drécoll's black taffeta and black velvet suit.

10

11

9

12   *13*

9. *Thurn's peacock-blue duvetyn, bell-skirted coat and skirt, trimmed with sable-dyed kolinsky and a dark-brown velvet hat decorated with a heron feather.* 10. *Paquin's blue gabardine coat with flared skirt and shorter overskirt with red embroidered tricolour motifs and a stock-like collar.* 11. *Callot's geranium-red velvet 'Minaret' coat trimmed with black fox and worn with an ankle-gathered skirt.* 12. *Martial et Armand's skunk-trimmed scarlet velvet coat with a black crêpe-de-Chine cape, striped with narrow silver bands to match the coat's fastenings.* 13. *Chéruit's close-fitting Bordeaux-red cloth dress with narrow, upstanding collar and long, tight, set-in sleeves.* 14. *Resplendently beaded 'Minaret' dress.* 15. *Drécoll's black charmeuse puffed tunic with black net embroidered with jet and pearls. The simple black velvet bodice has a deep white yoke and strands of jet from the sleeves.* 16. *Poiret's 'Tango' dress with split sides and the hem sewn together between the legs, like a bag.* 17. *Callot's short, wide evening skirt trimmed with white fox and roses.*

14

15

16   *17*

be paid for with the order, rather than on delivery, and in cash. Furthermore, it was impossible to guarantee delivery anywhere outside France. These changes restricted many foreign buyers, especially as there was a cash shortage following a money panic in the first week of the war. The couture income was significantly reduced as a result. Any foreign buyers who were in Paris could pay cash for gowns or obtain credit at Premet – the only couturier to ignore the Chambre Syndicale's decisions on trade – and could take the clothes in their personal baggage, particularly to America, stood to make a fortune, for women there were still hungry for Paris designs.

Clothes which appeared late in the autumn clearly showed the influence of the war. Military collars, braid, sword-belts and other details were added to suits and coats, and were worn even in America, which was relatively unaffected by the war. Khaki was popular for street wear, tailored as plainly as possible; Victorian styles and trimmings were completely *démodé*.

In America, a 'cotton crusade' began. America produced three-fifths of the world's cotton but during the hostilities Europe, which made up two-thirds of the foreign market, classified cotton as contraband, since it could be converted into gun cotton by the enemy. Consequently, America's supply far exceeded demand and the price started to tumble. American women were asked to buy a bale of cotton, or at least cotton garments, to help the industry.

By the end of the year few sumptuous evening gowns were being made in Paris, with the odd exception for a traveller or bride. Paris evening wear had become extremely simple. Fashionable ladies soon became aware of cut-backs on lace, feathers and frivolous trimmings. The Turkish-style sleeveless Tango frocks were typical of the few dance frocks that were still made.

The war had had only a superficial effect on the lives of fashionable women by the end of the year, but couturiers were clearly affected. Some abandoned their work to fight for their country and it was largely the female couturiers who continued in their salons. Few, however, believed that the war would last longer than a couple of months and so little thought was given to the possibility of fabric shortages (hence the full silhouette) or to the strenuous tasks that women would have to perform.

1915

1

1. Tappe's yellow velveteen sports jacket and black-and-yellow skirt.   2. Premet's taupe faille suit with a bustle and a mole-coloured velvet collar and hat.   3. Lanvin's warm grey cloth suit with a seven-eighths-length jacket. The turban and muff are of moleskin and ribbon.   4. Redfern's military touches. Left: black faille peplumed jacket and overskirt of figured voile. Right: blue gabardine suit trimmed with blue braid and officer's straps on the shoulders.   5. Jenny's simple suit trimmed with self-fabric ruffles.   6. Lanvin's black charmeuse coat with white-and-gold bead motifs, white fox collar and cuffs and the white charmeuse frock beneath.   7. American flared coat of Hudson seal trimmed with opossum.

With the torpedoing of civilian and merchant ships – the British liner *Lusitania* was sunk by the Germans in May – trans-Atlantic travel became increasingly difficult. The spring collections in Paris were very poorly attended by the American buyers, but the autumn collections were better organized and gained more attention, partly because buyers who could not cross the Atlantic used their European-based commissionaires to order collections on their behalf.

The transportation difficulties inevitably restricted American imports of French fashion, to the chagrin of the French couturiers and manufacturers. A 'Made in America' movement developed, stimulating the American clothes industry, but the very wealthy continued to wear high fashion from Paris, imported despite the difficulties. Lanvin's entire autumn collection was purchased by the American department store Bonwit Teller and Jenny was sending 125 garments a day to America, Russia and England by the end of the year. Jenny, who moved to the Champs Elysées this year, was the first couturier in Paris to have a purpose-built salon. Specializing in very comfortable, elegant clothes, her success was instant. She was one of several French couturiers who showed at the San Francisco Exhibition of Design.

The tailored suit was plainer and more severe this year, owing its line and colour rather than trimmings to the military influence. Most of the summer and winter models were in sombre fabrics, such as dark blue or black serge and velvet, lifted in a number of cases by white trimmings. Callot was an exception, delighting in bright colours and

8　　　　9

11

12. *Premet's dramatic black-and-white velvet cloak is lined with rose-coloured velvet. The deep yoke is beaded with pearls, gold and black roses.　13. Martial et Armand's Victorian-style sprigged evening frock.　14. O'Sullivan's silk and chiffon gown with a full, ankle-length skirt and cap sleeves.*

10

8. *Lanvin's black chiffon afternoon frock worn with a red taffeta jacket.　9. Doeuillet's black velvet and taffeta dress with a tiered, hand-kerchief-flounced skirt.　10. Callot's lemon-yellow pongee dress embroidered with black, worn with a black satin vest and red patent-leather belt.　11. Jenny's black velvet coat-dress with a tight bodice, flaring at the collar and cuffs; the tiered skirt has tassels of antique gold braid to match the girdle.*

voluminous skirts for the spring. Soldier blue or *lie de vin* shirts with high linen collars which flared on each side of the face were worn with the military-style suits and braiding was often the only decorative device. Fashionable accessories included the type of slender bamboo cane used by British officers, the forage cap and the baton hat.

The typical suit jacket was tight-fitting at the waist and worn with a full, short skirt. Basques and peplums accentuated the normal waistline. Paquin experimented with the full, early-Victorian, tiered skirt. Only Callot and Chéruit favoured narrow skirts for the autumn. In Paris the tailored suit was reserved for country wear and the coat was generally worn in the city over a velveteen dress for the morning and a softer frock for luncheon. In London, by contrast, the suit held undisputed sway.

The long coat was considered the most economical choice for cold months, replacing the wrap-around coat. Despite the war and the rising costs of furs, these were still used lavishly for winter coats. Many houses showed leather coats for travelling and sportswear. Paquin tailored leather into redingotes, three-quarter- or full-length coats open from neck to hem, usually belted at the waist, seamed and fitted like cloth, while Doucet favoured oilskin as an alternative.

In general there were two daytime dress shapes: semi-fitted and fairly straight, or waisted with a full skirt. Few dancing frocks were shown in London and Paris this season. Fashionable European, especially French, restaurants frowned on gay attire, now associated with war profiteers. Women dragged the most passé outfits out of their wardrobes, one suspects more for patriotic effect than from actual need. Social life in America was relatively unaffected by the war, although fund-raising balls for the Allies filled the social calendar, so American designers still offered a great variety of dance and evening dresses. Most dinner gowns had trains and were exceedingly narrow at the hem, lacking even the concession of a split. They were generously décolleté and usually sleeveless. Many of Lanvin's frocks, by contrast, were stiffened with hoops and decorated with lace and crystal embroidery. Poiret's evening gowns were ornamentally theatrical.

12

13
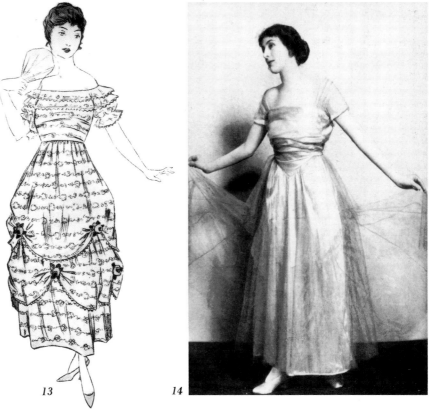
14

1916

This year saw an important evolution away from the curvaceous pre-war silhouette towards the sheath of the twenties. The chemise, a straight dress hanging loosely from the shoulders, was heralded in *Vogue* this autumn as 'the modern dress'. The spring collections had abounded with voluminous skirts, contrasting tight bodices and small inset sleeves. Skirt width was emphasized with horizontal trimming. There was great indecision over the precise location of the waistline. Worth concluded that it could be placed at the designer's discretion, and some houses completely ignored the waistline, anticipating the chemise. Chéruit reduced it to a beltless seam on some spring dresses, while others had a high waistline at the front curving down low at the back.

As a result of the continued popularity of gowns with trains in America, couturiers continued to show this feature, which they had introduced several seasons ago. The theatre was a source of inspiration for period fashion. The Comédie Française in Paris and various

1

1. *Stein and Blane's mauve linen frock with capacious pockets.* 2. *Paquin's full-skirted frock with fringed ruffles, worn with a veil swathing the neck.* 3. *Lanvin's black satin chemise embroidered with white beads, worn with a purple velvet drum-major's hat.* 4. *Summer models from the Boué Soeurs, with full, unstiffened skirts.* Left: *blue taffeta and white embroidered organdie.* Centre: *old-rose taffeta with white polka dots.* Right: *white net and white batiste with insertions of filet lace.*

playhouses in New York produced a number of plays dating from the late seventeenth and early eighteenth centuries, which led some couturiers to show bodices tapering to a V at the midriff, trimmed with bows and lace, over pannier skirts. Señora Gallenga, the creator of one-off studio gowns, experimented with period influences. Her lavishly stencilled and painted dresses were inspired by the narrow, gentle lines of Ancient Greece and Oriental dress.

The three-quarter-length jacket was the most fashionable for the suit this year. In general suits were not subject to the medieval, Renaissance and Empire period influences which affected dress design. Corduroy was a practical, durable new material that was experimented with for suits and coats. Street costumes were usually cut in navy blue serge or broadcloth, sometimes sporting military features, such as epaulettes or gauntlet cuffs. Some houses, such as Lanvin, showed kilts and tartans this spring.

By the late spring slimmer gowns were appearing – last year's hoops, which had been so unpopular and were particularly uncomfortable in the summer, were removed. Skirts were still full, but they fell, unstiffened, close to the body.

The narrow, modern chemise of the autumn was better suited to wartime: it used less material, gave ease of movement and was more practical – many women were taking jobs in hospitals and factories to serve their country. The chemise was offered in every colour and fabric for every hour of the day: velveteen or cloth for motoring, silk or jersey for the afternoon, satin georgette or organdie for the evening. Its simplicity made it relatively easy to copy. 'Made in the seclusion of the sewing room, to be worn later with the air of having been issued from Les Grandes

5. *Napoleonic-style coat of dark-green ratine braided in white and trimmed with opossum, and a black felt tricorne.* 6. *Chanel's old-blue jersey coat with a deep shoulder cape and matching turban.* 7. *Green cheviot morning coat with black taffeta scarf and a pantaloon skirt of black cloth.*

8. *Paquin's blue serge suit with a fitted jacket and full skirt.*   9. *Lanvin's natural-coloured Japanese pongee suit decorated with bands of embroidered, self-coloured soutache.*   10. *Redfern's cream suede suit with lavender suede collar and pocket flaps.*   11. *Bergdorf Goodman's blue jersey suit, yellow hat and white enamel stick.*   12. *Lanvin's full kilt worn with an embroidered blue serge jacket and black straw beret.*

Maisons', observed *Vogue*. Chanel, who had actually introduced the chemise in 1914, presented her first complete collection this autumn, concentrating on loosely girdled chemises that were embroidered at the hem and often cut in a black jersey. By the end of the year Paris and London women were spending their days in jersey: 'War and jersey; jersey is no longer a fabric, it is an obsession,' reported *Vogue*.

However, London couturiers were slow to adopt the narrow chemise: full-skirted dresses and suits still abounded there this autumn and the waistline was still placed at its natural level. Lucile showed Russian-inspired, full-skirted suits with simple tunic tops or tie-belted jackets. Practical sweaters were popular in England for morning wear. The more ornate versions were trimmed with fur, and Delysia and Poirette showed silk smock-shape sweaters with wide sleeves and patch pockets, similar to those worn by Chanel just before the war.

Once again Parisiennes chose to wear fur with summer frocks and costumes. Perversely, in view of the scarcity of pelts, couturiers made huge fur collars,

12

16–18 inches deep, and deep fur hems and trimmings on coats and suits. Dœuillet used narrow bands of American mink and dyed and clipped rabbit to trim summer costumes. The pelts of labradors and cats were even resorted to under the guise of some fancifully named fur. The fashionable evening wrap was usually a combination of fur and velvet. By the end of the year there was a practical reason for warm, fur-trimmed coats – horses and taxis were scarce in Paris, so women were forced to walk or cycle. There were two fashionable lengths: a few inches shorter than the skirt, or hip-length.

'It may be the result of the feminist movement or merely a whim,' observed *Vogue*, 'but women are claiming the masculine advantage of pockets.' They appeared this year, large and small, on many frocks, coats and suits. The walking cane fad, which had started in Paris at the beginning of the war, was now imitated in America and Britain. Fashion leaders, such as Mrs Vernon Castle, who returned to America from Europe this autumn, carried many fashion ideas across the Atlantic.

13. Elspeth Phelps's evening gown: the diamanté-edged train is cut in one with the bodice, and the white tulle bouffant skirt ends in silver-threaded lace.
14. Gallenga's Grecian tunic in deep-gold silk embroidered in white at the neck and hem, with an orange crêpe-de-Chine wrap stencilled lavishly in gold.
15. Chéruit's gold-and-blue lamé evening gown embroidered with blue and red beads. The full, short skirt has a train at each side. 16. Paquin's simple pink bengaline gown girdled with marine-blue brocaded satin. The silver lace train ends in two tassels.

1917

The war was directly responsible for the sober, adaptable clothes which now dominated the Paris and London collections. Patriotic service had become women's first thought, social life their second. The couturiers responded accordingly, providing functional attire for women working out in all weathers and in unheated buildings. Practical colours dominated the collections: browns, beiges, blacks, blues and, most popular of all, 'hopeful' green. The need for smart simplicity led designers to borrow clothes styles from masculine attire; waistcoats, rainproof gabardine coats, mannish hats, stout boots and umbrellas, walking canes, ties, and simple tailored suits were widely worn. Silks and satins were the most acceptable daytime materials even in winter, due to the scarcity and high price of woollens, which were needed for soldiers' uniforms.

The narrow lines of the chemise held sway and led to the 'plumbline' evening gown, which fell simply in diaphanous layers from the shoulders. However, some Paris couturiers tried to introduce the 'barrel' line, evolved from the more exaggerated pannier style. The fullness from waist to knee was often achieved with the addition of large, loose pockets which hung out over each hip. It had initially been shown by Callot, and was now available at Paquin and Dœuillet. Only the American buyers, seeking another Paris novelty, seized upon the

1. Lucile's black satin restaurant gown with plunging neckline.   2. Black crêpe-de-Chine mourning frock trimmed with black beads. The mushroom hat has a white crêpe brim and a long black chiffon veil.   3. Pyjamas in black foulard spotted with white and tied at the shoulders with red velvet.   4. Orchid-coloured crêpe-de-Chine negligée lined in salmon pink. The fan-like ornament is of gold and white silk braid.   5. Dœuillet's barrel-line evening gown in pale-blue-and-black figured taffeta.   6. Cream velvet restaurant gown draped with coffee-coloured hand-made lace. 7. Lucile's plumbline-straight lace-and-tulle gown decorated with flounces of silvery flowers.

8

8. Burberry's severe brown tweed suit with a sweeping cape. 9. Paquin's 'hopeful' green wool-velour coat trimmed with caracul and worn with a Russian toque. 10. Maupas's red velvet cloak with sealskin hood, collar and cuffs. 11. Poiret's quilted brown faille coat stitched in navy blue and girdled with blue velvet.

barrel line with avidity and popularized it in New York.

American designers favoured plaids in light, cool materials for the summer. By the late summer lace had returned to high fashion, though it was not worn in Paris, being saved for the export market. The most fashionable laces were black and white Chantilly, Valenciennes, Lyons and Malines.

Many fashionable European women now remained at home in the evenings, as both travel and entertaining were limited, which encouraged the fashion for tea gowns and pyjamas. The grand evening gown had failed to appear in Paris society for several seasons, since the French government had decided that formal evening wear was unnecessary at official functions for the duration of the war. As a result the restaurant gown evolved. Similar to an elaborate after-

11

noon frock, it was cut rather low across the bodice and teamed with a large picture hat. The dress could also be used for entertaining at home.

As the casualties of the war escalated, mourning became a common and public act and consequently formality was relaxed. For instance, touches of white were now permitted with black for first mourning.

Warmth was a major consideration for coats this winter and the quilted hood was popular. The latest coat was the manteau, which fell straight from the shoulders and had vast kimono-style sleeves. Brown, beige and brick were popular colours and a new 'beetroot' shade was introduced. Due to the confiscation of private automobiles for the war effort, motoring as a sport continued only in America, where the suede sports coat was the most fashionable attire.

12. *Lanvin's simple white summer frock trimmed with sky-blue ribbon.* 13. *Beer's black satin frock with an embroidered panel and tassels of orange, blue and silver.* 14. *Jenny's beige dress and jacket embroidered with grey cord. The skirt has a grey batiste panel that matches the lining of the jacket.* 15. *American black-and-white chiffon dress trimmed with plain black chiffon to match the black lace hat.* 16. *Maupas's short-sleeved plaid coat and matching dress.* 17. *Lucile's simple beaver-coloured wool suit with a stiff basque.* 18. *Kenneth Durward's tobacco-brown suit with stitched tab waistband and leather-covered buttons.* 19. *Doeuillet's barrel-line suit.*

1918

2   3

By 1918 there were acute fabric short-ages. No designer could use more than $4\frac{1}{2}$ yards of cloth per suit, dress or coat. Wool was very scarce and *Vogue* attempted to unite women under the banner, 'Wool will win the war: conserve it'. There was not a spring garment that was not made, in part at least, of silk, the most readily available material. British looms in the north of England produced thousands of yards of silk, but Germany was the major source of dyes and with the ban on imports, manufacturers and the trade press forecast dreary colours. However, rich materials were still exported from Lyon, where, despite shortages of coal and labour and the difficulties of transportation, high-quality silks of the latest designs were produced.

'Plain', 'severe' and 'austere' were the adjectives used to describe this year's clothes. Simple was deemed smart by patriotic fashion editors, and money-saving advice was constantly given to readers during these dire days. They were advised to give up eccentric dress-ing, avoid complicated gowns that dated quickly, and use practical, dark colours such as black, blue and brown.

There was a noticeable stan-dardization of attire now. Adaptability was the most important fashion cri-terion; almost every outfit was expected to have at least two functions and women began to change only once, or at most twice, a day. This led to a relax-ation and eventual abandonment of the strict pre-war rules regarding what was to be worn for each occasion of the day. The faithful jersey dress and loose coat or tailored suit became linchpins of most women's wardrobes. The practical sports suit was the most widely adopted form of tailored suit.

The Americans joined the war in April 1917. There was a noticeable difference in skirt lengths in Europe and America; the Paris and London houses were showing shorter skirts, but in America shorter boots were worn as a result of government regulations to save leather,

4

1. Quaker-style dress of oyster-white satin and pearl-grey charmeuse. 2. Doeuillet's short, slim silhouette – a black crêpe-de-Chine dress with a bolero-style bodice and high collar, worn with a waistcoat of rose satin and white angora. 3. Lanvin's new cap sleeve on a black satin and jet gown. 4. Royant's white silk-jersey dress with a matelasse bodice and beige silk-jersey coat trimmed with beaver fur.

5

6

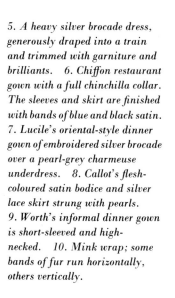

7

8

9

10

5. *A heavy silver brocade dress,
generously draped into a train
and trimmed with garniture and
brilliants.   6. Chiffon restaurant
gown with a full chinchilla collar.
The sleeves and skirt are finished
with bands of blue and black satin.
7. Lucile's oriental-style dinner
gown of embroidered silver brocade
over a pearl-grey charmeuse
underdress.   8. Callot's flesh-
coloured satin bodice and silver
lace skirt strung with pearls.
9. Worth's informal dinner gown
is short-sleeved and high-
necked.   10. Mink wrap; some
bands of fur run horizontally,
others vertically.*

so skirts had to be longer. The American tradition of the shirtwaister, a tailored dress with a bodice like a mannish, tailored blouse, which had been introduced many years earlier, was ideally suited to the present requirements of simple practicality. It was to appear repeatedly throughout the twentieth century. Alternatively, the tailored blouse and simple skirt was much worn in both America and Europe.

Vests or shirts inspired by various European peasant costumes, such as pleated blouses, were worn with many fashionable French suits. The silhouette was very short and severe. The waistline was either in the natural position or lowered, and sleeves generally followed the natural line of the arm closely. Dress and skirt drapery was reduced to a minimum now, though Lanvin did experiment with details of the 1840s dress, trimmings in organdies, muslins and sprigged cottons for summer, and there were a few examples of *directoire* and Victorian styles at other houses.

Checks were popular for casual summer gowns. Serges and silks and silk-and-wool gabardines were basic early spring materials, lightened with white trimmings. Peasant silk handkerchiefs, which had been introduced last year, were draped across the front of black silk dresses, to add much needed colour.

Paris coats for the spring followed straight, narrow lines, and were often cut in satin with the new fashionable features of wide sleeves, narrow cuffs and deep collars. The two most popular designs were the wrap-over and the high-necked, buttoned coat. Worth's spring collection showed a series of military-inspired coats fastened with toggles. The rubberized cape, with practical large pockets, was worn on rainy days in the country or even in town. Heavy raincoats had detachable aprons and ambulance drivers and nurses wore oilskin waistcoats with woollen sleeves and linings.

Many designers such as Premet were using ingenious substitutes for fur to band the hems of their winter coats and dresses. The most conspicuously extravagant furs were now worn during the day only in New York. Practical, high Russian boots topped with fur were worn with tailored suits and dresses.

Less formal evening wear led to what the Americans called 'reception' gowns

11. *American corduroy jacket with an asymmetrical collar and long pleated velour skirt.*
12. *Lucile's Victorian-style black velvet dress collared and cuffed in lace and black velvet hat trimmed with pink ostrich feathers.* 13. *Jenny's black serge and white piqué suit with black satin cravat, girdle and revers.* 14. *Jenny's fur-trimmed black satin coat.* 15. *Worth's full coat and slim skirt of brown duvetyn fringed in Chenille. The brown satin waistcoat is embroidered in gold.* 16. *Callot's cinnamon tweed coat with a brown-and-white check lining.*

and the French called 'demi-toilettes'. Trailing hemlines and minimal bodices were the most distinctive features of more formal evening gowns. By the autumn, with the hopeful news from the Front, there was a new note of elaboration evident in Paris evening gowns.

Chanel, for instance, used rich embroideries, rivalling the most elaborate Oriental tissues, to decorate her simply cut, sleeveless evening gowns. Stage influences reappeared in couture gowns, particularly in the work of Callot, who was a successful stage costume designer.

1919-1925

Maisie was horrified when she saw the new boyish line in 1923! But she managed it at the cost of her health and looks!

Angus Wilson, *For Whom the Cloche Tolls*

Cecil Beaton's caricature of the skinny Flapper; the sway-backed and breastless Miss Elizabeth Ponsonby.

A confusion of styles reigned immediately after the war. Brightly coloured, lavish clothes to celebrate victory appeared in *Vogue* alongside the emancipatory, shorter, plainer suits and tunics that had been ubiquitous in the previous five years. Which mood would prevail? Between the close of hostilities and the end of 1922 a number of designers attempted to revive pre-war hooped and panniered evening dresses. Only Chanel, Molyneux and Patou championed the straight, simple chemise, ignoring these retrogressive styles. American *Vogue* believed that the corset would return for the evening, but that for day wear the corsetless relaxation which most women had recently enjoyed would continue. In fact, the restrictive corset was not revived, though some now wore a modified version, which created a straighter silhouette.

By 1922 the controversy over hemlines was at its height: should skirts continue to rise or should they fall? *Vogue*, responding to the varied practical requirements of its readership, advocated consumer choice: 'Women are coming to recognize that there is no fashionable length, that one cannot give a definite measure of so many inches from the ground, which will be invariable for all figures. All women, it seems, agree that the revival of the really long skirt for street wear would be a mistake.' The magazine recognized that its readers wanted options, not dictates.

The post-war slump directly affected the clothing industry: there were shortages of materials, dyes, fuels and manpower; markets shrank; cotton and silk imports from India, Egypt and the East flooded in and Europe's textile industry lay devastated. The woollen industry of northern France was virtually destroyed; Lancashire's cotton mills were heading for the cotton slump of 1922 and the emergent clothing industry of the United States was still getting over its teething problems of organization and standardizing production and distribution. Couture prices soared.

The war and its effect on the world economy precipitated a redistribution of income and *Vogue* experienced a significant change in its readership as a result. The *nouveaux riches*, the wives of the war profiteers, craved the ostentatious fashions with which Poiret and other couturiers celebrated the end of the war. 'At Worth, Pacquin, Dœuillet, everywhere, in fact, women go in and out all day long dressed in an elegance which has no suggestion of

48

the past months.' However, the prevailing social and economic climate censored such immodest indulgence. There were fewer customers who could afford these clothes, and the old society was very wary of the *arriviste* and her taste and lifestyle. For instance, the young actress Miss Tobin was described by American *Vogue* as 'the daughter of a war profiteer in search of manners'. Partly in reaction to this new element in society, it became smart to assume poverty, or at least a Bohemian lifestyle. Women cultivated alternatives to preoccupation with dress – literature, politics and, in some cases, careers. Fashion responded to this social evolution. The war had changed everything radically, especially women's place and expectations within society. Many broke with convention and those seeking responsibility outside the home were encouraged by the success of the suffragettes. Bills enfranchising married women over thirty were passed in Britain in 1919 and in America in 1920 and a Sex Discrimination (Removal) Act was passed in Britain in 1919.

Women had proved their worth during the war and, for a while, their emancipationist views were tolerated and deemed newsworthy. The traditional preoccupation of women with children and home was questioned and Margaret Sanger and Marie Stopes campaigned for wider access to birth control. However, as the men returned from the trenches, women had to fight hard for their jobs, being blamed for mass post-war unemployment. Dorothy Parker writing in *Vogue* described the situation thus: 'The heroine is no more. No longer does she potter about touching the house all day long, no more does she wait at the gate in the evening ... No, it's the hero who's waiting for her these days. You see, she has taken his job in the factory. When the men went to war, the women just naturally went right into men's jobs: when the men came back from the war, the women just naturally stayed right on doing men's jobs. It is, according to them, the only life.'

Sadly, despite the determined efforts of some modern women, there were proportionally fewer women at work in Britain, for example, by 1921 than there had been before the war. However, marriage was no longer inevitable. One in seven men had been killed in the war and many shared Vera Brittain's reaction: 'Marriage, I decided, was not for me, nor ever for me the maternal joys of tender patience and pity and understanding ... I was destined for permanent spinsterhood' (*Testament of Youth*, 1933). Action and political consciousness were deemed alternatives to marriage. These non-domestic women tended to eke out a living in mundane jobs as stenographers, shop assistants and nurses. They were no more likely to adopt a pre-war fashion than to accept the discredited lifestyle and mores of their parents' generation.

Vogue was aware of two new factors in its readers' lives: the need to work and lower incomes. American *Vogue* had started a column during the war entitled 'Dressing on a War Income' and British *Vogue* responded with 'Smart Fashions for Limited Incomes' in 1916; after the war both suggested practical wardrobes for the impecunious and the business woman. Tailored suits and sports clothes dominated the collections and ostentatious day wear was viewed askance. *Vogue* commented that 'no fantastic adornment attracts attention to one woman more than another. Indeed their appearance suggests that they are almost clothed in a uniform which changes in colour and proves that the present generation cannot be reproached for frivolity or vanity.' In 1921 Worth considered that 'the modern designer must devote his greatest effort to clothes for ordinary occasions ... simplicity is praiseworthy and suited to our present conditions of life'.

Nancy Astor, Britain's first woman Member of Parliament.

Marchers on the famous American women's suffrage parade in 1917.

The Vogue artist Edouard Benito depicts The Rape of the Lock (or the passion for short, bobbed or shingled hair) on the contemporary stenographer. 'Stern is the demeanor of Miss Gifford – at the office. But if you could see her picknicking at Coney Isle! Giddy is not the word!' 1924.

The tennis champion Suzanne Lenglen.

The man–woman styling of Miss Julie Lentilhon depicted by the artist Mme de Launx.

Radclyffe Hall, author of the novel The Well of Loneliness.

Active lives, whether in the office, on the golf links or in a car, required practical apparel and Chanel, Patou and their followers obliged. 'I make clothes women can live in, breathe in, feel comfortable in and look young in,' explained Chanel. Many other houses followed her lead and opened shops specializing in sportswear. In 1923 *Vogue* pointed out that 'a few years ago the sports costume was ignored by the French couturiers; now it appears in the collection of almost every house'.

The most popular expression of liberated clothing was the tailored suit. According to *Vogue*, after the war 'many found it hard to go back to ordinary habiliments, which called for arbitrary changes so many times a day, for the joys of standardized dress, once tried, could not be abandoned'. With simple changes of accessories, the suit could be worn from nine in the morning until six in the evening, a godsend for the woman of limited income and busy lifestyle.

Many women interpreted emancipation as the freedom to dress as much like a man as possible – in a smoking jacket, waistcoat, necktie, tailored suit, stout shoes or pyjamas. Some chose the masculine manner to underline their political views or to hide their sexuality. Contemporary literature explored the situation of the lone woman, whom *Punch* referred to as the 'man-woman', poking fun at her assumed masculinity. The feminine, curvaceous figure was hopelessly out of fashion and the 'sweetly slinky' was admired. In 1922 *Vogue* wrote, 'Men and women are becoming every year more indistinguishable. The distinction between the sexes has been discovered to be grossly exaggerated.' The cry of Sodom and Gomorrah was heard from many a pulpit, voicing a fear that this androgyny would damn society. Some idealized the androgynous gamine. Victor Margueritte's scandalous novel of 1922, *La Garçonne*, is an example, while Radclyffe Hall's *The Well of Loneliness* (1928) touched upon the anguish and social ostracism of the lesbian.

Post-war haute couture in Paris was now dominated by women: Chanel, Lanvin and Vionnet. 'The First War made me. In 1919 I woke up famous,' recalls Coco Chanel. She anticipated the market's needs; for common sense, appropriateness and simple chic were her guidelines. Her clothes typified the first half of the twenties. Chanel introduced the sports suit in jersey or tweed, with an easy-fitting cardigan jacket and softly pleated, short shirt, characteristically worn with a combination of bold, obviously fake costume jewellery and real gems. As a chief promulgator of this practical masculinity, she looked to men's tailoring, especially the traditional English tweed suit, as a source of inspiration. Her clothes were so comfortable because she tried styles out on herself, rather than dreaming up creations on paper, divorced from the realities of cloth, cut and mobility.

Vionnet had trained with Mme Gerber of Callot Soeurs and at Doucet before opening her own house in 1912. It had closed during the war but reopened in the Avenue Montaigne in 1922. Like Chanel, Vionnet did not sketch, but draped and wrapped cloth round her mannequin, imbuing her clothes with the simplicity of classical Greek dress. The glorification of the free, uncorseted body was her philosophy. In 1919 *Vogue* acclaimed her plain crêpe de Chine dress with long sleeves, trimmed only with hemstitching and initials on the left of the blouse, as 'the sartorial Ford'. Her bias cutting was to become supremely fashionable in the late twenties and early thirties.

Jeanne Lanvin trained as a dressmaker and a milliner. At the turn of the century she began to make clothes for her younger sister and daughter which were greatly admired by her friends. This prompted her to open her own couture house, which became renowned for its mother-and-daughter ensembles. Though she was subsequently patronized for her feminine, romantic picture frocks, which were beautifully embroidered and appliquéd, she was one of the first couturiers to present the modern chemise at the beginning of the First World War.

Jean Patou's career had been interrupted by the war. He had opened Maison Parry in 1912 and it closed during the war; in 1919 his business reopened under his own name as a couture house. Like Chanel, Patou concentrated on modern, linear sports clothes, in navy blue, beige, black, cream or apricot, decorated with simple embroidery, such as Russian peasant motifs or geometric details and Cubist patterns. Experimental cutting techniques became his post-war hallmarks: godets and concealed pleats and decorative panels. Patou's close association with the leading tennis star of the twenties, Suzanne Lenglen, consolidated his position as an important designer of active sports wear. She wore his short pleated skirts, simple jumpers and cardigans at Wimbledon and other international tournaments. He also dressed her rival, Helen Wills, and in 1924 he opened shops in Deauville and Biarritz offering sports attire for morning and luncheon wear. At its height in the twenties, Maison Patou was one of the largest houses, presenting up to 350 designs a season – more than Chanel – which would take a whole day to show. He and Chanel were fierce rivals, but Chanel managed to court the press more effectively and hence won greater acclaim.

Lucien Lelong opened his house in 1923. Though not a great originator, he became an important businessman and organizer of the couture. His house offered fine quality clothes and employed many young talented designers; their creativity, combined with the house's professionalism, proved a successful alliance.

A number of pre-war designers who continued their businesses after the war found it hard to tune in to the simple style of these years. Inevitably houses such as Chéruit, Dœuillet and Drécoll were no longer in the vanguard and attracted an older clientele. Poiret was the most tragic victim of the watershed in style created by the First World War. He reopened in 1919 and his taste for the Oriental satisfied the immediate post-war craving for colour and luxury, but he failed to adapt to new demands and continued to overload

Gabrielle 'Coco' Chanel, c.1925.

Mannequins on display in the Parisian department store Printemps, demonstrating the change in ideal figure from the voluptuous Edwardian to the svelte flapper of 1925.

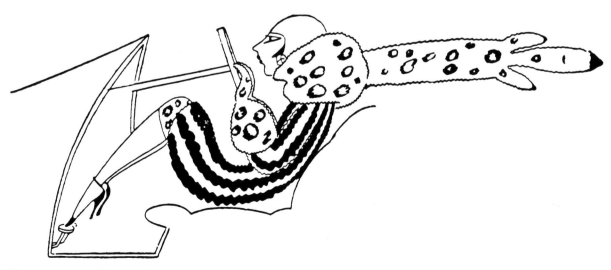

Fish, the Vogue *cartoonist, illustrates the contemporary 'Speed Queen' of 1925.*

The Spanish singer Racquel Meller, sporting the fashionable bob and ethnic jewellery.

Two negro jazz dancers by Covarrubias.

even simple sheath dresses with excessive decorative detail. By the mid-twenties he suffered serious financial problems and during the Wall Street Crash of 1929 was forced to close.

The English couture benefited from the contemporary international demand for masculine sports clothes. Reville & Rossiter had the advantage of royal and aristocratic patronage, designing both tailored clothes and court and ball gowns. By 1922 the firm had expanded into premises on Oxford Street. Though not a house of great innovation, it satisfied the needs of many discriminating clients. Redfern served a similar market.

The prevailing straight, simple line led to what *Vogue* described as a 'rage for the proper culture of the body, and the determination of modern woman to look as youthful as she can'. In 1922 Leon Bakst, Diaghilev's chief designer, emphasized the importance of the slim silhouette: 'In the art of costuming, it is the main essential. If one can attain the correct silhouette, the battle is won; the rest is but a trifling matter of technical artifice: artistic arrangement of colour, a clever coiffure and suitable make-up.' He thought the current mode tyrannical in its determination to oust the curve, but proclaimed, 'Let us, like Diana, be thin.' He recommended art as a remedy for unsatisfactory proportions. Black could be used to minimize an undesirable feature or shift attention to other parts of the body, and he illustrated the disastrous effect of using horizontal stripes instead of vertical ones.

Others believed in 'banting' ('reducing') and exercise to eliminate the inadequacies of the figure, or used corsetry – the rubber girdle and the brassière were the modern alternative to the old-fashioned corset. In 1922 *Vogue* observed that 'the pursuit of slimness is one of the chief labours of the modern woman'. The ideal was the physique of a young boy: straight, hipless, bustless, waistless. Madge Garland, fashion editor of British *Vogue*, remembers that any girl endowed with a large bust might as well have stayed at home and shut the curtains during these years. A spate of advertisements for slimming foods, health clubs and spas appeared, and dining was regarded as a dangerous indulgence for the fashionable woman.

Women flocked to the golf links, the tennis court and the beach to keep in trim and to bare their fashionably lithe bodies. One gentleman remarked, 'The opulent curves associated with the Victorian age have been supplanted by straight simplicity of design once considered masculine: it makes a day on the beach somewhat confusing!' Travel to exclusive resorts, such as the Lido in Venice, the French Riviera or Florida, was a new form of conspicuous consumption for the rich; sunbathing in revealing swim wear was the latest craze. Noël Coward cynically remarked that 'the blazing sun brings out the worst traits of character, like a heat rash, so that the beach is an excellent place to see how the smart world quarrels'.

In 1924 Diaghilev's *Le Train Bleu*, a modern ballet based on sport, crystallized the sports craze. Chanel designed the costumes, creating real sportswear, such as knitted bathing suits, rather than dance clothes.

Jazz music and dancing entertained the young. Young girls, 'flappers', went out unchaperoned with their 'boyfriends' to nightclubs, hotels and restaurants, a trend which had started during the war. Fashion responded; the couture evening frock now became almost exclusively a dance frock or cocktail outfit – diaphanous, figure-revealing and extremely décolleté.

The Bright Young Things personified the post-war moral laxity and new decadence, or attempted decadence, of the young. Evelyn Waugh satirized their behaviour in *Vile Bodies* (1930): 'Oh,' said the Bright Young People,

'Oh, oh, oh. It's just exactly like being inside a cocktail shaker.' The cocktail party was one of their new sports, introduced to England, according to Waugh's *Diaries*, by his brother Alec in April 1924, 'to fill the gap in London social life between 5.30 and 7.00 p.m.'. The cocktail was an American import: a symbol of the age's preoccupation with alcohol.

Despite the notoriety they achieved, the Bright Young Things were never more than a very small coterie. Angus Wilson recalls in *For Whom the Cloche Tolls* (1973), 'It's strange how the illusion persists that those who make the most noise are the most important ... there was only a fraction, of course, who went on behaving as though the whole of life was one long Armistice celebration.' In the long run, however, society was affected by their indulgence, and greater freedom was tolerated in manners, dress and morals. Women were free to express their sexuality, or at least to discuss it, and for a while the whole of life seemed to revolve around the discovery of 'sex appeal'.

Obvious make-up began to be worn and was even applied in public – was the powder room to become defunct? Michael Arlen, the author of *The Green Hat* (1924), described the contemporary look as 'a vermilion gash across a face of chalk'. *Vogue* reported in 1919 that 'No one thinks of leaving the house nowadays without powder and lipstick, purse, notebook and smoking paraphernalia, to which the latest addition is the gold briquet for lighting the perpetual cigarette in these days of scarcity of matches'. Stories circulated of young ladies getting 'blotto' in public bars. Their mothers' generation had regarded merely dining in public as somewhat suspect. Suspicions of 'petting' were whispered. Growing knowledge of contraceptive methods, which had been widely publicized by Margaret Sanger as early as 1914 in the magazine *The Young Rebels*, contributed to the defiant and carefree attitude of the young.

My Lady Nicotine *by Fish, 1925.*

The shock value of 'modern' dress appealed to them – clothes were as short and flimsy as they dared, even to the point of rolling stockings down just above the knees. The tradition of wearing stockings with bathing costumes was abandoned. As breasts were bandaged out of sight and clothing avoided the curve of the hips, legs became the new erogenous zone.

Short skirts focused attention on hosiery and shoes. Most stockings by the mid-twenties were flesh-coloured and the simulated nudity was initially considered outrageous – until then stockings had been opaque – hence Cole Porter's song:

> In olden days a glimpse of stocking
> Was looked on as something shocking
> But now, heaven knows, anything goes!

In the early twenties artificial silk brought the possibility of gleaming legs to every girl. Prior to this wool or cotton had been the norm; silk was only for the rich. D.C. Coleman's *Courtaulds: An Economic and Social History* (1969) concluded that 'the profits of the rayon industry and the social freedom of women were intertwined'. However, as the fashion historian James Laver pointed out, 'It would be difficult to say whether the vogue for very short skirts created the demand for silk (or artificial silk) stockings or whether it was the new method of manufacturing silk stockings at a reasonable price which reinforced the tendency towards the short skirt' (*Taste and Fashion from the French Revolution to the Present Day*, 1945). During the

The French couturier Mme Jeanne Lanvin.

Pola Negri, Hollywood star, is kohl-and-vaseline-eyed and beturbaned.

inter-war years artificial silk was also to become the major material for women's underwear.

American firms such as Steine & Blane, Bergdorf Goodman, Lord & Taylor, D. M. Tighe, Thurn, Gidding, Franklin Simon and Wanamaker were importing original Paris models as well as mass-producing Paris-inspired high fashion for their large home market. International buyers and commissionaires, especially Americans, flocked to the Paris shows; they bought one or two gowns from the houses but also sketched and noted details of the famous collections. By the mid-twenties the problem of plagiarism had become so acute that Vionnet organized a couture numbering system; each model was photographed, in an attempt to establish a patent. However, the lack of an efficient policing system to catch offenders made this system merely a symbolic recognition of the problem.

Paris reigned supreme as the centre of fashion, but by 1923, according to British *Vogue*, the American way of life and New York fashions had begun to influence Paris. The consolidation of the American fashion industry had begun in 1918, when over fifty manufacturers leased land on Seventh Avenue. Two buildings, numbers 498 and 500, were completed in 1921, to house the core of New York's fashion industry, on what became known as 'Fashion Avenue'.

French *Vogue*, launched in 1921 by Condé Nast, fared very badly in the twenties, as few houses advertised in the magazine. The French system of advertising consisted of a couture house dressing a socially prominent and beautiful woman for next to nothing. The couturier's advantage was that the gowns would be seen at the most exclusive venues. The society woman had to guarantee to wear only the clothes of the one house; if she reneged on the deal, she was liable to be sent a hefty bill for her season's wardrobe.

Immediately after the war ethnic and exotic styles inspired fashion. 'Fashion weaves tropical spells ... books and paintings have vied with each other to bring the tropical spell home to our Northern world, and who has not in spirit travelled with Gauguin to admire the subtle coquetry of dusky beauties?' asked British *Vogue*. Cubism, which originated in Paris in 1907, followed the exotic as a source of inspiration. The fashion world had been slow to appreciate the decorative value of Cubist forms, although Poiret had

The Mangbeta woman's headdress, which inspired the Parisian milliner, Agnès.

Agnès's ethnic-inspired turban of 1925, titled 'Croisière Noire'.

experimented with them before the war. Designers such as Sonia Delaunay began to use Constructivist motifs inspired by machinery and skyscrapers and geometric Cubist patterns for fabrics. Princess Lucien Murat applied embroidered geometric motifs to her clothes and Patou designed a successful range of Cubist-patterned sports sweaters in the early twenties. The straight, simple sheath was an ideal canvas for Cubist designs, which became popular with the advent of the new silhouette. Cubism was particularly well expressed on fur coats during the twenties, most notably at Fourrures Max. Exotic pelts were cut and matched to create Cubist effects using two methods. Either contrasting pelts, such as mink juxtaposed with sable or monkey fur, were cut and laid side by side to create a pattern, or, more subtly, pieces of the same fur were patchworked together so that the pile on each piece lay in a different direction to that of its neighbour, creating the effect as the fur caught the light.

Line rather than colour predominated. The vivid hues of the previous years had given way to beiges, black, white and browns in the mid-twenties. Subtlety was required in the choice of beige. *Vogue* stated that 'the ideal is like a pale, dead leaf, not rosy, not yellow, but a kind of faintly toasted neutral'. *Punch* depicted an old-fashioned gentleman in a draper's shop saying, 'I want a dainty scarf for a lady, in some pretty colour.' 'Certainly, sir, we have them in mud, rust, clay and old brick.'

The straight silhouette had been perfected in 1925, the year of the Exhibition of Decorative Arts in Paris. Having gained widespread popularity, it immediately began to decline; in September 1925 *Vogue* reported that the straight line was dead; 'a softened, supple, sophisticated simplicity has replaced the simplicities of yesterday, that now appear tight, hard and lacking in invention'. Full skirts, curves and clothes with movement were evident in the autumn collections. Bias cut, uneven hemlines (dipping at the back as far as the heels at the houses of Patou and Louiseboulanger), a natural waistline (at Patou) and an abundance of superfluous trimming, long absent, began to reappear. Straight lines were largely confined to sports and casual wear, as the genius of Vionnet's bias cutting and svelte, flowing clothes ushered in a new era of design.

Agnès modelling her Cubist printed toque with matching muff, 1925.

Arnold Ronnebeck's Cubist-style The City of the Future, *1925.*

1919

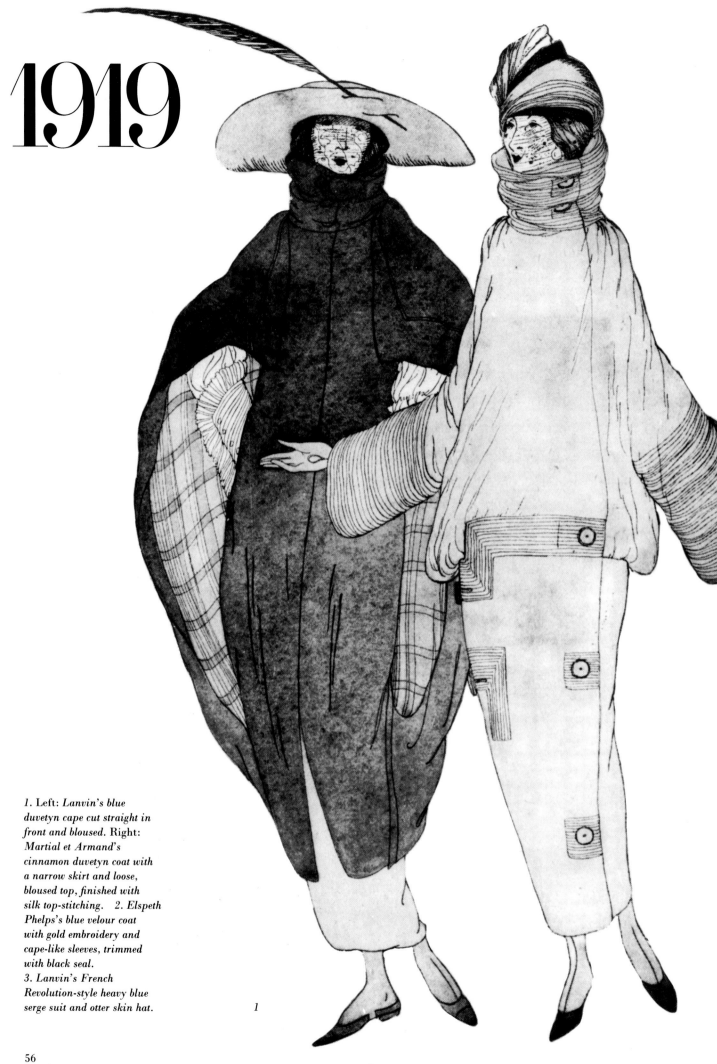

1. Left: *Lanvin's blue duvetyn cape cut straight in front and bloused. Right: Martial et Armand's cinnamon duvetyn coat with a narrow skirt and loose, bloused top, finished with silk top-stitching.* 2. *Elspeth Phelps's blue velour coat with gold embroidery and cape-like sleeves, trimmed with black seal.* 3. *Lanvin's French Revolution-style heavy blue serge suit and otter skin hat.*

1

There was great speculation about what the post-war silhouette would be. *Vogue* expected fashion to follow the Tanagra line – loosely draped, waistless robes, sometimes girdled about the hips, based on the costumes of Hellenistic grave figurines – which Fortuny had been experimenting with for some years. In fact the beginning of the year was characterized by variety and confusion: there was the Empire waistline, the medieval look, the Oriental line – dropped below the hips – and the 'normal' waisted shape. Sleeves were equally varied: there were tight sleeves, eighteenth-century-style puff sleeves and the Eastern sleeve, slit along its length and tied at the wrist. Women took advantage of this variety to pursue their own personal styles.

Many women remained economy-con-scious for some time after the war, due to the immediate post-war slump. British *Vogue*'s 'Dressing on a Limited Income' column featured versatile garments like the coat-dress and advocated separates dressing, as a result of which the lingerie blouse returned to fashion. Its plain, rather severe neckline, popular for the last few seasons, could be softened by a lace collar, and was recommended as a cheap way to cheer up one's wardrobe. Another practical contemporary fashion was the jumper dress, which could be knitted at home.

Suits based on Louis XV male costumes were considered chic. (Demobilization meant that men were again available to tailor suits.) An alternative was the longer, beltless suit jacket, which in some cases, notably at Paquin, was very narrow at the bottom. The post-war skirt was slightly longer than its wartime counterpart; it was close-fitting at the back and tight at the front. The cape, appreciated during the war for its practicality, was still widely worn, though more decorative versions were now introduced. An alternative was the waisted redingote with a tight bodice and full skirt.

In celebration of the victory dresses became less sombre; the skirts of both afternoon and evening dresses received

4. *Molyneux's 'Slav' look: belted, fur-trimmed tunic coat and tight-fitting cap.* 5. *Three American 1860s-style outfits.* Left: *fringed jacket and billowing, burgundy linen skirt.* Centre: *sheer cream batiste with a lace shawl collar.* Right: *charmeuse outfit with an exaggerated black-and-white fringe.* 6. *Lucile's navy wool street outfit, trimmed with navy and royal-blue stripes and worn with Russian boots and royal-blue velvet hat.*

7

8

special attention. They were elaborate and flounced, or draped and puffed into panniers, though the more practical day dresses remained straight. In general the very short evening skirt was abandoned and, as a compromise, transparent hems were adopted. The fitted bodice was the most popular shape; although the waist was wrapped more snugly, there was no indication of a return to the tightly corseted figure. Embroidery was generally unpopular; ribbons and edged trimmings were preferred and a number of novel methods of fabric decoration were introduced, such as fringes, self-fabric piping and cut-outs.

Transparent and fringed wraps were luxuriously ostentatious. The Far East was a particularly potent inspirational source for designers, and large fans, often of feathers, made a return this year as a fashionable accessory.

Chanel's popular chemise gown reappeared this year in blue satin or beige wool jersey. *Vogue* admired her *nonchalance de luxe:* 'the sort of simplicity that always has been and always will be expensive'. She was very aware of contemporary influences; for instance, her collection of fringed coats and dresses were inspired by American Westerns.

7. *Lanvin's 'slouch-back' black satin dress with green velvet collar and sash. 8. Chanel's black satin coat-dress with cowboy fringes of black silk and simple handkerchief tie. 9. Lucile's simple, narrow, short-sleeved white marquisette summer dress decorated with key patterns. 10. Renée's black satin gown trimmed with coin spots of blue velvet pasted on to the material. 11. Poirette's hyacinth-blue crocheted dress decorated with beads and cherry kid tam-o'-shanter.*

The house of Molyneux opened in Paris this autumn. The imagination and talent of this young Irishman were to challenge the supremacy of French dressmaking. Madeleine & Madeleine and Augustabernard also opened. The former was especially popular with tall, slender women, while the latter became the favourite couturier of French *Vogue's* editor, Main Rousseau Bocher; she was a great influence on him when he took up dressmaking under the portmanteau name Mainbocher.

9

10

11

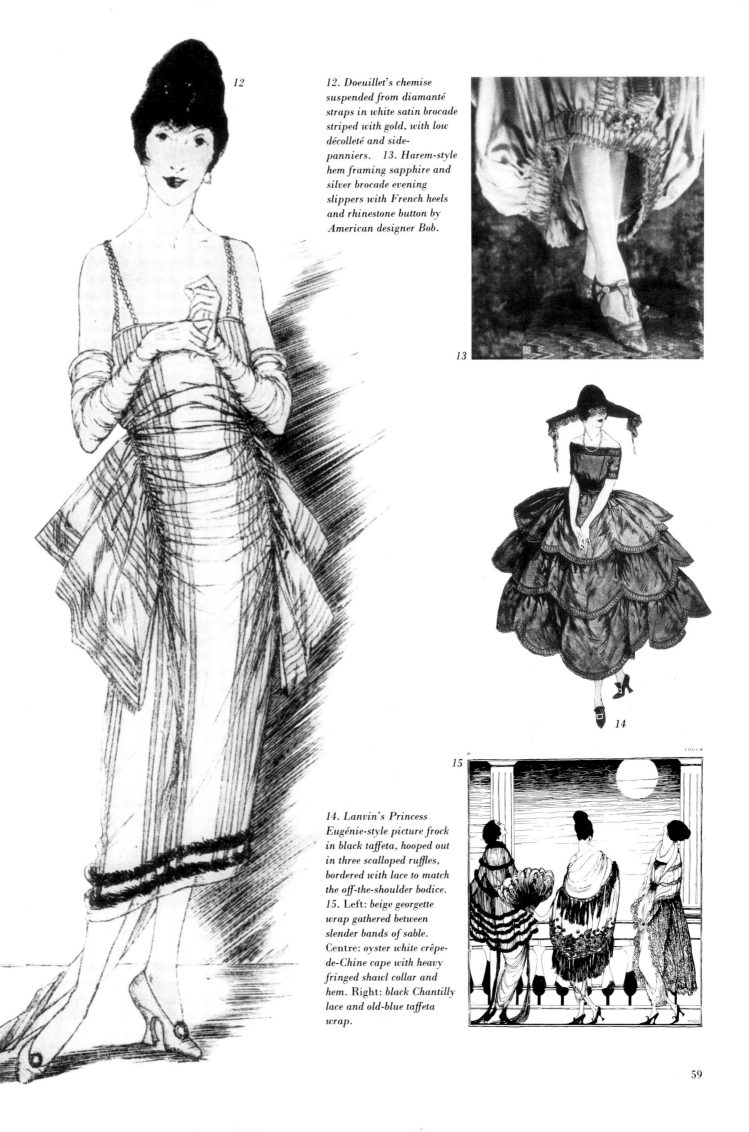

12

12. Doeuillet's chemise suspended from diamanté straps in white satin brocade striped with gold, with low décolleté and side-panniers. 13. Harem-style hem framing sapphire and silver brocade evening slippers with French heels and rhinestone button by American designer Bob.

13

14

14. Lanvin's Princess Eugénie-style picture frock in black taffeta, hooped out in three scalloped ruffles, bordered with lace to match the off-the-shoulder bodice. 15. Left: beige georgette wrap gathered between slender bands of sable. Centre: oyster white crêpe-de-Chine cape with heavy fringed shawl collar and hem. Right: black Chantilly lace and old-blue taffeta wrap.

15

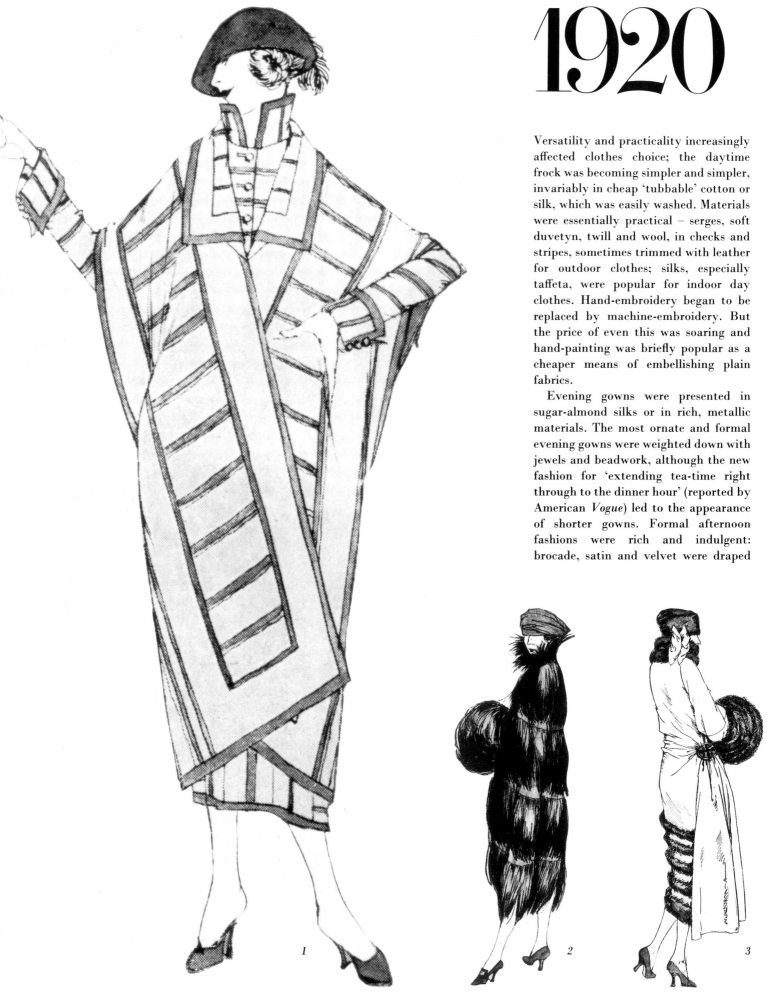

1920

Versatility and practicality increasingly affected clothes choice; the daytime frock was becoming simpler and simpler, invariably in cheap 'tubbable' cotton or silk, which was easily washed. Materials were essentially practical – serges, soft duvetyn, twill and wool, in checks and stripes, sometimes trimmed with leather for outdoor clothes; silks, especially taffeta, were popular for indoor day clothes. Hand-embroidery began to be replaced by machine-embroidery. But the price of even this was soaring and hand-painting was briefly popular as a cheaper means of embellishing plain fabrics.

Evening gowns were presented in sugar-almond silks or in rich, metallic materials. The most ornate and formal evening gowns were weighted down with jewels and beadwork, although the new fashion for 'extending tea-time right through to the dinner hour' (reported by American *Vogue*) led to the appearance of shorter gowns. Formal afternoon fashions were rich and indulgent: brocade, satin and velvet were draped

5

6

into classical lines. Of all the dress luxuries lace continued to be a particular postwar favourite. Summer frocks stepped back into the Victorian or medieval era, although the simply embroidered overblouse in a variety of colours was also popular, being casual and functional.

The natural, uncorseted figure and the linear silhouette dominated high fashion, in a variety of guises – the recurring

1. Lucile's black-and-white blanket coat based on the traditional Indian guapile, with slits for armholes and straight, low-waisted dress with long sleeves. 2. Madeleine and Madeleine's monkey-fur cape mounted on black chiffon. 3. Jenny's straight, mouse-coloured velvet coat-dress trimmed with skunk fur. 4. Chanel's cape in pale grey crêpe-de-Chine trimmed with deep bands of dark flying-squirrel fur, worn with a matching two-tiered dress. 5. Martial et Armand's frock and cape-grey velour wool skirt edged with skunk fur, and a mouse-grey velvet bodice. The matching skunk-collared cape is appliquéd. 6. Black wool velour suit, worn over a white organdie blouse with a deep, face-framing pleated frill. Soft flamingo feathers droop from the small flamingo-coloured velvet hat. 7. Chanel's two-piece charmeuse suit veiled with black chiffon and banded with blue tissue with manteau d'abbé.

4

7

8. *Alternating panels of blue and black chiffon form the skirt of Chéruit's dress; Chantilly lace drapes the hat.* 9. *Madeleine and Madeleine's modern version of the fourteenth-century high-collared dress.* 10. *The gathered sleeves and neck of the black velvet dress were inspired by Russian peasant dress, as was the vivid cerise embroidery.* 11. *Lanvin's black-and-white medieval page-style dress.* 12. *Bonwit Teller's black velvet dress with a large bustle-like tied sash and fox-fur trimmings.*

medieval theme, the Empire line at Callot and the Infanta line at Poiret. The mode for 'Egyptian' dresses, which employed Egyptian girdles, Pharaoh emblems and lotus embroidery, predated the discovery of Tutankhamun's tomb in 1922.

Only Chanel remained untouched by the styles of the past. Her suits this year continued to be black, beige or grey with short rather than long jackets. A key feature was the fullness of the skirts, drawn up to the sides and secured by a button or strap, thus increasing the width of the silhouette at the hips.

Chanel was one of several couturiers to show Russian boots, Russian peasant blouses and cossack-style hats. The Russian Revolution of 1917 and its aftermath had affected fashion and was reported on coyly by *Vogue*: 'Recent unpleasantness in Russia has at least called attention to the charm of its native costume.' Another effect was that the USA became the chief supplier of fur, as trade with Russia had been suspended.

There were two major jacket shapes this year: the short, square, free-hanging style, usually referred to as the Eton jacket, and the longer, loose or belted shape with wide sleeves. Various period references were also used both in Paris and London. Redfern designed the costumes for Sasha Guitry's play *Béranger*, produced in Paris, which were a great success, and as a result modelled his suits on the Louis XVI period. High collars were seen at Jenny, Paquin and Martial et Armand, and pleats abounded. All houses offered shiny trimmings: polished braids, patent leathers, oilcloth and lacquered ribbon.

Callot, Martial et Armand and others challenged the previously fashionable wrapped coat this autumn. They showed the short cape, which had appeared during the war but now became high fashion. Callot was also the originator of the *manteau d'abbé* – the short cape flying from the shoulders of suits, coats and evening wear.

Vogue considered Lanvin and Poiret to be the two great contemporary designers. 'The mode of Lanvin is simple and youthful, for all its subtle art, while at Poiret's the mode becomes a thing of gorgeousness and splendour.' Nicole Groult, Poiret's sister, opened her own house this year, as did Jacques Heim.

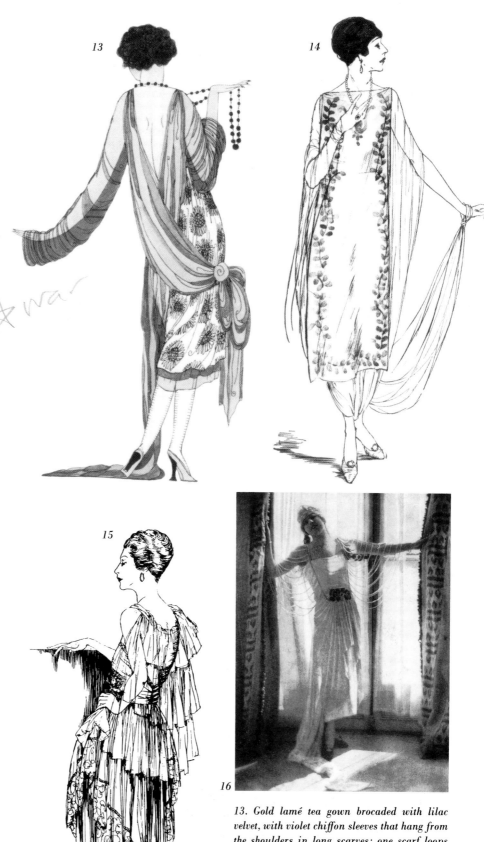

13. *Gold lamé tea gown brocaded with lilac velvet, with violet chiffon sleeves that hang from the shoulders in long scarves; one scarf loops into a knot and the other falls into a train.* 14. *Piguet's cerise satin gown with Turkish-style underskirt; the cerise chiffon draperies are painted with silver leaves.* 15. *Callot's rose chiffon and dull-silver lace gown girdled with a shining band of silver ribbons and tulle manteau d'abbé.* 16. *Worth's coral-coloured velvet gown with brilliants at the waist and pearl rope wings. Diamond and black paradise feather headdress.*

1

1921

The spring colour was black. 'If a French frock isn't black, it's more than likely to be black and white,' observed *Vogue*. Simplicity of line was regarded as high chic and two-tone colour-ways accentuated this. Slip-on frocks and chemises all had a minimum of trimming and decoration. Pleats and gathers tended to concentrate fullness on the hips, waists were lowered and the hemline for day and evening wear descended. Worth continued to accentuate the natural waistline and Patou attempted to highlight the waist in his autumn collection, but a general return to the defined waistline was not made until 1925. Sleeves remained short, or were long and slashed. Crêpe de Chine and marocain were the leading materials at French houses, accompanied by the return of high-lustre taffeta, wools from the house of Rodier and French serges.

Alongside a growing preoccupation with Futurism and Cubism, and materials and trimmings inspired by them, such as steel buttons, the influence of the French Directory (1795–9) refused to die. It inspired simple, classic clothes in reaction to the over-ornate Louis XVI styles: coat-style dresses with wide lapels, gauntlet cuffs or small, tight sleeves, high-sashed waists and low décolletés.

Day wear was relatively free from period and ethnic influences, with the notable exception of Lanvin, who based her entire spring collection of Riviera clothes on Aztec art. In contrast evening wear was more lavish and eclectic. Most houses showed very long evening gowns with trailing sashes and uneven hemlines, especially in London, registering an indecision as to whether the evening hemline should rise or fall. By the autumn the silhouette was plumbline straight, virtually unwaisted, with a deep décolleté and long tight sleeves. The pannier and full-skirted gowns of the immediate post-war years were now completely outmoded.

2

3   4

5

1. Lucile's black organdie summer dress trimmed with white lace of varying widths, patent-leather belt decorated with a pale-blue motif. Black ciré ribbon hat with osprey feathers.   2. Three dresses from Patou's autumn collection. Left: grey cloth dress trimmed with grey chiffon, steel beads decorating its wide sleeves, and steel-and-turquoise-fastened girdle. Centre: a black crêpe marocain dress with coral-edged slashes, cuffs and buckle. Right: a black crêpe satin frock and short tunic. The sleeves are decorated with steel-and-red embroidery.   3. Navy-blue twill Directoire-style frock with large collar and turn-back cuffs, edged with pleated frills.   4. Princesse Lucien Murat's striking, Léger-inspired design in red, blue and yellow on the black jersey frock.   5. Lanvin's black-and-white broadcloth dress with skirt split to reveal the white underskirt. A shot rose-and-silver ribbon highlights the broad black velvet hat.

6. *Reville's navy-blue serge tunic worn with a pleated fawn crêpe-de-Chine petticoat. 7. Madeleine and Madeleine's blue serge dress with pale yellow tussore bodice and matching seven-eighths-length coat. 8. Vionnet's black duvetyn cape lined with ermine and black charmeuse embroidered dress. 9. Grey fox collar, cuffs and hem on Doucet's Russian-style flared black kasha coat, which blouses over the fitted waist and then falls into flaring godets. 10. Lanvin's Aztec collection: burnt-sienna wool jersey frock with a capuchon collar and embroidered skirt under a buccaneer's jersey cape (back view shown). Centre: grey silk jersey dress with intricate embroideries, and scalloped hem with a row of silver grelots – small bells. Right: loose, dark-blue embroidered jacket. 11. Inverted pleats in the back of Revillon Frères' trimmed grey broadcloth coat. 12. Chanel's maize-coloured grey check homespun sports cape. 13. Jenny's cardinal-red gabardine cape lined with blue taffeta and tasselled with red silk. 14. Dark-brown reversible leather trench coat and brown suede hat. 15. Vionnet's fringed black crêpe marocain gown draped over a tight bodice of black lace. 16. Madeleine and Madeleine's Egyptian collection: a lamé brocade, black velvet, dull-silver and grey silk gown, girdled with pearls and emerald beads. 17. Pearl-white chiffon gown with short skirt and a black velvet ribbon girdle, a single loop of which acts as a train. Black velvet and bead motifs edge the long, wide sleeves. 18. Madeleine and Madeleine's medieval-style white chiffon gown oversewn with white crystal beads and belted low with a band of pearl and diamond embroidery. 19. Chéruit trails a loose twisted girdle from a coral chiffon gown.*

Four styles of topcoat were fashionable: long and straight, snugly belted, circularly cut, or gathered at the hips with fullness above. Short capes continued to be popular instead of coats and many winter suits consisted of a cape and dress, rather than a jacket and skirt. Alternatively the suit had an unbelted coat, or bolero jacket.

Some houses this autumn were experimenting with the novelty of circular-cut skirts, occasionally adding an apron panel at the front, and the inverted pleat was widely adopted in Paris. London suits remained very conservative and the most distinctive designs came from Redfern, who adopted the Empire line for some jackets.

This year Chanel launched her famous perfume, Chanel No. 5; she regarded five as her lucky number, partly as it was the date of her birthday.

10

17

15   16

18

19

1922

The silhouette hardly changed at all; skirts were longer and the line even straighter, emphasized with decorative seaming and bands of braid. The most fashionable dress was slim and sleeveless or had long, wide sleeves and a simple neckline. To balance the narrow line, Reboux ordained that hats should be wider than before. Drapery lifted the monotony of this straight line. It was arranged horizontally across the pelvis and down one side, across the back, down both sides, or across the sleeves in a kimono style, as at Martial et Armand. Dresses at Worth were very simple: only moderate embroidery or very modest drapery distracted the eye from the tubular line. In London Lucile accentuated the hip-level waistline of her dresses with stand-out pockets and patent leather belts.

Despite the taste of both Lanvin and Doucet for the bouffant (there was always a market for the pretty picture

frock, which these houses satisfied), the chemise prevailed for evening wear. All the autumn collections showed chemises with bateau necklines and a bow on one hip or at the back. Evening head-dresses and turbans were high fashion accessories this year.

Printed crêpes and patterned fabrics were favoured, as was plain or striped kasha (a soft mixture of wool and goat's

hair) for spring clothes. There was a renewed interest in the famous eighteenth-century *toiles de Jouy*, which were based on Indian hand-blocked prints.

Suits also followed straight lines and were belted at an exaggeratedly low waistline. The sports suit skirt was shorter and retained the practical, masculine cut acquired during the First

1. Vionnet's covert-cloth sports dress piped with white to match the belt and fastened by one button on the shoulder. The straw hat is wide-brimmed and trimmed at the crown with old straw lace. 2. Lanvin's simple dress with a black bodice trimmed with yellow and brown chenille and velvet bloused jacket with summer ermine collar and cuffs. 3. Knox's grey-and-red-striped kasha ensemble: dress with low girdle in red bugle-beads mounted on elastic, striped and plain grey kasha cape. 4. Molyneux's crêpe-de-Chine frock girdled with straw daisies, and white organdie, lily-trimmed, Reboux hat. 5. Narrow bias bands, ruffled and applied in regular ovals to Vionnet's petal-blue dress with brief petal-shaped sleeves. 6. Left: Worth's black crêpe dress, over which hang two panels of pleated black-and-gold lace. The chemisette and sleeves are also in pleated and gold-patterned lace. Centre: black crêpe model. Right: black broadcloth dress with white, soutache-trimmed sleeves.

7

8

9

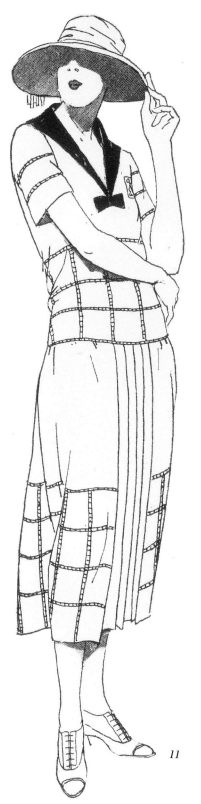

10

11

World War. The 'slouch' suit, with the jacket blousing over a low-slung belt, was first introduced by Lanvin in 1919, but now gained fashionable acceptance. Jenny offered several interpretations of this line. The street skirt, in contrast to the less formal sports skirt, was noticeably longer with the return of private cars in Paris. This summer Redfern showed short, feminine coats worn with white pleated serge sports suits; Jenny and Douet showed the paletôt jacket:

short and flared, it swung out at the back and was worn over a straight skirt.

American designers were particularly fond of knitted silk summer ensembles in yellow and white. In Paris there was a greater variety of bright colours for summer than the previous year.

Overcoats this autumn were long, straight and wrapped close to the body, especially at Lelong, Patou and Worth. Lanvin experimented with Russian-inspired redingotes. Alice Bérnard,

Martial et Armand and Doucet offered the circularly cut coat swinging from the shoulders. Jenny and Beer presented a novel skirt cut flat at the back and flared at the sides or front, worn with a three-quarter length jacket, often trimmed with a fur collar.

Short, bobbed hair had outmoded the chignon and was now considered the most fashionable style for women of all ages, although some found the bob difficult to carry off successfully.

12

13

14

15

16

7. *Redfern's blue duvetyn jacket and white serge pleated skirt.* 8. *A selection of American brightly coloured knitted silk suits.* 9. *Lucile's black silk velvet Directoire suit. Soft lace decorates the neck, and the white satin bicorne is veiled with grey lace to match stockings and shoes.* 10. *Jenny's 'slouch-back' silhouette, with tight hipband curving up towards the front and plain black broadcloth skirt with triangular godets. The organdie blouse is trimmed with lingerie points.* 11. *Redfern's yellow serge sports costume, which is hemstitched in squares. The pleated panel down the skirt front is faced with black satin, as is the cape, which is made of two yellow serge squares, one plain, the other hemstitched.* 12. *Poiret's black satin pyjamas with a yellow-and-green printed satin blouse.* 13. *Molyneux's evening gown in dull and bright silver and black brocade, and sleeveless blouse-jacket of bright silver, bound with bias folds and a steel-studded belt.* 14. *Martial et Armand's black velvet evening gown with cerise velvet-lined train.* 15. *Taupe velvet embroidered wrap with beaver-edged cuffs, and Suzy's velvet turban trimmed with a gold silk tassel.* 16. *Duchess Sforza wears Chéruit's balloon-shaped black satin cape – a puff-ball silhouette – gathered at the top on to a monkey-fur collar and at the bottom into a slim lining.* 17. *Aquascutum's all-weather, brown-check waterproofed tweed coat.* 18. *Poiret's beige wool coat with striking geometrical black velvet insets.*

17

18

1923

Paris declared that the chemise was dead. It had been superseded by the *robe collant*, which was so narrow it was almost glued against the body, in contrast to the loosely hanging chemise. However, the straight silhouette was elaborated in a great variety of ways. Sleeves could be puffed or plain, wide or tight, necklines cut close to the throat or scooped wide. Belts were either abandoned or very pronounced, emphasizing the fashionable dropped waist.

Equally varied ethnic and historical influences – Breton, Algerian, Second Empire, Chinese and Indo-Chinese – were evident. The Eastern kimono sleeve, for example, was used for some straight-line coats, while Callot, inspired by Indo-Chinese costumes, showed gowns that were full at the front and perfectly flat at the back. Jenny, Drécoll and Doucet all showed Egyptian styles for the evening. Some of Jenny's evening skirts had godets and were gathered at one side into a decorative bow or chou. Chéruit's evening silhouette was highly distinctive: it was based on the Cambodian national costume, which was wide through the hips.

Evening accessories received great attention and the evening scarf was reintroduced by one of the smartest women in Paris, Mme Letellier. Scarves and handkerchiefs tied about the throat also accompanied day dresses.

This year's materials were rich and warm in colour: rich green, brown and black velvets and embossed and figured materials, such as silk broché, for the

1

1. Patou's full cape and straight, pleated dress.   2. Drécoll's coats. Left: dark-green matelassé trimmed with brown unplucked seal and fastened to one side. Right: perfectly straight, black silk broché coat-dress with tab fastenings held with giant jet buttons.   3. Patou's full black wool short coat, trimmed at collar, cuffs and pockets with white and green detailing, contrasts with the narrow pleated skirt.   4. Philippe et Gaston's castor-coloured (greyish-brown) duvetyn wrapover coat with cony-fur cuffs.   5. Chanel's printed foulard suit: cardigan-like, hip-length jacket with braid edges and straight, pleated skirt.   6. Shirring accentuates the vertical line of Paquin's dress worn with a fur-trimmed jacket.   7. Chéruit's wide-jutting panniers, inspired by Cambodian national costume, stiffen out the straight jacket.   8. Doeuillet's dark-red wool cape suit buttoned in silver with red, white and silver cuffs and pocket details, red glacé kid shoes and red-and-white-striped taffeta hat.

9. *Premet, Jenny and Drécoll's Indo-Chinese modes.* Left: Premet's string-coloured crêpe-de-Chine dress with red and brown bands at the neck and an inserted, Indian-inspired girdle. Centre: Jenny's black crêpe-de-Chine frock under a straight, shorter coat in a red-and-green Rodier chintz. Right: *Hindu native dress inspired Drécoll's black-and-white printed crêpe unlined coat and straight, unbelted dress.* 10. *Vionnet's straight, low-waisted summer dresses printed with naturalistic motifs.* 11. *Harry Lichtenstein's orange sports frock embroidered with white, and Bonwit Teller white straw and satin hat.* 12. *Lanvin chose gaily coloured handkerchiefs for the neck and cuffs of his navy-blue twill dress.* 13. *Paquin's sleeveless, straight black dress with dark-green-lined chou attached to the back.* 14. *Lanvin's white crêpe-de-Chine dress with black velvet bodice inset, encrusted with crystal beads and contrasting panels of white, like braces, over the shoulders.* 15. *Arrow-narrow, black velvet sheath dress, embroidered above the dropped waistline with crystal beads; wing-like panels are inserted into the sides in contrasting chiffon.* 16. *Callot's jade-green taffeta evening cape draped with black Chantilly lace and closed with ribbon. The wide pleats fall from a shoulder-revealing yoke.* 17. *Patou's bateau neckline and deep décolleté at the back, on a cardinal-red moiré evening gown. The circularly cut skirt is attached diagonally to the bodice and faced with royal-purple satin. The chignon at the nape of the neck was an alternative to the bob.*

winter, while bright pastels and white, especially in patterned crêpe de Chine, were worn in the summer.

The tubbable gingham sports frock was popular in America. At summer resorts American *Vogue* advised readers to wear straight jackets in a brightly coloured figured material over pleated white or cream sports skirts. American designers such as Harry Lichtenstein and Dobbs presented casual, simple flannel and jersey sports dresses.

Most sports and casual skirts were pleated. Accompanying coats could be plumbline straight, as at Worth and Chanel, or circularly cut, as at Lenier. The fashionable suit was usually a three-piece, with a hemline between 8 and 10 inches from the ground, and a tunic blouse or waistcoat. The bolero or the three-quarters-length jacket were seen at Jenny, Beer, Dœuillet and Béchoff. Jenny showed long, straight, close-fitting skirts worn with long tunics. The most popular spring coat shapes were short and wrapped to one side. For the cost-conscious wardrobe *Vogue* recommended a velour, wool-mix or flannel tailored coat teamed with a jersey frock.

Louise Boulanger, having trained at Chéruit, opened as Louiseboulanger in Paris.

13

14

15

12

16

17

1924

Chanel's association with the Grand Duke Dimitri of Russia led her to admire and copy rich Russian embroideries, moujik tunics, low-slung belts and fabulous fur, all included in her 1923 and 1924 collections. She also presented costume jewellery, crafted by Gripoix, based on classic Russian jewellery; one of the early examples of costume jewellery being included in a couture collection. British *Vogue* even entitled 1924 the 'Soviet Season', partly because of these fashions but also because the first Labour Government had come to power under

Ramsay Macdonald (which *Vogue* supposed had Russian undertones!).

Most of the clothes featured in *Vogue* were élitist, luxurious and inappropriate to a busy working life. However, there were a few articles that did cater for working women and those of slender means, coyly referred to as the 'nouvelles pauvres', which recommended such garments as the reversible coat, the informal suit, the practical jersey dress and sports clothes. The chic business woman was warned that, for the office, 'the sleeveless street gown is unspeakably vulgar', as were short, tight dresses. *Vogue* also condemned the drab shirt and serge skirt, traditionally associated with the suffragette, bluestocking or war worker, and recommended the one-piece, preferably black, frock as the ideal compromise, as it could easily be accessorized with a fresh scarf, gloves and perhaps a flower

at the waist when one left the office.

Sportswear was now *de rigueur* during the day and hence was represented more extensively in the couture collections. Jackets were normally semi-fitted and worn with a straight skirt and simple white overblouse.

Coats for the spring were either three-quarters or seven-eighths in length, belt-less, straight and worn with a dress rather than a suit. The latest coat for the autumn was double-breasted. One notable fashion characteristic was a plaid coat lining to match the dress.

The severe tailored suit was fashionable, worn with a tiny cloche and a long scarf. Women were loath to relinquish the suit's practical advantages. Not only was it chic for every daytime occasion, it was more hardwearing than a dress, being cut in tweed, flannel, Oxford cloth or homespun. Chanel presented a

2

3

4

5

6

1. *A selection of Maria Guy's straw and satin small hats worn low over the brow and trimmed with grosgrain ribbons. 2. Small-brimmed Directoire-style hat by Reboux. 3. Georgette and black Milan-straw turban trimmed with grosgrain ribbon, black rep coat-dress and patterned satin scarf threaded through the left shoulder. 4. Alex's small steel-grey felt hat trimmed with drooping feathers. 5. Agnès's beige high-crowned felt hat trimmed with a double-headed crystal and onyx pin. 6. Vogue upholds the reign of the cloche.*

1

7. Patou's white chiffon dancing frock with a deep, crystal-beaded bertha. The full handkerchief skirt is similarly beaded.   8. Lelong's straight, unwaisted crêpe evening dress beaded with crystals and pearls.   9. Chanel's simple white crêpe georgette evening dress.   10. Chanel's brown velvet evening coat with shirred panels and marten-fur collar and cuffs. A separate, peach-coloured satin inner-coat is lined with matching fur.

number of sensible, short-skirted Oxford-cloth suits. Skirts in general were shorter this year: tailored morning clothes were 10–12 inches from the ground, formal afternoon dresses 8–10 inches and evening wear 6 inches.

Most day dresses were simple, straight and devoid of fussy drapery. Tunics were ornamented with rows of buttons and were often cut to flare out over the hips. The popular summer shift was white and the summer collections abounded with white or cream sports dresses. Crêpe de Chine dresses with matching printed coats, notably from Patou, were worn for more formal wear, while white gabardine was a popular choice for the Riviera. The alternative to the more usual tweed sports frock for the autumn was velveteen, which Chanel showed, as it was functional, washable and relatively cheap.

Chanel was the most daring promoter of the short chiffon dance frock, cut with a very deep décolleté. Low necklines and bare backs were flaunted by the fashionable young. Lace and chiffon, or velvet dresses, usually in black, beige and for the winter, were popular for evening green, and some were heavy with lavish gold and crystal embroidery. In some cases flounced or feathered hemlines or caped effects added variety to the straight lines. Flesh- or apricot-coloured silk stockings and buckled brocade sandals completed the evening ensemble.

The formal afternoon ensemble returned this autumn, in velvet and fur, ottoman, or satin and fur, while many houses offered the silk knitted dress, with slight over-blousing above a drawstring belt on the hips.

Marcel Rochas opened in Paris.

11. Callot's black satin and white crêpe-de-Chine jabot frock.   12. Groult's afternoon/informal dinner dress in beige toile embroidered in black and deep rose.   13. Lanvin's black georgette crêpe dress resembling a blouse-and-skirt outfit with high-collared bodice fastened with loops and steel discs.   14. Eve Valère's sailor-collared black velvet and white georgette dress and black-and-white felt hat.

15. Renée's seven-eighths-length autumn coats. Left: double-breasted black-and-grey wool and civet-fur collar. Right: cut with pointed revers suggesting a jabot when the cut is open but closing diagonally when buttoned up. 16. Chéruit's Cambodian-line, yellow and green sports coat. 17. Sonia Delaunay's geometrically patterned kasha coat. 18. Vionnet's bias-cut suit with geometrically patterned lining. 19. Hickson's tailored suits. Left: single-breasted suit in brown, tan and brick-coloured tweed. Right: black broadcloth; the jacket is cut like a tuxedo. The matching skirt is trimmed with white bias/hairline stripes.

15

16

17

18

19

1925

The Exhibition of Decorative Arts in Paris this year focused international attention on the geometric decorative style in furniture, fabric and interior design which now became known as Art Deco. Sonia Delaunay's work provides good examples of Art Deco. From 1924 she created Cubist-inspired geometric patterns for the textile house of Bianchini-Férier and worked with Jacques Heim on a collection of patchwork and appliquéd cloth-and-fur coats that juxtaposed different colours and textures like a collage.

Numerous American designers, including the Colour Studio, experimented with Art Deco and Cubism, which were acclaimed by the American press. However, just as they gained widespread acceptance, the most avant-garde couturiers, notably Vionnet, now created a different mood, abandoning a strict linear emphasis, such as geometric seam details or Cubist decoration, in the autumn collections. By the end of the year the silhouette was softened by means of more intricate construction. Bias cut, jabots, flying panels and softer, more pliable materials all emphasized

1. *Chéruit's casual silver-gauze evening gown with tight, straight sleeves painted with lacquer-red, grey and black Cubist designs.* 2. *J. Suzanne Talbot's cloth-of-gold dress veiled with white chiffon. Gold braid trims the diagonal décolleté, and the girdle is of gold-braid bands with a pleated ruffle of chiffon beneath. Delman's gold-and-silver kid sandals.* 3. *Lanvin's simple two-piece gold-and-green lamé evening suit.* 4. *Louiseboulanger's blue satin frock with trailing panels and tiered skirt.* 5. *Chanel's short, full dancing frock in black and pink chiffon with flounces highlighting the side, leaving the back and front quite flat.*

6. *Vionnet's motoring ensemble: collarless, reverless black grain-de-poudre jacket closed with six buttons and cut low to reveal white crêpe-de-Chine blouse and vast cape lined with white crêpe-de-Chine, fastened with two silk tassels at the collar. 7. Ina Claire in Chanel's tailored tan-and-white herringbone tweed sports suit with brown leather belt, beige felt hat, beige gauntlet gloves. 8. Agnès's silk jersey blouse stencilled with grey and white Cubist patterns and simple, straight, pleated skirt. 9. The otter skins on Heim's coat are laid in opposite directions to achieve a geometrical effect. 10. Poiret's myrtle-green velvet coat with wrist-flaring sleeves trimmed with long-haired bear pelts. 11. Patou's grey gaberdine coat with raised waistline and white piqué shawl collar and cuffs.*

women's curvaceous figure. Afternoon frocks at the Paris autumn collections flattered with a new, youthful grace.

Another major development was Patou's decision to raise the waistline, while Chanel, Chéruit, Paquin, Worth, Dœuillet and Lanvin showed various expressions of the uneven waistline – usually higher at the front and sloping downwards at the back.

The natural proportions of the body were revealed again. The straight, figure-less fashions of the early twenties had not only been a reaction to the Edwardian S-bend line, but were also an expression of the cult of boyish youth that followed the demographic imbalance created by the war. Fashion was now gradually emerging from this neurosis.

English wools and kasha were popular for spring suits, which were very fluid and feminine at Lelong, Vionnet and Patou. Chéruit's suits were soft yet simple, sometimes with front pleats, godets and fullness in the skirt, which was worn with a coloured blouse and contrasting jacket.

The evening décolleté, in general,

12. *Patou's circularly cut white georgette frock with black Chantilly lace inserts, which also outline the inside of the shoulder wings.* 13. *Chéruit's black and pink Riviera frock.* 14. *Lelong's long-sleeved afternoon dress of chiffon velvet in 'Lézard d'Afrique' (one of the new cloth approximations of animal skin) is slightly flared and illustrates the style of waistband that was cut higher at front than back.* 15. *Lanvin's black crêpe, coat-like roma tunic with shirred skirt front and rose-coloured crêpe roma slip beneath and a rose crêpe bow. The tunic and the sleeves are embroidered with rose-shaded circles.* 16. *Vionnet's tobacco-coloured crêpe-de-Chine dress with masterful tucks.* 17. *The Eton collar, the tailored kid-leather jacket and the straight tweed skirt were popular sports attire. The washable suede jacket,* right, *has knitted sleeves.*

remained lower at the back than the front. The most popular evening materials were crêpe, chiffon, mousseline, supple metal cloths and lace, or velvet for the colder months. By the autumn there was a move towards longer, more elaborate evening gowns, particularly at Louiseboulanger; the sheath or short chemise now seemed too simple.

This year's coat was generally buttoned; wrapped styles were now considered dated in Europe, although they continued to be worn in America. The cut of coats also became more intricate: the back of the silhouette was flattened and the front and sides emphasized with jabots and flaring godets. Fur trims in both Paris and London were used in more artistic ways than the usual cuffs, collars and hems, for instance as inserted bands. Leather and suede were hardy materials for sports clothing and were now highly fashionable, styled like masculine sportswear.

The luxury leather luggage firm of Fendi opened in Rome.

1926-1933

Beware . . . Because Princess Obolensky wears a Tyrolean peasant's jacket with complete success while drinking her hot chocolate at the Café Bazaar, little Miss Anybody must not be under the impression that she can stroll out upon the golf links sporting a pair of sailor's pants . . . There are many pitfalls, for every detail must be right . . . The right shoes have to be worn and also the necessary swank. You must not wear an African necklace unless you wear it with an air; you must be cocksure in your Saint Tropez shepherdess hat. You must not blush when your Lederhosen are remarked upon.

Cecil Beaton, British *Vogue*, 1932

The Princess Obolensky in a Tyrolean jerkin and hat, 1932.

She wears gold and scarlet kid evening slippers fastened with brilliants, cream velvet and gold lamé wrap from Drécoll, he wears black tie.

By the mid-twenties colour, shape and sex appeal had returned to clothes. Skirts became fuller, initially through the use of pleats and godets, hemlines gradually lengthened and the tall, leggy silhouette became the ideal. According to Vionnet, the pioneer of this new line, '. . . the dress must not hang on the body but follow its lines . . . and when a woman smiles the dress must smile with her.' Womanly sexuality outmoded adolescent boyishness. 'The hard, finished mode is a thing of the past. No longer are we all boys, dauntless and uncompromising Sir Galahads,' observed British *Vogue* in 1926.

Lingerie and discreet corsetry were essential to this smooth bodyline. Some women rolled their stockings over a garter rather than use a suspender belt, which caused unsightly bumps under clothing, and perfectionists had undergarments made for each gown to avoid the slightest wrinkle. Rayon, now widely used for lingerie, was no longer 'designed to shroud but rather to display the hopefully attainable!' (D. C. Coleman, *Courtaulds: An Economic and Social History*, 1969).

The use of the term 'rayon' instead of artificial silk raised the status and acceptability of viscose and acetate fibres, but spinning techniques had not yet been perfected and fabrics creased easily and had an unpleasant sheen. However, the low cost and durability of rayon appealed to the ready-to-wear manufacturers and even couturiers such as Vionnet, Schiaparelli, Louiseboulanger and Patou began to experiment with it, no doubt prompted by favourable deals with manufacturers. It was mixed with natural fibres such as wool and woven with a cotton warp to make brocade.

With the economic prosperity of the twenties, class distinctions became more prominent as the monied élite were no longer loath to display their wealth. The fashionable took pains to stand out from the crowd and appeared in lavish furs, glittering jewellery and intricately beaded and bejewelled dresses. By 1927 *Vogue* was rejoicing at the return to style and individuality: 'No longer need a woman conform to type, she can and does express her own personality.' *Vogue*, like so many of its readers, was tired of cost-consciousness. It recommended buying a completely new wardrobe, rather than trying to work in a still wearable garment from a previous season that did not harmonize with the new colours and lines – a far cry from the instructions for alterations and tips on separates dressing that had stretched the wardrobe during the post-war slump.

Style had ceased to be the prerogative of the privileged few, as magazines, newspapers and films communicated fashion information to all sections of society. By the mid-twenties women could buy a wide variety of fashionable garments of reasonable quality at a range of prices; they spent more on cheap ready-made clothes and were less prepared to make their own dresses.

Vogue increasingly showed a selection of ready-to-wear garments, at the higher price range, from Peter Robinson, Harrods, D. H. Evans, Marshall & Snelgrove, Lord & Taylor, Bendels and Bergdorf Goodman. However, British *Vogue* warned readers who shopped in the big stores not to buy *the* model of the season, 'for it is discouraging to see yourself duplicated on every street corner, fat, thin, tall or short!'

In the United States there was a phenomenal development of the ready-to-wear industry. Millions of yards of domestic and imported materials and a large skilled workforce were available. Machines cut through a hundred layers of cloth, sewed a thousand stitches at a time and ironed in bulk. Road and rail links between industrial and commercial centres ensured efficient distribution of products. By the twenties ready-made clothes departments were firmly established in all the big city stores and there were outlets in many smaller towns. Department stores often leased their clothes departments to ready-to-wear specialists, who installed and managed large-scale operations at lower profit margins. The fashion industry, based on Seventh Avenue in New York, dominated this section of mid-town Manhattan for twenty blocks.

In 1928 seventeen women met in the Mary Elizabeth Tea Room in New York to discuss plans for setting up an important fashion institution, the Fashion Group of America. Its aim was 'to add dignity and standing to the job of stylist and to serve as a clearing house for information'. In 1931 the Fashion Group was incorporated, with bye-laws, officers and a place to meet. There were seventy-five eager members and Marion Taylor, editor of American *Vogue*, was its first president. It has now become an international fashion organization, with a headquarters in New York and offices in most American cities and many capitals around the world. It brings together all levels of the fashion industry: designers, manufacturers, retailers, publishers and magazines. Serving as an information bank, it organizes seminars and workshops. After both the European and American ready-to-wear collections it sets up presentations for the industry to discuss and act upon the work that has been shown. In 1954 it instituted an annual fashion training course, giving lectures on fashion careers.

American designers such as Hattie Carnegie, Omar Kiam, Edward L.

Stylized dummies found in fashionable department stores.

The fashionable interior of Mr John Hay Whitney's two-motored Sikorsky Amphibian aeroplane, 1929. The rich craved travel after the restrictions of war.

Classic mid-twenties sportswear.

Elsa Schiaparelli.

Jean Cocteau at work.

Mayer and Richard Heller were acclaimed by American *Vogue* for creating 'a mode which is definitely American, as it is definitely of our era', and which laid the foundations for the wartime success of American couture. In 1926 Hattie Carnegie opened on East 49th Street, New York. She changed her unpronounceable Austrian name – Henrietta Kanengeiser – to something that had a Fifth Avenue ring – Carnegie was an industrialist reputed to be the richest man in America at the time, and she chose Hattie because she began her career as a milliner. Astutely, she realized that people were no longer able to pay high couture bills and opened a ready-to-wear department copying the very best Parisian couture.

Chanel continued to offer simple sportswear, though her evening ranges did satisfy the yearning for lavishness. Her friendship with the Duke of Westminster from 1925 to 1931 widened her knowledge of and interest in British textiles and styles. She concentrated on superbly tailored suits, learning cut and technique from Savile Row tailors. She perfected the inset of the sleeve to allow maximum movement and copied men's hunting-jacket revers which lay flat regardless of the wearer's movement.

Chanel's arch rival Elsa Schiaparelli, an Italian, had been designing one-off gowns for herself and friends since 1915. She opened in the Rue de la Paix in 1927, following the success of her *trompe l'oeil* bow sweater, an early example of her taste for surrealism. The chief buyer at Straus in New York placed a bulk order for the sweater and matching skirts, to be delivered in a fortnight. Schiaparelli accepted the challenge, setting up a workshop with Armenian knitters. Some attempted to deter her, maintaining that she had 'neither the talent nor the *métier*' for fashion designing; one of Maggy Rouff's staff commented that she had 'better plant potatoes than try to make dresses'.

Schiaparelli regarded designing as an art, not a profession: 'a most difficult and unsatisfactory art, because as soon as a dress is born it has already become a thing of the past'. Sportswear, co-ordinated beachwear and matching bags and shoes characterized her early work. By 1930 she was using upholstery material and terry cloth for beach wear and zippers on ski ensembles. Her chief fashion contribution was witty vulgarity.

Another rival, renowned for her fluid line and feminine cut, was Maggy Rouff, the pseudonym of Maggy Besançon de Wagner. She set up in 1928 in the Champs Élysées, with immediate success. She loved draped, bowed and puffed clothes – a reaction to the straight, simple lines of Chanel in the twenties – and was most closely associated with the wave of romance in the thirties.

Meanwhile the London couture was developing a reputation for well-cut, practical, casual clothes and traditional ball gowns. Two major British houses opened: Norman Hartnell in 1927, and Victor Stiebel in 1932.

Captain Edward Molyneux, an Irishman who had trained at Lucile, had opened his own house in Paris in 1919. His pared-down, feminine clothes established his reputation as the master of understatement and fine, subtle colour. His wardrobe for Noël Coward's *Private Lives* in 1930 became the envy of the fashionable world. Molyneux's pale grey salon on the rue Royale was renowned for its exclusive ambiance and restrained styling. He was the only couturier to insist that the staff, 600 in his Paris branch alone, wear uniforms – pale grey to match the décor. The collections at the London branch were exact replicas of the Paris ones, so that a customer could order the same ensemble from either branch. Molyneux was blind in one eye, but

Molyneux's costume for Noël Coward's play, Private Lives, *1930.*

John Cavanagh, who worked with him between 1932 and 1939, recalls that 'he could see more with one than most of us could see with six'. When Cavanagh joined the house at eighteen he thought that the 'collection' referred to a staff money box.

Sports boutiques opened in many cosmopolitan cities. Worth opened a sports boutique in London in 1927, sister to the one in the Rue de la Paix in Paris. Realizing the importance of a fast service, he offered a range of ready-to-wear sports clothes in a variety of sizes, 'so that one may decide today to go to the Lido and appear there two days later in the smartest of such pyjamas from a great couturier, without the necessity of fittings or delay'. Other élite establishments such as Lanvin and Patou also opened boutiques offering 'instant' couture clothes that required only minor alterations, and were highly successful. In the early thirties some of the most interesting summer sports clothes were created by the small houses servicing the Côte d'Azur, united under the Union des Créateurs de la Mode Côte d'Azur, rather than by the large Parisian salons.

Tennis was a particularly fashionable pastime. In 1927 *Vogue* attributed this to the Centre Court at Wimbledon and the French couturiers: 'the former has brought the prestige of tennis and the interest in it to a higher pitch among the world of fashion ... and the latter have seized this opportunity to show still another proof of their theory that great chic is only the logical result of great practicality'.

White was the most acceptable shade for tennis clothes but pale peach and yellow were considered to look better against sunburnt skins. Tennis shoes, generally of canvas with rope soles, were worn with thin, white or pale beige lisle stockings. Each year tennis outfits became freer, a far cry from the cumbersome long dresses worn by the previous generation.

The young and privileged continued to enjoy the fruits of their new-found freedom, but in 1929 the American government introduced Prohibition, the outlawing of the manufacture and sale of alcoholic drinks for common consumption. Prohibition lasted until 1933, but the prosperous classes, who set the fashionable standards, continued to use alcohol freely. Men and women were seen drinking together in 'speakeasies' and similar dives and alcohol lubricated an unprecedented informality in manners.

Make-up was now widely worn by the fashionable. *Vogue* admitted in 1931, 'We are all painted ladies today. It would be sad to reflect what our status would be if we were suddenly transferred to that era when rouge made a dangerous woman of anyone who used it. Now we feel undressed unless we have the right shade of face powder, and if we lose our lipstick, we lose our strongest moral support.' The cosmetic industry boomed. In 1917 in the United States there had been only two people in the cosmetics business according to the tax returns; by 1927 there were 18,000 firms in the field. In 1930 American women were spending $750,000 on make-up.

The late twenties were the most prosperous years of the couture and all related industries. Never again were houses to have such long and prestigious lists of clients; 1929 was an Indian summer for the whole industry. The fortunes and security of many crashed in the wake of Wall Street's financial collapse. Some prominent Parisian houses such as Doucet and Dœuillet were forced to merge to cut costs. In America the number of dress companies on Seventh Avenue fell from 3,500 in 1929 to 2,300 in 1933, while many ready-to-wear firms in the Midwest folded.

Fashion houses became more cost-conscious. For instance in 1932 even

Madge Garland, the fashion editor of British Vogue, *painted by Edward Wolfe in 1926. When lunching one afternoon with the beautiful Virginia Woolf, Miss Garland inquired why Mrs Woolf hated dining in public restaurants. 'Because I feel so badly dressed. If I had an outfit like yours I would feel more confident.' Mrs Woolf was later delighted to receive a copy of the Nicole Groult outfit from Paris, courtesy of Miss Garland.*

Chanel, whose clothes tended to be the most expensive, cut her prices by half. *Vogue* ran sensible articles for those with limited incomes, those now working and those prepared to revive knitting or dressmaking for economy's sake. Numerous knitting patterns were offered for inexpensive, fashionable outfits.

Aesthetically, fashion 'grew up' – triviality was démodé. Only the creations of Schiaparelli retained a sense of humour and fun – this was perhaps the root of her success. Conservatism prevailed, with longer skirts, lace, long gloves and feminine stances. Readers were steered away from the temptation of novelty. Traditional values returned, radical behaviour and dress were frowned upon and, as so often in times of crisis, the past was looked to for security. The styles of classical Greece, Persia, the French Directory and the 'upholstered' fashions of the prosperous 1880s were revived. 'We shall never look like our old selves again. Much as you may detest period effects, you might better look like your grandmother than like yourself of last year,' commented American *Vogue* in 1930. British *Vogue* was rather more sceptical, warning its readers not to go 'too picturesque, too whoopsy-droopsy, too 1860, 1870, 1880', but it chastised those who refused to adopt the new styles of flowing gracefulness – probably the same women who had screamed at the leg-revealing fashions of the mid-twenties.

Vogue expected a dramatic metamorphosis of women from the adventurous, rebellious youth to the genteel lady. American *Vogue* advised the new super-woman to be 'a combination of a fashionable beauty and the Byzantine Madonna, turned towards what used to be called a woman's life: home, society and those frivolities which are essentially woman's. The brave and clever face looks out with wisdom and eagerness at the world of work. Toiler, spinner, she nevertheless retains the grace of a lily.'

The beach pursuits of the smart world that had typified the recreation of earlier years were now tempered. Few could afford jaunts to the resorts and those that did found conditions changed. American *Vogue* in 1930 recorded that in Palm Beach 'there is a wholesale reversion to the more casual and simple life ... No one is trying to live up to a delusion of grandeur and

Knitted jersey bathing suits from Spalding, left, and Fauvety, right, 1931.

Buy British propaganda, 1931.

pomposity.' By 1931 the return of white-skinned beauty was proclaimed and *Vogue* suggested that 'we bleach our precious suntan so that we have swan necks for the rumoured tulle-edged décolletés'. Throughout the thirties, as a result of the Depression, the sportswear industry developed in America, partly in recognition of a shorter working week and greater outdoor activity. California became the focal point of this business.

With the new gentility that pervaded the social scene, sex talk was now considered boring and unsophisticated. Robert Benchley observed in the *New Yorker* in 1930, 'I am now definitely ready to announce that sex, as a theatrical property, is as tiresome as the old mortgage'.

Fervent economic nationalism and trade barriers were the result of the Depression and led American *Vogue* to ask in 1933, 'Will we place a moral ban on French ideas and develop a new national style? ... The American designer is more important today than ever before. First, because of the tariff difficulties, we have imported fewer things each season. Now, because of the *crise*, every buyer sent to Europe is strictly budgeted. More and more, then, we need to create designers in New York.' Similarly in 1931 British *Vogue* encouraged its readership to 'Buy British'.

Severe unemployment affected the couture industry. Augustabernard, who had been enthusiastically promoted by Mainbocher, was one casualty of the Depression. Clients, notably South Americans, no longer placed orders, while others failed to honour theirs, and by 1934 she was forced to close. Exports of French haute couture fell by 70 per cent between 1929 and 1935 and it was reported that the losses of the French dress industry had reached 2 billion francs by 1935, aggravated by a sharp decline in tourism – by 1934 the number of American tourists had fallen by a quarter. In addition to restrictions between various countries, American ready-to-wear firms and department stores now bought fewer original French gowns to copy, cutting their costs by joining together to buy only one or two models.

Cautious designing and decreased demand led the couture into the doldrums. Fashion was in desperate need of inspiration and verve. Schiaparelli was to satisfy this need.

The radical change in dress demanded a change in posture, reported Vogue in 1930. 'As soon as she comes from dinner, she hurls herself upon the first armchair and flips her legs over the arm. She used to shock the dowagers with some success. They discussed her at mothers' meetings only a short year ago. But now no one pays attention to her antics. She has not been versatile enough to change her pose. She is no longer a sensation.

'Knees apart, a spine like asparagus, and a drooping head, what used to be the life of the party, once more sets out of charm. Life is not what it used to be for this young lady. Her orchids are getting thinner. No one compliments her on her gown. She does not know quite what to make of it, so she pouts and slumps even lower than before. She should be told to mend her ways. World weariness is unfashionable.'

The inevitable consequence of Prohibition in America – the Speakeasy.

1926

Femininity had irrefutably returned to fashion. Bloused bodices, softer necklines and a thousand tiny details – bows, buckles, jewels and pretty accessories – made for grace and charm. The virtually brimless small cloche was *the* accessory, pulled right down over one eye. Accordingly to Edna Woolman Chase, 'to show the forehead would have caused a scandal. Chic started at the eyebrows.'

This transition period had no prominent silhouette, although a new fullness and more intricate treatment of fabrics were common features – materials were gathered into puffs, loops, bows and cascading draperies. Flared fullness, emphasized by tiers, was now fashionable, while straight silhouettes were softened by jabots, flying panels or pleating.

Despite Patou's introduction of the natural waistline last year, there was still general uncertainty about its position. In general, the hemline of day dresses was 14 inches from the ground, although it was longer at Poiret, Paquin and Vionnet. With these shorter skirts there was a greater emphasis on shoes: high-cut pumps or one-strap shoes for dresses and Cuban-heeled two-tone Oxfords for tailored suits. Beige or skin-tone stockings were fashionable.

Prominent colours for summer afternoon dresses were black, white, red and green and the pastel tones of Riviera clothes – mushroom pink, yellow, mauve or blue – lifted with touches of white. This was a relief after the dull palette of the early twenties. The most widely used materials were soft chiffon, georgette, crêpe, tulle and voile, often printed with small flowers, polka dots or confetti – the new motifs.

Three quarters of the daytime fashions shown in Paris were sports outfits – simple, practical clothes without the feminine touches added to formal clothes. The pleated skirt and the longer jacket were still key elements in a woman's wardrobe. Molyneux showed a collection of braid-trimmed yachting blazers worn with circular-cut skirts, while O'Rossen combined long blazers with straight short skirts. Jane Regny

1. Left: *Gunther's grey tweed coat.* Right: *Gunther's neutral-to-brown tweed cape with a tan sangha Martha Norden hat.* 2. *Lanvin's loose, cardigan-style velvet sportscoat and crêpe-de-Chine dress.* 3. *Madame Champcommunal in her crêpe marocain suit.* 4. *Chanel's green, three-quarter-length Crêpella coat edged with green braid, and matching skirt.* 5. *Callot's white crêpe-de-Chine cape-coat, lined with black, with a red, black and white scarf effect.* 6. *Artelle's pale-green short cape-coat and figured silk dress.* 7. *Callot's green-and-yellow tweed cape.*

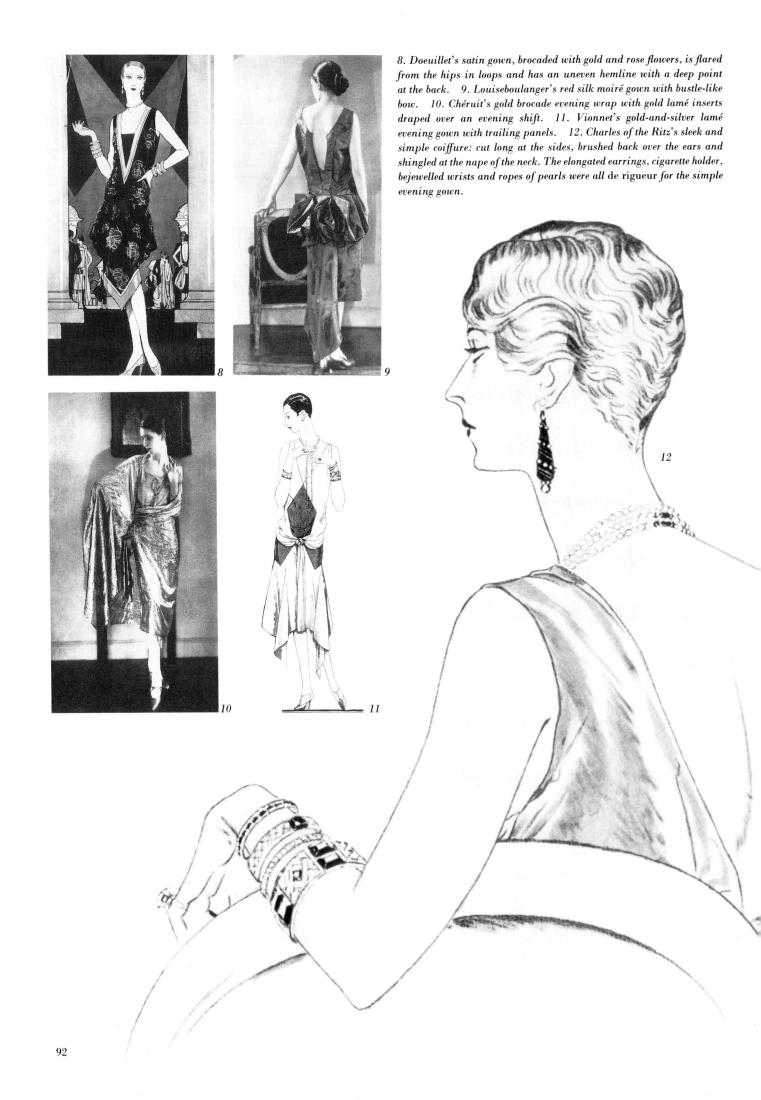

8. *Doeuillet's satin gown, brocaded with gold and rose flowers, is flared from the hips in loops and has an uneven hemline with a deep point at the back.* 9. *Louiseboulanger's red silk moiré gown with bustle-like bow.* 10. *Chéruit's gold brocade evening wrap with gold lamé inserts draped over an evening shift.* 11. *Vionnet's gold-and-silver lamé evening gown with trailing panels.* 12. *Charles of the Ritz's sleek and simple coiffure: cut long at the sides, brushed back over the ears and shingled at the nape of the neck. The elongated earrings, cigarette holder, bejewelled wrists and ropes of pearls were all de rigueur for the simple evening gown.*

13. *J. Suzanne Talbot's knitted wool motoring dress trimmed with black, beige and rust grosgrain ribbon, long jumper with pleated grosgrain basque and trimmed hood.* 14. *Poiret's white georgette crêpe dress flounced with fine, rippling pleats along the collar and skirt sides. The fichu collar is tied at the front with a black velvet bow.* 15. *Left: Chanel's three-tiered silhouette: dark-red Crêpella dress and bolero coat. Right: Chanel's black-and-white spotted crêpe dress with a plain Crêpella coat.* 16. *Left: Chéruit's bold flower-print dress with flaring sleeves. Centre: Molyneux's polkadot-print georgette crêpe dress, tied with a low-slung black satin sash. Right: Poiret's green silk dress with delicately pleated panels.*

presented novel knitted sweaters, typically in dark red and beige, over skirts made in Crêpella – a popular wool crêpe.

Fashionable holiday resorts had become so sophisticated that city formality was required, particularly at race meetings. The slightly flared, three-quarter-length coat was very chic, wrapped to one side across the body. The cape was an alternative and was considered particularly appropriate for travelling.

American designers such as Kurzman, Gunther and Franklin Simon principally showed wide-lapelled coats to just below the knee, cut in decorative panels, in fur, wool or tweed. Stein & Blaine chose to trim even the simplest coats with fur collars and cuffs. The American business woman was advised by *Vogue* to opt for the simplicity typified by Chanel and Molyneux. Copies of their original models could be bought at the major New York department stores.

For the summer the three-quarter-length jacket was important and Chanel popularized the cardigan-style sports jacket. Last year's suit tunics were cut longer and wider below the waist to stand out over the hips rather than lie close to the body.

For the evening every conceivable form of jewellery and bead-work was applied to pastel-coloured fabrics such as chiffon, lace, crêpe, satin or taffeta.

Deep décolletés and uneven hemlines were fashionable details. Louise-boulanger's autumn collection featured a number of evening gowns with large puffed bows at the back and trailing panels, which were the precursors of Patou's floor-length hemline of 1929. London evening gowns from Violet Norton, Eve Valère and Cécile were very simply cut compared with the elab-

orately trimmed French and American styles. Silver or gold brocade slippers, lozenge earrings and quantities of bracelets – journalist Nancy Cunard popularized ivory ones – were fashionable evening accessories.

Champcommunal opened in Paris, Charles James opened as a milliner – Bouchéron – in Chicago, and Hattie Carnegie opened in New York.

17. *Mary Nowitzky's black waterproofed Cheviot coat with scarf collar, waterproofed serge skirt and Agnès hat, for skiing.* 18. *J. Suzanne Talbot's chine wool air-travel ensemble trimmed with grosgrain ribbon in several colours. The helmet is attached to the two-piece frock and suggests a sailor collar when the coat is removed and the helmet slipped off.*

1. Left: *Paquin's princess-line black cloth coat with fox-fur collar and cuffs.* Right: *Vionnet's dark-blue princess-line coat with one-sided shawl collar.*

1927

Couturiers now applied greater elegance and richness to clothes without abandoning the recent lessons of comfort and clean-line tailoring. Women's day wear combined appropriateness and ease with renewed formality – characteristics that were to become typical of the thirties.

The coat and dress ensemble was now the most acceptable afternoon attire. Feminine, colourful, printed chiffon was popular for summer afternoon frocks worn beneath a full-length coat which was wrapped to one side, collared, cuffed and banded in fur. For the autumn the fashionable woman typically wore a long-sleeved frock in lamé, crêpe, marocain, satin or silk jersey, either plain or printed with a small design. The smart hemline was always irregular – festooned or handkerchief-pointed. Many Paris houses showed hip sashes and scarf details draped to one side on day dresses with narrow sleeves. Louiseboulanger added bows and mock-bustles to her day dresses and Vionnet designed dresses with double panels falling on each side, like streamers, to the hem. An obliquely

closed coat inset with triangular godets for movement, light shoes in patent leather or buckskin and a small, flat, rectangular bag completed the outfit.

Wrap-over coats were fashionable for spring. They were either collarless and sleeveless or had velvet collars, raglan sleeves and jabot details. By the autumn the princess line, fitted under the bust, was popular for coats. Vionnet designed

a series of English tweed, velvet and wool-velour travelling coats, many of which were three-quarter-length, widening to the hem. The back and the sleeves were cut in one piece with a top seam detail rather than the more usual underarm seam. The most luxurious daytime coat in America was the dark eastern mink offered at Stein & Blaine. Lelong designed an unusual raincoat in heavy

2. Hayward's full top coat in red, black and grey tweed trimmed with fox, box-pleated skirt suit and bright-red jersey jumper. 3. Goupy's waterproofed beige kasha coat with baby calfskin collar and distinctive large, single, oblique rever. 4. Dancer Edwina St Clair models Patou's blue printed chiffon summer frock with tiered skirt. 5. Left: Louiseboulanger's black satin dress with pleated effect on one hip. Right: Louiseboulanger's grey satin dress with hip fullness gathered to a point at the front, becoming flat at the back and ending in two points. 6. Left: Lanvin's olive-green mousseline dress with gold lamé trimmings and green crêpe-lined black kasha coat trimmed with black silk tassels and stitching. Right: Lanvin's black crêpe marocain suit, white crêpe-de-Chine blouse with white picot and black ribbon edging. 7. J. Suzanne Talbot's two-piece outfit in light wool jersey, with simple box-pleated skirt and diagonally shoulder-fastened jumper.

silk, with a rubberized lining.

Cardigans and collarless jackets in horizontal stripes were offered by Chanel, who opened a shop in London this year. Jane Regny, Chantal and Goupy showed semi-sports frocks with decorative panels and pleats and belts emphasizing the natural waistline.

Tweeds were tailored into softer suits and pleated skirts in Paris, while London continued to favour a more masculine cut: straight, severely tailored, plain jackets and straight skirts. Jackets no longer had to match the skirt; a light jacket contrasting with a darker skirt or dress was considered very smart. The bolero, which had returned to the fashionable wardrobe last year, was now high fashion for day and evening wear.

There were four distinct evening lines this year: the crisp dress in stiff satin, faille, moiré or velvet; the very sophisticated dress constructed in circular tiers; the dress with a puff or chou; and the picture frock with a wide, full skirt. Décolletés ranged from a deep V at the back or front to the oval or square neckline. Black and white were the most popular shades, closely followed by yellow, pink, lavender blue, turquoise, pale green and terracotta. Chanel, innovative as ever, promoted 'lipstick red'.

London evening gowns were elegant and simple. Norman Hartnell, who opened in London and showed his collection in Paris, presented the most spectacular flowing gowns for the 'season' in chiffon, satin and lace. His designs still bore signs of his experience of theatre costume. His clientele largely consisted of English society ladies, for whom he designed grand ball dresses and serviceable country tweeds.

By the autumn detailing was focused on the back of the gown with flying panels, choux and lavish mock-bustle bows. Wealthy Americans still chose to buy French evening dresses.

Details were now the essence of high fashion on both day and evening wear and included black velvet collars, fringes, crêpe bands, the sunburst motif, the square or V neck, or the bateau neckline in America.

Elsa Schiaparelli arrived on the fashion scene this year with a black wool jumper with a dramatic white *trompe-l'oeil* bow motif. *Vogue* featured the garment and its success led Schiaparelli to set up a business in the Rue de la Paix.

8. *Patou's black crêpe-de-Chine beach coat lined with white towelling and matching swimsuit.* 9. *Henri's grey suiting skirt with flat, tailored, cuffed hem, brass-buttoned, double-breasted blue hopsack blazer, white crêpe-de-Chine blouse with blue-and-grey checked tie.* 10. *Schiaparelli's famous hand-knitted black-and-white jumper with bow motif.* 11. *Jane Regny's white silk piqué tennis shift.*

12. *Lanvin's black taffeta picture frock with a huge black-and-white taffeta bow trimmed with a brilliant ornament at the centre back.* 13. *Patou's black-and-white Japanese-patterned 'jumper' suit for the evening: the black satin skirt has inverted pleats lined with white satin.* 14. *Louiseboulanger's black mousseline and beaded-tulle gown with a garland of multi-coloured flowers on the corsage and new, longer back hem.* 15. *Chéruit's orange-glacé taffeta gown with hip flounces that fall in irregular lines. 'Modernistic' buckles clasp the shoulder straps.* 16. *Patou's dress in black Chantilly lace and black chiffon with a circular bolero to match the tiers on the skirt, trimmed with rose and mauve ribbons.*

1928

The trend towards long, elegant evening gowns was mirrored by a similar fall in afternoon hemlines this spring. The length of skirts was accentuated by the rise of the waistline. Lelong advocated its natural position for evening wear. The neckline and sleeves of an outfit were highlighted by details such as double or triple strips of material edging the décolleté, loops, bows, ribbon-like scarves or handkerchiefs.

Spring fabrics, especially crêpes and satins, were brightly coloured and there was a profusion of small patterns such as polka dots, leaves and floral motifs, geometric designs, plaids and ginghams, although plain crêpes and satins were seen at Lecomte and Louiseboulanger. The combination of black and beige was offered by Louiseboulanger, Lelong and Paquin. Chanel favoured Chinese silk and the Americans used washing silk for resort wear.

Hairstyles were gradually lengthening; the Eton crop was now démodé. Small-brimmed hats, such as the cloche, or turbans were fashionable for casual

1. Chantal's printed crêpe etamine dress. 2. Madame Lelong in a black-and-white satin one-piece, collarless dress. 3. Chantal's white silk tussore sports dress. 4. Louiseboulanger's reddish-mauve, artificial-silk-mix tiered dress. 5. Patou's navy-blue crêpe-de-Chine dress with two flounced tiers. 6. Redfern's dress. A circular panel falls in uneven folds from beneath a curved, yoke-like band. 7. Yteb's figured satin suit, with plain bands of satin around the coat and skirt. 8. Lady Abdy wears Molyneux's sports outfit: grey-blue tweed coat, blue wool skirt and red, white and blue striped jumper. 9. Chanel. Left: fingertip-length jacket and skirt in bright-red kasha lined with red-and-black striped jersey to match the blouse. Right: two-piece dress and fingertip-length jacket in almond-green Rodier jersey, striped in dark brown and lined with beige jersey.

10. Louiseboulanger's black-and-white printed taffeta pannier dress. 11. Worth's wide, pleated taupe satin trousers and velvet-lined gold lamé jacket fastened with a gold tassel. 12. Vionnet's blue rayon-and-silk velvet evening gown, swathed tightly about the hips, hanging in long panels. 13. Gertrude Lawrence in Molyneux's georgette crêpe evening gown, embroidered with fine crystal beads.

fashionable women in London tended to buy their sports underclothes, handkerchiefs and scarves from traditional men's outfitters, for, by and large, these were unisex requirements.

In New York the printed silk suit with a pleated skirt and cardigan jacket was considered charming worn with a tiny cloche hat and flat shoes.

Slinky materials such as satin and crêpe, cut on the bias, sometimes with a train, continued to dominate evening wear, though some houses, notably Molyneux, preferred straight, simple, shorter evening dresses based on sportswear lines. Both styles aimed to create a long-limbed look, and *Vogue* emphasized that 'the straight silhouette which accents the slender column of the body – the result of the twentieth century pursuit of youth – is the newest and smartest silhouette'. For the autumn red or burgundy silk velvet was chosen for evening wear at Patou, Louiseboulanger and Lelong; Molyneux favoured a deep midnight blue. Printed and cut velvet evening gowns were also fashionable. In London brocade evening wear, for example by Dove, was popular.

The black crêpe day dress reigned supreme for city wear at Chanel, Molyneux, Carette, Martial et Armand, Jane Regny and Redfern, and was worn with higher heeled shoes. The princess line and uneven or asymmetric hem reinforced the spring trends.

Like dresses, coats dipped at the back. Various lengths and silhouettes were fashionable: straight, wrapped, flared or full and slightly fitted at the waist. Louiseboulanger featured contrast colour peplums on her coats. Rainwear was now less masculine in cut. Schiaparelli used a variety of rubberized materials, particularly those from Rodier.

The Chambre Syndicale de la Couture set up the École de la Chambre Syndicale de la Couture to teach and maintain the standards of craftsmanship in the couture. It became the centre of couture apprenticeship and was open to both French and foreign students.

Schiaparelli opened her shop Pour le Sport in Paris and Digby Morton, a young Irishman, joined the small sportswear house of Lachasse (founded in 1900) as a designer. Valentina and Elizabeth Hawes opened in New York, while Charles James began designing clothes as well as millinery.

day wear, but more formal ensembles required a larger brimmed hat.

Sportswear continued to be prominent in the international collections. Premet's spring collection included a variety of sports ensembles worn with sleeveless cardigans in varying shades of the same colour; while Chéruit and Lelong promoted the corduroy sports coat; and

Paquin showed the fur-trimmed sports coat. The London collections favoured the cape and cape details on sports coats and ensembles and the two-piece, knitted 'frock-suit' was offered by the major department stores. Tweeds with a woven diagonal, zig-zag or chevron pattern were used for sports and day suits. American *Vogue* reported that

14. Left: Schiaparelli's grey rubberized Crêpella coat with loose sleeves and flyer's helmet. Right: rubberized ensemble fastened diagonally across the bodice and skirt with 'corozo' buttons (a bone-like substance). 15. Left: House of London Trade's turquoise culotte skirt and angora twinset. Agnès's blue jersey cloche with triangular felt insertion. Right: Schiaparelli's black-and-white costume – serge culottes and knitted jumper with a white front and a black back. Lacquered black lambskin jacket with furry lining. 16. Saks's white jersey blouse with navy-blue flannel bands, white flannel skirt, navy-blue flannel reefer, navy-blue-and-white polkadot scarf and Bangkok hat. 17. Chantal's coats in different tweeds, for town and country. The collars are traditionally cut with modest revers, and there is a slight suggestion of a normal waistline. The sleeves are skilfully moulded at the shoulders, all the seams being emphasized with top-stitching.

14

15

16

17

1929

1. The tricorne, the basque and the section blouse are all fashionable details on this spring ensemble by Paquin. The fine black cloth suit is trimmed with black caracul. 2. Lelong's black cloth coat with details in fashionable astrakhan, and Maria Guy's soft felt hat. 3. Paquin's black crêpe dress and beige cloth coat trimmed with Persian lamb and cut with an uneven hem. 4. The high-fashion accessory: sable scarf by H. Jaeckel and Sons, made from eight skins. Mado's black velvet, shallow-crowned hat with long, pleated sides and back.

The tricorne (replacing the cloche), basque and blouse were all fashionable spring features and *Vogue* put great emphasis on accessories, such as handbags, hats and ostentatious furs slung over shoulders, which gave a mature, sophisticated image. Gloves were *de rigueur* for all occasions. The newest glove was 6–9 inches long, was worn wrinkled at the wrist, and had prominent hand-stitching outlining the fingers. Flesh-coloured suede was the most popular with navy-blue or black ensembles.

The sun-tan fad affected fashionable colours: gloves, stockings, and clothes appeared in a variety of sun-tanned hues ranging from honey to praline to set off a tanned complexion. Augustabernard, for instance, designed the simplest shell-pink dresses with deep, tan-revealing décolletés. For spring coats and suits black and red were favourite colours, while feminine, pastel colours were fashionable for the summer months, although contrasting black and white were still in vogue.

Long-legged slimness was now the fashionable ideal, set off by close-fitting, moulded dresses, which defined the curve of the upper thighs and made corsetry a necessity, as *Vogue* pointed out: 'Corsets of some sort ... mould the figure to more gracious lines, less harsh and boyish ... less casual and unconfined.'

Jutting flares and irregular hemlines were confined to late afternoon dresses and coats, though the basque was seen on many daytime clothes. A soft blouse, particularly the new sleeveless blouse, was tucked into the top of the skirt to emphasize the waistline, replacing the straight overblouse. Semi-tailored jackets were now more fashionable than

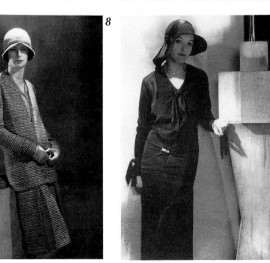

5. Molyneux's crêpe marocain suit in navy-blue-and-grey check, with sleeveless jacket and Reboux straw hat. 6. Fifinella's grey-blue, semi-tailored cape-shouldered jacket in lightweight wool, and simple one-piece dress with Agnès's light-blue jersey turban. 7. Lady Victor Paget's classic rust-and-beige tweed suit and beige crêpe-de-Chine blouse. 8. Chanel's striped jersey suit, close-fitting cloche and bold blue, greige and black jersey scarf. 9. Lenief's black crêpe-de-Chine dress, tightly moulded from the waist to below the hips. The skirt reaches eight inches below the knee. The shallow-crowned Agnès hat in felt and satin has an oblique, side-swooping brim.

the casual sports cardigan or jumper. Skirts, which were cut in a circle or loosely pleated, continued to lengthen, and some houses, notably Patou, offered the ankle-length afternoon dress. Charles James showed his bias-cut 'taxi' dress, made in only two sizes.

The sleeves of dresses were detailed, tucked or cuffed, or a floating trumpet shape, and in general tended to be longer than in the recent past. Lelong showed distinctive bell-shaped sleeves. However, sleeveless summer dresses were also fashionable; they had a double waistline – a hybrid of the normal waistline and the princess line – which was still in its embryonic stage. White detailing was applied to many summer dresses, coats and jackets, usually at the collar and cuffs but sometimes also at the hem. Period influences, for example Victorianstyle lace details, became important.

Winter coats of all lengths had a great deal of back detailing. The smart city coat was wrapped across the body, fell to just below the knee and was trimmed at the collar and cuffs with fur. Astrakhan was a favourite fur trim, especially for basques on smart coats and jackets.

British fashion followed Paris lines – skirts were longer and the silhouette slightly fuller. Even the tailored tweed suit began to admit feminine curves and softness, emphasizing the waistline. Horizontally striped tweeds were especially popular for London suits, the most practical being designed by Ulick.

The return of sleeves for evening marked the increased formality of the

10   *11*   *12*   *13*

mode. Elegant and intricately cut gowns were worn with furs and evening gloves. Most gowns reached the floor at the back and some reached it at the front as well. The sumptuousness of Hollywood film clothes, which created a feminine, untouchable image, affected the couture, and many emerging American couturiers concentrated on this look for many years to come.

However, as a result of the Wall Street Crash on 30 November the profits of the

couture and related industries nosedived. Janet Flanner, Paris correspondent for the *New Yorker*, wrote that 'In the Rue de la Paix the jewellers are reported to be losing fortunes in sudden cancellations of orders, and at the Ritz bar pretty ladies are having to pay for their cocktails themselves. In the Quartier de l'Europe little firms that live exclusively on the American trade have not sold one faked Chanel copy in a fortnight.'

10. Chanel's black net gown. 11. Patou's soft silver lamé gown brocaded in pastel colours. The skirt's back fullness is released from curving hipbands and emphasized by the downward movement of the cowl. 12. Dolores del Rio in Hollywoodstyle evening ensemble: three-quarter length, pale-grey/beige velvet and white-fox evening cape with shirred inserts at the elbow. 13. Lady Ashley in a black taffeta dress by Hartnell. It reaches the floor at the back; the ruffles, which can be worn up or down, accentuate the slenderness of the bodice. The décolleté has scalloped edges.

14   *15*   *16*   *17*

14. Chantal's tweed bouclé dress with asymmetric neckline. 15. Chanel's tiered caped-sleeve dress. 16. Chanel's three-piece jersey sports costume worn by Gertrude Lawrence. 17. Patou's long-sleeved black velvet afternoon dress. 18. Lelong used a Raoul Dufy print for this black-and-blue crêpe marocain coat and matching blue pyjamas.

1930

A mood of emphatic femininity prevailed. The fashionable soft coiffure, which was rolled at the nape of the neck, reflected the draped, gentle lines of clothes. Real gems supplemented the costume jewellery of the twenties, giving a discreet and expensive look: pearl neck-laces, tiny dress watches and diamond dress clips. Other chic details included turbans, berets, gloves pulled over cuffless sleeves, fur collars, crystal embroidery and sequinned flowers.

The patterned, usually floral-printed, dress was more popular in America than in Britain and France, where the plain morning dress was favoured, in silk, jersey, velvet and satin. Some dresses had intricate, swathed necklines, kimono or raglan sleeves and swirling, bias-cut skirts. Tunic dresses and blouses in contrasting colours and materials created a layered effect that was considered an effective way of breaking up the silhouette. The afternoon dress was at its smartest combined with a three-quarter-length coat: the most striking versions were shown at Vionnet, Lanvin, Bruyère and Maggy Rouff. Worth and Callot Soeurs designed three-quarter-length coats that were interchangeable with shorter jackets or tunics, to extend one's wardrobe. Hickson, Jay-Thorpe and

1. Louiseboulanger's black-and-yellow check marocain dress and jacket with white chiffon fichu, from Bendel, bordered once again with checks. The felt hat is by Bouchéron (Charles James). 2. Edward L. Mayer's sinuous gold-and-black brocade dress. 3. Vionnet's transparent, pale-turquoise crêpe romain dress. 4. Hartnell's chartreuse-green crêpe romain tucked dress and small coatee faced with a darker shade of the same material.

Bonwit Teller all showed afternoon dresses in luxurious materials usually associated with evening wear: lamé, satin and velvet, in black or rich brown. Hattie Carnegie combined dark dresses with white hats for city summer wear.

In contrast to Paris and America, most London designers, with the exception of Hartnell, concentrated on informal sports and tub frocks rather than very formal afternoon dresses or ensembles. Fine wool, heavy crêpes and tie silk (silk that can be tied or knotted) were

popular fabrics.

The length of skirts increased as the day wore on. Hems were 12 inches from the ground for the afternoon, 10 inches for teatime, just clear of the ankle for dancing and to the toes for grand evening occasions; 15 inches from the ground was normal for travelling clothes and a hand's width below the knee for sports clothes. Higher heels were worn with the longer skirts, while sports skirts were worn with flat shoes and waisted wide-shouldered jackets.

5. Vionnet's light, diagonally buttoned top with dark skirt. The loose cowl neck of the blouse hangs over the deep 'V' of the neck of the jacket.
6. Ulick's bolero over a high-waisted, slender-hipped fine black-and-white tweed dress. The bolero revers are faced with black taffeta, and the dress's white organdie vest is trimmed with black-and-white buttons.
7. Chanel's striped, brown-and-beige three-quarter-length jersey tweed cape lined with contrasting green jersey.

8. *Schiaparelli's pale greige, rough tweed coat with patch pockets and tied scarf ends, and Agnès's natural-coloured lace straw hat.* 9. *Callot Soeurs' dark-brown kasha coat with one-sided shoulder cape detail cut in one with the back.* 10. *Madame Martinez de Hoz, a South American beauty, models Vionnet's white ermine and black broadcloth coat and black Reboux beret.* 11. *Brown astrakhan trims Lelong's brown cloth coat.* 12. *Gertrude Lawrence in Molyneux's black-and-white gathered and draped tweed dress, cut like a coat. Grey fox borders the scarf.*

Practicality continued to be the main criterion for beach and active sports clothes. The more masculine the better was the rule for Antibes or the Lido in Venice: long, tailored trousers, sailors' jumpers, fishermen's blouses, mechanics' overalls and Boy Scouts' shorts and shirts. Spectator sports clothes, however, admitted feminine touches and gentle blousing softened the most functional sports suits, which had either waisted or bolero jackets. Even the jackets of Chanel's little town suits were fitted through the waist and briefly flared below it.

The sensation of the autumn was Vionnet's transparent gown, moulded to the body, showing a hint of flesh colour as the wearer moved. Usually worn over a *maillot* or body stocking, the drawbacks for less-than-perfect figures were only too obvious, but the fashion for crêpe or satin bias-cut gowns revealed every curve of the body. There were variations on this evening line: Lelong and Augustabernard favoured drapery; Lanvin and Augustabernard gathered peplum flounces standing out between the hip and the knee; Chanel and Chéruit showed skirts with tiny ruffled tiers; Molyneux and Irene Dana favoured the Empire line. Evening gowns at Hartnell, Augustabernard and Germaine Lecomte featured spiral, asymmetric effects and Augustabernard and Germaine Lecomte used intricate seaming across the hips and along the thighs to create sinuous gowns reminiscent of the robes of the 'Nike of Samothrace' in the Louvre. Other period influences included 1850s and 1880s styles; the American designer Omar Kiam featured mock bustles and Schiaparelli showed Victorian-style puff sleeves.

The 'semi-demi', which looked like a sophisticated tea gown, was also popular for evening, worn with a short fur or fabric evening cape. Some evening dresses had matching boleros. The most popular evening colours were black, white, pink, lacquer-red, pale green and lilac.

Fur and fabric were combined to create dramatic coats in Paris this autumn – Patou and Augustabernard showed the most memorable versions. Hattie Carnegie used flat fur and brown velveteen for three-quarter-length coats teamed with a skirt or dress that flared below the knee, as did Philip Mangone. Astrakhan and sealskin, which could be applied with tailored control, as they had a shallow pile, were the most fashionable fur trims.

Mainbocher opened in Paris, specializing in strictly formal clothes of complex cut and simple line. Charles Creed opened in London and in New York the Fashion Group was established to co-ordinate the various sections of the fashion industry and provide a bank of information and advice.

13. Left to right: *Jane Regny's blue and green chiffon dress with draped, cowl neck. Augustabernard's grey, lemon-yellow and black chiffon afternoon dress has a shoulder bow holding the bodice drapery and circular godets adding fullness to the skirt. Callot's yellow, rose-and-grey chiffon dress has a draped jabot.* 14. *Lucile Paray's turquoise tunic with prominent revers and black, crinkled panne velvet skirt.*

15. Centre: *Schiaparelli's moussa tuslic (a soft, spongy wool) belted beach pyjamas, with beige blouse and blue trousers worn with crêpe-rubber sandals. Right: Yteb's white woollen two-piece bathing suit: a step-in top with a deep back décolleté and braid-trimmed shorts.* 16. *Schiaparelli's washable white linen summer dress and Agnès's natural straw hat.* 17. *Left: cotton piqué sports frock, with white shantung lace beret. Right: sports dress with pale-blue tussore and white cotton piqué cloche.* 18. *Maggy Rouff's sports suit: white cotton piqué jacket over intricately tucked and pleated sleeveless dress, worn with Marie Alphonsine's cloche.*

16

1931

The Great Depression that followed the crash of the American stock market in 1929 was now influencing high fashion. *Vogue* responded in two ways: on the one hand editorials offered advice on money-saving chic for those with a limited income and on the other they instilled in their readers a spirit of patriotic support for native designers. In these dark, miserable days fashion predictably responded in a supportive, conservative and feminine manner, offering the palliative of highly romantic and glamorous fashions.

London designers were particularly aware of economy-consciousness, and British *Vogue* advised those with a limited income to purchase a simple suit, which could be made smarter for formal occasions with a bias-cut satin blouse or a tunic blouse with a decorative basque.

Both British and American *Vogue* promoted cotton after the slump in the cotton industry. Leading couturiers such as Chanel, Lelong and Hartnell now used cotton even for evening wear, partly to promote the interests of their national textile industries and partly because it was so versatile. Chanel showed thirty-five cotton dance frocks in her summer collection and Patou designed cotton-organdie dance dresses with patent-leather belts. Cotton lace was applied to romantic ball dresses, which were ideal for young débutantes – the social season had been revived in all its formality. 'Ball gowns are ball gowns again and come home in massive boxes; materials are going to be noticed,' reported *Vogue*

under the heading 'The Triumph of Cotton'.

Most evening dresses were slim through the waist, wide at the shoulders and very figure-revealing. White was *the* colour for evening in the international collections; fabrics ranged from luxurious satin and crêpe at Vionnet, to simple cotton at Hartnell. Redfern was renowned for his débutante frocks in frothy white georgette. American designers such as Carnegie continued to favour the printed evening gown, teamed this year with a brightly coloured jacket.

The white top coat was a fashion essential in Miami and other American resorts. Spring and summer coats were, in general, long and slinky like the dresses worn underneath. Flannel was now often chosen as a sports fabric and was expertly handled at houses like Patou. Sweaters were back in fashion for sportswear and modish accessories

1. Lucien Lelong's wife models his black-and-white striped wool dress and Maria Guy's white piqué hat. 2. Vionnet's white crêpe dress and Reboux's wide-brimmed hat. 3. Mainbocher's black-and-white crêpe dress, Agnès's hat with knitted silk crown. 4. Mainbocher's models for formal tea wear or restaurant dining. Left: black crêpe pedove dress. Right: black velour suit, trimmed with ermine. 5. Madame Isobel's navy-blue wool morning frock with flared basque and puff sleeves above deep cuffs striped in red, white and blue. 6. Geene Glenny's fine red wool jersey crêpe dress, with puffed sleeves and draped neckline.

included white plaid espadrilles, large, floppy beach hats, bulky white gloves and horsehair bags.

The prevailing silhouette was long-limbed and curvaceous; hats – worn pulled down over one eye – and bodice details focused attention on the upper half of the body, while long skirts flaring below the knee emphasized narrow hips. Hemlines for the late afternoon were now as long as those of evening gowns, brushing the ankles. Vionnet's crêpe dresses made their wearers look particularly tall and thin, for she cut skirts on the bias and deepened the waistline, creating a sense of spiralled length.

By the autumn the long-legged look had become more angular. Schiaparelli and Rochas introduced militaristic, wide shoulders, using shoulder pads for coats and jackets. Both Rochas and Schiaparelli were influenced by the 1931 Exposition Coloniale in Paris, which showed wide-shouldered Japanese and Balinese costumes and Bangkok temple dancers with winged shoulders and tiny waists. Schiaparelli entitled her autumn clothes her 'Wooden Soldier' collection, which established the silhouette for several years to come.

The autumn collections ousted glossy, shiny materials such as satin in favour of matt fabrics such as *peau d'ange*, a satin-faced silk or rayon fabric with a suede-like, soft, downy finish. Woollen day dresses were brightly coloured and often striped, while velvets in deep

7. *American sports suits: Left: bright-green, basket-weave woollen suit, crêpe-de-Chine blouse with gargantuan monogram from Saks. Right: yellow-and-brown country wool dress and velveteen jacket, with plaid silk scarf, from Stein and Blaine.* 8. *Sable bands across the bodice, basque, peplum and cuffs of Paquin's black cloth suit create a fashionable, top-heavy look.* 9. *Derryls's orange light-wool jacket, brown wool skirt and short, fitted tussore waistcoat.* 10. *Chanel's beige sports suit with brown-and-beige striped blouse and Rhavis's felt hat.*

11. *Two Schiaparelli coats. Left: wool coat accentuating shoulder width and seal-lined front. Right: figure-hugging coat with detachable baby-seal collar.* 12. *Molyneux trims his straight, beige tweed wrap coat with a pilgrim cape of beaver to match that on the upper arms. Brown leather Hermès gloves.* 13. *Patou's light-green wool crêpe coat, white tussore frock and sailor hat of rough white straw.*

colours were popular for the afternoon.

Like dresses, autumn coats were cinched tightly at the waist and reached the lower calf. The slightly shorter tailored redingote from Creed, Busvine, Redfern, Martial et Armand and Jane Regny was deemed ideal for travelling. The more formal coat was elaborately trimmed at the neck and shoulders with long-haired fur, or alternatively was cut entirely from a flat fur such as broadtail (similar to Persian lamb but with a texture like cut velvet). Goupy, Bruyère, Lucile Paray, Maggy Rouff, Germaine Lecomte and Yvonne Carette all showed coats in half fur and half fabric. The soldier coat, with broad shoulders and bodice fastened right across both shoulders, was very fashionable.

The most sought-after accessory in Paris was the fur stole, slipped over the head like a figure of eight, and worn with most daytime outfits. Throughout times of financial or political instability, status items such as fur are craved by fashionable women.

14. *Artelle's pale pinkish-mauve peau d'ange halter-neck dress, with novel neckline coming to a point at the base of the throat in the front, while the back is cut very low, with a short basque and skirt flaring from the knees.*
15. *Augustabernard's beige-and-black pyjama dress.*
16. *Chanel's romantic, red velveteen evening dress with puff sleeves and a jutting overskirt.*
17. *Mainbocher's heavy, cream-coloured faille short tunic cut into a V-shaped point and edged with a band of grey-beige marten continuing down the back. The skirt gradually widens in overlapping sections. The cape scarf is worn over one shoulder.*
18. *Vionnet's grand white crêpe marocain evening coat, tightly sealed by a draped collar, tapered at the waist and widening into loose folds, hiding the gown underneath.*

18

14

15

16

17

1932

1

1. Schiaparelli. Left: *wool jacket with raglan sleeves, clipped waist and peplum panel over grey silk blouse and wool skirt. Centre: check wool jacket on silk crêpe background with satin ribbon edging. A leather belt marks the high waist. Right: fantasy jersey coat-dress, styled like a suit, ribbed silk jersey blouse and holster belt fastened with dagger clips. The knitted woollen caps are distinctive Schiaparelli touches.* 2. Mainbocher's wide-shouldered autumn suits. Left: *black tweed suit with scarf and sweater in red, black and white jersey. Right: dropped-shoulderline suit extending into full sleeves at the lower arm, three-quarter-length black wool coat.* 3. Molyneux's red-and-brown striped sports suit. *The three-quarter-length coat has a scarf collar.* 4. Schiaparelli's sunset-rose-coloured tailored coat with *wide revers and nipped-in waist; banana-beige jersey dress and plaited scarf.* 5. American swagger coats. Left: *two-tone-blue English wool swagger jacket collared in polar wolf. Right: herringbone tweed skirt and swagger coat trimmed with red fur.* 6. Lanvin's autumn styles. Left: *beige woollen coat, corded on each pocket and sleeves. Centre: wool dress with velvet collar and sleeves and organ-pleated shoulders. Right: pale-blue woollen top, encrusted at front and loose as cape at the back.*

Vogue announced the foundation of the London Fashion Group, comprising members of leading wholesale houses in London whose aim was to establish London as a world-recognized fashion centre.

Since most women would not be able to afford as many clothes this year, *Vogue* advised its readers to treat their wardrobe like a carefully chosen portfolio of investments and to beware of cheap bargains. The clothing industry had been severely hit by the economic crisis and was making cheap clothes to be sold at apparently reduced prices. However, there were also widespread legitimate reductions in clothes prices, especially at the higher end of the market. Mink coats, for instance, that once would have cost $3,000 could now be bought for $1,200. Another symptom of the Depression was the renewed popularity of the sweater, which had fallen out of favour in the late twenties. It was now worn for more formal late-afternoon and cocktail functions as well as for sports and casual dress. *Vogue* offered money-saving advice on home knits, while several houses showed knitted late-afternoon suits.

All the editions of *Vogue* tried to encourage their national fashion and textile industries. British *Vogue*, for example, celebrated the English talent for dressmaking as exemplified by Molyneux, Hartnell, the young Victor Stiebel (who opened this year), Isobel, Lachasse, Busvine and Geene Glenny. French houses were now bringing their designs over to London to be made up in British

7

7. Lanvin's sequinned silver short cape worn over a long shaft of dull black crêpe.   8. Stiebel's slinky, hyacinth-blue chiffon and ribbon velvet Grecian-style dress, sunray pleated and cummerbunded high up under the bust.   9. Ilka Chase poses as a Gibson Girl in a black taffeta evening jacket over a black chiffon dinner dress with roses marking the décolleté from Saks.   10. Dress with cowl neck in Courtelle's Courgette, an artificial silk.   11. Isobel's ermine and black velvet evening dress.

8   9   10   11

workrooms, rather than showing French-produced dresses. British fabrics were gaining world acclaim. In Paris, British guardscloth was very fashionable, following Schiaparelli's promotion in 1930, as were Scottish tweeds, Bradford wools, Irish lace and Lancashire cottons.

Military details appeared in abundance this spring, notably at Schiaparelli, but even at houses renowned for femininity, such as Vionnet and Worth.

The new spring dress silhouette was mushroom-shaped. Elbow capes and cape sleeves concentrated width at the elbows, while the body below was stem slender. The typical waistline was high under the bust and sometimes emphasized by a wide sash. One-piece woollen dresses buttoning up one side were smart in colours such as beige, yellow, tangerine, cornflower blue and greyish-green – the spring palette.

The autumn collections accentuated this high-waisted princess line. Hips had to appear as narrow as possible and the day-length skirt fell straight to mid-calf level. The fashionable neckline was high: scarves were knotted under the chin, fur pieces were worn like boas, and many coats buttoned up to a high neck. Schiaparelli used some unconventional autumn colours – cabbage red, hyacinth blue and deep yellow – and showed waistcoats with frilled jabots reminiscent of Beau Brummel, and skirts and coats with pleated bustle panels.

Patou's autumn collection was dramatically different from the prevailing silhouette: he showed long, medieval-style dresses with a dropped waistline.

12. Joan Crawford models Schiaparelli's lacy knitted woollen dress with white-and-heliotrope matelassé crêpe jacket. 13. Heim's blue-and-white striped crêpe-de-Chine dress with scarf collar, which wraps around the neck and falls down over one shoulder. 14. Stiebel's brown-and-white striped woollen dress and brown coat lined with matching material and collared in beige fox.

However, the style did not catch on.

Coats were cut to look like dresses. The formal coat-dress ensemble had given way to the blouse and skirt, often in contrasting colours and materials. In America the swagger coat – an easy-fitting, beltless, flared coat – was very fashionable.

Suits were more popular than coats. Skirts were high-waisted, day jackets stopped at the hip, sports jackets at the waist and Schiaparelli's models at mid-rib. There was a profusion of boleros for day and evening wear.

Water-colour mauves, blue-greys and rosy-reds were prominent spring evening colours. Cotton was still important and the washable cotton evening gown appeared at many houses: Louise-boulanger showed flowered organdie dresses, Lanvin candy-striped organdies and Chanel rose, white and blue piqué gowns. By the autumn evening wear echoed the day silhouette. Shoulders were wide and sinuous materials used to create a moulded effect, enhancing the leggy grace of the fashionable figure. Necklaces were not worn with the most chic evening ensembles, attention being concentrated on the novel décolleté, which was cut high at the front, like a choker, and in some cases very low at the back.

This year Madeleine de Rauch and Nina Ricci opened in Paris and John Cavanagh joined the house of Molyneux. The young Claire McCardell began to design for Townly Frocks in America.

15–17. Three stages of Mainbocher's polkadot beach ensemble. 18. Hand-knit for American Vogue *readers: moss stitch, tie-waisted pyjama top.*

1933

The cinched waist emphasized by soft, full bodices and cravat bows dominated the evening collections and was attributed to the influence of Hollywood and to Mae West's costumes in particular.

The year's most significant trend was that towards a straighter daytime silhouette, accentuated by knee-length box coats fastened at the neck, which hung straight and wide over slim skirts. Coats with contrasting sleeves, for instance a cloth coat with velvet sleeves, or a velvet coat with black Alaska seal sleeves, were fashionable. Mainbocher showed loose, high-necked black wool coats and Molyneux showed a similar line in bold tweeds. Maggy Rouff favoured the straight cloth coat with basket-like hips and heavy fur trim. Bruyère's novel line was the coat with an unbroken front line, achieved by placing the fastening under the arms. Vionnet favoured full yet sleek capes in distinctive checked tweeds. In America the three-quarter-length *directoire* coat was seen at Jay-Thorpe and Blum's of Chicago.

Prints for summer day dresses included bold, primitive stripes and checks, a dramatic alternative to floral patterns. Summer evening gowns were very flowery – airy dresses of tulle, organza or chiffon. The slinky sheath of recent seasons was now démodé; gowns were becoming more romantic and extravagant, while the tunic was high fashion for formal evening wear.

Mainbocher designed a series of dinner suits this spring consisting of toe-length skirts, which were full enough to allow

2

1. Schiaparelli's Tyrolean-style tailored suit: heavy, hand-woven grey-and-yellow tweed jacket, granite-grey wool skirt, silk jersey blouse with a stock-like, stiffened yellow taffeta collar and knitted Tyrolean hat.   2. J. Suzanne Talbot's white piqué accessories with Augustabernard's black wool dress.   3. Schiaparelli's three suits. Left: heavy black silk ensemble with the foxes on the cape adding volume to the shoulders. Centre: angora wool ensemble with wrinkled sleeves, navy-blue crêpe blouse speckled in white. Right: thick navy-blue silk dress and bolero with gilet of foxes attached snout to snout, and small blue knitted clown hat.   4. Paquin's black wool suit with modest revers and inverted-pleated skirt worn with lavish white feather boas wrapped across the body.   5. Chanel's black ciré satin afternoon suit cinches the waist under a bloused bodice and is moulded over the hips.   6. Philippe and Gaston's Negondo suit (Siberian ponyskin). The jacket has a scarf collar and a short basque flaring from a nipped-in waist. Matching fur toque.

3

4

5

6

7. *Callot Soeurs' shorn brown lamb, three-quarter-length coat, waisted with a large leather belt.*   8. *Maggy Rouff's beige crêpe romain dress with satin crêpe bodice under loose ribbed velvet coat, the raglan sleeves cuffed in summer ermine to match the collar.*   9. *Creed's panelled, beige-and-white tweed travelling ensemble. The coat is raglan-sleeved, scarf-collared and loose.*   10. *Lanvin's flung-back, mottled-grey astrakhan cape with a monk's hood at the back, closed with one button under the chin and lying open to expose the brown cloth dress underneath.*

ease of movement and short jackets or capes, worn with pert little pill-box hats. Hattie Carnegie showed Victorian-style 'speakeasy' costumes. Schiaparelli attached taffeta 'dust catchers' to the hems of her dresses (in Victorian times the hems of skirts were bound with tape, or 'brush braid', to protect them from dust and fraying as they swept along the pavement). The Hollywood-influenced white satin evening dress and the white fur wrap continued to be a mainstay for the evening. Evening gloves were *de rigueur*, often matching the gown. Molyneux and Mainbocher succumbed to the Oriental influence for evening wear, designing Japanese-print kimonos with dragon-like tails trailing behind.

The high point of the Paris autumn collections was the demise of shoulder padding – exaggeration was now démodé. Only Schiaparelli continued to pad her jacket and coat shoulders. Her choice prevailed. Capes emphasized the softer, sloping shoulderline, the short fox cape being particularly fashionable.

Fur collars and cuffs were popular trims, while some houses showed tailored suits or jackets cut in fur and leather.

Autumn fashions continued to emphasize the neckline, with guardsmen's collars, bows, stocks, foulards, jabots and fur chokers. Hats added height, which was compensated for by lower heels. Laced Oxfords with low Cuban heels were smart with morning outfits.

Molly Parnis opened her house in New York. Digby Morton left Lachasse to open his own house in London.

11. *Lelong's simple, bias-cut, matte crêpe dress with a black-and-white striped three-quarter-length coat tied at the waist and the bodice with bows.*   12. *Vionnet's grey velour Leda coat-dress arabesques about the body. All details are focused at the back; grey fox collar, velvet back yoke and antelope belt. Sectioned beret by Maria Guy.*   13. *Geene Glenny's ankle-length, dark-green rough crêpe afternoon dress with a metallic waistband, high, straight neckline draped into a 'V' at the back and long, triangular cuffs.*   14. *Mainbocher's black wool dress decorated with a pleated bertha of crinkly black satin ribbon. A pleated white chiffon jabot is added to a little guimpe about the throat.*

15. *Augustabernard's close-fitting sheath dress enveloped in a dramatic cape tied across the poitrine.* 16. *Augustabernard's black crêpe back-split evening dress with dramatic gold-lamé stripes.* 17. *Miss Constance Bennet wears Carnegie's black velvet, Victorian 'speakeasy' costume: double-breasted jacket, finished with white piqué collar and cuffs, and black velvet hat trimmed with a fine mesh veil.* 18. *Lelong's tulle and navy-blue velvet evening sheath traced with navy and silver threads and silver embroidery.*

1934-1945

Mind my duvetyne dress above all! It's golded silvy, the newest sextones with princess effect. For Rutland blue's got out of passion.

James Joyce, *Finnegan's Wake*, 1939

I Dream About an Evening Dress, *by Salvador Dalí.*

Lady Elsie Mendl and the Duchess of Windsor photographed at the Duchess's Paris home.

The Hon. Reginald Fellowes in her Schiaparelli outfit and Antoine's decorative coiffure photographed at the 'Bal Oriental' in 1935.

I belong to the useless, superficial class of society, whose importance lies in its ability to inspire luxury – demand it in fact. We are the ones for whom new and exciting jewels are designed, extravagantly beautiful furs and clothes are created, more luxurious and faster cars are made. We nudge the creative instincts of the tradespeople of the industry. Without us fashion would have little motivation,' a prominent socialite told *Vogue*'s Bettina Ballard. Princess Faucigny-Lucinge, Princess Natalie Paley, Mrs Ernest Simpson and the Honourable Mrs Reginald Fellowes were amongst these headstrong, demanding leaders of style, whose ostentation expressed the mode.

Strict sartorial conventions now firmly replaced the frivolous novelty of the late twenties, and wardrobes were planned down to the minutest detail. Skirt length, quality of material and mode of dress – even the sheerness of stockings – were so clearly defined for each hour of the day that one observer declared that he could tell the time of day by the length of a fashionable woman's skirt.

Society yearned for the luxury and precise social etiquette of the past, and designers responded quickly to this nostalgia. Two weeks before her autumn show in 1934 Vionnet scrapped her entire collection and replaced it with gowns of taffeta and velvet, bustles and full-skirted picture frocks, all drawn from the nineteenth century. In 1935 couture collections, inspired by an exhibition of Italian Renaissance paintings in Paris, showed Fra Angelico aureole hats, plunging Medici necklines under rich velvet cloaks and pages in velvet jerkins and berets. Mae West visited Paris in 1936, having first sent Schiaparelli, who was to dress her, a life-sized, naked replica of her figure in a Venus de Milo pose. The arrival of the busty, hour-glass-shaped film star promoted a tidal wave of Nineties gaiety and fuller-figured fashions. 'Falsies' were worn to pad out the bosom. Edwardian costume balls and styles became all the rage. This fancy-dress escapism lingered on in the subconscious throughout the war until its reappearance as the inappropriately titled 'New Look' of the late forties.

In contrast to the previous decade, the couture presented a clear division between day and evening wear. Alongside the fantasy by night, the mainstream daytime silhouette established by 1934 prevailed until the end of the war: a tightly waisted line with wide, if not padded, shoulders, and a straight, narrow skirt. The skirt was gradually shortened by about four inches during the war years and the jacket lost its military details. Tent and redingote coats, which appeared in the mid-thirties, were also stalwart items of clothing during hostilities.

The tailored daytime mode was elegantly epitomized by the American Mainbocher, who worked in Paris until 1939 and dressed the Duchess of Windsor. Mainbocher, like Molyneux, hated 'over-aggressive fashions and people', exaggeration and too obvious period dressing. He preferred to 'try to blend mystery rather than to rave and rant with my shears'; the trousseau he designed for Mrs Simpson on her marriage to the Duke of Windsor in 1936 earned him worldwide acclaim.

Mainbocher had been the editor of French *Vogue* from February to September 1929. Following a disagreement over salary, he left the magazine to open his own house in the Avenue Georges V, a new address for the couture. A battle of wills with his successor at *Vogue*, Michel de Brunhoff, commenced. Mainbocher claimed that Schiaparelli's designs dominated the fashion pages, so he decided to set his own terms for editorial coverage of his collections, as Patou had tried to do in the twenties. Initially, he insisted that his clothes always appear on a full page and never opposite those of another house. He then demanded that four consecutive pages be devoted to his clothes. De Brunhoff eventually capitulated. Mainbocher's good taste and unrestrained chic, along with pure egotism (which has always appealed to the fashion world), perfectly counterbalanced Schiaparelli's dramatics.

The increasing popularity of the cinema, particularly following the introduction of 'talkies' in 1929, contributed a new source of inspiration to the world of fashion. Hollywood films presented a type of beauty and a style of clothes that women everywhere emulated. Until recently, to greet an outfit with 'Whew! Pretty Hollywood,' had been an insult. Hollywood clothes were inevitably flamboyant compared with the couture, but they became more restrained as certain actresses refused to be dressed like 'Christmas trees' and prided themselves in setting fashion standards.

The sophisticated temptress became a feminine ideal and sex appeal was a woman's front-line weapon. The fashionable woman of the mid-thirties was slender, long-legged, small-breasted, narrow-hipped, heavily painted, and sexy. As artifice replaced nature, page after page of beauty tips adapted from film and stage make-up appeared in *Vogue*. A plague of beauty spots and tattoos, false eyelashes, plucked and pencilled eyebrows, and garish lipstick streaked across the Western world. *Punch* sneered, 'The newest shop girl has a mouth like a bad inflammation.'

Acknowledging the impact of films on fashion, Schiaparelli declared, 'What Hollywood designs today, you will be wearing tomorrow.' Styles could be directly attributed to specific films and film stars. Jean Harlow, dressed by Adrian, popularized the sheer white satin ball gown in *Dinner at Eight* in 1933. Low necklines followed the appearance of Mae West in *Belle of the Nineties* and Jeanette Macdonald in *The Merry Widow* in 1934. Masculine clothing designed by Travis Banton – broad-shouldered, outsized jackets, shirts, ties and tapered trousers – was worn by Marlene Dietrich with such penetrating femininity that it too was widely copied.

Although many Paris couturiers, including Paquin, Chanel, Worth, Patou, Rouff, Lanvin and Alix, designed wardrobes for the stars, they were not always successful, as film chic required exaggeration rather than refined understatement. Chanel believed that Hollywood overdressed its stars, but

The Indo-Chinese costumes at the 'Exposition Coloniale' in Paris in 1931 inspired Schiaparelli and Rochas to imitate the extended shoulders by introducing shoulder pads.

The Cinema *by William Roberts, 1920.*

Beware of becoming a Hollywood clone, warned Vogue; *several Garbos and Marlenes.*

her casual sports clothes for Gloria Swanson seemed flat and unmemorable alongside Hollywood wardrobes. *Vogue* warned its readers not to be overwhelmed by Hollywood's influence, to maintain an individual style rather than become an imitation Dietrich or Garbo.

In America, however, the copying of Hollywood fashions and Paris couture became a vast and powerful industry. American *Vogue* responded by creating a special label – a blue-and-white celluloid tab with a silver seal – for the ready-to-wear dresses that met *Vogue* standards. New York and California were the two American sources of ready-to-wear fashion. New York concentrated on cosmopolitan styles of urban dress, while Californian firms such as White Stag, Catalina and Jantzen specialized in sports and casual wear.

The British eventually adopted American methods such as standardized sizing. In the early thirties a number of British manufacturers invited a group of American specialists to apply a systematic and comprehensive sizing system to their projects. As demand for American ready-to-wear increased in Europe, some British stores bought complete American ranges and three Americans – Marjorie Castle, Peggy Morris and Rose Taylor – opened stores in London. By 1936 British ready-to-wear companies began to emerge, notably Dereta and Dorville, which both adapted French couture styles, and Windsmoor and Berkertex. This was the beginning of ready-to-wear's challenge to the couture, but it was not until the war, with the streamlining imposed by government requirements, that this sector of Britain's fashion industry would be fully developed.

For the British couture, which lacked the artistic and imaginative daring of its French rival and rarely attracted the custom of the well-dressed international woman, the thirties was a formative period. Norman Hartnell consolidated his position as court dressmaker to Queen Mary and the Duchess of Gloucester. In 1933 26-year-old Hardy Amies took over from Digby Morton as manager and head designer at Lachasse. Giuseppe Mattli, born in Switzerland and trained in Paris, opened his house in London in 1934. Victor Stiebel, who had opened his own house in 1932, joined the ready-to-wear company Jacqmar in 1939, as did Bianca Mosca, an Italian of considerable influence, who had trained at Schiaparelli.

The French couture continued to be dominated by successful and colourful women, particularly Chanel and Schiaparelli. Schiaparelli shocked and amused the public; to her, 'good taste' was subordinate to outrageousness and humour. She was infuriated by coy attitudes to dress, believing that '90

Copenhagen women selling fish. Their newspaper hats inspired Schiaparelli's fabrics.

Bonwit Teller created first surrealist windows, 1938: models' faces are sheet music.

per cent [of women] are afraid of being conspicuous and of what people will say, so they buy a grey suit. They should dare to be different.' No matter how plain or unattractive a woman might be, Schiaparelli insisted, with a fine figure and attention-seeking clothes, she became chic.

Having dared to be different herself, it came to be expected of her. Schiaparelli had been the first couturier to show brightly coloured zippers, featuring them on sportswear since 1930, and in 1935 she used them again on evening dresses. She collaborated closely with fabric houses to create novelty prints and materials. She made glass-like tunics in 'rhodophane', a cellophane material invented at the fabric house Colcombet. Her other famous fabrics included 'anthracite', a coal-like rayon; 'treebark', a matt crêpe crinkled in deep folds to resemble bark; and a fabric printed with newsprint. Schiaparelli also commissioned major contemporary artists, including Christian Bérard, Jean Cocteau and Salvador Dalí, and their association led to such memorable eccentricities as the lamb-cutlet hat, the brain hat, the shoe hat and the coat with pockets simulating a chest of drawers. She used crazy, outsized buttons in the shape of peanuts, bumble bees and rams' heads. Her idiosyncratic novelties prompted Cocteau, in awe of her work, to comment, 'She knows how to go too far.'

In 1934 Schiaparelli opened in Grosvenor Street, London, and the following year moved her Paris premises from the Rue de la Paix to Chéruit's old salon in the Place Vendôme. Her basic silhouette, like Chanel's, was simple, but she lavished it with witty trimmings on a number of themes, such as the military, the zodiac and the circus. Despite her outrageousness Schiaparelli did appeal to the more cautious woman of fashion with her severe suits and plain black dresses. 'Shocking Pink', a luminously bright pink, was launched in 1936 and became the hallmark of the house.

New houses were founded and established houses nurtured the development of a number of designers who were to become the leading lights of post-war fashion, one of whom was Madame Grès. Details about her past are unclear but she originally wanted to become a sculptor. Having trained at Premet and opened a shop under the name Alix Barton around 1930, she became joint owner of Maison Alix in 1934. She was internationally acclaimed as the master of the draped silk-jersey evening gown. Working alone and refusing to sketch, she created her designs in linen on the mannequin. By respecting the natural lines of the body and the intrinsic qualities of her chosen material, she never forced or contorted her models. Grès also respected

Chanel and Serge Lifar.

André Breton's surrealist chest standing on human-style legs, 1938.

Salvadore Dalí and his wife Gala in 1932.

The red-lipped mondaine for whom heavy lipstick was a fashion prerequisite.

Aage Thaarup's designer gas-mask case of 1939, holding a gas mask, poker dice and a flask of brandy. The case is pasted with clippings of his favourite poems, for extra cheer.

The arrow-straight stocking seam.

talent in others; it was she who encouraged Balenciaga to open his own house in 1937 rather than work for her.

Robert Piguet, who had trained at Poiret and Redfern, opened his own house in 1933. Like Lelong, he was a dressmaker who employed others to design for him. Piguet bought sketches from Balmain and gave jobs to Givenchy and Dior. Marc Bohan was given his start by Raymond Barbas, who employed him at Patou after the latter's death in 1936.

The collections during the mid-thirties were inspired by the national costumes of 'Mittel Europa', highlighting the charm of peasant dress and illustrating the attention that Germany was attracting through its propaganda campaign. Tailored Tyrolean styles – green loden suits, feathered trilbies, stout walking shoes and canes – were considered very chic. Rearmament moves and dictatorial machinations affected writers and designers, and even *Vogue*'s editorials were infused with military jargon: 'Paris demands that you march to the sound of drums ... Regiments of strict fitted suits file by ... The fiery Schiaparelli called out a batallion of martial ideas.' But while the totalitarian regimes had their impact on high fashion, they could not rule it. An article in the Italian newspaper *Popolo d'Italia* quoted Mussolini as advising the Nazi regime, which had banned lipstick and rouge: 'Any power whatsoever is destined to fail before fashion. If fashion says skirts are short, you will not succeed in lengthening them, even with the guillotine.' 'This statement, by one dictator to another, acknowledging a power before which both are helpless, is of peculiar interest,' commented *Vogue*.

The Soviet authorities also had to bow before the force of fashion. Despite the government's intentions to crush Western-inspired 'bourgeois' styles and beauty aids, Russian women still demanded them. In response, the regime initially issued cargoes of bright orange lipstick to women on collective farms and industrial compounds, followed by pretty blouses and silk underwear. The revered Order of Lenin was awarded to the head of the State Cosmetics Trust and a Soviet fashion magazine was launched in 1935.

As the reality of war approached, the military styles retreated. Fashion cast aside the strict little suits and sheltered women behind layers of lace, corsets, full crinoline skirts, picture frocks and mock Edwardiana. Clothes took on the appearance of pure fancy dress, with horsehair underskirts and frou-frou accessories, which virtually parodied femininity. Women adopted a supportive role, instead of challenging 'the supremacy of man'.

When war came, Paris designers exported the full skirted ballgowns to the United States and South America, and created shorter, more practical restaurant/dinner dresses for the home market. Schiaparelli devised a clever compromise, a long skirt that could be hitched up so that a woman could walk comfortably when no taxis were available. She also designed a 'cash and carry' collection: each garment had huge pockets to free women from carrying bags.

Despite the war the spring 1940 collections in Paris were attended by some Americans, who placed a staggering number of orders. After the fall of France, however, Paris couture was no longer available to the Free World. Although many couture houses remained open, they designed for internal consumption only, which included the wives and associates of the German occupying forces. The great exception was Mme Grès, who refused to dress the Germans. She was accused of designing patriotic blue, red and white collections, and was constantly threatened with closure. When Goebbels arrived with stormtroopers and demanded access to order clothes, her *vendeuse* sent them away, claiming that Mme Grès was preparing her next collection. In fact she was sitting on the floor of her room with yards of silk from Lyons, sewing a huge tricolour. Defiantly, she hoisted the flag out of the window. Her house was closed.

In Britain paper was one of the first commodities to be rationed during the war. Publications were not closed down, but the government allocated them paper based on the amount that they had used in 1938. British *Vogue* dedicated its pages to supporting the important fashion and textile industries, to encouraging normal activities whenever possible, and to pursuing a useful and intelligent attitude to everyday affairs, with advice on how to cope with rationing, hardship and the care of oneself and one's family. It offered tips on beauty treatments, since many beauty parlours had closed. A large overcoat and a gas mask bag became essential parts of every woman's wardrobe, and *Vogue* suggested ways of coping with the exigencies of war, such as keeping trousers, jumper, tweed jacket, wool socks, gloves, torch, keys, money and gas mask by the bedside at night in case of an air raid.

'*She works in all weathers, reclaiming downland*' for the war effort.

Some designers seemed to take the war in their stride, even creating custom-made gas mask cases. The milliner Aage Thaarup combined a gas mask, poker dice set and a brandy flask in a case covered with clippings of his favourite poems, Elizabeth Arden offered a waterproof white velvet gas mask-cum-vanity case to be carried with evening clothes and Schiaparelli delighted in creating clothing and accessories for the woman at work.

Britain began to suffer fabric shortages early in the war. Curtains and upholstery materials were turned into clothing and by 1940 shoddy (coarse, reprocessed woollen cloth) was in use. The government issued pleas for the public to 'Make do and mend' so that the soldiers could be adequately clothed and shod. It introduced clothes rationing in May 1941, not because clothes were scarce but in order to release factory space for the manufacture of military equipment and munitions. An exhibition of 'The Use of the Clothing Coupon' included a poster explaining that 'If everybody took a pair of scissors and cut out and gave to salvage one coupon, it would release 8,000 workers, 5,000 tons of raw material, which could be used to make 2,000,000 battle dresses or clothe 500,000 soldiers from head to foot, including underwear, boots and greatcoat!'

Women employed in factories; '*It must go on,*' urged Vogue.

The government tried to ban cosmetics at the outbreak of war, but fortunately withdrew this ruling, for lipstick and rouge were to become the last unrationed, if scarce, indulgences of feminine expression during austerity, and were vital for morale. By 1941 silk stockings were banned, as all available silk was needed to make parachutes. *Vogue* reassured women that there was no need to panic. Manufacturers had anticipated this problem, producing a collection of rayon, cotton and woollen alternatives. However, the following year hosiery shortages became so acute that women were reduced to wearing socks with dresses and suits.

The Utility mark introduced on British clothing in 1941.

With restrictions imposed on both the manufacture and purchase of clothing in Britain, the fashion industry required organization and leadership. Margaret Havinden, a director of Crawford's advertising agency, encouraged co-operation between the leading couturiers and was instrumental in bringing them together. In 1941 a group was formed to co-ordinate an export drive and in 1942 this became the Incorporated Society of London Fashion Designers (I S L F D). Led by Edward Molyneux, its members were Hardy Amies, Champcommunal at Worth, Norman Hartnell, Digby Morton,

American Vogue *cover admonishing women to 'Take a Job! Release a Man to Fight!'*

Working on the farm.

American Vogue Victory *cover.*

Peter Russell, Bianca Mosca and Victor Stiebel. After the war it came to include John Cavanagh, Charles Creed, Angèle Delange, Lachasse, Mattli, Michael, Ronald Paterson and Michael Sherard.

The I S L F D created austerity couture, a series of designs for the nation that were functional and warm but saved as much fabric and labour as possible, in accordance with the Utility Clothing Scheme introduced by Hugh Dalton, President of the Board of Trade, in February 1942.

Cloth manufacturers were required to allocate 85 per cent of their output to Utility clothing, which was sold at a fixed price and not subject to purchase tax. The remaining 15 per cent could be made into 'general' garments, which were sold on the free market and subject to tax. From 1 June 1941 each person was issued with sixty-six clothing coupons a year, which were gradually reduced to forty-one by 1945. Additional coupons were available on the flourishing black market. To buy clothes one had to use both money and coupons. The initial reaction was a rush to the shops in anticipation of falling coupon values. Men and women in the armed forces and others who were issued with uniforms because of their occupation had to surrender some of their coupons to their employers; for example, a nurse had to give up ten coupons and a policewoman, six.

Vogue explained to its readers what coupons could buy: a London designer suit from Lachasse, for example, was approximately 18 coupons, a blouse 4, a waistcoat or jumper 5, stockings 8, shoes 10 and sandals 5. Since trousers were only seven coupons and were worn without stockings, they became a very popular wartime fashion. As clothes rationing became more stringent, the magazine observed that 'only brides and babies start the winter with a new wardrobe', and offered ingenious tips on how to use the few fabrics and accessories available. Separates, for versatility, and the tailored suit were recommended, in jersey and serge for winter and cotton and synthetic mixes for summer. However, *Vogue* warned its readers not to fall for the hard-wearing tweed suit just because it would last longer, for it could not be worn at dinner or on formal occasions.

Many London houses closed as designers joined the war effort. Hardy Amies served as an intelligence officer in Belgium, and Stiebel and Cavanagh joined the same regiment, naming tanks after memorably cantankerous or well-endowed customers.

America took advantage of Europe's isolation to promote its own designers. One of its greatest, Mainbocher, returned to New York from Paris. Two important talents emerged in 1941 – Norman Norell, the master tailor, and Claire McCardell, the innovative sports and casual wear designer. Released from the American indifference to its own fashion heritage, they sought inspiration in every corner of the continent. Together with Hattie Carnegie, who had trained both McCardell and Pauline Trigère, and Charles James, they confirmed America's standing as a serious and original fashion source.

America entered the war in December 1941. Fashion's role in the changed circumstances was widely discussed. Edna Woolman Chase, editor of American *Vogue*, was quoted throughout the American press under such headlines as 'Sensible Fashions Urged for War' and 'Industry Has Grave Responsibility in Bolstering Public Morale'. Until the middle of 1942 Americans were relatively free from the deprivations and clothing restrictions that their allies suffered. American *Vogue* reminded its readers how lucky they were to have plentiful soap supplies, and American women virtually lived in the 'tubbable' cotton frock. In Britain, by contrast, *Vogue* reported that 'the soap shortage has not yet brought squalor, but planned economies abound. The day of white gloves and the sheer white or pastel blouse is doomed.' American women were encouraged to buy both British fashion and the comparatively plentiful clothing designed and produced at home, in order to help the war effort. Self-denial was unproductive, explained *Vogue:* 'Arms and munitions, boats and planes are made by workers who are paid from the money that comes from Defense Bonds and taxes; a sizeable part of these taxes comes from the clothing industry ... But use discretion and buy clothes of suitability and taste.' Gradually the Americans began to suffer shortages and the L 85 rulings, introduced in the summer of 1942, were less stringent versions of the British Utility measures. People were advised to treasure woollen clothes and the industry endeavoured to create new fabric blends and synthetic fibres.

In France during the Occupation no French woman was allowed to wear a uniform or badge that showed that she was serving her country, so she flaunted the irresponsible, frivolous clothes of a fashionable coquette in front of the occupying forces. According to *Vogue*'s Lee Miller, the rebellious signs of fashion bravado were rampant by 1942. Colours were garish, jackets lengthened, skirts shortened, hair was worn longer and hats more and more absurdly decorative, sometimes standing 18 inches high. Saving and rationing only benefited Germans; the more material the French used, the less was left for the invader; the more workers French industry employed, the fewer would be conscripted into German industry; the more the Germans attempted to restrict them, the more defiant the couture houses became. This frivolity was seen as the French woman's way of saying to the invaders that although they had taken her country, her liberty and her peace, they could not break her spirit.

The Germans appointed Maggy Rouff's husband, Besançon de Wagner, fashion dictator, with Lelong as his deputy, dealing with artistic aspects of the industry. Lelong became chairman of the Chambre Syndicale de la Couture and is officially credited with dissuading Goebbels from closing the Paris couture and relocating it in Berlin. However, conversations with those involved at the time suggest that credit for this belongs not to Lelong but to the courageous Mme Grès and her friends.

It was ironic that despite hostilities the affluent French woman was still better dressed than her American counterpart. 'While we are wearing rayon,' grieved American *Vogue*, 'she is wearing yards of silk.' War-torn France never stopped being the centre of fashion, producing creations reminiscent of Degas, Renoir and Boldini. In stark contrast, American fashion was active and convenient.

With the liberation of Paris in 1944 the first glimpses of Paris couture for four years were revealed to the world. The end of the war also signalled the arrival of new fashion houses. In 1945 Hardy Amies opened in London and Balmain in Paris. The closing of Vionnet led to the establishment of three new houses: Marcelle Chaumont, a former *première* at Vionnet; Charles Montaigne, who had been a tailor; and Mad Carpentier. Despite the crippling austerity restrictions in Britain and the remaining fabric shortages affecting designs in Paris, fashion at the end of 1945, particularly in France and America, was softer, fuller and more feminine. Luxury began to return after a six-year exile.

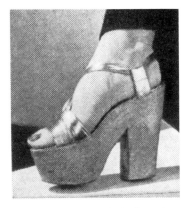

The cork and gold kid platform shoe, a wartime, leather-saving fashion introduced by Salvatore Ferragamo.

A set from Christian Bérard's Théâtre de la Mode; two white tulle dresses from Bruyère and Mad Carpentier, 1945.

1934

Movement – forwards, backwards and sideways – was the primary theme of the Paris spring collections. It was achieved by the use of oblique revers, cape details, basques and trailing panels. Most spring coats, notably those from Schiaparelli and Mainbocher, appeared blown forward with protruding revers. Patou created movement at the back with wings from the shoulders, volants from the hips and training along the floor.

For evening wear Worth and Rouff introduced long, sinuous trains and a suggestion of a bustle, while Lelong revived the oblique waistline, higher at the front than the back. Many skirts, for evening and day, were split up the front or side, and Lanvin inserted gold medallions in the splits of black crêpe dresses. Mainbocher flared evening skirts and used whalebone to support the bodice, the lack of shoulder straps emphasizing the bare shoulders. An extravagant décolleté was permitted for late evening attire, but the tailored suit imitating masculine evening wear – a long black skirt, a pussycat-bow blouse and a dinner jacket – was worn for dining.

Several leading houses showed spring suits in the *directoire* style, romantic yet practical: snug jackets with high collars, frilly jabots and stocks à la Danton. Vionnet's interpretations were sprightly suits with crisp bows under the chin, redingote coats and dashing tricornes. Schiaparelli showed both three-quarter-length and short tunic jackets.

1. (p. 131) Left: *Augustabernard's black chiffon dress, Paquin's fox cape and Agnès's lace hat.* Centre: *Vionnet's print dress, velvet cape and Suzy hat.* Right: *black crêpe Chanel ensemble, ermine cape and Suzy hat.* 2. *Molyneux.* Front: *black wool cape-dress and cartwheel hat.* Behind: *bamboo-coloured wool coat and coolie hat.* 3. Left: *Molyneux's black wool coat with Persian lamb revers.* Right: *Rochas's moujik-style dress in black silk with inch-long hair like a fur.* 4. *Schiaparelli's spring coats.* Left: *dark-blue tweed with ocelot collar.* Right: *bright, checked wool.* 5. *Vionnet's black wool greatcoat, lined with black seal. Amber-coloured wool dress with black satin bow and Maria Guy seal-skin hat.*

6. *Schiaparelli's violet-blue tweed suit trimmed with mink bands, the jacket skirt flaring over a narrow, straight skirt. Plumed Talbot hat.*
7. *Mainbocher's wool dress and three-quarter-length cape.*
8. *Augustabernard's tweed cape ensemble worn with Rose Descat's pink panama.*
9. *Schiaparelli's black taffeta jacket and Treebark crêpe directoire dress and cellophane scarf.*

10. *Victor Stiebel's deep-blue woollen skirt and plaid taffeta blouse worn outside the waistband of the skirt.* 11. *Mainbocher's caped-sleeve black wool dress, red-and-white polkadot silk scarf, matching gauntlet gloves and beret.* 12. *Saks Fifth Avenue's tailored taupe velveteen dress with loose sleeves and big, cone-like buttons, worn with Florence Reichman's light taupe hat.* 13. *Left: Yvonne Carette's black, white and yellow silk print dress has a cut-away peplum. Right: Mirande's black-and-white surah tunic jacket has a large bow and is worn over a black crêpe dress.*

Accessories assumed such importance that many outfits included gloves and scarves of the same material and print. Gingham was popular for blouses, scarves, jabots and gloves. Large buttons were fashionable too, echoed by large, distinctive hats.

Linens, crêpes and cottons in pastel shades abounded for summer. Cottons were particularly popular for garden dresses, playsuits and dinner suits, and American designers used gingham for dresses as well as accessories.

By the autumn, romanticism was high fashion. Many of the 3,000 garments from the Paris autumn collections were aglitter with gold, sequins and paillettes. Vionnet modelled her dance dresses on every historical era – Greek, Medici, Louis XV, French Directory and Second Empire – while London couturiers favoured the picture frock. Worth designed stiff black moiré gowns with cut-away backs, but in London and New York many evening dresses were still slinky.

Molyneux and Mainbocher played down costume themes to reflect the long, simple, elegant lines of the East. Their day and evening clothes were accompanied by Eastern-inspired accessories: swathed sashes, split skirts, Japanese winged draperies instead of sleeves, kimonos and dragon-embellished bamboo-coloured materials. Molyneux created the caped long-line tunic style for the tall, slender Princess Marina when she married the Duke of Kent in November, bringing his work to the forefront of fashion.

Once again a new material – rhodophane – inspired a new fashion. The great novelty of the season was a 'glass' dress from Schiaparelli. Although it was not accepted as a serious fashion contribution, the House of Alix, which opened this year, also showed full-skirted cellophane dresses. One journalist quipped '… people who live in glass dresses should not throw parties'.

A tunic over a narrow skirt was one of *the* winter daytime outfits, especially at Mainbocher and Lanvin. The alternative was the simple, straight, long woollen or crêpe dress, seen in bold, royal colours at Schiaparelli. Rochas and Molyneux showed simple woollen morning dresses, slightly shorter than their afternoon counterparts, worn with flat fur coats. Augustabernard designed silk crêpe dresses with bias-cut cowl collars, while

14. *Lanvin's black georgette crêpe dress slides completely off the shoulders, yet the arms are discreetly hidden under tight sleeves lined with stitched silver lamé.* 15. *Piquet's satin frock with shoulder wings caught in at the waist.* 16. *Mainbocher's blue Chinese-rose print, tunic and narrow skirt.* 17. *Lanvin's big, stitched, red velvet detachable bertha over a simple black crêpe dress with full sleeves and a train.* 18. *Bergdorf-Goodman's black-and-white printed satin evening dress with matching gloves and ostrich-feather cape.* 19. *Maggy Rouff's Russian-style evening ensemble – a huge black taffeta skirt attached to a black-and-white striped basque cape, faced and collared with white taffeta, and vast, tail-fringed ermine muff.*

Lelong and Goupy's crêpe dresses were tailored. Hartnell used black-and-silver striped lamé for a collection of formal afternoon dresses with decorative jabots.

Cossack hats and coats charged down the catwalks at Molyneux, Rochas, Schiaparelli and Andrébrun. Most Paris houses showed the three-quarter-length wool coat with backward movement inserted at the hem or cape back. Full capes were seen at Vionnet and Paquin, while Schiaparelli, Molyneux and Lanvin showed wrapped, slender versions. Narrow tunic-line coats were shown at Molyneux and Mainbocher. Fitted, slightly shorter redingote coats with no trimmings were favoured by Jaeger in London, but Saks in New York trimmed them with huge astrakhan collars and military turn-back cuffs.

Giuseppe Mattli, who had trained at Premet in Paris, opened in London.

1935

3

2

4

5

6

The French collections were witty and light-hearted this spring, clearly reflecting the improved economic climate. Schiaparelli, who opened her boutique in the Place Vendôme in Paris this year, burst forth with novelties, adding colour to simple black gowns with coloured plastic zippers, using tweed for evening clothes, padlocking suits and mocking the French devaluation by using gold sovereigns as buttons. Her memorable accessories included oversized silver-fox gauntlets and warrior-plumed helmets. Pre-empting the op art dresses of the mid-sixties, she designed clothes printed with hallucinatory dots rimmed with tones of the same colour.

There was an emphasis on splendid materials. Floral prints rambled across spring frocks, particularly at Mainbocher and Patou, while Chanel favoured butterflies, and Schiaparelli popularized the 'Garden of Eden' print. Despite the scepticism that had greeted the use of rhodophane last autumn, Schiaparelli persisted with a collection of cellophane dresses, evening jackets, belts, bags, hats and even shoes.

Most spring dresses had pleated skirts, which were shorter and wider than last year's. Necklines vacillated: some dropped right off the shoulders, some sported simple, child-like collars, and others clutched the upper neck. Sleeves were inflated. Rouff showed shirred, peasant and pleated sleeves; Patou's were huge and pailletted, and Alix's sculpted and draped.

Suits were the main focus of the spring collections. The check suit, nicknamed the 'Bookie' suit because it resembled those worn by racecourse bookmakers, was particularly popular in London. Strictly tailored suits with single-breasted bellhop jackets were shown at Lelong and Schiaparelli, while Mainbocher's short, fitted jackets had prominent peplums standing out over full, swirling, shin-length skirts. Lanvin concentrated on bell-shaped jackets and capes, and Geene Glenny's day clothes featured capes of all sizes and materials. Nina Ricci, who specialized in casual and sports clothes, designed a weekend wardrobe of two-piece dresses with a selection of accessories for a more formal effect.

Evening clothes glorified styles of other cultures. Vionnet's draped gowns were distinctly Nordic, Alix's Greek, and Mainbocher's Turkish, with skirts that

1. Schiaparelli's black wool suit, bulky, paw-like gauntlets and a stiffly quilled hat.   2. Stiebel's stiff black faille suit jacket, shirred at the waist and flaring at the hip, and straight skirt. 3. Chanel's irregularly ridged black satin dress, ruffed at the throat and cuffs. Rhinestone racquets clip sleeves, bodice and belt, and velvet beret plumed with ostrich feathers.   4. Paquin's dark-beige Leda velour coat trimmed with kolinsky and matching fur muff.   5. Piguet's bleached-linen suit trimmed with green leather elbow patches and collar, and Blanche and Simone panama hat.   6. Left: Knize's yellow flannel waistcoat jacket, brown whipcord skirt and brown-and-red print scarf, with Marthe Valmond yellow felt hat. Right: O'Rossen's black-and-white check suit, white silk blouse and Rose Valois's natural baku hat.

7. Left: *Nowitzky's zouave beachcomber outfit has a straw braid bolero over white crash trousers. Nowitzky's white linen sand boots have flat leather heels.* Right: *Lastex ink-blue satin fitted swimsuit from Marion Jacks.* 8. Left: *Nina Ricci's blouse and skirt in piqué with striped trimming.* Right: *blue-and-white wool suit trimmed with stripes of its own selvage.* 9. *Rouff's beige shantung dress with burst of sunray pleating across the bodice, sleeves and skirt, and Agnès's straw hat.* 10. *Paquin's white toile yachting costume and navy-blue wool cape.* 11. Left: *tweed plus-fours, woollen socks, cord shirt, man's tie and knitted half gloves.* Right: *jodhpurs, short boots from R. R. Bunting, sweater from Old England and gloves by Hermès, felt hat from Willoughby. The fashionable alternative to jodhpurs for sports was the jupe-culottes.*

were gently gathered at the hem. Schiaparelli and Alix delighted the spring couture audiences with their heavily draped, Indian-inspired ensembles: seductive saris, Ihram headscarves, gauzy draperies and nautch-girl sandals.

In London Victor Stiebel, the rising star of the British couture, showed Greek- and Edwardian-inspired gowns in pastel colours and matt materials, plain or strewn with enormous wild flowers. His day silhouette of a fitted bodice, slender, wide-belted waist and flaring basqued jacket was reminiscent of the pre-First World War style. Hartnell's evening wear was somewhat dated, as most of his dresses were still cut on the cross and clung to the figure. The vogue for dinner suits continued throughout the fashion capitals, now touched with feminine accessories.

12. *Alix's white rayon jersey Roman-style toga and matching cape, which leaves the shoulders bare.* 13. *Stiebel's frogged, fitted and flared black slipper-satin evening gown.* 14. Left: *Patou's mauve, violet, green and white blossomed print, styled into a slim dress elongated with a train.* Right: *Worth's giant burgundy and brown roses strewn across a yellow taffeta frock with skirt spreading like a peacock's tail.* 15. *Vittorio Crespi wears Schiaparelli's dress and three-quarter-length glass tunic.* 16. *Karinska's evening skirt with high, boned corsage, pleated silk shirt, toreador tie and yards of black leather galloon, in Spanish style.* 17. *Vionnet's magnificent black wool coat, trimmed at the revers with leopardskin to match the cuffs and scarf that falls to the hem.* 18. *Mainbocher's flowery black taffeta coat and dress.* 19. *Geene Glenny uses bands of silver-grey fox round the shoulders and cuffs of her heavy silk crêpe coat.*

Seaside pursuits and health had become very fashionable and the design of beach and swimwear was taken seriously. A slim body was a prerequisite for the two-piece bathing suit, first seen in *Vogue* this year. Lastex, a fabric woven with elastic, was widely used in this briefer swimwear to control the figure.

Europe bristled with war scares and in autumn the couture reflected the prevailing mood. Shirred breastplates put a brave front on evening dress, crowns and cocks were printed on blouses, epaulettes broadened shoulders, and braid or frogging adorned almost every chest. Even Vionnet, the queen of femininity, had sharpened her lines, widened her shoulders and brassed her buttons.

There was a mania for black, occasionally lightened by pink, particularly at Schiaparelli. Bags were big and pouchy, jewellery heavy and loud, and to enhance the femininity of masculine or military suits hats were trimmed with ridiculous appendages – canaries, kingfishers and overblown flowers.

Persian lamb, the pet of Paris, was flaunted on winter suits and coats, rendering the French ensemble more formal than its British or American counterpart. In New York suits had neat, slender, long skirts and short belted jackets; coat silhouettes were variously straight, cowled, flared, swaggered and semi-moulded, or tailored in black wool. Both the box coat and the three-quarter-length free-swinging coat were popular for morning wear.

1936

1. Charles James's evening capes and coats. Left to right: *white whipcord marshall cape; sculptured green billiard-table-felt coat; another in deep grosgrain; pale blue-grey grosgrain cape.* 2. Piguet's black-and-white jersey evening ensemble worn by *Madame Khairy Bey.* 3. Black tulle frock from Bergdorf Goodman. *The skirt foams in layers to the heels at the back and just to the knee at the front, where it reveals an ice-white sheath.* 4. Schiaparelli's black bengaline cocktail suit festooned *with gold and coloured paillettes, which arabesque down the front of its short, fitted jacket and black, glycerinized ostrich feathers on the Mongolian tribesman's hat.* 5. The fashionable basque is featured on Lelong's shaved lamb jacket worn with a *full black skirt. The rolled hairstyle, creating a sculpted headline, is now à la mode.*

Fashion continued to requisition masculine attire, as tailored suits worn with trilbies or homburgs and stout shoes appeared on most couture catwalks. In Paris Schiaparelli led the promotion of masculine chic – her padded shoulders were the widest, her military detailing the most eye-catching. Everywhere wide shoulders hovered over tiny waists, which were either fractionally lowered or raised up under the bust. Revers and peplums added width to an essentially straight silhouette and many designers, notably Alix and Rouff, used tunic tops to add fullness to the front. Mainbocher called attention to the sleeves, adorning them with a whole field of flowers, his 'poppy harvest'. The white piqué waistcoat, not widely seen since the First World War, reappeared to add another touch of masculine detail.

In London suits and coats remained casual and wearable, with masculine tailoring that admitted little of the fantasy found in their French counterparts. Charles Creed offered very masculine, tailored chalk-striped suits. Elsewhere the Tyrolean theme prevailed, and embroidered waistcoats in broadcloth, grey flannel and suede were worn under dark jackets with divided skirts and heavy ribbed stockings. Printed crêpes arrived in a new guise – slim dresses with straight skirts and inset front pleats.

Many American designers used dotted, striped, flowered or plain piqué with dark wool skirts or dresses. They showed a consistent talent for sports and fun clothes, the most popular of which were to be found at Altman's, Marshall Field, Abercrombie & Fitch, Peck & Peck, McCreery, Lord & Taylor, and Bloomingdales.

Schiaparelli's recent experiments with surrealist accessories, such as 'brain' hats and 'telephone' handbags, were now widely imitated, and ornate buttons looking like lobster claws and fox heads made their appearance.

Brightly coloured wools and felt were tailored into sharply cut dinner suits, jackets and capes for the evening. Schiaparelli launched her 'shocking pink', a luminously bright pink, which caused a sensation and became a hallmark of the house. For colder evenings knitted suits styled like smoking, riding and bolero jackets with wide revers were worn with large cummerbunds. Most fashionable women wore an evening

2

3

4

5

6. *Vionnet highlights the sleeves and shoulders of her white rayon piqué coat. The shoulders stand square and high, with folded fullness at the top of the sleeves.* 7. *Paquin's monkey-fur coat and soaring Agnès hat.* 8. *Hermès's deep, thick lambswool coat, white fleecy mittens, green leather belt, buttons and hood.* 9. *Jodelle's thick, white blistered piqué redingote with an inverted pleat in the back of the skirt and long puffed sleeves, and white straw hat from Louise Bourbon.* 10. *Rouff's black wool afternoon cape embroidered in gold, dress and Suzy checia (cylindrical scull-cap).*

headdress or hat; *Vogue* advised its readers to wear something dramatic – a cap, a hat, or a brooch in their hair.

In London evening gowns were swathed and draped, sometimes leaving a shoulder bare in the Greek style, then falling in soft pleats to the floor. In Paris the costumes of the play *Margot* popularized the wasp-waisted triangular silhouette, accentuated by deep V insets on the bodice. Sleeves were short and hemlines tended to be shorter at the front than the back. High shoulders were favoured by Vionnet and Rochas, and Piguet's were shaped like canoe paddles, rising nearly to the ears.

Practicality was the keynote for many American evening gowns, such as the prim red-and-white striped piqué shirtwaisters at Saks. At Carnegie one ingenious evening outfit featured a front-buttoned dress, tailored jacket and fox-edged cape to be worn at dinner, but for grand occasions the jacket was removed to reveal a diving décolleté. The Eastern influence also appeared in many collections, with mandarin coats and Chinese silk jackets proving popular.

The Lace Ball in New York in February created a demand for lace gowns, and romantic ball dresses with *mille feuilles* tulle skirts and fitted taffeta jackets were available at Bendel's and Carnegie.

Autumn dresses were plain and black, invariably mimicking a suit. At Vionnet the waistline was still high, accentuated by the skirt continuing above the belted waistline. Lelong preferred the princess line, while Schiaparelli promoted the Empire line with the use of bustline yokes. Fine pin pleats were a major dress feature at Molyneux, Mainbocher, Lelong and Lanvin.

By the end of the year hats were high, skirts were short and there was a 'lust for gold'. All the couture centres showed glitter, sequins, lamé and embroidery on gowns, and emblazoned plain day and evening suits and dresses with loud costume jewellery, from large semi-precious or junk jewel brooches to armfuls of thick gilt bracelets worn over gloves.

In Italy Zoe, Nicol and Giovanna Fontana took over their father's couture house and moved the business from Parma to Rome.

11. Left: *white linen tennis dress, green linen jacket.* Right: *blue-and-white cotton beach pyjamas and red linen coat. Bergdorf Goodman.* 12. *Alix's white and green stiff albebe beach suit, with Arab pantaloons.*

13. *Having watched parachutists in Russia, Schiaparelli designed a skirt opening like a parachute for her crêpe dress with an intricately seamed high waist.*

14. *Rochas's spring suit has stiff shoulders and sleeves on the short jacket, with inverted pleats at the back. It is edged with fluted piqué ribbon on the revers and pockets that match the waistcoat. The straight black skirt is pleated over the hips and hangs in a straight line to just below the knee. The hat is by Maria Guy.*
15. *Left: Alix's matte crêpe tunic jacket with a velvet front matching the underlying dress. Right: Rouff's tunic is longer at the front and edged with astrakhan along the zig-zag hem and collar. The pencil-slim skirt is slit at the side.*
16. *Piguet's black-and-white suit with built-up shoulders and Talbot's cavalry-plumed hat.* 17. *Creed's masculine chalk-striped and blue wool suit and short, cocoa-coloured wool coat and trilby.*

1937

Sex appeal, or its cartoon caricature, flourished at most houses, and *Vogue* advised its readers to wear 'anything that suggests allure' now that fashion's mood was moving away from feminine independence 'back to charm and seductiveness'.

Paris and London were aflutter with gauzes, muslins and organzas, shirred and draped to emphasize the body's natural lines, whether in a narrow sheath of folds reminiscent of an Egyptian mummy or the romantic bouffant style recalling the Empress Eugénie. Molyneux split skirts and plunged the décolleté to new depths, Schiaparelli built a brassière into the bodice of her dresses, and Lelong placed brassières on the *outside* of evening dresses, for decorative detail. Valentina showed classic waisted evening dresses with severe nun-like wimples, while Paquin and Mainbocher promoted the alluring 'come hither' veil. Charles James sewed $6\frac{1}{2}$ inch Colcombet ribbons in rainbow colours for the bodice of an evening gown and an entire cape, which caused a furore when worn to a Paris garden fête by Mme Arturo Lopez.

1. The Duchess of Windsor on her wedding day, in a white wool Mainbocher suit. 2. Heim's pastel-rose flannel suit. 3. Molyneux. Left: grey wool Polonaise dress and short jacket. Right: grey wool and nutria zipped-up tube jacket over a fitted dress. 4. Hattie Carnegie's brown wool suit trimmed with black lamb and braid. 5. Matita's suit with a small, bolero-like black wool jacket, blue gilet and black leather eyelet embroidery. 6. Marshall Field's black-and-white, chevron-striped piqué dress. 7. Alix's Persian-style purple crêpe dress wrapped at the waist with a fuchsia tie. 8. Bust emphasis. Left: Schiaparelli's black cloqué crêpe dress with high cowl neck jutting under the chin. Centre: triangles of shirring on the bodice give Schiaparelli's black matte dress a Junoesque line. Right: Rouff's cinnamon-coloured sheer matte crêpe blouse with a band shirred like a curtain across the bodice. 9. Creed's black woollen dress with red, white and blue piqué. The Rose Valois straw hat has a matching crown.

10

11

12

13

10. Chanel's pleated lamé bolero and skirt, and rose hat perched on the front of the head, aflutter with soft veiling.   11. The Mittel–Europa influence: his-and-her après-ski evening suits, grey-flannel jackets with green facings and green/grey striped trousers.   12. Piquet's rayon satin evening gown with a novel gathered corsage.   13. Cocteau, working with Schiaparelli, decorated the back of her royal-blue rayon spring coat with pink taffeta roses.   14. Lanvin's full-length shaved-beaver coat, sashed like a bathrobe in the front only, and matching beaver hat 15. Francevrament tailored wool paisley into a collarless coat flaring gradually to the hem. The taffeta toque is by Suzy.   16. Vionnet's half-and-half black wool coat is lined with white sheepskin and hangs straight from the shoulders.   17. Rochas's grey-and-blue plaid fine wool coat with a matching, slightly flared skirt.

Sequins, gold-thread embroidery, colour contrast bands and piping were prominent, and huge dress clips and bracelets were worn with the simplest dresses. Following Schiaparelli's lead in surrealist buttons, Mainbocher used metal clips, Patou flower pots, and Rochas open books.

Colour had returned to the couture palette. Now it was difficult to find a totally black outfit; yellow, tangerine, brown, mauve and purple dominated evening wear, and beige, mustard, tomato red, and plaid mixes were popular for day. There were fine wools and heavy silks from the East printed with bold paisley patterns. Chanel contributed a series of jersey and flannel suits without collars or revers, worn with bright plaid or striped blouses. Navy blue and black shirts sported bright piping and were worn with harlequin-print blouses. The coat-dress appeared, slim and usually single-breasted, and Breton hats, narrow pleated skirts, wasp waists and boxy reefer jackets were all fashionable.

In America the peasant influence was again seen in clothes from Carnegie and Amado. Cross-stitching, lapel embroidery, flower-printed dirndls and cotton headscarves for day and Tyrolean bibbed and aproned dresses for evening were available at Bonwit Teller, Marshall Field and Saks. Also at Bonwit were trailing chiffon evening dresses in flame, acid green and yellow, inspired by Bérard's designs for Massine's ballet *Symphonie Fantastique*. By day many American women chose to wear the simple shirt-waister with a pleated skirt, invariably in printed crêpe.

By the autumn waistlines were either high or low. The former were inspired by the Directoire Ball in Paris, and the latter brought to mind the styles of the 1920s. There was a marked emphasis on the draped *directoire* bosom and many hemlines swung up at the front. Individualism continued to be expressed through wild, violently coloured jewellery worn over long evening gloves.

The top-heavy look so fashionable last year was now reserved for suits and outerwear, and swirling arabesques of fur continued to emphasize line on both day and evening wear. Paquin loaded suit jackets with fur and used fur bands to break the smooth lines of materials. Half fur and half cloth outfits were

14

15

16

17

popular too. Schiaparelli and Heim cut coats with woollen fronts and fur backs, and Molyneux gave a woollen dress a fur bodice. The ever-innovative Schiaparelli trimmed fox furs with mermaids' and rams' heads, and introduced suits in daring pink and purple tweeds celebrating the Scottish moors.

British *Vogue* presented its first fashion feature for students, and included in its selection Lelong's inex-

pensive new fur: wild sheepskin dyed to look like nutria.

Military symbolism persisted alongside the dominant mood of romance and became more nationalistic. *Vogue* claimed 'We are now in the dark before the dawn of a great era of uniforms.'

This year three important couturiers opened in Paris: Jacques Fath, Cristobal Balenciaga, who had emigrated from civil-war-torn Spain, and Jean Dessès.

1938

Frank femininity was afoot this spring. Nothing jutted, flared or clung too obviously. In Paris day dresses were shirred or sheathed, skirts were slightly longer than last year, and jackets either followed an Edwardian line or were short and pinched at the waist. Chanel showed navy-and-beige suits with only very slightly shaped skirts and hip-length jackets. In contrast Schiaparelli's iron hand carved suits as straight as ramrods in black, navy blue and bright colours. Redingote coats with *directoire* detailing were cut away in front to reveal frothy blouses, rustling tussore and taffeta skirts and lace petticoats. Coats with full, relatively short skirts were cinched at the waist and brightened with bands and panels of a contrasting colour.

To emphasize the feminine image, Edwardian-style trimmings and accessories abounded: feathers and soutache, dainty Dorothy bags, modesty vests, Tango shoes and muffs. Hair was piled into high chignons bedecked with miniature fruit and flowers. Colour continued to be in high fashion. Creed brazenly combined mustard and amber, fuchsia and red, and Paquin presented a ripe raspberry red worn with deep fern green.

For evening the essence of femininity was satin corsetry worn *outside* a crinolined dress, first introduced by Lelong

1. Schiaparelli's circus theme. Bérard designed for her a merry-go-round of circus themes on textiles, which she cut into jackets, hats and blouses. Schiaparelli's evening jacket from the Circus collection is nipped in at the waist, from which flares an upstanding peplum; it is worn over a satin skirt. 2. Lanvin's white crêpe jacket embroidered with clusters of gold beads, worn over a black crêpe skirt. 3. Vionnet's silver slip is shadowed by a bouffant net skirt studded with rows of glittering black sequins. 4. Alix's soft, plaid wool evening dress with a Scottish sealskin bodice. 5. Giant poppies are printed over fifteen yards of Duchamp's silk dress by Patou. 6. Lelong's two evening models. Left: a brassière top placed on a black lace dress, and starched cotton skirt. Right: a strapless bodice of watered blue taffeta, which shines over a billowing black net skirt.

2

3

4

5

6

149

8

7

9

7. *Debenham and Freebody's navy-blue, black and pink check coat, cut on the cross, barely meeting at the front and flared at the back.*   8. Left: *Rouff's coat: a deep, wine-coloured body with purple raglan sleeves, green shoulders and a diamond brown inset at the neck. The off-centre beaver collar is detachable. Right: Alix's two-coloured collarless coat in navy blue with bands of rust.*   9. *Lelong's black coat panelled in electric-blue crêpe and decorated with frogging.*   10. *Tilly Losch has garlands of wild spring roses climbing the edges of her evening jacket from John-Frederics.*

in 1937. Fashion favoured either drapery from head to foot or the lowest possible décolleté and a bare back coyly veiled by a lace fichu. Designers took their inspiration from art and history: Molyneux, for so long associated with the understated rather than the picturesque, looked to Winterhalter and showed romantic 1890s-style dresses, while Lelong favoured Watteau; the House of Patou chose Madame Pompadour; Alix, Queen Victoria; and Lanvin, the Empress Eugénie. Alix and Chanel showed organdie gowns trimmed with yards of candy-coloured ribbons. Long evening coats were revived.

The London collections showed similar styles for the evening, but for day wear they maintained a sobriety that Paris had thrown to the wind. The tailored suit continued to be the mainstay of the classic English wardrobe. Spontaneity was encouraged by mixing and matching skirts, blouses and jackets. Skirts were generally shorter and swung free from stitched pleats, which were also featured on dresses, especially at Glenny, Strassner and Rahvis. Jackets remained short and trim and coats were either plaid and flared or plain and straight.

In America tweed suits were cut on very square lines across the shoulders and back, and the latest colour was a rusty red teamed with plum-coloured accessories. The shirtwaister dress was as popular and widely adopted as the Ford motor car – *Vogue* continued to refer to fashion 'Fords'. Claire McCardell pre-

sented her famous 'Monastic' dress: a dartless tent shape, which, when belted, acquired an easy, feminine line. For day wear the simple blouse-and-skirt ensemble sported a shirt-style bodice, while the evening version featured a ballooning

10

rumba-style blouse. American *Vogue* tried to persuade its readers to wear their hair in the European fashion, but this coiffure was mature-looking and American women were loath to adopt it: 'How we Americans rebel against looking our

age. The French will trade adolescence for sophistication any day.'

By the autumn fashion had become a confused mixture of period styles – Renaissance, French Revolution and Edwardian – and the fanfare greeting the visit of King George VI and Queen Elizabeth to Paris was reflected in the collections by tartans and Victorian trimmings. The Renaissance emphasis brought in a lower waistline – Alix and Molyneux showed evening dresses with long fitted torsos and full skirts flaring from the hips. Balenciaga chose a *Little Women* theme of long sleeves, buttoned bodices, high necklines and Victorian wraps and shawls. Schiaparelli's novelty for the season was her 'Circus' collection and a number of woollen capes with shoulders like an admiral's epaulettes, also seen in more modified versions at Alix and Molyneux. Paying tribute to Edwardiana, Paris dragged up all the come-hither details of the early twentieth century: jewelled side combs, leg o'mutton sleeves, tiny hats, veils, muffs, hoods and other 'heartbreaker' accessories. Woman was to be as mysterious, alluring, witty, veiled, gloved, corseted and even button-booted as any romantic, fairytale queen.

11. Front: Molyneux's brown-and-white printed crêpe jacket-dress. Behind: Molyneux's white-and-brown crêpe dress. 12. Agnès's black felt skull-cap decorated with a large ornamental gardenia, worn with Balenciaga's black marocain dress. 13. Left: Alix's sheer blue-and-green jersey dress and large side-tilting blue straw hat. Right: A dress with an intricately draped white jersey bodice and blue skirt.

11

12

13

14

14. Lelong's simple, wrapped and shirred marine-blue dress with gold collar and undecorated harlequin hat. 15. Rhavis's grey suiting outfit with a red over-check has a very close-fitting short jacket and a strict pleated skirt. 16. Balenciaga cut the neckline of his white tussore suit so that it could be either fastened up high or folded back and worn, as shown, with a silk scarf at the throat. Legroux's matte straw hat is decorated with ears of corn. 17. Vera Boreas's smoking suit in white albene with short sleeves and wide, sailor-style trousers. The organza blouse is printed with large flowers.

15

16

17

1939

The Paris spring collections were snowed under with paper-white lingerie touches on rather girlish dresses. When modified for the street this fashion was interpreted by many simply as a means of brightening up last year's dresses and suits. The printed frock also flourished in Paris this spring; cherubs were a favourite motif at Schiaparelli, ducks at Chanel and leaves at Lelong.

The London couture ignored the frou-frou of Paris and displayed 'a perfect sense of suitability, elegance and restraint', according to *Vogue*, in the simple, classical outfits, which were designed with particular, often conservative, clients in mind – sensible, tailored woollen and tweed suits for day wear, with softer versions for more formal occasions. The latest wools were in 'Kipling' colours: burnt grass, dark jungle green and bamboo yellow. Suits varied from the classic, straight-skirted silhouette to those with nipped-in waists and flared skirts. Jaeger showed a collection of plaid suits with wide belts, long jackets and pleated skirts. By night the young débutante was dressed in a tight-waisted, full-skirted ball gown in stiff white satin or organza with narrow

1. Darlings of Glasgow's short box jacket and straight skirt with a kick pleat in black, grey, maroon and tan checked tweed. 2. Three Jaeger outfits. 3. Chanel's black velvet, Watteau-style suit with long, waist-cinching jacket and flared short skirt.

shoulder straps; by contrast, the London siren wore a gold fishnet gown and snood.

Designers were highlighting the hips in Paris for the mid-season collections. Schiaparelli used wide tucks on day and evening dresses, while Alix padded the hipline with stiffly draped panniers. Bustles protruded and peplums were gathered at the front and back. V-necklines were considered the most flattering and echoed the nipped-in waist. Skirts swung short, often 15 inches from the ground, and were full, some requiring hoops to hold them out.

Americans relished the younger look from Paris, but found their own designers now offered them a wide choice of styles. For day they preferred the tailored redingote or a sporty three-quarter-length coat in a bright plaid over a hip-length jacket and knee-length skirt with box pleats. For the city the black jersey dress, draped and wrapped across the bodice with white piqué collar and cuffs, was also popular. For the evening the simple shirtwaister – straight, unadorned, practical and modern – continued to be popular. Alternatively,

4. Tamara Toumanova wears a striped zebra coat, which swings out from a small collar, a loosely swathed black turban and gold gypsy jewellery. 5. Lanz of Salzburg's baby-lamb hooded jacket. 6. Vionnet's velvet coat with a silk jersey stole matching the dress underneath. Talbot's wool-mesh turban is draped and helmeted like a Knight Templar's.

there was a full-skirted peasant dress in fifteen-colour rayon gingham by Carnegie, who also showed zouave-style pyjamas with gold-braided boleros. Nettie Rosenstein offered naive, orchid crêpe dresses with tucked bodices and simple scooped necklines filled with brightly coloured costume beads. Shades of white and cream were favoured by the Hollywood designer Irene, who combined white lace with blond tulle for full-skirted ball gowns with 'sweetheart' necklines. Bergdorf Goodman stocked cream fishnet dresses and slinky gowns of artificial silk and mock sharkskin, to be worn with brightly coloured silk turbans and vivid costume jewellery.

Despite the outbreak of war on 1 September, the Paris autumn collections were well-attended. There were a limited number of models and the catwalks looked like an old-fashioned variety show, sporting dresses with hooped and hobbled skirts and tight and shirred bodices featuring every form of trimming from tassels to admiral's braid. Soft, smooth woollens, spongy crêpes, lavish velvets and miles of jersey were combined with pelt upon pelt of fur.

In general, suits had thigh-length jackets and straight short skirts, but there were some variations. Piguet's skirts were narrow at the knee with softly draped hips, and Molyneux showed swinging short skirts with short boleros, which were practical and popular. In contrast, Schiaparelli dropped apron-fronted jackets almost to the knee and presented the 'cigarette' silhouette, a long, tubular jacket over a back-draped skirt. Rouff maintained an accentuated backwards flare on her jackets and used bustles to push out skirts.

Afternoon dresses and restaurant hats inundated Paris for the early evening and the tweed suit travelled right through the day to the cocktail hour, as blackouts restricted social activities to earlier hours. Formal evening dresses covered the throat and wrists, and bare shoulders were banished. Fabrics were still luxurious and emphasis was concentrated below the waistline. Molyneux designed such beautifully proportioned ankle-length evening dresses that he demolished the previous resistance to this slightly shorter style. Balenciaga oscillated between pannier skirts and 1880s bustles, and both he and Bruyère showed Second Empire styles. The most

7. *This year's college girl wears knee socks, gabardine jacket, short skirt, long sweater, in combinations of wool, plaid and flannel.* 8. *Détolle's laced evening corset with exaggeratedly cinched waist.* 9. *Balenciaga's black satin pumps perched on Japanese-inspired black wood pedestals.* 10. *Schiaparelli's blue wool 'alert' suit could be zipped up and is worn with damp-proof canvas boots.* 11. *Carnegie's Oriental-style drapery on a slim silhouette with full crêpe skirt that loops through the ankles, veiled turban and embroidered bolero.* 12. *Bruyère's silk faille dress, satin jacket and tiny felt hat.* 13. *Chanel's white piqué bolero dress with eyelet embroidery daisies.* 14. *Saks's evening shirtwaisters. Left: black-and-white striped jersey belted in red. Right: flower-printed foulard dress with ample sleeves and a tailored collar.*

fashionable accessories were muffs, fans, coloured gloves and amusing handbags, like Balenciaga's giant medallions and velvet sunflowers.

Grand ball dresses shown at the London collections were to be worn rarely because of the war, and British women began to adopt some Continental habits. 'It's taken a war to teach English women to wear restaurant clothes in a Continental manner,' commented *Vogue*. Black was the most popular colour, but there were foggy and sea-storm greys and threatening blues as well as strong clear greens, cherry reds and oranges.

Parisian women stopped wearing hats by day and hooded coats were seen everywhere. Loose, mandarin-collared coats in bold stripes or plaids were also popular, and large tweed overcoats with roomy pockets became a wartime must. The essential accessories for these hostile times were a large bag for carrying a gas mask and solid, low-heeled, square-toed shoes for striding with purpose.

Chanel closed at the end of the year and Mainbocher returned to New York.

15. *Molyneux's short-skirted jersey dress.* 16. *Mainbocher's tight-waisted polkadot surah dress with tiny bodice and gently rounded hips. The shoulders are slightly padded, and the skirt is tiered and pleated.* 17. *Piguet's green wool coat-dress, with a full skirt and piqué collar.*

1940

The Paris couture was the life-blood of French exports, so the government gave designers who had signed up two weeks' leave to create their collections before returning to the front. The spring collections were aimed at two distinct markets – women at war and women at peace. They were a triumph of suitability: colourful but not gaudy, rich but never ostentatious, gay yet far from frivolous. The outbreak of war put an end to the fashion for feminine frippery. To be chic was, more than ever, to be suitably dressed for the occasion; easy-fitting, light-coloured town suits replaced dark, wasp-waisted clothes, and British and French women strode out in clumsy-looking lace-up shoes and ample-hooded coats with large kangaroo pockets. Fashion was responding to the needs of the time, but alongside *Vogue*'s advice on practical styling came a plea to maintain femininity to please the soldier on leave.

Hips were the focal point of the spring collections, with swathed polonaise skirts, the fullness gently gathered and released at the back and the bodice extended into a point. Balenciaga and

1. Left: *Hattie Carnegie's blue and black coat braided along the skirt.* Right: *Saks's navy-blue wool crêpe coat with a whole yoke of black soutache and a navy-blue Breton.* 2. *Creed's square box jacket in beige-and-white checked herringbone tweed.* 3. Left: *Russek's black wool suit with leopardskin peplum and collar.* Right: *Pattullo's brown wool suit has large Persian lamb peplum pockets.* 4. *Matita's mahogany tweed top coat and boldly barred suit.* 5. *Schiaparelli's brown, beige and red plaid tweed jacket.* 6. *Digby Morton's beige tweed top coat lined with small brown-and-yellow checks.* 7. *Revillon's full, check tweed tent coat has padded shoulders.* 8. *Charles Montaigne's wool coat with bag-like pockets.*

Germaine Monteil revived the Renaissance protruding stomach (which Balenciaga considered beguilingly feminine) by rolling and draping fabric across the midriff.

Evening clothes designed in Paris and London for export, mainly to the United States and South America, were still flounced in lace and tulle in white and pastel shades, while those for the home market were simpler, more suited to a quiet dinner in a war-time capital. Last year's bouffant skirts were ousted in favour of a much slimmer silhouette, for fabric shortages were already taking their toll. Many houses offered practical day-into-evening clothes formalized by more luxurious materials; Hattie Carnegie in New York, for example, showed sweaters and pleated skirts, while Balenciaga and Schiaparelli presented jet-adorned separates such as evening cardigans. In London dinner dresses were generally black, hats were a must and small pouched bags like Victorian reticules were carried on the arm. In Paris, where there was a concerted move away from black, Lelong campaigned against too strict *tailleurs* and promoted light grey with softening details.

When the London couture began to suffer from the fabric shortage British *Vogue* reported that there were huge stocks of wool in the country: the government had bought the entire 1940 clip from Australia and New Zealand as well as a large proportion of South Africa's output. However, most of this was reserved for military use and the vital export trade. Nevertheless, British *Vogue* concluded, at this point the civilian would still be able to 'dress in the style to which she is accustomed'.

Following the occupation of Paris in June, the New York and London collections eclipsed those from the former fashion capital; though many Paris houses remained open, communications and trade became increasingly restricted. The Paris collections promoted a bloused look above a tiny waist and slim hips. Skirts were as narrow as pencils, especially at Schiaparelli (the house still operated though Schiaparelli was living in America), where a number of them were topped with bands of woven Lastex, eliminating the need for zips and openings. Pleats and slight fullness at the back of skirts hung from pointed or rounded hip yokes or were cowled across

the stomach. Jet collars and yokes were featured on dresses and suits, particularly at Balenciaga and Monteil, and the subdued shimmer of jet beads on evening wear compensated for the dowdiness of covered arms and shoulders.

Suits in Paris were cut on a curved, fitted line, while in London they were more severe, less fitted and longer, but both styles sported large pockets. Coats, too, boasted roomy pockets and were either tailored and fitted, a look particularly favoured by the Americans, or full and tent-like to suit European needs. London designers turned from sleek black fitted coats and furs to brave, bright colours and sensible tweed coats.

The American collections were far more extensive than their European counterparts and included ready-made as well as made-to-order clothes. The American silhouette for daytime was slim and sleek, broken only by the slight flare of a fur peplum on a jacket or the sudden flounce from a tubular bodice. Hair was worn framing the face or brushed off the temples with a fine, feathered hat perched on top.

The evening silhouette followed the same slim line. Dresses were long-sleeved and high-necked and the dolman sleeve was fashionable. Peplums were more pronounced, the long torso was exaggerated with clinging sheaths, and dresses with hip-tied effects were popular. Many designers showed Renaissance dresses with little page-boy hats and gave dinner attire lingerie touches with net and satin.

American designers dominated American *Vogue*. Norman Norell, who was to become the wartime king of American couture, launched his first collection to great acclaim. Claire McCardell, free from the influence of French chic, based her clothing on the life-style of active American women. Her casual, easy-fitting clothes, which could be worn all day long and for any occasion, were dubbed the 'American look'. She cut her sleeves in one with the bodice by extending the shoulder seam down the arm. When she insisted on removing shoulder pads, which had prevailed since the early thirties, so that the shoulders could drop naturally, her backers, the wholesalers Geiss and Klein, considered this uncommercial. McCardell arrived at a compromise; she tacked shoulder pads inside so that they could be easily discarded.

9

10

9. Molyneux's evening suit: above the narrow waist the jacket is bloused, effecting a slimming line to the hips clad in an arrow-narrow skirt.
10. Best's 23-carat gold kid trench coat with buttons down the front and a casual tie belt.

Britain continued to produce and export fashionable clothes despite the Blitz and American *Vogue* was eager to encourage its readers to make their own special contribution to the war effort: 'Here is one way that a woman can help support democracy's fight. Buying a British suit is as much a contribution to British defence as a sum of money. A new sweater puts another nail in a plane for Britain.' After the fall of France Charles Creed returned to England and began designing for Fortnum & Mason, where he popularized the finger-tip length jacket. In Italy Schuberth couture opened in Rome.

11. *Charles James's broad Colcumbet ribbon cape slit at the side to make wing-like sleeves.*   12. *Balenciaga attached black paillette bands to this black chiffon dress.*   13. *Valentina models her own black dinner dress with a Crusader-style dinner hat.*   14. *Charles James's black Celanese rayon crêpe dress with wide collar, which turns imperceptibly into a panel. The gilt-threaded wool-jersey turban looks like a tasselled cushion.*
15. *Left: Dickens and Jones's striped corded silk jacket with a wool skirt. Right: Dunkerley's spotted red-and-white crêpe-de-Chine dress with bloused bodice, bow neck and pleated apron skirt.*   16. *Balenciaga's folded peplum dress in red-brown and beige silk crêpe of geometric design.*

1941

2

1. *McCardell's black sweater, hood, magenta felt knee skirt and black lisle stockings.*
2. *Boiler suit streamlined from the neckband to the ankle cuffs, buttoned down the back, with patch pockets.*

Isolation from the influence of French styling provided American fashion with an artistic and economic boost. Designers found inspiration in their own culture and, no longer relying so heavily on European textiles, were the first to use synthetic fibres on a large scale commercially. The expansion of ready-to-wear fashion within their massive home market turned fashion into big business and accelerated the rise to stardom of a large number of designers. Ben Zukerman was the master of good tailoring, the Hollywood designers Adrian and Omar Kiam provided glamour, and there was an abundance of casual sportswear from Pauline Trigère, Claire McCardell, Nettie Rosenstein, Bonnie Cashin and Claire Potter. Norman Norell began his collaboration with the manufacturer Traina, bringing the principles of couture into the commercial showrooms of New York's Seventh Avenue.

For spring the Americans favoured the 'tailorknit', a tailored, 'citified' knitted jacket worn with a fabric skirt or dress. Suits tended to have deeper armholes, longer jackets and a less fitted silhouette than last year. Deep armholes were also evident on summer dresses, which were distinguished by Regency jabots, boleros, peplums and harem drapery.

Sweater dressing was part of the new all-American cult, especially for the young. Lightened by accessories, it could expand one's wardrobe for day and night. These evolving American traditions were soon communicated across the Atlantic.

A number of Paris-based designers, including Creed, Molyneux, Paquin and Worth, had moved to London, which struggled on as the most prolific source of European fashion despite fabric shortages (rationing was introduced in June). Most designers chose to accentuate the waist and allow sleeves plenty of movement, and the dolman style dominated. Spring dresses tried to be gay, with skirts gathered on front yokes and flared discreetly, while maintaining a simplicity of cut.

Grey was the staple wartime colour, and designers made contrasting colour a prominent theme to fight the drabness. Dashing jackets in gay checks and plaids brightened skirts, and coats in pillar box red, buttercup yellow, and bright green were worn over plain and print dresses. Strassner used contrasting colours for the back and front of ensembles, and Rahvis experimented with sleeves that contrasted with the bodice. Coloured stockings were another popular way of cheering up wartime clothing.

Molyneux, like McCardell in America, removed shoulder padding and let sleeves follow the gentle slope of the body. He softened the lines of his coats, suits and dresses, and the silhouette he presented was approximately the same width at the shoulders, hips and hem,

3. Hard-wearing double-breasted Scotch tweed Utility coat with broad, shoulder-high revers and wooden buttons. 4. Spectator Sports' red coat with bat-wing sleeves, a tie-waist and full skirt. 5. Molyneux's huge yellow coat with raglan sleeves over a black-and-white print dress. 6. Madame Valentina models her black wool coat with a trio of capelets. Felt and jersey hat.

3   4   5   6

7

8

9

Brown with Black 10

11

7. John-Frederick's blue-and-black hand-knitted jackets and halo hat and turban.
8. American putty-coloured corduroy suit with dolman sleeves, a snug waist and velvet beret. 9. Rhavis's black velvet suit and Argyll socks. 10. Harrods' beech-brown tweed suit lifted with braid scroll work and heavily embroidered motifs. 11. A war bride in Bradley's pale-oatmeal wool jacket-dress, buttoned up to a Peter Pan collar. The shoulders are slightly padded, and the line is slim and narrow. 12. Bonwit Teller's navy-and-white Enka rayon dress in a ribbon-knot print with dolman sleeve and gently padded shoulders. 13. Brigance white rayon mesh and Truhu (washable) silk-and-rayon faille burnoose-top dress with sloped shoulders, wide, short sleeves and wide, bright belt.

12

13

with a natural waistline. Lachasse followed the softly tailored trend by cutting deep subtle revers and soft collars on coats, and by offering simple cardigan jackets.

The elaborate short dress was worn on most formal occasions. Embroidery was unrationed and often used to enliven dinner dresses. Black gloves were considered an essential formal accessory, and shoulder-length styles were introduced in an attempt to re-establish coquetry in dress.

By the autumn the fabric shortage forced the introduction of the 'skimp' silhouette – tight and short. British *Vogue* tried to persuade its readers that the new line was not reminiscent of the 'grotesque' skimpiness of the mid-twenties, and reported that 'Most of the London designers agreed that skirts should not go more than 18 inches from the ground, for the kneecaps seldom please.' The magazine also advised women to put away their finery and stop behaving like ostriches – timely words, as silk stockings disappeared and rayon substitutes were hard to get by the end of the year. As necessity became fashion's touchstone, woollen stockings were worn in town with smart suits and dresses as well as in the country with much less formal attire.

14. Germain Monteil's ballet dress, a new length for semi-formal occasions, in pink organdie bordered with black velvet, worn with pink stockings and black slips. 15. Winston Churchill's daughter, Sarah, models Strassner's black crêpe dinner dress with a 'sweetheart' neckline embroidered with gold. 16. Molyneux's filmy, sequin-dotted tulle dress for South America with a snowdrop bouquet on the bodice. 17. Hattie Carnegie's formal black-and-white evening gown with silk satin skirt and embroidered silk crêpe bodice.

14

15

16

17

1942

In Britain neat, simple grooming was the current fashion, for few new clothes were available. Dressiness was démodé and ostentation was considered unpatriotic and selfish. The collections were extremely coupon-conscious as the designers in the ISLFD pooled their experience to create durable, fabric-saving, inexpensive Utility clothing. Each designer was required to produce his or her interpretation of four basic items: a top coat, a suit, an afternoon dress and a cotton overall dress. The Board of Trade and the clothing industry then chose thirty-two most suitable designs, which were produced in 1943. There was a great reliance on multiple-purpose clothing, with dresses cut to look like jacket or bolero suits, and late afternoon dresses that doubled as evening gowns.

Strict tailoring was reserved for the battlefield, and the civilian line became easy and bloused despite the fabric restrictions. Sleeves were treated economically, tending to end just at the wrist. Any skirt fullness was gathered into a lowered waistline at the front and seaming carried the eye down to the hem,

1. Two autumn Utility dresses. Left: red crêpe cut on classic shirt lines, softened with a tucked skirt and flap pockets. Right: blue dress with a small collar and revers.   2. Bergdorf Goodman's washable white cotton piqué suit-dress.   3. Non-rationed sequins decorate Traina-Norell's black Rodier wool jersey. The black wool coat is lined with unrationed rabbit fur.   4. Magnin's black Enka rayon dress with a prominent bustle. 5. Molyneux's 'Tulip' line. Black-and-white checked dress of British wool, worn with a pert sailor hat.   6. Bergdorf Goodman's double-breasted, nylon fleece, back-belted coat.   7. Right: military-style white wool dope-skin trench coat. Left: trench coat in green tweed with a cut-in belt and push-up sleeves. Both were from Lord and Taylor.   8. Utility coats. Left: navy-blue wool overcoat shaped at the waist with 'V' inset panel. Right: dark-brown topcoat with deep, shawl-like revers.   9. American boldly checked wool box-coat lined with black sealine (dyed lapin).

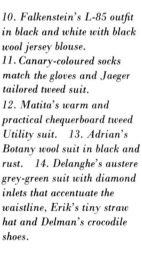

creating an illusion of length. Hip seams and large, low hip pockets with belts slotted through them were used to break the austere line of coats. Big sturdy coats were either back-belted and double-breasted or swung wide, like tents, from padded shoulders.

Ingenuity turned necessity into creative opportunities. Cords and strings of beads, for example, were used instead of elastic to hold hats in place, and tea was used instead of dye to colour shirts. The Board of Trade's admonition that if women continued to wear stockings in the summer, there would be none available by the winter led to what British *Vogue* called the 'Sock Shock'. The magazine tried to show models wearing a tailored formal suit with socks as charmingly as possible. It advised that in town socks should be pulled up the leg, so as to appear unsportslike, while for the country socks could be worn folded over.

While Britain was preoccupied with 'Make do and mend', American *Vogue* continued to exhort its readers to buy clothes to help the war effort. The L 85 restrictions, introduced by the American

government this year, banned wool linings and decorative flaps and pockets, but fur linings were permitted and unrationed sequins and braid adorned suits. Colour was another means of brightening up outfits; mix and match themes teamed different brilliantly coloured jackets and skirts. Black and white were also popular because of their versatility.

Restrictions on fabric resulted in generally narrow and short-skirted silhouettes for day and evening, but a number of designers managed to promote slightly wider widths and longer lengths for afternoon dresses while complying with the L 85 rulings. Falkenstein showed uneven hemlines, Magnin offered draped and dipping skirts and Herbert Greer's striking 'long-short' dresses measured 18 inches from the ground at the front and 9 inches at the back.

Cotton was America's most plentiful fabric and washable white dresses were much sought after. The alternative, linen, was still available from neutral Ireland but the general fabric shortage

10. Falkenstein's L-85 outfit in black and white with black wool jersey blouse.
11. Canary-coloured socks match the gloves and Jaeger tailored tweed suit.
12. Matita's warm and practical chequerboard tweed Utility suit. 13. Adrian's Botany wool suit in black and rust. 14. Delanghe's austere grey-green suit with diamond inlets that accentuate the waistline, Erik's tiny straw hat and Delman's crocodile shoes.

10

11   *12*   *13*   *14*

encouraged the development of more synthetic fibres. Even milk, unrationed in the United States, was processed to make a new material called 'Aralac'; it was used for coats.

In order to conserve materials, the length of the evening dress, especially in Europe, was raised to mid-calf no matter how formal the occasion. Mixing and matching evening skirts and beaded jumpers was a way of extending an evening wardrobe, while the jumpers also provided some protection against bitter cold in restaurants and dining rooms affected by the fuel shortage. The prominence of black, that most versatile colour, was also a symptom of the need to mix and match.

Fabric houses in Britain and America offered prints with patriotic slogans, symbols and colours, for clothing was deemed a worthy weapon of politics. News of Paris fashions was intermittent, but the couture continued to resist the pressure from the Germans to move to Berlin. Pauline Trigère opened in New York.

15. Traina-Norell's warm, grey kidskin pants, hand-knitted sweater and black accessories. 16. Left: Marshall and Snelgrove's black rayon moiré jacket tied over a black crêpe dress, the bow fastening to the front of the skirt. Right: late afternoon/early evening ensemble. A bouffant ballet-style rayon moiré skirt with a softly draped bodice of black jersey – an American design. 17. Jay Thorpe's black silk crêpe dinner dress with extremely slim skirt decorated with sequined flowers, long, black gloves and large jewels. 18. Vivien Leigh models a 'Coupon 66' dress printed with rare and rationed items. 19. Lord and Taylor's Mexican-style white blouse and red-and-white striped skirt in Mallinson's Miami cloth.

15   *17*   *18*

16   *19*

1943

'Fewer, simpler, better' was the rallying cry as the war dragged on. British *Vogue* advised its readers to make the most of their coupons by choosing a blouse and a skirt rather than a dress. American *Vogue* estimated that between 12 and 15 million metres of material had been saved as a result of the L 85 restrictions. The economic designs that were responsible for this saving included the short, sleeveless dinner dress, a revival from the First World War, and very straight, Chinese-inspired outfits, such as the cheongsam and narrow trousers.

With practicality a high priority, fashion favoured 'Luxable' cotton and rayon clothes that could be washed without shrinking; vivid prints, bright Tattersall plaids and checks that disguised wear and tear; hats that could be wiped clean with a sponge; and 'portable heaters' – quilted or flannel-lined cotton skirts, worsted jackets and jersey tops – for the evening. Lace was used to trim a variety of American suits and dresses, and coloured stockings were worn to brighten formal, especially black, outfits.

Utility and L 85 regulations affected shoes too. Heels were a maximum of 2 inches high in Britain and 1½ inches in America. Open toes were banned because they were unsafe and impractical. The dire shortage of leather, particularly in Britain, resulted in wooden-soled clogs being worn everywhere, even by the most fashionable women.

American *Vogue* warned its readers against the American 'newness neurosis': 'We moved to new flats every year,

1. Peck and Peck's balloon grey officer's coat in merrimack (hollow-cut velveteen). 2. Jay Thorpe's short, sulphur wool coat over a two-piece green-and-wine coloured wool ensemble. 3. Molyneux's narrow black wool city coat with a back yoke that forms a cape, falling into bell sleeves. 4. Wetherall. Left: rubber-backed, lined cotton raincoat. Right: black rubber-backed hessian raincoat. The hood was fast replacing the hat for protection. 5. Tatiana de Plessix's Persian lamb Breton hat and matching laced-up spats. 6. Utility dressing: grey bouclé wool cardigan suit by Spectator Sports. 7. Traina-Norell's Tattersall-check waistcoat jacket with black sleeves, men's-wear wool skirt and blouse banded in red. 8. Traina-Norell's beige-and-black checked blouse attached to a black crêpe skirt.

acquired new cars and new husbands
every other ... we bought new hats every
week or so and several new dresses each
season.' Because of the prevailing shortages readers were encouraged to value
the not-so-new, such as the dearly loved
and serviceable jacket, classic jumper or
headscarf.

The four styles of suit this year – the
waistcoat, the bolero, the box jacket and
the hacking jacket – were teamed with
Utility or L 85 blouses. The most successful blouse designs were bowed at the
neck, styled like a jumper, or low-necked
for formal occasions. The bare-backed
blouse was demure by day, covered by a
suit jacket, and seductive by night.

In London most suits were double-
breasted with door-crack narrow skirts,
and shawls were often substituted for
jackets to save material. A new design
alliance emerged as strong, hard-wearing
tweed was softened at the collar and cuffs
with velvet, often in pastel shades.

Warmth and practicality were the
primary considerations of most European designers in their winter collections.
The coat was either buttoned to the chin,
as were many jackets, or closed with a
single button at the throat and wrapped
round the body. In America double
collars were banned, no coat collar was
to be more than five inches wide, and
many coats were collarless. Yellow, grey,
brown and plum were popular colours
for coats, while black, grey-green and
brown predominated for suits. The

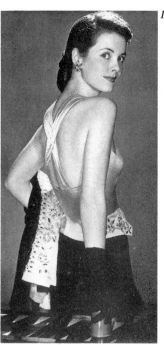

double-breasted coat was allowed in Britain, but some designers compensated for the material it used by offering a short sports coat. American *Vogue* hailed this variation, to be worn with stem-slim skirts and dresses.

The low neckline was prominent on simple, invariably black, evening dresses, worn with plenty of costume jewellery and a hat. In America, despite the restrictions, the covered-up look, from top to toe, was the alternative to the low décolleté, and fuchsia pink provided a welcome lift to ubiquitous black.

9. Left: *Siegal's nautical navy-blue reefer.* Right: *Travella's brown, blue and clay-coloured double-breasted reefer.* 10. *Blue-denim overalls and canvas shoes for the Land Girls.* 11. *Joseph Halpert's Rodier block-print rayon crêpe dress.* 12. *Traina-Norell's off-the-shoulder black silk shantung dress.* 13. *Bright-pink satin evening blouse, fitted over the shoulders and reaching to a neat waist, long satin gloves and jewels.* 14. Left: *Henri Bendel's black rayon crêpe evening dress flaring out with a double puffed peplum of bright-pink silk satin.* Right: *Carnegie's black silk crêpe dress with a giant-sized pink slipper-satin bow perched at the centre back and worn with long, cover-up gloves.* 15. *Carnegie's short skirt, black jacket encrusted with gold revers edged with Persian lamb and warm-pink satin blouse.* 16. *Carlwynn's blue-and-white striped cotton dress.* 17. *The Vogue artist designed a print, as though made from scarves, for a simple dress. As another solution to the fabric shortage Vogue asked, 'Why shouldn't we get a similar effect by seaming scarves together?'* 18. *Susan Small.* Left: *vivid-blue crêpe dress fastened with silvery medallion buttons.* Right: *skirt flares into fashionable front-centre fullness in black wool.* 19. *Délanghe cleverly arranged spots into solid lines across the yoke and sleeves of her brown-and-white smocked crêpe dress to give a rich, honeycomb effect.*

1944

After the liberation of France in August Paris rejected the extreme and frivolous fashions it had produced during the Occupation and stepped into line with the British and American restrictions. The silhouette narrowed as the Paris couturiers now designed to save their own cloth rather than waste the Germans'. The Chambre Syndicale de la Couture ruled that a collection be limited to forty models – as opposed to the usual 150 – only half of which could be in fabric containing 30 per cent wool. Dresses were restricted to $3\frac{1}{4}$ metres of fabric, suits to $3\frac{3}{4}$ and coats to $4\frac{1}{4}$. Since wool was scarce, it was often mixed with rabbit's hair or rayon. In Lyons the fabric makers even wove fantastic cloth from wood pulp.

Among the French houses still operating were Paquin, Piguet, Lanvin, Alix/Grès, Heim, Lelong and Jacques Fath, who was the rising star. Schiaparelli had left for America in 1940 but her house did not close. The couturiers' talent for working within the restrictions showed in their judicious use of bias and straight cut, stitched skirts to imitate pleats, and the artful combination of narrow skirts and full bodices, or full skirts and tight bodices, to make three metres of material appear six. Although

1. *Traina-Norell's short-sleeved, collarless Rodier black jersey tube.* 2. Left: *Peck and Peck's slim pink-and-blue striped cotton dress with a deep, square neckline back and front, gathered into cap sleeves.* Right: *Stern's denim pinafore, braided on the pockets.* 3. *Molyneux's two-duty dress, which could have a short skirt by buttoning the hem under in a zouave manner.*

sleeves tended to be narrow, the batwing shape was a common feature on dresses at Piguet, Marcelle and Dormoy. *Vogue* delighted in the work of an exciting new house, Mad Carpentier, which favoured apron basques and introduced a 'lean on the wind' silhouette, with the back of the dress bodice slightly bloused and the skirt drawn gently forward into flat folds or drapery over the stomach. Only heavy

overcoats were extravagant, with wide, balloon-shaped sleeves.

International tailoring became more feminine with the re-entry of French influence. The look was still discreetly understated, but now touched with some romance. Skirts began to be less severe and waists more slender and tops clung to the figure. In London Hartnell's jackets were a little longer and Molyneux

4. *Molyneux nipped in the waist of his brown wool suit with panelling. It is worn with a mustard crêpe blouse with a brown trim.* 5. *Mad Carpentier's black wool jacket with truncated cape line formed by a plain, chin-high yoke, cut in one with balloon sleeves. It is worn with a full-fronted, plaid skirt.* 6. *Mainbocher's suit has flat mink banding on a slightly Graustarkian black crêpe jacket, straight and narrow over a simple straight dress.* 7. *Piguet's tailormade suit with leopardskin basque and Paulette hat.*

8

9

10

11

used back panelling to nip in the waists of his jackets. The selection of dresses for the British home market was very limited and usually undecorated, as the designers' finer, more expressive work continued to be for export only. Coat designs had changed very little during hostilities and black remained Britain's favourite colour.

Women had started wearing trousers in Britain because they could be worn with socks, thereby saving on the tightly rationed stockings. Necessity made the fashion acceptable and as women came to appreciate the ease and comfort of trousers, it spread worldwide. For summer resort wear Americans chose to wear shorts or trousers or alternatively the little cotton dress, which now had a slim rather than dirndl shirt.

Balenciaga, designing from Spain, continued to promote the Renaissance figure: small bodices, tight waists, slightly bloused stomach, rounded hips and curvaceous bottom. The sleeves were absolutely straight and narrow. His feminine wool or velvet redingotes were single- or double-breasted, occasionally hooped or yoked and nearly always collarless; square box coats trimmed with large appliquéd patch pockets; and rounded-hip coats with flared skirts.

In America the tube jersey dress was standard attire twelve hours a day, four seasons a year, and its most creative exponent was Charles James. His forte was an architectural approach to tailoring combined with artful drapery of

8. Juillard's Melton cloth coat with chinchilla rabbit collar and straight Jay Thorpe skirt. 9. Lachasse's wide-revered top-coat in Heather Mills tweed. 10. Paquin's ample red pleated coat. 11. Mad Carpentier's beige gondolier coat with bulky bishop sleeves. 12. Though uncredited in the magazine, Claire McCardell designed the big-pocketed skirt striped in black, grey and red worsted wool and sleek, slashed black wool blouse. 13. Rose Barrack's Enka rayon crêpe two-piece dress: tunic and underdress. 14. Marlene Dietrich models Schiaparelli's evening coat with a mandarin collar. 15. Lelong's black velvet sheath dress with a low-slung sash of black jersey. 16. Charles James's ink-green dinner dress, which had been presented in England sixteen years earlier (originally it was ankle-length), and Suzanne and Roger's hat of black wired lilacs. 17. Train-Norell's 'Wilsonian era' rayon crêpe evening gown. 18. Madame Eta's Enka rayon crêpe gowns, pleated and scrolled with a frieze of gold and white sequins.

14

15

16

12

13

cloth. Like all the other designers he had to abide by the L 85 restrictions, but his dresses were never mere tubes – offbeat drapery or seaming lifted them above the commonplace. One of his most interesting coats had no front edges but rolled inwards to make a double-layered coat.

In anticipation of the imminent Allied victory, by the end of the year clothing,

and particularly evening wear, was less sombre. The leading French houses showed a range of grand ball dresses aimed at diplomatic circles, while for more modest evenings angora dresses decorated with sequins were offered. Traina–Norell in America was inspired by the lines fashionable during the Wilsonian peace-making era, 1918–19.

17

18

1945

The Paris collections continued to follow a functional line this spring. It began at the top with a page-boy hat, feathered or ribboned, worn well to the back of the head. The silhouette was slim and uncluttered, usually with one point of emphasis. If the bodice was sweater plain, the hips were draped and the skirt was straight or had narrow pleats; if the skirt was plain, the top had deep kimono armholes or caped sleeve tops. Most French houses preferred a fairly straight skirt, but the poor quality of the cloth and the need of many women to cycle made this style impractical, and the rounded hipline found favour in both Europe and America. Waists were generally small but not exaggerated, and tunics and boleros were popular.

The Chambre Syndicale de la Couture staged a worldwide promotion of French fashion on doll-sized mannequins in a *boutique fantastique* known as the Théâtre de la Mode. The dolls were exquisitely attired by the top couturiers and posed in scenes on tiny stages designed by Christian Bérard, Jean Cocteau and others.

The couture was yearning to reinstate feminine dress and the opportunity finally arrived with the end of the war in Europe. Clothes were rounded to the female figure and softness was achieved with dolman, batwing and kimono sleeves; open-necklines on blouses; and rounded, stand-up collars on tailored tops. The womanly silhouette was aided by seaming and belting, and padding the bust and hips to accentuate the slim, nipped-in waist. Skirt fullness, still within the Utility and L 85 regulations, was concentrated at the front. Prints, satin blouses and diagonal buttons counteracted the severity of tweed suits.

When Schiaparelli returned to her salon after four years' absence, she found that fabric restrictions were so severe that muslin and voile could not be wasted on *toiles*; fur was in such short supply that cat and rabbit furs were offered as if they were gold; and there was enough leather only for trimmings,

1. *Omar Kiam's rayon crêpe two-piece with a loose Russian blouse and Florence Reichman hat.*
2. *Décolleté grey jersey and circular flannel skirt from B.H. Wragge for après-ski evenings.*
3. *Cole of California's off-the-shoulder top and skirt of red-and-white print batiste. The midriff is wrapped in ribbon like a spool.*   4. *McCardell's spun rayon and cotton casual sports dress is stitched in white.*   5. *Molyneux's blue crêpe coat-dress has a softly gathered skirt. The straw halo is decorated with cock feathers.*   6. *Lelong's black wool dress with a black taffeta bustle-bow.*
7. *Lelong's straight, kimono-sleeved beige wool dress with black buttons and a black belt.*

12

8. *Hattie Carnegie's banded mink coat.* 9. *Bergdorf Goodman's soft-red velveteen Directoire coat with three-quarter-length sleeves.* 10. *Mainbocher's infantry cape and plumed hat.* 11. *Schiaparelli's black drap coat lined and trimmed with sable.* 12. *McCardell's 'Future Dress', stitched in brown shantung with a kid belt, made from two triangles tied at the neck, back and front.*

8

9

10

11

not to make bags or garments. The designs Schiaparelli showed now went contrary to the general trend. She lowered the waist and introduced the tubular jacket, and trimmed jackets, coats and dresses with lowered martingales. These styles did not find favour.

In July the Russians held their first fashion show since the beginning of the war, to choose models for mass production. The main considerations were that the clothes should be practical to wear, easy to produce and attractive. It was reported that the designers based their work on American sportswear, which did not require a great deal of material, the traditional Russian silhouette and the English tailored tradition.

In Paris great excitement greeted the opening of Pierre Balmain, and his arrival was acclaimed in *Vogue* by his friend and admirer Gertrude Stein. He showed short dinner dresses with straight zipped-up woollen over-shirts, but his major contribution was the romantic, full-skirted ball dress, which was to become a hallmark of his house. At other couture houses grand evening dresses were as scarce as the occasions to wear them, although Lelong offered full-skirted brocade gowns with Romney-like folds enveloping the shoulders.

In the autumn Balenciaga helped to change the direction of fashion when he dropped his hemlines to 15 inches from

the ground, thus pre-dating Dior's 'New Look' of 1947. He also softened and dropped the shoulder farther than any other couturier and offered bouffant evening gowns flounced with Gainsborough-style ruffles.

America also reflected the mood of change in fashion. American *Vogue* reported on two popular trends that were worlds apart, which it referred to as 'personal futurama' and 'typical traditionalism'. The modern functional style, which *Vogue* assumed would prevail, was typical of designers like McCardell, who favoured neat, smooth-waisted clothes, sweaters and simple flat shoes; but in the post-war era women preferred the highly ornate, ultra-feminine fashions emanating from Paris. As a result, modern designs, such as McCardell's, did not gain international fashion recognition until the mid-fifties, when Balenciaga's influence in Paris eclipsed Dior's.

13. Schiaparelli's black velvet dress with a tiered front and slightly gathered skirt, worn with a velvet drum muff and toque.
14. Mainbocher's slender black evening dress with deep décolleté and gilt, petal-shaped belt and matching headdress.   15. Balmain's foaming white tulle 'robe de style', pleated across the strapless bodice and decorated with a spray of holly.   16. Schiaparelli's navy-blue Directoire-style felt hat and navy-blue topcoat.   17. Madame Rubio of Mexico wears Balenciaga's oatmeal-coloured, sloping-shouldered box jacket over a sleeveless jacket and white ottoman top with black velvet sleeves and black velvet skirt.

1946-1956

> But now as she stood before the stunning creations hanging in the wardrobe she found herself face to face with a new kind of beauty – an artificial one created by the hand of man the artist, but aimed directly and cunningly at the heart of woman. In that very instant she fell victim to the artist; at that very moment there was born within her the craving to possess such a garment . . . a Dior dress.
>
> Paul Gallico, *Flowers for Mrs Harris* (1958)

Dior's black cocktail dress from the 'New Look' collection sketched at Maxim's by Nobili, 1947.

In the late forties mainstream fashion failed to confront post-war reality and cowered behind pre-war myths, in stark contrast to contemporary architecture, paintings, textile or furniture design. Nostalgia in British art was washed away by the 'kitchen sink' school, which relished the grey, almost brutal post-war reality. In America and Europe the action painting of Jackson Pollock and the colour abstraction of Mark Rothko, Joan Miró, and Paule Vesarley shocked the world with their modernity. There was no room for retrospection in the celebrated buildings of the day, such as Brazilian architect Oscar Niemeyer's 1950 Auditorium, based on the 'beautiful horizon', or R. Buckminster Fuller's geodesic domes, which dispensed with massive supports and relied on the principles of stress and tension for stability. While Dior's New Look was still relying on old-fashioned underpinnings like boned corsetry, architects and furniture designers were inventing new construction methods.

Fashion, however, pandered to society's yearning for the security and peace associated with *la belle époque* by reviving the mock-Edwardian style first presented in the late thirties. In an understandable reaction to the demands of war, women now wanted to masquerade as decorative ladies of leisure, retreating into the styles of the past. Longing to cast aside the mean fashions of the war, they welcomed the lavishness of the Paris line: a softened silhouette, a defined, normal waistline and a longer hemline. Highlighting the mood of retrospection and romance, *Vogue* presented the 1946 collections like Boucher or Fragonard paintings. Pierre Balmain's début collection of full-skirted ball gowns smothered in lavish embroidery made him the darling of Paris. A richness that had been out of the question for the last five years was now displayed at peace-welcoming balls, especially in diplomatic circles. At last luxury, unapologetic luxury, was available again, at least in Paris.

Christian Dior accentuated these shapely, full lines in his 1947 début collection. The press dubbed his 'Corolle' line the 'New Look' and it became front-page news. The tighter waists, longer, fuller skirts and more pronounced

Jacques Fath's evening dress photographed against a Jackson Pollock 'action' painting.

hips were in fact the maximization of an old style, but these charming, flattering clothes appealed because they differed so dramatically from the austere fashions of the war and because they were in tune with contemporary women's fantasies. Backed by the textile industrialist Marcel Boussac, Dior dressed women in ankle-length skirts, corsets, opera pumps, cocktail hats and umbrellas as coquettish as parasols. Dior and his followers stole the limelight from those pursuing more modern design. He claimed that he was conducting 'the eternal fight against the demoralizing and mediocre influences of our time', but far from being an innovator, Dior was in fact trapped in a constant effort to create more changes and more publicity. As a result each collection seemed to be more complicated, more constricting and more artificial.

Buckminster Fuller overlooking his geodesic dome.

The Americans, who had already put an end to wartime austerity by lifting the L 85 restrictions in 1946, embraced Dior's look. The business community was delighted, for the New Look boosted not only the clothing industry but the mass-production of all the accessories that were so much part of the look; milliners, manufacturers of umbrellas, gloves, shoes, stockings and corsets all enjoyed a boom. Overnight Dior became a hero. The Neiman-Marcus store in Dallas invited him over to promote the New Look.

Dior was a reserved, shy, self-effacing man, more like a country parson than an international couturier. John Cavanagh, who dined with him on the eve of the launch of the New Look, was struck by his quiet modesty and beautiful manners but felt sure there was a volcanic drive under the temperate surface. On seeing the collection the following day, Cavanagh was 'transfixed, in tears. The relief was overwhelming; that relief of seeing total beauty again, from the tips of the little shoes to the feathers on the hats – it was a total glorification of the female form. Everything was important, the ankles, the gloves, the umbrella, the hat.' During Chanel's era it had been impolite, almost indecent, to draw attention to the bust, waist or hips; the silhouette was modest. Dior radically opposed this. The impact was so immediate that every designer was affected, even Norman Hartnell, who declared of the New Look, 'No Englishman would ever do that,' but promptly began designing clothes in the same style.

British *Vogue*'s Sheila Wetton recalls how essential correct accessories, such as white gloves, were then. Members of the staff who transgressed would receive rebukes from Harry Yoxall, the Managing Director, such as this stern memo: 'It has been brought to my attention that you were seen on Pollen Street without hat or gloves. This is not good enough.'

Christian Dior, 1947.

In 1945 Britain opted for the 'New World' of Labour government. Unnecessary luxury was inevitably considered unpatriotic and wasteful, as it had been after the First World War. All industries, including textiles, were understaffed, so cloth shortages continued and the wartime restrictions were maintained. British women had to 'make do' with their Utility fashions; the New Look was considered a political outrage, a calculated defiance against austerity controls. Never before had fashion been so newsworthy, so controversial. Sir Stafford Cripps, the president of the Board of Trade, commented, 'It seems to me utterly stupid and irresponsible that time, labour, materials and money should be wasted on these imbecilities.'

None the less, the New Look was on the British streets by 1948. Miss M. Ridleagh, MP, was outraged; she recognized it for what it was: 'reminiscent of the caged bird attitude ... I hope that our fashion dictators will realize the *New Outlook* of women and give the death blow to any attempt at

Sir Stafford Cripps.

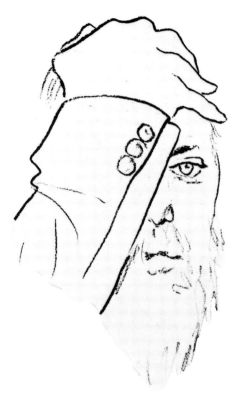

Christian 'Bébé' Bérard by Eric.

curtailing women's freedom.' But the earnest Miss Ridleagh overestimated the importance that most women would place on physical freedom and the psychological implications of their dress. Fashion is a capricious form of sensuous expression, rarely influenced by intellectual considerations.

The New Look was impractical. Baroness Rothschild, realizing that her wide-skirted ball gown would get crushed in even her largest limousine, was forced to travel in a horse box. She arrived at the ball a little late, but with the dress intact and uncreased. The story may be apocryphal, but it certainly conjures up the delightful absurdities of such fashions.

The New Look coincided with a return to the traditional lifestyle of marriage and motherhood for many women who had worked during the war. The narrow-waisted, wide-hipped silhouette acclaimed fertility, in contrast to the androgyny of twenties clothes. Many working women retired to their homes and contributed to the 'Baby Boom' of the late forties, reassured by the findings of such medical experts as John Bowlby and Benjamin Spock. Dr Bowlby warned of the dangers of 'maternal deprivation' in the first five years of a child's life, and pronounced that therefore the 'mother of young children is not free ... to earn'. Dr Spock preached the importance of 'togetherness'.

In Britain the 'season', that great marriage market, was revived in 1947, when presentations at court were reinstated and it became a top priority for fashionable young women to 'come out'. Female careerism was shelved as a contemporary ideal; more than fifty per cent of female university students in America dropped out at this time to marry and encourage their husbands through college and career. After 1949 'career woman' became a pejorative term denoting a 'ball-busting, man-eating harpy, a miserable, neurotic witch from whom man and child must flee for their very life' (Betty Friedan, *The Feminine Mystique*, 1963).

The popular press, especially women's magazines, condemned young wives who wanted more than motherhood. Compared with the twenties, there was a dire lack of information and advice for career women in magazines, which concentrated exclusively on fashion and beauty. The dominant role of men not only as breadwinners but as the arbiters of taste was reinforced; the leading couturiers at this time – Dior, Fath, Balmain, Balenciaga, Adrian and Norell – were men. Chanel had retired in 1939, and Elsa Schiaparelli's influence waned dramatically; only Madame Grès continued, presenting flowing, Greek-inspired, uncorseted clothing.

The corset industry was booming, as fashion emphasized the bust, cleavage and waist, which were the erogenous zones of the period. The number of sex-goddess filmstars whose ticket to success was a voluptuous figure, such as Jane Russell, Diana Dors and Marilyn Monroe, bears witness to this. The 'waspie' was introduced by Warners in 1947 and the strapless brassière, the strapless all-in-one and later the roll-on girdle became wardrobe necessities.

The corsetry business used discoveries in synthetic textiles, in both America and Britain. British firms such as Courtaulds and British Celanese had been pioneers in this field, but it was America, and especially the Du Pont company, that became the post-war leader. However, the couture still preferred to use natural materials for most of its clothing.

Artifice 'perfected' the figure. Many dresses had built-in corsets and an evening dress could virtually stand up on its own. Madame Marguerite, who worked with Dior, described how a couture gown in the early fifties was constructed: 'The scaffolding was put under the dress itself. First the famous

Anti-Dior reaction in America.

No. 132 tulle from Brivet, then a very sheer organza from Abraham to prevent the tulle from scratching and making ladders in the stockings, a very fine silk pongee added to line the skirt. But that was not all ... there were the tulle corsets made to give them the shape we wished them to have.' The inside of couture clothes of the time often reveals many of the faults of their owners' figures.

The New Look transformed the streets of Europe and the United States, from the suburbs to fashionable Fifth Avenue and the Champs Élysées. Its impact was partly a reflection of the power of the post-war ready-to-wear industry. Chainstores like Marks & Spencer, C & A in Britain, Prisunic in France, and Macy's, Bloomingdale's, Woolworth's and J. C. Penney's in America were now spreading post-war consumerism to a wider market.

By 1950 the economic situation was improving. British Utility restrictions were abolished for clothes in 1948 and rationing of most other goods in 1952. Many women were gaining access to a more affluent lifestyle, and it was on the strength of this mass market that the famous ready-to-wear manufacturers such as Frederick Starke, Dereta, Harry Popper, Koupy, Susan Small, Fira Benenson, Mark Mooring, Czettel, Valentina, Carnegie, Adrian and Sophie Gimbel made their names and fortunes. They catered for the new fashion-conscious meritocracy, who did not mind everyone looking the same so long as they had a variety of easy-care quality clothes.

The English ready-to-wear producers were centred in Leeds, Manchester and London. The Austrian and mid-European Jewish refugees working in the clothing industry brought an expertise and an eye for quality that was to stand Britain in good stead as a mass-producer of quality clothes. (A similar influx of immigrants benefited the American industry.) Gradually through powerful promotions in daily newspapers and fashion magazines, the top ready-to-wear companies built a reliable, high-fashion image to which women became very loyal.

Starke, founded at the turn of the century, was a notable example of top-class ready-made clothing. In 1947 Frederick Starke was responsible for setting up the Model House Group in London to co-ordinate the wholesale industry, recognizing the need for 'a shop window for the houses with a view to export'. There were fourteen original members, and it evolved into the Fashion House Group of London. The export trade earned valuable foreign currency from the colonial markets, which had been secured before the war, and from the more competitive American and European markets. As a member of the Dollar Export Council, in 1948 Starke took a large British ready-to-wear show to America and clothes were bought by Lord & Taylor, Bonwit Teller and other leading stores.

Until the late fifties the French did not tackle mass-produced fashion and their ready-to-wear industry was tiny; fashion-conscious French women either dressed at a couture house or employed a local dressmaker. The couture did produce boutique collections, but these were expensive and primarily intended as an outlet for a designer's scent, handbags, shoes, gloves and general accessories, which were more lucrative than the clothes themselves. Many of the goods were emblazoned with the house motif, a very saleable commodity in these status-conscious times. Boutiques, like the couture, were regulated by rulings laid down by the Chambre Syndicale: all items had to be clearly labelled 'boutique' and as they were to some extent mass-produced, they should not be copies of the couture collection. However, boutiques did not represent a consolidated attack on the mass market.

The crinoline, the power behind spinny skirts. A petticoat to be worn two or three deep, advised Vogue, *in stiff net by Sidney Bush.*

The Hon. Mrs Reginald Fellowes at the Beistegui Ball in the Palazzo Labia, Venice, 1951.

Lady Pamela Berry.

A crowded Dior opening.

The midwife of the French prêt-à-porter (a term introduced only in the late forties) was Maime Armodin. She observed the style and importance of ready-to-wear while working on British *Vogue*, and after returning to Paris to join *Le Jardin des Modes* in 1951, she encouraged the emergence of a French version by giving repeated editorial coverage to young ready-to-wear designers and guiding them according to the market's needs. As a result of this, by the end of the fifties, Gérard Pipart and Emanuelle Khanh at I.D., Germaine and Jane, Côte d'Azur (and later Cacharel and V de V) were established, offering high-quality, high-fashion ready-to-wear. Shops such as Prisunic set up sections specializing in these clothes.

The Incorporated Society of London Fashion Designers was the couture equivalent of the Model House Group. After the war the ISLFD, under the chairmanship of Edward Molyneux, provided a framework to attract foreign buyers and speak with one voice to both the government and the consumer. It organized the London Fashion Week just before the Paris shows (this was later changed to after Paris) so that the international buyers could easily visit both capitals. But post-war attempts to centralize the whole industry failed and it remained financially weak compared with the French couture. Hardy Amies believes that the ISLFD was 'founded on a fallacy and doomed to failure'. It made no enquiry into the financial strength, capital assets, workers and business acumen of each house; only the creativity of the designer was regarded as a worthy gauge of success. There was no official training scheme for designers until 1958, when Madge Garland was asked to found the Fashion School at the Royal College of Art to offer instruction by designers, cutters, tailors and milliners working in the trade.

The British couture houses remained essentially court dressmakers; only the ready-to-wear won international acclaim. Many couturiers went bankrupt, lacking the knowledge and ruthlessness to set the British couture on a sound enough footing to challenge Paris. Furthermore, unlike the French and Americans, few English couturiers attracted major backing from textile industrialists or ready-to-wear manufacturers. But Lady Pamela Berry, who in 1954 became the first woman president of the ISLFD, was successful in handling international public relations and attracting interest and investment in the couture from the government (she was a friend of Peter Thorneycroft, President of the Board of Trade, and his wife Carla, who had been a *Vogue* fashion editor). However, this energetic initiative soon foundered on the old problems of apathy, long-term disregard by the government and a myopic notion of style by the very rigidly traditional London couturiers.

For the Paris couture, the forties and fifties were the last great days, inspiring the showmanship of its greatest contributors. Jacques Fath showed in the Eiffel Tower or at his country house, others in the open air or in theatres. Only 200 or so guests attended each show in the private salon. Successive shows over the following weeks catered for the less important clientele. (Today's collections are shown to as many as 3,000 people at once, in a setting resembling a metropolitan discothèque.)

The models were an essential part of the glamour of the couture, and each couturier tended to have a favourite. Jean Dawnay was one of the first English girls to enter the circle of favoured models in Paris, and her break came as a result of her typical and charming impetuosity. Stepping off a Venice–London train in Paris with £5 and the address of a cheap hotel in her pocket, she went to Dior in the simple cotton frock and tired-looking sandals she had been wearing in Venice. Dior's house was very imposing, and in the inner sanctum rows of immaculately dressed models were waiting to be seen. But Dawnay's natural style shone through her weary attire and Dior offered her a top modelling job.

The most important couture customers were no longer the fabulously rich but the store buyers and ready-to-wear manufacturers, who bought toiles to copy and mass-produce for all the great stores of the Western world. Professional buyers, such as the American Ethel Frankau of Bergdorf Goodman in New York, Sir Charles Abrahams of Aquascutum, the buyers for Harrods, Saks and Ohrbachs, and Madame Pedrini of Rina Modelli in Italy, became the honoured customers of the great houses.

Collections were shown first to buyers and then to private customers, this new order showing the change of emphasis after the war. For the trade the cost of a ticket, known as a deposit, was about £300 in the fifties. This entitled a buyer to a seat and would be deducted from the price of any models bought. The buyers would be charged from 50 to 100 per cent more for the gowns than private customers; if they did not buy an original they would take some toiles or paper patterns rather than waste their deposit.

However, piracy continued to be a major problem. Hysterical secrecy veiled the collections until the very last moment, and the couture staff went to extraordinary lengths to avert plagiarism. Even after the collections, the press were barred by the Chambre Syndicale from reproducing any photographs for three weeks or so, until the first gowns had been delivered to the buyers. Professional copyists forged passes to the collections and were rarely caught. In 1952 the National Assembly, lobbied by the Chambre Syndicale, passed a law establishing that a couture collection was copyright for only one season; it made sharp distinction between the relatively harmless copying by local dressmakers and professionally organized plagiarism.

Great snobbery still coloured the reception of clients in the couture, but no matter how dubious a woman's background she was always served so long as she honoured her bills. Ginette Spanier recalls that when she was working as a *directrice* at Balmain, a woman who was unable to speak the 'President's French' arrived wanting a fur coat. Having fitted her, Spanier enquired how she wished to settle her account and was presented with a copy of *Paris Soir* stuffed with thousand-franc notes. The cash was discreetly taken down to accounts and the transaction completed, but the woman continued to loiter in the foyer, waiting for her newspaper to be returned!

Vogue fashion editors played a powerful role in linking the couture with the wholesale ready-to-wear houses. Madge Garland remembers making deals with the heads of wholesale companies, such as Olive O'Neill at Dorville, whereby *Vogue* featured a particular couture gown and mentioned the manufacturer who bought the toile or pattern; help in distributing copies of the gown to the most important stores was also provided. Thus the choices of the editors to some extent determined which gowns would be mass-produced.

By the mid-forties Charles James's prominence was assured in the fashion world. He was an artful master of cut but his flaring temper destroyed almost every working and social relationship, and he proved to be an atrocious businessman. He rarely broke even and on occasions actually ran out of material because he had no money. His clothes were works of art, he believed, which justified taking them apart time after time, even if this meant they would not be ready on the night they were wanted by his clients (who included Millicent Rogers, Mrs Cornelius Vanderbilt Whitney and Mrs Harrison Williams). On such occasions he secured their willing co-operation

Charles James.

Claire McCardell, the doyenne of American modernism in dress.

Hattie Carnegie at home in black gabardine trousers and a gold-braided linen shirt.

Emilio Pucci in his Florentine palazzo.

Gabriella, Countess di Robilant of Gabriellasport.

Roberto Capucci.

to do the unheard-of – borrow couture gowns from each other. Their respect for him was absolute.

James loved spiral drapery, prominent revers, dramatic choux and peplums; he used heavy materials for his strong architectural shapes. Among his most famous innovations were the 'Petal' dress of 1949, the 'Arc' sleeve of 1951 and his abstract 'Clover Leaf' dress of 1953.

American women were at last prepared to support their own designers, and American folklore, traditions, sportswear and Hollywood provided an exciting source of design inspiration. America jettisoned the constantly dressed-up look and showed women how to wear the simple shirtwaister with great style even on formal occasions, the importance of the event being registered only by the colour and quality of the cloth. Style was no longer dependent on elaborate accessories and formality.

Claire McCardell led this trend. Aware of the economic and design limitations of mass-producers and sympathetic to the freedom of movement required by women's bodies, her major contributions were mix-and-match, casual sportswear and, specifically, the dirndl skirt, the elimination of the brassière and girdle, the kitchen-dinner dress, the diaper bathing suit, the ballet pump, the 'popover' dress with side slits and ties, the leotard and playclothes. While other couturiers were 'out-luxing' each other with lavish silks and wools, McCardell was using denim, seersucker, wool jersey and mattress-ticking. She said of her style, 'It looks and feels like America. Its freedom, its democracy, its casualness, its good health. Clothes can say all that.' And hers did.

American talent now received its due acclaim. Adrian brought the glamour of the film world to the wider public, and Norell was experimenting with novel lines. Hattie Carnegie and Mainbocher offered fashion classics based on specifically American requirements. American ready-to-wear still kept a sharp eye on Paris, but there was now an alternative, presented with confidence, style and patriotism.

Like the Americans, Italian designers gained international acclaim after the war, mainly for their resort clothes, boutique collections and leather goods. The editor of British *Vogue*, Audrey Withers, travelled to Rome immediately after the war and reported in amazement that the Italians no longer wore city clothes: the fashionable were wearing brief resort clothes with bare, brown legs and thong sandals in town. Suddenly young people everywhere were tempted to dress in this attractive, youthful manner.

American *Vogue*, reporting on the Italian collections of 1947, pointed out that the Italians had two great advantages: a seemingly inexhaustible pool of hand labour and wonderful materials. Their use of textiles was artistic and experimental, and their strongest contributions to post-war fashion were innovative prints, off-the-shoulder and 'doric column' evening dresses, and resort clothes, as from Gabriella, Countess di Robilant of Gabriellasport.

Italian designers were becoming very aware of the American market, and one of the Italian pioneers in this field was the Marchese Emilio Pucci. In 1947 he was photographed at a ski resort wearing a ski outfit he had designed. As a result Pucci began designing sports and resort clothes. He changed the look of the well-travelled *mondaine*; she abandoned masculinely cut linens and sailor-style resort wear in favour of slinky, radiant silks. Pucci's daring juxtaposition of acid yellows, lime greens, Aegean turquoises and fuchsia pinks made him the first master of psychedelia. Pucci trade marks were sexy, narrow-legged pants, easy tunic tops, blouses worn outside the waistband.

Giovanni Battista Giorgini was another pioneer of Italian high fashion. Realizing that the American buyers were becoming interested in Italian style (many designers had been presented with Coty and Neiman-Marcus awards), he visited the well-known *ateliers* in Rome and Milan, suggesting that they stop copying the Parisians and create their own designs. He succeeded in persuading ten couturiers to show at his villa in Florence in 1951: Simonetta, Fabiani, Fontana, Antonelli, Schuberth and Carosa of Rome, Marucelli, Veneziani, Noverasco and Wanna of Milan. Four boutique designers, Emilio Pucci, Baroness Gallotti, Avolio and Bertoli of Milan, also showed.

Roberto Capucci, who opened his own house in 1950 at the age of twenty-one, presented a tableau of ball gowns at Giorgini's show that earned him worldwide attention. Like Charles James, he became known for architectural structure and proportions and novel line. His 'Dove' collection in 1952 used upholstery materials and the models wore white wigs; it was considered too extraordinary and was not well-received. The suits and dresses contradicted contemporary lines: seams and godets created forward rather than backwards movement and the effect was stiff and geometric. However, his 'Rose' line of 1956 won international acclaim.

By 1953 *Vogue* was acclaiming the Italians for their talented innovations in outerwear, suits and ball gowns, as well as for their shoes and boutique sportswear. Simonetta, who had opened in 1946, Mirsa, Fontana and Camerino followed Pucci across the Atlantic, where they found commercial success in the fifties. The first concerted display of Italian fashion in America took place in 1956, when to widespread acclaim nine aristocrats organized a show and modelled the clothes.

Meanwhile in Paris Dior's sheaths were shown in the spring of 1950. Sometimes described as the precursor of the sixties shift, they were in fact very restrictive; although the silhouette was dramatically different from the New Look, there was no note of real freedom.

It was Balenciaga who was developing the lines of the future. Cristobal Balenciaga was master of the arresting simplicity that is the most elusive of tailored effects. His gowns were bold, pure drama, characterized by quiet, strong, prophetic silhouettes and apparently effortless distinction. Balenciaga's work remains the pinnacle of couture art, and he was admired by every couturier, no matter how competitive.

'*Quand la charpente est bonne, on peut construire ce qu'on veut*,' Balenciaga told his protégé Hubert de Givenchy. Having mastered all the known tailoring techniques and invented many more, Balenciaga applied his craft with breathtaking effect. While other designers used geometry for sensationalism, defying rather than enhancing the body, Balenciaga applied radical shapes to flattering ends, for his clothes echoed movements and gestures, never determined them. He achieved the perfect harmony between the body and the garment, freeing the spirit of the woman within.

His designs were widely copied for the mass-market. The 'Bulle', the 'Sac', the kimono-sleeved coat (one of his most copied lines), the 'marinière' (also a favourite of Chanel), knee-high boots, culottes – these were Balenciaga's legacy to all women. But despite his indisputable talent Balenciaga's name was relatively unknown to the world-wide audience. He did not seek popular acclaim, shunned publicity, rejected the commercial options of a boutique or licence operation and repelled the press. He was a shy, proud and private man. It is said that Barbara Hutton, the Woolworth heiress, having patronized the house for several years, was so desperate for an audience with this

Simonetta Visconti.

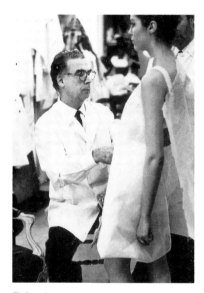

Balenciaga at work.

Balenciaga's fainting client, the American heiress, Barbara Hutton.

The textile entrepreneur Zika Ascher.

Santa Casilda by Zurbarán, a source of inspiration for Balenciaga.

Zurbarán's St Francis.

retiring maestro that she staged a faint at his show to gain admittance to his private office to recover.

Archive film demonstrates his meticulous concentration and perfectionism. A model girl would stand before him for many hours while he inspected, rejected, ripped apart and reconstructed, without any sense of time or impatience. He was a complete couturier – drawing, cutting, constructing, draping, sewing. And the final light touch of wit, a full-blown flower, an alluring hat, was always his.

One day Zika Ascher, an important textile entrepreneur, presented Balenciaga with a thick shaggy mohair, regarded by other couturiers as 'a complete fantasy, an outrageous material', which could not be used by the couture because of its extremely loose weave. Balenciaga looked at it. 'Yes, but how will we make the buttonholes? Shall we try?' Ascher's sample was taken away, and when it came back from Balenciaga, 'Well, it was perfect', recalls Ascher. 'One couldn't understand how it was done. Then I showed it to Gérard Pipart at Ricci and he turned it around, this buttonhole in the cloth, he studied it, turned it left and right and said, "You should frame it: buttonhole by Balenciaga."'

A distinctive Balenciaga touch was to focus the eye on a single dramatic point: the up-in-the-front hemline framing beautiful feet slippered in satin; the sleeveless bodice defining a regal shoulderline; the dramatic yet softening 'choux' enveloping an imperial head; the slightly protruding, Renaissance-style stomach, which he thought very becoming, very feminine.

Reflecting his respect for women, Balenciaga never contorted or restricted their bodies. His clothes seemed to rest on a fine cushion of air – a suspended halo crowning the whole body. He did not depend on hoops and petticoats to hold out the skirts of his evening dresses but on well-balanced, architectural construction. He did not use the typically skeletal couture models but chose small, plump, Spanish ladies. He believed imperfect figures to be as worthy of his attention as perfect ones. Two of his tailoring techniques to flatter small heavy women have been widely adopted: a collar cut away from the base of the neck, which elongates the neck and allows a woman and her pearls to move comfortably inside her clothes; and the nine-tenths sleeve, abbreviated above the wrist to create a more feline look.

Balenciaga married the precise elegance of France with Hispanic passion – the tailoring of the sixteenth *arrondissement*, the bullring, the serenity of the church, the art of Velázquez and Goya. Though renowned for his dark clothes, he had a brave flair for colour deeply rooted in his Spanish origins, bringing to Paris the red and fuchsia pink of matadors and flamenco dancers, the muted greens of olives, the grey-black of mussel shells lying by his father's fishing boat, the stone-grey of a monastic cloister, the black of the church in Lent, and the richly embroidered golds and silvers of saints' festivals. Struck by the seventeenth-century painter Zurbarán, he reinterpreted the angularity and smooth density of his almost super-realist devotional paintings, the cupola-like curves of religious robes, the full-bodied rich satins and rough sackcloths. These two Spaniards shared a sensibility for the sacred. Just as the paintings of Zurbarán, the music of Bach and ogival Gothic architecture belong to the church, so the wedding gown was the most inspiring medium for Balenciaga's mastery, for he imbued it with a sense of mystery, sacramental ceremony and, above all, dignity.

There is much controversy over who designed the first shift, the symbol of youth, ease and modernity. Balenciaga, Dior, Fabiani, Quant and others have all been credited with this new style. In the autumn of 1951 Balenciaga introduced a collection of untailored suits, the 'Gentle Look', and the 'Midi' line, reminiscent of the twenties in its loose waistlessness. Many people loathed this reminder of the shapeless mid-twenties silhouette, and it was ridiculed by some critics in the press, who were still blinkered by the New Look silhouette. Balenciaga persevered; his youthful drawstring jacket of 1953 was a positive statement of free line and a rejection of stiff, clinging, structured clothes. Balenciaga himself normally worked in a painter's smock, which he found so comfortable and practical that he offered a magnificently tailored version for women. He was the master of non-fit and counterpoint cutting, while maintaining absolute control of the garment's silhouette.

Hubert de Givenchy at his début collection in 1952.

Dior admired and was clearly influenced by Balenciaga's work; one only has to look at their Chinese collections of 1951 to observe the similarity (Pierre Cardin, working alongside Dior, realized this). Dior started to lose spirit and verve after his first four or five collections. He made one last stab at the past in 1956, when he tried to lower the hemline to the lower calf, but *Vogue* commented, 'Is it a stunt or a serious development? Should we, can we, do we *want* to revert to the pre-emancipation femininity in the uncompromisingly emancipated world we live in?'

In 1952 a new young designer opened in Paris; Givenchy had been trained at Fath, Piguet, Lelong and Schiaparelli. He was in tune with the age, significantly launching his first collection through the boutique medium rather than the couture. The collection was shown in cotton shirting and consisted of mix-and-match blouses, skirts and trousers for a casual, yet impeccable, wardrobe. As Givenchy says, 'I think it was quite a novelty thirty years ago to have everything separate. I used cotton because it is a simple and true fabric.' He also wanted to offer a contrast to the formal clothes of Dior, and he had little money.

The couture was justifiably criticized by Chanel on her return in 1954. She felt that the lessons in comfort and ease learnt three decades ago had been forgotten. In an interview with *Vogue* she explained, 'A dress must function. Place the pockets accurately for use; never a button without a buttonhole. A sleeve isn't right unless the arms move easily. Elegance in clothes means freedom to move easily.' Chanel abhorred impracticality: 'These heavy dresses that won't pack into aeroplane luggage, ridiculous! What is the point of going back to the rigidity of a corset?' The waspie she considered to be 'an exaggeration on a wasp'!

British *Vogue* saw Chanel's first collection as a pre-war revival without contemporary relevance. It was wrong. Chanel's ideas became international fashion currency again, especially in America. In 1957, aged seventy-four, she went to Dallas to receive a Neiman-Marcus award; to the Americans she was Paris's greatest designer.

In 1954 the young Karl Lagerfeld's entry in a competition organized by the Wool Secretariat was the epitome of the youthful chemise. The style that was to be abbreviated in the sixties had arrived. By 1955 there was a 'significant struggle taking place in Paris', as *Vogue* observed. On the one hand there were the clothes with instant 'hanger appeal', firmly structured, hanging stiffly on the rail. These 'clothes of character', or imposition, were designed by Dior, Fath and Balmain. On the other hand, clothes from Balenciaga, Chanel, Givenchy and Lanvin (where Castillo was designing) had to be worn for their charm to be realized — one was conscious of the body moving underneath them. The latter prevailed, inspiring future design.

1946

The French were determined to reinstate Paris as the centre of international fashion and restore the prosperity and fame of the couture. This spring the first French collections to be exported since 1940 featured effortlessly graceful clothes that made a woman look pretty and feel elegant. The spring collections showed an almost naked look for the afternoon – full skirts and deep décolletés – while for the day most designers chose the straight silhouette, varied with tunics and drapery swathing the hips. Hats returned: 'Whatever the silhouette, there's a hat to match it. Trim sailors and cloches for the 1910 look, big cartwheels, Queen Mary, wing-trimmed toques, Van Meer handkerchief head-dresses,' reported *Vogue*. Paris also overflowed with amusing details such as birds and flowers pinned into chignoned hair.

Paris evening dresses were either slender columns or grand, bouffant skirts with deep décolletés. There was an attempt to revive the hobble skirt, but the meanness of line hinted at austerity, and therefore it did not become a popular silhouette. There was a bold use of colour and material and a proliferation of stripes, which was echoed in Britain and America.

London, Paris and New York all craved elegance. Mock Edwardian details were revived in Paris and copied in New York: 'The plumed head is a symbol: to Paris it is the essence of the old elegance,' commented *Vogue*.

American designers had been moving towards a less constricted line during their isolation from French couture, but they now immediately followed the lead of Paris. Bustle-like effects were prevalent and Howard Greer's strange anachronism, the hip hoop, was introduced just a year before Dior crystallized this mode. 'A small waist is money in the bank – rounded hips are an asset – good bosom and shoulders are jewels – the flat midriff worth a ransom,' commented American *Vogue*.

The American made-to-order collections also emphasized the tiny, feminine waist. Nearly every collection showed the 'Spool' torso, introduced last year, which ended in the shapely fullness of a pannier, peplum, hip hoop or edge of twisted fabric. Only Claire McCardell continued to create easy-fitting, modern clothes.

American *Vogue* was very patriotic about its emerging designers. Castillo, Fira Benenson, Mark Mooring, Adrian, Hattie Carnegie, Valentina and Mainbocher had achieved international acclaim, but *Vogue* believed that American women's talent for style still lagged behind the designers' talent for creating it – most American women bought too many clothes without enough thought.

American *Vogue* sponsored the

1. The essence of post-war elegance: large hat, bare black dress and courts. 2. Legroux's big, black-feathered cartwheel hat for the evening and Balmain's décolleté dress. 3. Countess 'Niki' Visconti models Ventura of Milan's white silk jersey evening dress with draped skirt knotted at the waist. 4. Piquet's navy-blue and white striped crêpe dress splits the hobble with a spool torso. 5. Hartnell's single-shouldered gown, based on the oblique line, has a jutting hip-line beneath a draped black velvet, diagonally cut bodice. The hobble skirt is in black faille, with a stiff hipline bow. 6. Lelong's short black wool crêpe dinner dress with neckline, necklace and drapery all swung to the back in deep loops.

7. *Balenciaga's long écru cotton shawl over a simple, black sheath dress, which is very tightly belted.* 8. *Greer's thin grey wool dress with a hip hoop, edged in white and worn with white accessories.* 9. *McCardell's grey striped wool jersey dinner dress, unorthodox evening wear, modern in the way that it softly delineates the figure without artifice. It is worn with casual, flat, gold sandals.*

'Young Dandy' look derived from the American 'preppy' tradition: the dapper elegance of crisply tailored suits and neat accessories – short white gloves, gentlemanly umbrella, lapel pin, cravat and low-heeled 'Mary-Jane' shoes.

The wartime silhouette prevailed in England, as the country still suffered from austerity restrictions, although the London collections did include a group of luncheon and late-afternoon dresses influenced by the easier line established in Paris last year: softly swathed or draped dresses with circular or sun-ray pleated skirts. Colour outshone black: rosy-red, blue, gold and all the sherry browns. London evening gowns tended to be very traditional; following Paris's lead last autumn, many houses showed dresses reminiscent of portraits by Romney, Gainsborough and Sargent, in full-skirted satin, billowing tulle and tiered lace, with low décolletés to display the family diamonds. Hartnell's oblique line was more prophetic in silhouette than most, for it was to appear as a major theme in Paris in 1948. Amies's autumn collection featured hip padding.

Coats from the London collections were as traditional as the evening wear. They were either boxed or full, and great attention was paid to small details. Stole shoulders were seen on some coats (stoles were very fashionable – wrapped over a suit or a simple wool dress, or worn in the evening over a pencil-slim dinner dress). Giant plaids and checks were the most prominent fabric patterns for day coats.

Paris offered a variety of coat lines in the autumn: fitted coats with nipped-in waists; greatcoats, which had proved their worth during the war, with huge suitcase pockets; and the wrapped silhouette, hugging the hips, which tended to be the most popular.

For daytime Paris chose the narrow swathed silhouette, varied with tunics and hip draperies. Miniature corsets, which just pulled in the waist, were built into dresses to achieve the fashionable hourglass figure.

A strong influence of Madame Grès appeared in the work of the doyen of Italian fashion, Ventura of Milan. He draped and moulded jersey to create simple dresses like Doric columns.

Charles Creed, son of Henry Creed, and Michael Sherard opened in London this year, and Molyneux re-opened in Paris.

10. *Lelong's 1910 style ensemble: a dolman-sleeved jacket over a slim dress, topped with a massive cartwheel hat.   11. Left: a dry-brush suit in black-and-white Onondaga rayon crêpe by Capri, worn with a Milan straw cloche. Right: Adèle Simpson's tweed-print suit and straw braid cloche. Both hats are by Hattie Carnegie.   12. Springtime wool stole.   13. Monte-Sano's short, bright-yellow wool coat with a high collar and prominent seaming.   14. Lelong's wrapped greatcoat with plaid lining and large kimono sleeves.   15. Creed's tan, beige and dark-bottle-green plaid swing coat for travelling with an inverted back pleat, tabbed and buttoned across the back, and turban.*

193

1947

'My dream is to save [women] from nature,' announced Christian Dior, who opened this year. The ultra-feminine details of his 'Corolle' collection – corsets, high pumps, sleek gloves, cocktail hats and umbrellas – caught the public imagination. Dior's silhouette, with its long skirts, nipped-in waist and sloping shoulders, was heralded as a watershed, making wartime fashion obsolete. It was christened the 'New Look' by journalists, although the trend towards longer skirts, smaller waists and feminine lines had begun in the late thirties and was seen in America in the early forties; hence Dior was not the originator of this mode, but its rejuvenator and popularist.

Dior accentuated the New Look in his autumn collection. 'Without foundations there can be no fashion,' he insisted. The petticoats, padding and built-in corsetry that underpinned these clothes made them very heavy – Valerie Mendes of the Victoria and Albert Museum has estimated that the pleated skirt alone of the model 'Bar' weighs eight pounds. The billowing ankle-length

skirts, some of them knife pleated, were often slightly shorter at the front to draw attention to a finely turned ankle, and were worn with the Gibson Girl blouse, which was boned around the neck (Laura Ashley showed a similar look, without bones, in the early seventies). With the new, sloping shoulderline, necklines were a focus of interest: there were Bonaparte roll collars at Schiaparelli, stand-away and face-framing collars at Piguet and Lelong, and simple, collarless necklines at Balenciaga. In the midst of the retrogression that characterized Paris fashions this year, only Balenciaga, with

his pure line and easy-fitting, modern clothes, remained the champion of understatement.

The gap between the world's fashion centres was closing fast and the New Look made an immediate impact on London and New York. Despite the continuing fabric restrictions in Britain, skirts were longer, made of stiff, rich materials, particularly silks and rayon mixes imported from France; jackets were padded over the hips and fitted to emphasize a tiny waist. Some American designers also favoured the short bolero or 'bell hop' suit jacket.

1. Dior's 'New Look'. Black wool suit, fitted jacket padded out over the hips and full skirt. The gloves, slender umbrella and opera pumps complete the elegant look. 2. Dior's 'Five o'Clock Dress', epitome of the New Look. A low-cut, fitted bodice, a cartridge-pleated waist, a curved leather belt and large solitaires at the wrist. It is worn with a felt toque, elbow-length black gloves and high-heeled shoes. 3. Taffeta dinner dress made from twenty-five yards of material – 'Your own shoulders plus padded hips.' 4. Dior's padded and boned corset. 5. Dior's 'Gibson Girl' blouse, boned around the neck, with a flat, boned cummerbund. 6. Dior's formal afternoon surah dress. The polkadots are printed on a green-beige background. The simple shirtwaister has a very full skirt, falling from unpressed pleats, and a wide sash tied into a bouffant, knotted bow. The chiffon-draped straw hat is also from Dior. 7. 'Bar', Dior's best-selling New Look suit; a pale tussore silk jacket and black knife-pleated skirt.

9

8. Castillo's suit being sketched by Erik: long black jacket and an equestrian skirt caught up over one hip; large picture hat and long umbrella.
9. Carnegie's silk shantung suit with dropped shoulders, accentuated by rippled shirring.   10. Adrian's square-shouldered suit, diagonally striped in green and brown, with tweed wings and spindle, which ends fourteen inches from the floor.   11. Balenciaga's loose, straight white jacket and slim, box-pleated skirt.   12. Creed's tight-waisted, grey-blue tweed jacket split up to the waist to produce curved panels and straight skirt.

10

11

12

13. *Gattinoni of Rome's brilliant-green brocade padded evening coat with a high, double-back collar.*   14. *Rhavis's black faille picture dress has a billowing skirt swept up to a severely straight velvet underskirt. The cream lace over the velvet corselette falls into small sleeves.*   15. *Molyneux's long, black jersey coat, giving the appearance of a double cape, over a white draped jersey dress.*   16. *Adrian's evening shirtwaist: a silk print blouse and black, raw silk skirt.*   17. *Fira Benenson's dove-grey satin evening dress with a flower-strewn skirt, and Newton Elkin's gold kid, strapped sandals.*

Charles Creed was one of the few British designers who refused to embrace the New Look. Disliking close-fitting, corseted lines, he chose to pursue his tailored style, which was typified by jackets with a masculine cut, black velvet collars and shirts with stocks.

Coats in London had an asymmetric feel: pockets on only one side, or one side of the coat turned back to reveal a contrasting lining. Capes were also popular, while cape collars and graceful cape sleeves were used to accentuate the sloping shoulderline. There were two coat shapes in America. The 'Cocoon' was a straight coat that was wrapped

and held in place by the hand – it demanded flat hips, long legs and a not-too-ample bosom; the 'Infanta' had a close-fitting bodice and a skirt that flared over the hips.

Most coats in Paris were tent-shaped, with large buttons and the full, deep pockets of wartime styles, although Dior's alternative was the tightly belted redingote, accentuating the feminine curves of hips and bust.

The Paris houses showed two lines for evening wear this year: the full-skirted picture frock and the sleek, draped gown. Drapery was used in a much more lavish manner as fabric became more readily

available. Black and white was widely regarded as the most chic and formal combination; formality was *de rigueur* again. In all the American ready-to-wear collections evening dresses were full-skirted, while London evening wear was distinctly Edwardian, with bare shoulders, defined waists and rustling skirts.

Having worked with Balmain at Molyneux during the thirties, Cavanagh now joined Balmain's house in Paris. Schiaparelli licensed her name – one of the first designers to do so – with the Chester H. Roth company in America. In Rome Princess Giovanna Caracciola opened Carosa couture.

18. *The Cocoon coat.*
19. *Paquin's beige wool greatcoat has a stitched hipband forming a pocket ledge. The collar is rolled down over the bodice.*   20. *Nettie Rosenstein's hooded, full-back red gabardine coat.*   21. *Gunther's Russian broadtail Infanta coat with shawl collar and frogging, and Hattie Carnegie's plumed hat.*

1948

Ready-to-wear manufacturers on both sides of the Atlantic seized on the New Look and offered a wide range of Dior-inspired clothing. However, since the war the Americans had become more critical of the dictates of Paris – according to American *Vogue* 'although the new Paris collections vary from 15 to 18 inches off the ground for day, spring skirts in America take a somewhat steadier view'.

A new tweed with a light, almost silky, texture was now available in America in a variety of patterns and colours. Quite different from 'the old, almost Tory tradition tweed', it was considered smart for town suits. The New Look suits in the London spring collections featured front- and back-fastening boleros, but by the autumn the classic tailormade suit with a pleated or kilted skirt had returned, notably at Morton, Creed, Molyneux and Russell. A number of jackets and dresses were designed to look like traditional suits.

London coats were impressive this year, whether full length, wrapped, loose, fitted or *directoire*-style. Some were trimmed with flat furs, others were quilted or embroidered. Many coat styles were shown in Paris, but the tent variety held its own, being useful and versatile. Dior and Lelong both offered a number of pyramid-shape coats for the spring.

The Paris collections this spring explored variations of the New Look. Dior introduced the 'Envol' line, which featured jutting wings and accentuated back interest, particularly on jackets. Skirts ranged from Fath's test tubes to full stiff skirts with uneven hemlines at Dior. Pleated skirts were fashionable everywhere – pressed, unpressed, box, inverted, sun-ray, accordian and knife – worn over taffeta petticoats in bright colours. Balenciaga reintroduced the high waistline, showing Empire-line summer dresses and coats.

Spring evening gowns with panniers – an extension of New Look fullness – were featured in the London collections; Stiebel styled his panniered evening

1. Dior's winged-back décolleté on a back-buttoned wool dress, close velour cloche and suede gauntlet gloves.   2. Balenciaga soars pleats high up under the bust of his shell-pink wool dress with a crossover bodice.   3. Dior's pale-pink chiffon shirtwaist, chiffon cartwheel and fall of pearls. 4. Griffe's fluid, grey, accordion-pleated, smocked dress.   5. Dior's double-apron skirt drawn back, with half-fabric matching opera pumps from Perugia.   6. Peter Russell's schoolgirl theme. Left: sunray-pleated skirt of fine navy-blue and white wool pin-check, navy-blue jacket with buttoned bodice and check revers. Right and centre: navy-blue dress with a full flared skirt and double schoolgirl collar. Both models wear navy-blue and white boaters with beekeepers' veils.   7. Griffe (for Swansdown's) Juillard woollen cloth tent-coat with jutting collar, taffeta scarf, octagonal-brimmed hat from Legroux and high black pumps.   8. Balenciaga's melon-coloured, high-waisted wool coat with back fullness and double-quilted leather hat.   9. Charles Creed's brandy-coloured cotton velour all-year coat with knife-pleated skirt and cape sleeves.   10. London coats. Left: Wallace's dark-brown heavy velour coat with large quilted cape collar and cuffs, tufted with jet. The Venetian hat is trimmed with a black taffeta ribbon. Centre: Michael Sherard's honey-yellow velour coat has welted front panels forming pockets and seal under cuffs and revers. Right: Helena Geffers's back wrapover facecloth coat in embossed velvet with taffeta bands at the hemline, large cape collar and kimono sleeves.

12

13

11. *Charles James's black faille suit and hat derived from a Yugoslavian cap.*
12. *Dior's pencil-slim black wool dress topped with a black-and-white checked wool 'envol' jacket. The Peter Pan collar is tied with a large black taffeta bow. Black beret and Perugia's check wool and patent-leather boots.*
13. *Schiaparelli's arrow-narrow silhouette: jutting collar, peg-topped skirt, wide belt and high-crowned cloche.*
14. *Schiaparelli's exaggerated heavy cotton sou'-wester with a stiff, stitched brim rolled up at the front and dipped in a kick pleat at the back to meet the low décolleté of the simple, one-piece white linen beach dress.*

14

skirts like those of a nineteenth-century washerwoman. Bodices in general were tight, with deep décolletés. British ready-to-wear firms such as Frederick Starke offered young and simple fairy-tale dresses for summer evenings. In the autumn the romantic Empire line and crinolined dresses abounded.

By the autumn the Paris daytime silhouette had become less padded and exaggerated, except at Dior. Skirts were slimmer and slightly shorter. Schiaparelli offered the 'Dandy' look – suits accompanied by enchanting accessories: stoles, gaiters, cloches, *directoire* hats, Venetian bicornes and jewels of Byzantine magnificence.

Dior's autumn collection was entitled 'Zig Zag'. It emphasized an asymmetrical line, particularly on evening gowns, some of which had one-shoulder and one-sleeve bodices and wrapped and draped torsos. Day skirts were cut with uneven or handkerchief hemlines and skirts were caught up on one hip.

Charles James now showed both in New York, his base, and in London; his evening gowns were especially innovative. Maggy Rouff retired this year, and Louis Féraud opened in Cannes.

15. *Schiaparelli's plaid taffeta skirt, wired out in spiral flounces, and a black polo-necked silk jersey top. The short coiffure and long earrings were new fashion details.* 16. *Dior's pearl-grey satin swathed evening gown with asymmetrical wrapped neckline and a single sleeve.* 17. *Charles James's apricot faille silk and aubergine satin dress over an edge of black velvet.* 18. *Matilda Etches's full-skirted, blue-printed organdie dress, over a pale-pink net petticoat, has a strapless bodice and a dropped shoulder bolero.*

15

16

17

18

1. Salvador Dali caricatured the extremes of the moulded and flared fashions. He had anticipated the importance of this look in 1948 (the date of the drawing). The figure was wrapped with a gown that flared out intermittently, producing kite-like shapes, sharply angular, down the torso.   2. Black Hurel grosgrain Paquin gown, spirally wrapped from neck to knees, where it ends in two pleats.   3. Lanvin's white organdie evening stole.   4. Dior's cascading grey brocade cocktail dress folded deeply at the front to pour out over the slim underskirt, with a brown sash.

5. Traina-Norell's tunic dress with a double silhouette, fullness spread over a sheath.   6. Schiaparelli's deep, rich velvet sheath dress is straight and slim and completely bare-shouldered save for a large, contrast-coloured leaf that covers one shoulder.   7. Paquin's cut velvet dress, the swirls of its skirt stiffened and ruched with taffeta.

1949

The Paris spring collections showed two different yet equally sophisticated lines. One was narrow and moulded to the body's natural silhouette, with angular, asymmetrical interruptions such as sharp revers and back-wrapped skirts. Schiaparelli was the chief exponent of this line. Dior showed the alternative: an ample silhouette, with soft bulk in the skirt or torso, neatly belted in. This was an extension of his New Look. He used *trompe-l'oeil* devices such as huge jutting revers on dresses, giant collars which reached out beyond the shoulders, pockets placed high on the bodice or on the bust itself to emphasize the width of the bust.

7

The bust and hips, emphasis points for the last two years, were accentuated by the London couture as well as the French and American. The London collections had an air of formality and skirts were slightly shorter than those in Paris: Hardy Amies's were 15 inches from the ground.

Flare was a common theme throughout the international collections, and was a development of Dior's 'Envol' and 'Zig Zag' collections last year. A hint of flare, whether at the collar, at the back of the skirt or jacket, or in a jutting pocket, contrasted with and highlighted the

8. *Paquin's black wool suit with a sling of curved folds at the back.* 9. *Leathermodes' polished tar-black calfskin parka, tweed skirt.* 10. *Molyneux's grey-and-yellow check shirt dress and fringed stole with armhole slits.* 11. *Dior uses dropped shoulders and flounced sleeves to emphasize the width of the bodice above a tiny waist.* 12. *Mainbocher's short, double-collared Oxford grey wool jacket and silk crêpe drawstring blouse.* 13. *Jeanne Lafaurie's pale-green linen summer dress with a flared skirt and crossover bodice.* 14. Left: *Nina Ricci's black poplin dress. Rodier's fringed wool stole.* Right: *Bruyère's navy-blue wool dress and a navy-blue and white surah 'pied-de-poule' cape stole.* 15. *Hand-knitted stocking bodice with a long, lilac-pink rayon skirt.* 16. *Creed's black, braided zibelline redingote has a shoulder-wide, shingle-high Napoleonic collar.* 17. *H. & D.'s navy-blue rayon faille coat-dress.*

general simplicity of line. This, rather than any major innovation, was the overwhelming mood. In New York it appeared in the form of the little peplum jacket over a pencil line skirt, which was sometimes barrel pleated. Parisians favoured the soft stole, or the spirally-wrapped skirt, for both late day and evening. Numerous straight skirts in Paris had floating panels attached to the back or the side to soften the line and pockets added angularity, particularly at Fath. Piguet and Fath showed a number of dresses cut on diagonal lines.

Paris cocktail clothes were either high-necked and provocatively fitted or deeply décolleté. Various designers, particularly Balenciaga, presented abbreviated sleeves, so American *Vogue* advocated the new long glove, to continue the line along the arm. Despite the influence of Paris fashions, however, the practical simplicity of the evening shirt-waister still held sway in America. The American ready-to-wear collections were very well received this spring.

Textures were news this spring. Dior's hairy tweed and silk, nylon or cotton matelassé – a fabric with a raised woven design – were important. Many woollens had a damask-woven pattern, such as dots, or else were corded, nubbly, or even striped with rayon.

In the autumn the moulded line continued to be interrupted by asymmetrical details. The shoulderline was dropped and extended. A number of winter suits had large soft epaulettes, or huge collars, the latter especially at Molyneux. Jackets with back interest continued to be autumn favourites in Paris. Balenciaga introduced the middy blouse, which continued the unfitted style he had been presenting since the war. Initially popular for casual wear, it represented a movement away from the very fitted bodice and tightly cinched waist.

Coats this year tended to be fitted and tailored. The London coats had dramatic collars and cape shoulders. Hardy Amies showed coats with Danton collars, while Bellciano's belted coats had large saddle-bag pockets, flaring collars and leather belts and buttons. Many Paris coats this autumn were trimmed or lined with fur, especially beaver and Persian lamb. Fake fur was popular in America, notably for *après-ski* wear.

Like the Americans, the Italians were designing easy-to-wear colourful casuals, and *Vogue* consistently covered the Italian sportswear collections, particularly their knitwear and resort clothes.

A new garment for casual wear – the knitted 'stocking bodice', known in the sixties as the 'boob tube' – hit the fashion headlines. It could be worn with shorts on the beach or with a skirt for the evening.

Princess Galitzine opened her house in Rome this year and Ronald Paterson opened in London.

13

14

15

16

17

1950

Body line was the key term this year, as the sheath superseded New Look dresses. A shapely silhouette with an emphasized but unexaggerated bustline, angular hipline and seemingly endless legs was attainable as a result of developments in corsetry, such as the use of nylon and light elastic net. The elasticated cotton roll-on, a girdle with suspenders attached, now superseded the boned and padded corsets.

The designers of the most uncompromising sheaths were Dior, with his 'Vertical' line, and Schiaparelli, with her close-fitting sheaths. Daytime skirts were plumbline straight and shorter than last year – Dior's were 16 inches from the ground – although later afternoon and evening ensembles still tended to have wide skirts. Shoulder lines were generally natural, although sometimes swathed with drapery, at Fath, Piguet, Balmain and Dessès. Fath's 'optical illusion' hipband emphasized both the natural waistline, where it began, and the low waistline, where it ended. The daytime sheath was seen at all three main fashion capitals, but in London it was adapted so that it was more sympathetic to the natural female figure. Paris seemed to shout out its latest designs in a larger-than-life way, while London designers spoke in a quiet, conventional tone, offering well-designed clothes that were appropriate to the occasion.

The new Paris clothes were far from casual. Everything had to be co-ordinated: blouses matched suits, or the suit

1. Balenciaga's grey wild sheep's wool coat with voluminous dolman sleeves. 2. Traina-Norrell's cream whipcord short coat. 3. Hardy Amies's barrel-shaped tweed coat with shawl collar. 4. Trigère's black worsted crêpe trumpet coat with black felt mantelet. 5. Grès's huge, velvety wool wrap coat. 6. Balenciaga's sand duvetyne mantle coat. 7. Balenciaga's mustard tweed box jacket and white doeskin sleeveless underjacket. 8. Fath combines a slender skirt with flared jacket. 9. Charles Creed's oatmeal whipcord suit with black braid trim and velvet collar and cuffs. 10. Dior uses a stole cut in one with the jacket to achieve the oblique line on his grey flannel suit.

11. Larry Aldrich's wool jersey bodice sheath, trimmed with black braid, clinging from the bust to the hip. 12. Tina Leser's brilliant deep-red, ribbed wool bolero.

collar; dresses matched coats or coat linings. Attention to accessories was as important for style as the fashionable figure.

The 'Vertical' line for dresses made the streamlined 'middy' blouse popular. The bolero, with the width and warmth of a shoulder-hugging shawl, was another body-revealing shape. There were three main suit jacket lines this year. The box jacket, which was very successful in America, appeared at Capri, Traina–Norell, B. H. Wragge, Etta Gaynes, and Fath in Paris. It could be hip-length, cut away or reach just below the waist. The second shape was close-fitting, low buttoned, often with a horseshoe collar, and was shown by Dior, Balenciaga, Grès, Griffe and Hattie Carnegie. The third, low-waisted and bloused or loose,

was seen at Piguet and Schiaparelli. The accompanying skirts were invariably straight and narrow. Fath continued to design oblique revers and exaggerated pockets on jackets and coats.

Coats were either hip-length or long and many were full. Sleeves were often cut in one with the body of the coat and in Paris were used to emphasize the bust. Collars were small or non-existent. Balenciaga was the master of the collarless coat, dress or suit. In London some houses showed shawl collars and double-breasted coats. In America the coat novelty was Trigère's 'Trumpet' coat: a brief jutting coat that stopped short of the skirt flare. It was also shown at Dior. Short coats were important in America this year, invariably in pale shades and tailored with masculine

details such as velvet collars. Morton, Schiaparelli, Dior and Dessès experimented with the diagonal coat fastening.

The sheath was the most fashionable evening line. Fath and Schiaparelli showed short, elegant evening sheaths, in orange and yellow. The alternative this autumn was the balloon-like gown. Balenciaga led the field, designing a pumpkin skirt, or puff-ball similar to a Chéruit model of 1922, which Marc Bohan at Dior was to revive again in the late seventies. There was a shorter version for later afternoon. In contrast to the lavish mood in Paris, Mainbocher's evening designs were clipped and understated. Similarly American daytime suits were shorter and less exaggerated than their European equivalents.

Fabrics for day and evening wear were luxurious. Transparent fabrics were revived: chiffon, net, tulle, organdie and muslin were tailored in unusual ways. White and a dark colour was a sophisticated and popular combination.

The Italian master of printed silks, Emilio Pucci, opened his fashion house, Emilio, this year. Ben Zuckerman, who became renowned for tailored suits and coats in bold textures and for bright, jewel-coloured winter wear, launched his independent company in America, while in London Molyneux, threatened by blindness in his remaining eye, retired. Courrèges abandoned architecture to join the house of Balenciaga. In Paris the Associated Couturiers – Carven, Dessès, Fath, Paquin and Piguet – showed collections for the Printemps store.

13. Marcel Rochas's white mousseline (Bianchini Férier) dress with blue and yellow silk bodice, straps and sash.
14. Hardy Amies's short lace evening dress with tight, corset bodice of guipure lace, back-sashed skirt with a swathed hipline in navy-blue figured silk. The cartwheel is by Erik.
15. Molyneux's stiff sheath-tunic in black taffeta decorated with a green bow at the hip.
16. Dessès's cherry moiré sheath spirals up the figure and velvet-line stole.   17. Peter Russell's slim dress with a convolvulus waist. The skirt is of pewter poult and the bodice of grey embroidered satin.   18. Bonnie Cashin's brown polished silk shantung dress with a purple cast, cut in two pieces, with a folded skirt, inserting room for ease of movement.   19. Balenciaga's shorter version of the pumpkin-like, inflated skirt has a back-dipping hemline and an enormous loop of crisp matching taffeta forming a jutting wing at the back of the fitted bodice.
20. Dior's black wool trumpet-skir dramatically juts behind the knee. The long-haired fur cap and swathe of pearls set the line off.   21. Hartnell's knife-pleated silver lamé sheath, with velvet collar, belt and armhole binding, is decorated with a large lamé bow.

1951

Dior and Balenciaga showed a remarkable similarity of mood, which was surprising, given that their images of feminine chic had differed so radically in the past. It came about as a result of a change in Dior's approach: he now removed all padding, which had been the essence of his New Look, and abandoned artifice in favour of simple line and natural, body-conscious design – two elements which Balenciaga had always revered. However, in imitating, even subconsciously, Balenciaga's style, one is inclined to believe that Dior had peaked, for he had contributed, with passion, the New Look, the only look he really admired on women.

Both houses drew upon Chinese styling, showing mandarin collars, straight edge-to-edge jackets and coolie hats. Dior carved oval dresses with slim skirts that had the slightest godet at the back to give ease of movement. He also used draped pleats to add rounded softness. Balenciaga differed slightly here, in that he ignored pleats and kept the line close to the body.

Pleats were still a major theme in Paris: there were accordion-pleated skirts and panels, and whole dresses were knife-pleated. Fath pleated his skirts emphatically, often in panels to give movement. Castillo, who was now designing at the house of Lanvin, showed an important new line in dresses: they were collarless and constructed with the minimum number of seams. Accessories and details were very distinctive this year. Many necklines in Paris were trimmed with white and hats were unanimously tilted forward. Flowers were scattered across dress materials or posies were pinned to the body. American *Vogue* reported that costume jewellery was enjoying a revival.

Dior promoted the 'not bare' evening look with baroque, quaint necklines on simple, demure dresses. As a natural successor to his bouffant skirt of last year, Balenciaga designed dresses with hems that dipped at the back and curved up at the front, ballooning out over a narrow

1 & 2. Two black-and-white suits, from Balenciaga's and Dior's spring collections respectively. Both give a Chinese note to the suit: a mandarin collar, straight jacket and coolie hat. The shoulderline is rounded and soft, rather than padded and emphatic. Balenciaga's Chinese collarless paletôt is in black shantung. Dior's ensemble has an oval movement created by the rounded shoulders falling from a straight, stand-up mandarin collar bordered with shantung. The dress beneath is of an alpaca mix by Lesur, which is worn under a spencer in Bianchini Férier's natural shantung.

2

3

4

7. Balenciaga's beige
Ducharne wool coat has low-
placed buttons and black straw
hat.   8. Ben Zuckerman's
black-and-white wool coat
with a bright-red lining.
9. Trigères's reversible straight
coat with a crisp, shoulder-
covering collar. The coat is cut
in double-faced Lesur tweed:
one side chiefly black with
beige, the other side vice versa.
Shell-shaped black velvet hat
from Henry Bendel.
10. Hardy Amies's black ribbed-
pile wool bell coat with a bright
kingfisher-blue taffeta lining,
a big roll collar, wide sleeves
and two flap pockets. The
blue-and-black velvet hat is by
Simone Mirman.

6

3. Hattie Carnegie's black-and-white petit point worsted suit, with strict jacket fastened with smoky, baroque pseudo-pearl buttons, and blue velvet beret. 4. Traina-Norell's directoire jacket stops short at the bust, revealing the waist of the slim dress underneath, with its black silk faille top and pussy-cat bow. 5. Martini's black-and-white silk shantung copy of a Patou costume, polkadot scarf façade and long white gloves. 6. For his grey tweed suit Traina-Norell teams a fitted jacket with a neat, flat collar and a cartwheel skirt. The effect is one of maximum skirt under minimum waist and is accessorized with a sailor hat.

sheath. In London designers continued to create débutante-style tiered ball gowns and evening frocks. This typical London style persists even today.

Two major coat lines prevailed at the London collections: the more formal, fitted, high-waisted Princess silhouette, and the full tent line. Balenciaga's autumn coats were buttoned well below the waistline and had the longest revers in Paris, and Chinese-style band collars.

New York's ready-to-wear industry copying the Paris collections was fast and effective by the early fifties. Many of the copies were based on the various interpretations of the New Look and therefore most American suits still clung tightly to the waist and coats tended to swing from fitted waists. Hattie Carnegie sculpted her jackets following the Paris lead, while Norman Norell promoted the *directoire* jacket. American raincoats were particularly flattering and practical, as fabric-proofing was advanced, and manufacturers employed Parisian couturiers to design for them.

Important fashion casuals to emerge in America were the smock, which could be worn over straight trousers or with flared or straight skirts, and denim, particularly Levi Strauss jeans.

The British ready-to-wear industry was also producing high fashion with great speed and economy. Now that the austerity of the war was over, women

7

11

12

13

had a wide choice of off-the-peg fashions derived from Paris, New York and London couture. Frederick Starke had outlets in London and throughout the provinces and Dorville, Dereta, Hurel, Aquascutum, Alexon, Ladies Pride, Matita and Jaeger were all securing a significant section of the ready-to-wear market.

John Cavanagh opened in London and was acclaimed for his gently tailored 'Claridges' suits (for taking lunch at Claridges). His preference for the more formal suit rather than the heavier, English 'tailormade' offered by Busvine, Russell and Lachasse stemmed from his French training at Molyneux.

In Florence the Italian designers showed their collections in a concerted way for the first time. The show included the début collection of the young Roberto Capucci. Veneziani sportswear made headline news, continuing to remind the world of the quality and superiority of Italian sportswear.

Jimmy Galanos, who had trained with Carnegie, Piguet and Davidow, opened in California, as did Rudi Gernreich, with two partners. Galanos and Gernreich were to add great weight to American fashion.

14

15

11. Freddie Starke's natural-coloured shantung spring dress with narrow black piping, buttons and belt. 12. Lanvin-Castillo's new dress line: a loose bodice with exceedingly sloped shoulders and a stand-away collar. 13. Fath's dark-blue silk shantung dress has lace cuffs and is worn with Fath's rhinestone pin explosions and a big, flat hat. 14. Dior's softly full, long-sleeved black satin dress has a wide 'V' neckline, tied with a bow at the back and worn with graduated pearls, mink stole and oyster-coloured felt hat. 15. Capri's black linen dress buttoned with rhinestones. Bragaard hat of pointed felt petals piped in black. 16. Dior's short, covered dinner dress with narrow skirt, baroque neckline and puffy, knotted sleeves. The matching straight coat is bare-armed to reveal the dress's sleeves. 17. Patou's ample taffeta coat with strass-studded sleeves. 18. Balenciaga's black taffeta hem balloons out over a long, lace-covered, taffeta sheath. 19. Schiaparelli's white organdie kimono blouse with a wide, turn-back cuff. The Dognin material is embroidered with striped flower garlands. 20. Dior's printed silk summer frocks have pleated skirts, pussy-cat bows and sweetheart necklines.

16

17

18

19

1952

The London collections focused on texture rather than colour, concentrating on monochrome greys and beiges. There were three silhouettes: straight and square, soft and round, or puffed, curved and extravagant. Hartnell, Russell and Morton upheld their preference for precise tailoring. Their soft suit jackets tended to have set-in sleeves, cut-away fronts and shoulder-wide revers extending down to a low waist fastening, or were straight, belted Norfolks; all were worn over pleated skirts. Box jackets were an alternative, seen at Michael at Lachasse and Charles Creed.

Unlike London, Paris opted for colour this year: reds, pinks, oranges and greens. Full-blown floral prints and Paisleys blossomed on spring dresses: Dior used Ascher's rosebud chiffon (called 'Rose pom-pom'), a Japanese garden on surah, poppies on shantung and silk crêpe. The most popular summer print was a design of black leaves on a white background, seen at Griffe, Fath and Givenchy.

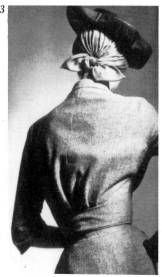

1. Michael at Lachasse's brushed velour jacket in a chessboard-check of olive-green and charcoal.   2. Balenciaga's stark poppy-red suit with flat-backed jacket and token belt at waist level.   3. Dior's mottled-grey wool blouson gathered into a high waistband and teamed with a matching skirt.   4. Givenchy fur-print, loose-hipped silk afternoon outfit.   5. Lo Balbo's pale-blue short jacket with a tiny waist and full skirt, and Tatiana's forward-tilting, blonde cartwheel hat.   6. Traina-Norell's pin-tucked fascia dress in fawn silk muslin.   7. Balenciaga's black wool dress with black satin bow.   8. Givenchy's black and white leaf-print dress.   9. Dior's jutting 'Profile'-line dress in grey empire ottoman, which stands out as two points of a square at the front and two at the back.

10. Ascher's famous 'Rose pom-pom' printed chiffon for Dior: a late day dress, bust-length jacket and belted red faille coat lined and scarved with chiffon. 11. Balenciaga's grey mousseline sheath dress encrusted with pearls and strass and tied with a wide, rose-pink faille ribbon. 12. Four bow-tied laces hold Herbert Sondheim's black silk peau d'ange dress to the rib cage. The midriff is lashed to its smallest circumference. Eisenberg jewellery. 13. Peter Russell puts a hug-me-tight stole, buttoning at the waist and tying at the back, over a black dress that has a fitted bodice. The immense whirling skirt is made of 200 graduated squares of Jacqmar material. 14. Schiaparelli's raspberry-coloured wool coat with a huge buckle strapped right across the bosom. 15. Dior's rever-less black wool coat and cone hat. 16. Lawrence's khaki-coloured poplin trench coat with raspberry poplin lining. 17. Dereta blanket coats in vivid colours are worn with Londonus drainpipe trousers and Gamba flat suede pumps.

The fashionable American summer dress featured the fascia – a wide waistband that drew attention to the rib cage. Alternatively, the 'middy-line' dress dropped the waistline to the hips, stopping on the way for a good cinch at the natural waistline too. London day dresses had halter necks and bodices that were soft over the bosom and hugged the ribs. Generously full skirts swept through the collections. The waist caught the eye at the Paris spring collections too. Low or high, its position was always emphasized.

Dior showed two very understated collections this year: his 'Sinuous' and 'Profile' lines. He now believed that 'the new essential of fashion is that it should be discreet'. The clothes were easy-moving and fluid. He showed three-piece sweater-look suits, reminiscent of Chanel's early work, and shirtwaisters with pleated skirts and high waists. Balenciaga presented the rectangular line this spring for suits and dresses: straight, completely unfitted box shapes. These were also seen at Lanvin–Castillo. Rochas, Schiaparelli and Dessès continued to show waisted suits, while Madeleine de Rauch showed both silhouettes.

American *Vogue* emphasized that 'clothes, like movies, are only good if they move. We want skirts we can step out of an automobile in without splitting their sides, sleeves that can reach for a telephone without straining their shoulders.' Skirts were easy-fitting, mostly styled on the triangle, cinched lightly at the waist. Traina–Norell showed the comfortable Norfolk jacket suit for the autumn, while Nettie Rosenstein combined slim dresses with loosely fitting cutaway jackets. Ben Zuckerman's dress-and-jacket ensembles were understated and unfitted. America provided the most forceful drive for comfortable, practical clothes, as Paris designers failed to satisfy these needs.

The autumn collections in both London and Paris featured the long supple torso, the neat little head. Some skirts were only 11½ inches from the ground. Waists were either moulded, bloused or fitted. The little black dress was recommended for every possible urban occasion. It could be either fitted like a sweater, bloused, double-breasted or have a deep V neckline, and in America often had a jewelled cowl and corset waist.

Navy blue was the alternative to black for evening dresses in France and America. Crêpe dresses of soft simplicity followed the line of the figure with gentle confidence, and relief embroidery was fashionable.

Givenchy opened this year, presenting his first collection in casual, inexpensive cotton. The prêt-à-porter company Chloé also opened in Paris.

18

pants, hemmed with a ball fringe and worn with Roman sandals.
19. Credo's yellow velvet trousers tapering to zipped ankles are worn with fitting black jersey blouse and black pumps.

19

1953

2 3 4 5

1. *Fath's round-shouldered silhouette: Leleu tweed suit.* 2. *Balenciaga's shantung bloused jacket with a white organdie bow at the waist.* 3. *Veneziani's red suit, cut loose through the waist and close to the hips, with a deep 'U' neck filled with a white-and-black polkadot taffeta scarf to match the little rounded hat.* 4. *Dior's black 'Tulip' suit with inflated bodice padded to curve out across the bust and to swell the shoulders into short, puff sleeves. The closely moulded waist slides into a straight stem skirt.* 5. *Harry Frechtel's matchbox jacket and skirt in water-blue bouclé wool.* 6. *Balenciaga combines the two high-fashion dress features, the unfitted neckline and the hip-level belt, on his beige and black print dress.* 7. *Dior's tweed princess-line dress.* 8. *Narrow lace tweed slate-blue dress by Elizabeth Henry, worn with a slate-blue pillbox by Elizabeth Hellier.* 9. *Viscountess Duncannon wears John Cavanagh's yellow silk print dress with a large wavy-brimmed hat by Simone Mirman.*

The coronation of Queen Elizabeth in June drew worldwide attention to London and its designers, who took the opportunity to create a series of court-inspired clothes and to promote traditional English fabrics. The colours and lines of evening dresses were clearly influenced by the coronation: white, pink, gold, mushroom and beige were offered in majestic silhouettes, and Hartnell, who designed the coronation gown, based his entire spring collection on white and gold.

English tweed was an important fabric for day wear in the Paris and London spring collections. Texture was more important than silhouette, since last year's high-waisted narrow line remained largely unchanged, although the unfitted neckline and the hip-length belt were two important fashion features. Dior showed his 'Tulip' line, the long body rounding out over the bust and shoulders in petal-shaped curves.

British *Vogue* applauded the work of the Italian designers. The spring collections of Veneziani, Fabiani and Simonetta included coats that were flat at the front and flared at the back, often with half martingales, and suits with skirts flaring slightly from the knees. Always renowned for their materials, this year's novelties were straw woven with cotton or wool, a white raffia laced with pink organza, and marbled and

6

7

8

9

10

12

11

chosen from the boutique or prêt-à-porter collections of the great houses, or came from the British ready-to-wear firms, but the column did not become truly exciting and young until innovative designers such as Mary Quant emerged in the late fifties.

The headline news from Paris this autumn was Dior's skirt – some 16 inches from the ground. Despite the fact that women had been wearing short skirts as recently as 1946, it was greeted with gasps of surprise. However, Dior offset the rise in hemline by raising the bustline to create an unbroken line, whether the skirt was full or straight, giving an illusion of length.

The autumn collections in London stressed the beauty of lace for the evening and the Americans presented grand evening dresses in a similar courtly style. However, Paris chose two other historical references: the Directory, with long, lean sheaths, and the Victorian, with huge bell skirts.

The stretch stocking was now available in America. Very sheer and flattering, clinging to the leg rather than wrinkling, and less likely to ladder, it changed the whole hosiery industry.

Bonnie Cashin opened her own studio in New York, collaborating with the manufacturer Philip Sills. Her distinctively avant-garde sportswear and layered co-ordinates, often made of leather, were prophetic of future decades.

double-printed silks. Straw accessories were popular.

British *Vogue* launched a new feature this spring entitled 'Young Ideas', inspired by American *Vogue*'s promotion of college and teenage fashion in its 'Under-Twenty Fashions' column started in 1947. 'We believe in an independent fashion for the young . . . a clean, uncluttered look, witty rather than frivolous, strictly practical and yet not incapable of fantasy.' The clothes were

10. *Grès's tight-fitting, long-sleeved jumper in shiny mohair bouclé over a sleek white jersey, roll-collared vest.   11. Fantasie's front-zipped boneless corselette in nylon elastic net and front-fastening, black nylon lace brassière.   12. McCardell's sleeved, clinging black jersey bathing suit with gilt-balled drawstring belt.   13. Hartnell's white and gold 'Coronation' range evening wear. Left: grosgrain evening coat. Centre: a chemise-topped white crêpe roman evening sheath decorated with chains of gold paillettes. Right: a white tulle débutante dress scattered with gold-centred lace daisies.   14. Dessès's white mousseline-de-soie sheath bordered with mink.   15. Germain Lecomte's draped rayon jersey evening gown.   16. Givenchy's bare-backed jersey sheath, shiny felt Chinese dish hat, giant lotus-flower earrings and Mancini's pagoda-toed satin slippers.*

13

14

15

16

17. *Givenchy's satin-bordered, mink-collared, four-fifths length black drap coat.*   18. *Balenciaga's beige wool patetôt jacket.*   19. *Silhouette de Luxe's copy of Dior's 'Dome Coat' in soft black-and-white tweed, broadly banded across the hips to emphasize the new length.*   20. *Fath's medieval-style grey flannel coat with Mandarin collar.*   21. *Hardy Amies's double-woven black-and-white tweed top coat, and velour hat by Vernier.* 22. *Grès's wool serge loose coat and dress, and Svend's little hat.*

1954

2

3

4

5

Chanel returned to the couture after a fifteen-year absence, partly due to the need to boost her scent sales by re-establishing fashion at the house, and partly to lead a rebellion against what she called the 'Fifties horrors' – the imprisoning, artificial fashions of the male couturiers. Her first collection was launched on 5 February and consisted of a return to the easy little suits that had made her name.

Jean Muir, who attended the launch, recalls how sceptical most of the fashion press was. Many journalists criticized Chanel for reviving fashions from her past and for offering little that could be considered innovative. Some, however, recognized that her easy, functional clothes might be a welcome relief from the tight-fitting, restrictive styles created by leading couturiers such as Dior, Fath, Balmain and Piguet. Muir was determined to see these liberating yet chic clothes made available to the ever-widening fashion-conscious public, and in fact Chanel's proven fashion phil-

osophy was vindicated – the house went from strength to strength. Chanel claimed that she no longer wished to dress just a few privileged women, but rather thousands of women.

Ease and softness characterized most collections, seeming to reflect Chanel's influence: nonchalant lines, soft bloused effects and simplicity. Dresses, for example, had tie belts rather than belts with buckles. Dior's spring collection was entitled 'Lily of the Valley'. Pale, subtle colours reinforced this relaxed mood, as did fabrics: new 'baby' tweeds, *cloqué* cottons, lace-printed organdies and non-iron fabrics like Orlon and nylon seer-

sucker. (Du Pont had introduced nylon in 1940 and Orlon in 1948.)

Fath and Balmain, however, were immune to Chanel's influence. Fath, especially, was marking time, insisting on dressing women in romantic Victorian jackets and skirts with flaring backs, which looked increasingly dated among the straight lines in Paris, London and New York.

The London collections saw the first set-in sleeves and square shoulders since the end of the war. Suits from Creed, Hartnell and Cavanagh were traditional in cut and colour. Beige was ousted by navy blue and grey. Tweed was the main

1. Chanel's navy-blue suit with square, slightly padded shoulders, comfortable, uncinched waistband, tucked blouse that buttons on to the skirt, neck bow and a sailor hat. 2. Charles James's black wool broadcloth princess-line coat. A satin panel runs from the shoulder yoke to the hip yoke. 3. Sybil Connolly's perfectly simple white-washed Donegal tweed coat with wide, shoulder-embracing collar. 4. Paterson's black-and-white printed facecloth seven-eighths coat with a large neck buckle to match those on the cuffs. 5. American spring coat: three-quarter-length in a very pale silver-beige moth-proofed cashmere and wool by Miten. 6. Michael's classic, tailored brown, white and grey tweed suit comprises loose, plumbline jacket with a stand-away neckline and slim skirt. Valerie Brill's tangerine hat. 7. Balenciaga's putty-coloured raw silk jersey suit with a stand-away tyre collar, kangaroo pockets and white starched cotton hat. 8. Sylvan Rich's black-and-white 'Kama Knit' tweed wool jacket and matching dress. The little hug-me-tight jacket is similar to a jumper. 9. Pertegaz's suit with enormous collar and piqué hat, folded like a table napkin.

6

7

8

9

10. Stanley Wyllin's black worsted jersey top and red-and-white cotton skirt, banded with black velvet rick-rack, open to reveal the underlying houseboy pants. 11. Chanel's formal dinner dress is tiered in a very modern material – bubbly nylon seersucker – in navy-blue and covered with full-blown roses. 12. Grès's white faille silk jersey dress is sculpted like an arum lily up across one shoulder, leaving the other bare. 13. Pertegaz's taffeta 'combining coat' is full-blown and flounced and bow-tied in bright sea-green. 14. Balenciaga's black wool sheath and white ermine bib.

fabric for American suits. 'She's hardly the horsey type ... yet there she is ... the smartest town suit ... in tweed.' The short, cut-off jacket was much more popular in America than in Europe.

One American contribution to fashion this year was the 'stocking dress' – a disposable version of the cotton-knit T-shirt dress. Several could be bought at a time and a fresh one worn every day.

The autumn collections from Paris were sharp and clean-cut, thanks to firm tailoring. Dior's 'H' line suggested 'the tapering figure of a young girl' by increasing the distance between the hips and the bust. His long, simple suits were reminiscent of riding habits, with narrow-shouldered, flat-fronted jackets flaring gently from the waist, over slender skirts. His dresses featured the 'Degas' and 'Tudor' bodices, which flattened the bust but were often balanced by wide ruched boat necks. Balenciaga also favoured the stand-away collar.

Loose, unfitted coats with martingales, placed high or low, were shown at Balenciaga and by Monte

Sano and Pruzan in America. Vogue approved of the ease and simplicity of this fashion: 'Ever since Balenciaga first took the tautness out of fashion, ease like this has been his going concern.' Softness prevailed at the London autumn collections. Many coats were narrow to the hem and collarless or had a huge collar the size of a cape. Fabrics continued to be the big story: tweeds of every weight

and texture, or towelling that was sometimes so fine it could be taken for silk. Fur, as in Paris, was an essential element. The ideal length for casual coats was two-thirds or seven-eighths.

Cardin opened his Eve boutique this year. Jacques Fath died and the house was taken over by his wife Geneviève, who continued to design the classic, feminine clothes for which it was famous.

15. Chanel's white wool jersey coat. 16. Fath's finest black nylon, lace-topped stockings, with rhinestones at the garter. 17. Left: beige Almanac stocking dress. Right: Garland's crew-necked black stocking dress. 18. Russek's copy of Balmain's leafy, paper taffeta jacketed dress. 19. Traina-Norell's 'Double Dress'. Left: a dotted blue and grey surah dress. Right: worn with a grey silk and wool sleeveless jumper dress.

1955

*The two silhouettes of 1955:
1. Dior's A-line: a two-part, late-day black faille dress with long torso tunic and high, square neckline. It is worn over a camisole dress that falls from the hips and a great black straw cartwheel. 2. Dior's straight, unwaisted line: a tunic coat in grey couvre over a straight sleeveless sheath that stops on the knees.*

Most designers were by-passing the waist this year and concentrating on long, straight, slender lines. Balenciaga showed tunic suits this spring, consisting of a tunic worn over a dress, while Lanvin–Castillo presented a twenties-influenced collection of long pleated skirts and simple jackets, worn with cloche hats. In London Cavanagh showed his 'Slink' collection – beltless, easy-fitting 'tube' dresses and suits. Traina–Norell showed a 'Pillar' silhouette this autumn – long narrow coats, dresses and suits. Contrary to this prevailing mode, Chanel decided to definitely waist her suits.

Natural colours and materials were the most fashionable for the spring, such as alpaca, linen, tweed and shantung in shades of grey, fawn and a new coppery-brown.

Dior evolved last year's 'H' line into the 'A' line, which was commercially successful and widely adopted. The 'A' line consisted of coats, suits and dresses flared out into wide triangles from narrow shoulders. The waistline was the cross bar of the A and could be positioned either under the bust in an Empire manner or low down on the hips. *Vogue* entitled it 'the prettiest triangle since Pythagoras'.

London lines were determinedly soft, enhanced by sashes, scarves and bows, flutters of pleats and gently rolled collars. There were a number of coat and dress ensembles, the coat lined with material that matched the dress or its sash. Fabrics and colours, too, were soft: tweeds, sheepskin, silks and surah in sugar-almond shades. Stiebel and Paterson both promoted flower prints. The exceptions to all this softness were the stiff, bright hessians that several houses used for top coats. The fashion show at the Mansion House organized by Lady Pamela Berry, president of the I S L F D, made the London collections the focus of a great social occasion.

By the autumn the close-fitting unbelted sheath was paramount in Paris.

Stoles and cape coats added bulk at the top, a silhouette similar to that of the early thirties. This top-heavy fashion was accentuated by hats pulled down over the brows and collars that rose up around the chin.

Maggy Rouff, Givenchy, Fath and Grès all presented asymmetrical lines of buttons on suits and coats. Many simple,

3

straight coats in Paris were merely vehicles for the opulent fur linings, collars and stoles that graced the catwalks. Racoon, nutria and mink were the most fashionable furs, whether in a full coat, collar, gilet or muff, and were cut to be as supple as fabric.

For the evening the full-length narrow sheath, coiled and draped at Dior, Lanvin-Castillo, Griffe, Heim and Fath, perfected the fashionable long slender line. Fath created the new wide-shouldered look with ballooning sleeves and Dior called his version the 'Y' line. Maxime de la Falaise showed a new line that Saint Laurent was later to evolve: the 'Bandeau' dress. It featured a décolleté shaped like a brassière, the cut-away back highlighted by a bow.

There was a pervasive Eastern influence in the autumn collections: mandarin collars, straight jackets and tunics all reappeared. Black and white continued to be important in Paris and white collars, bodices and pantaloons were popular.

American designers picked up Dior's 'A' line this autumn and applied it to coats. The alternative was the narrow coat, which was scarcely wider at the hem than it was across the sloping shoulders and cut in camel hair or a fur-trimmed fleece.

Bazaar, Mary Quant's boutique, opened on the King's Road, London, this year. Her clothes were selected and designed entirely for those under twenty-five. It was the first expression of the 'youthquake' that was to shake the fashion industry and evolve a totally new attitude to dress.

4    **5**    **6** 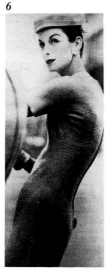   **7**

3. Left: *Ricci's grey polkadotted linen dress and paletôt jacket. Right: Montaigne's silk taffeta dress with large white dots has a side kick of godets at the knee. The sun hat is from Rose Valois. 4. Balenciaga's collarless, wide-shouldered sheath is double-buttoned below an unfitted waist. It is worn with a black velvet toque and sleek seal tie. 5. Givenchy's boutique collection: Orlon knitted tunic-sweater to be worn in the evening over the slimmest summer sheath. 6. Givenchy's long, lean collarless dress in oatmeal tweed is short-sleeved and semi-fitted. 7. Cavanagh's beige-and-white Shetland tweed 'Slink' dress. 8. Fath's Mongolian lambskin loose, shaggy coat. 9. Ronald Paterson's A-line parasol coat in white Irish linen. 10. A Traina-Norell 'Pillar'-line navy-blue wool coat worn with a slim wool and satin dress.*

8   **9**   **10**

11. *Chanel's simple white satin evening suit.*   12. *Capucci's red ottoman silk ball dress with sloping hemline.*   13. *Fath's lamé evening coat is collared and cuffed with mink and worn with a straight, brocade sheath dress.*   14. *Traina-Norell's evening pillar of black wool with a satin bodice.*   15. *Susan Small's narrow 'slink' dress in dusty-pink lace is swathed with satin at hip level to accentuate the long-bodied look.*   16. *Givenchy's slender off-white satin evening dress with a wide bâteau neckline. The coat is a sheath of pale-yellow satin, cut to stay open.*   17. *Lanvin-Castillo's twenties-style pleated skirt and slightly fitted, simple jacket with a scarf collar.*   18. *Balenciaga's mid-thigh-length tunic line is unbroken save for the low pockets in pale-beige herringbone linen.*   19. *McCardell's spice-coloured Jasco ottoman ribbed worsted jersey suit with blouse and lining of kumquat-coloured silk.*

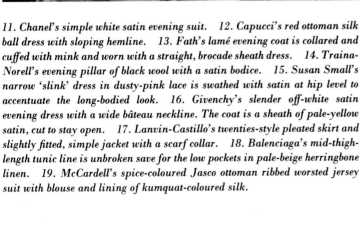

1956

The three dominant themes in Paris this spring all centred on the waistline: waists were raised for *directoire*-style dresses, jackets were cropped at Dior and Lanvin–Castillo, and bodices were bloused. Patou used blousing above slim skirts, Chanel above the hipbands of jumper suits and top coats, and Balmain's frocks were sometimes bloused only at the back. The young American interpretation of the bloused waistline was the drawstring.

Balenciaga softened his classic suit this spring into a slightly slimmer shape. Carrying this softer theme into the evening, he showed a series of flimsy lace dresses, with ribbon-threaded skirts. Givenchy's suits had pouch-back jackets tapered neatly at the hips. The pouch was achieved by a deep, inverted pleat or sometimes an over-panel. American *Vogue* considered the cropped jacket the answer for spring wear.

Colours this spring were gentle and natural and there was a profusion of flowered prints. Large hats as light as thistledown were frequently swathed in tulle. Jewelled brooches decorated the

hips, shoulders and *directoire* waistline.

In general most dresses in London were simply cut on clean lines. Stiebel presented a distinctive summer collection in deep, rich colours, in contrast to the greys and muted blues of other designers. For the evening he used rich satins in pale yellows, pinks and vivid marigolds. 'Diamond' cutting was this year's variation on the traditional London ball dress.

By the autumn ingenious drapery was widely used to accentuate the soft, flowing *directoire* line, notably at Givenchy, who used swathes of material at the front of dresses to create a tunic effect.

Fath, however, favoured the natural waistline. Dior's skirts shot down the leg, but there was too much eye-catching modern design available for this essentially backward step to succeed. As the chemise became shorter, more youthful and less restrictive it became mainstream fashion for the young. This simple shape was to be shortened and its formality discarded – the mini was perceptibly on the horizon.

The colour story in Paris this autumn was sombre: black was supreme, set off by grey, bronze and brown. The Prince of Wales check was a seasonal favourite. Accessories complemented the revival at some houses of an Edwardian style:

1. *Marie Rivetti's high-waisted redingote in grey-and-black tweed.* 2. *Patou's bloused black-and-white polkadot dress.* 3. *Givenchy's empire-line dress, with swathes of grey wool fabric pushed to the front to imitate a tunic, and grey suede belt.* 4. *Stiebel's navy-blue wool dress faced with white piqué.* 5. *Hardy Amies's black velvet dress and jacket.* 6. *Balenciaga's white linen nine-tenths jacket, tie-belted, and black dress.* 7. *Grès's kitten-soft camelhair coat with hood and two large breast pockets.* 8. *Left: a three-quarter-length yellow poplin coat; right: pink poplin seven-eighths-length coat by Quelrayn.* 9. *Hartnell's square, hip-length overjacket of white velour with red fox fur lapels.* 10. *Givenchy's putty-coloured, seven-eighths linen coat over a slim, sleeveless dress.*

235

muffs, and long, flat handbags. A pre-First World War mood also affected the ready-to-wear collections. Hartnell's autumn lines were asymmetrical and with a low flare, imitating last year's version in Paris and London. Suits were fitted, the skirts slim with hip yokes and a hint of drapery across the pockets.

Capes of all lengths were important, while in Paris top coats often narrowed to the hem, echoing the cape silhouette and last year's 'Y' line. For the autumn American *Vogue* promoted the 'cape-costume' – a cape that was as close-fitting as a suit jacket.

Coat sleeves were either set very low, as at Dior, or in a forward-thrusting armhole giving a curved outline, as at Balmain. A swaddled cocoon-like shape was also fashionable this autumn, achieved by lining capes and coats with fur. In Paris and London fur continued to be a favourite material, particularly for hats: busbies, shakos, cossack hats and Robinson Crusoe cones.

Capucci showed the outstanding 'Rose' line ball dresses in heavy, rich satin. The skirts were ingeniously cut from a single piece of material which was then tucked and folded to form the petals of a rosebud.

Italian sportswear from Morsa, Pucci and Spagnoli continued to be gay and colourful, while in London Teddy Tinling designed highly fashionable tennis outfits, many of which were worn by Wimbledon contestants.

11. Dianora of Florence's cotton shirt, hand-painted with brush strokes, and pirate pants painted black on white.   12. Teddy Tinling tennis outfits. Left: a thick white waggle piqué dress with a high scalloped neckline and scalloped skirt. Right: a trim dress of heavy white linen patterned with drawn threads, with a swirl of hip pleats.   13. Dior's classic Prince of Wales check suit.   14. Kasper's short black wool jacket and straight, black-and-white checked wool dress.   15. Leathermodes' black capeskin sweater and straight, knitted skirt.   16. Freddie Starke's scarf-stole, dipped at the back of the butter-coloured wool suit.   17. Lachasse's easy-fitting ginger-and-grey suit with draped shoulders.

18. *Fath's black-and-white early-evening dress. The bodice is of white organdie, and the dress is decorated with three black velvet butterfly bows.* 19. *Griffe bands white chiffon up under the bust of his high-waisted, balloon-shaped evening dress with sheer bodice and braid-edged cap sleeves.* 20. *Dior's dress in black wool, silk and Acrilan (a fabric from the British house of Seckers) with sarong drapery caught up under the bust.* 21. *Balmain's satin evening coat registers the high waist with a bow placed between the shoulder blades and a long, draped back panel.* 22. *Ricci's slate-grey taffeta cape and short, beaded sheath dress.*

1957-1967

Whaam! *by Roy Lichtenstein, 1963.*

Wow! Explode! The Sixties. It came to life in a pure, exaggerated, crazed out, wham, wham, wow way. The Beatles, Hendrix, Joplin, the Velvet Underground exploding so wonderfully.

Betsey Johnson, New York, 1983

Teenage street fashion – the winkle-picker boot.

Jack Kerouac, the pioneer of reckless freedom, depicted in On the Road.

In the late fifties, fashion was to defy: parents, society, even gravity, as it rose from the street to the couture salons, from daughters to their mothers. Contrary to popular belief, it was *not* Mary Quant who introduced the mini skirt – the fashion symbol of the era. It was born on the streets among art students and Mods. What Quant did achieve was fashion democracy; appropriate, witty clothes were now available, appropriately priced. The mini (between 4 and 10 inches above the knee) was a defiant statement by youth against its elders, encapsulating what the young chose to question. What relevance had couture to their lives? Why should they look grown up? Why couldn't girls look aggressively sexy and take the sexual initiative? Contraception was in their hands now.

The young have always been rebellious. The difference now was that they had independent incomes and could pay for the lifestyle they wanted. By the mid-fifties the real income of teenagers was 50 per cent higher than before the war. In 1956 there were five million teenagers in Britain, four million of them working. The average American teenager had $400 a year, most of which was spent on clothes, cigarettes, records and cosmetics. In Britain a young secretary or hairdresser earned £12 to £15 a week by the mid-sixties. Perhaps half that would be spent on clothes by the very fashion-conscious but prices had to be kept down. Novelty, not quality, mattered. The rule at Quant was that shirts were to retail at no more than £5 and use no more than $2\frac{1}{2}$ yards of material. The most expensive dress at Biba in the late sixties would have been about £7, and the average price £2 10s.

More teenagers were living away from home, gathering in large cities to work or study. They no longer questioned their elders; they simply ignored them. The codes of behaviour and modes of dress that evolved expressed their tastes, their values and their viewpoint.

Clothes were, as ever, a password to a chosen social set, and the counter-cultures that emerged throughout the period had their own dress distinctions, identifiable often by the men's styles. The beat generation 'dropped out' in

Greenwich Village, New York, emulating their idols Jack Kerouac, William Burroughs and Allen Ginsberg. These cool young intellectuals, who denounced materialism, professed anarchy, listened to modern jazz, read poetry out loud in cafés and experimented with drugs, were recognizably dressed in old jeans, loose jumpers and sandals, and had shaggy hair and beards.

A Parisian Beat café, the girls dressed like Juliette Greco.

In Paris the Existentialists, similarly attired, read Sartre and Camus, and congregated on the Left Bank to question not only de Gaulle's conservatism but also existence itself. In London the Teddy Boys mimicked the sartorial splendour of the Edwardians in drainpipe trousers and long, velvet-collared jackets. The Rockers, or Ton-up Kids, in thick black leather astride their motorcycles, seemed to threaten the public; the clean-cut Mods wore 'Chelsea garb' and cruised on motor scooters. Girls, influenced by American rock and roll fashion, wore tight jumpers over falsies, or torpedo-shaped brassières, and skirts that were full, held out by layers of nylon petticoats, or pencil slim.

For Madge Garland, who was Professor of Fashion Design at the Royal College of Art, the tremendous social changes in the late fifties seemed so profound that she decided to retire. Professor Janey Ironside, who succeeded her at the RCA, recalls that 'The students did not like the couture or what it stood for; they were nearly all working-class and had never known the life they saw pictured in *Vogue*.'

The young wanted to savour their youth and wanted clothes to reflect the way they felt. 'To me adult appearance was very unattractive, alarming and terrifying, stilted, confined and ugly. It was something I knew I did not want to grow into,' said Mary Quant. Young designers with various training or none at all began to design clothes for their peers. They had no allegiances to Paris couture or to manufacturers. Most were undercapitalized but achieved success through their hard work and enthusiasm, a press eager to feature these novelties, and a market hungry to buy new images.

There were three main avenues for young designers: they could set up a boutique, join a couture house and hope to rise to a position of design authority, or operate a wholesale business selling their wares to receptive department stores. There were all too few of the latter, but some designers who could not afford their own shop secured a 'boutique operation' – a couple of rails featuring their name – in big stores such as Woollands' Over 21 Shop and Peter Robinson's Top Shop in London, and J. C. Penney's in America.

Of the new designers, Mary Quant was the most articulate, businesslike and directed in her rebellion against the traditional bastions of fashion dictatorship. She, her husband, Alexander Plunket-Greene, and their manager, Archie MacNair, represented their generation's dissatisfaction with the squalor and boredom of the post-war world. 'We were rather socialist; partly because we had no money and partly because a lot of our generation thought that things were unjust,' explained Plunket-Greene. 'We wanted to increase the availability of fun, which should be available to everyone. We felt that expensive things were almost immoral and the New Look was totally irrelevant to us.'

Mary Quant.

Quant's Bazaar, which opened in 1955 on the King's Road, Chelsea, was the first boutique to offer cheap clothes designed to appeal specifically to the young. Originally Quant had not intended to make her own clothes but she could not find suitable stock and few manufacturers were sympathetic to

The dizziness of Bridget Riley's black and white Op Art, 1964.

Op Art decorates high fashion, Richard Anuszkiewicz's painted coat for Georges Kaplan's Fur Boutique and Moya Bowler shoes, 1965.

David Bailey.

her strange demands (for example, she asked established knitwear companies to lengthen their classic cardigans by eighteen inches so that she could sell them as mini dresses). She hurriedly attended night classes, bought material from Harrods and made up her stock in her Chelsea bedsitter. The 'gear' had to sell within twenty-four hours of arrival in the shop so that materials could be bought to restock. And it did. Bazaar was a sensation, with a permanent queue waiting to get in.

Amazed parental silence witnessed this terrific trade. The idea that teen-agers should choose their own clothes seemed to be a radical and defiant stand against propriety, and members of the Establishment were outraged by the clothes, which they thought perverse. 'Snobbery has gone out of fashion,' announced Quant. Her fashion democracy meant that girls and young women could have instant fashion that was made for *them*, not watered-down versions of designs for countesses and film stars. Dictates from Paris were now irrelevant. When the shift shape was shown in Paris salons in 1957, the fashion world began to take Bazaar seriously, for the new line had appeared there eighteen months earlier. Within seven years Quant's business was worth a million pounds and was supplying 150 shops in Britain and 320 stores in America. Bazaar became a well-known meeting place and Chelsea ceased to be just a part of London – it became a way of life.

Young designers emerging from the fashion and art schools were encour-aged by Quant's success to set up their own workshops. Kiki Byrne presented perfect geometric lines as early as 1960 in her King's Road boutique, Glass and Black. Her impeccably designed, well-made clothes were the strongest London fashion statement between 1960 and 1963. Sally Tuffin and Marion Foale graduated from Janey Ironside's course in 1960 and set up a workroom off Carnaby Street, which John Stevens was making fashionable. Their shift dresses were printed with modern American art, pop art, targets, triangles and zigzags of primary colours, and the silhouette became less important than the pattern on it. Along with John Bates, they were the first designers to present the mini, which had been creeping up art students' legs since 1959.

The mini officially arrived in high fashion circles in 1962. Its crowning moment was attended by Marit Allen, a junior fashion editor on *Vogue*, and Ronald Traeger, who photographed the two models wearing thigh-high minis in a street in Shepherd Market, London. The significance lay not only in the brevity of the skirts but also in the style of the photography – street reportage. The stunned looks of the passers-by were genuine: they had never seen anything like it.

The new manner of photography was influenced by William Klein's work in the late fifties, which used lamp-posts, scenes of urban dereliction or passing traffic. Static tableaux were superseded by active, aggressive photo-graphs taken with hand-held cameras, often using a telephoto lens for foreshortening, by David Bailey, Terence Donovan, Brian Duffy and Peter Knapp as well as Ronald Traeger. Bailey's photographs reinforced the sexuality of the girl; her attire was incidental. 'Well, a frock's a frock, isn't it?' (Bailey). Models became household names thanks to pop art and advertising's promotion of the cult of personality, and in turn, image-makers were idolized in the media. Antonioni's film *Blow Up* (1966) valorized Bailey and the photographer was now honoured with the status of a fine artist.

Bailey's raw talent, combined with his realization that a good picture could be ruined by poor layout, challenged the hierarchy of glossy magazine staff as he extended the photographer's influence within the magazine: 'You see, the difficulty with editorial people is that they're not visual people, they're basically writers. The visual is at the mercy of the pen.' Now fashion editors associated with designers, photographers and artists in a period of cross-fertilization.

London was completely self-absorbed. There was less interest in waiting for clothes to arrive from Paris collections to be reverently recorded on the glossy pages of the magazine than in participating in fashion being invented on the spot. Page after page of home-grown fashion was shown in British *Vogue* as editors spent their days scuttling from studio to studio, getting a milliner, for example, to make a hat to match the coat made by one designer to complement the dress made by another. This was one of British *Vogue*'s most creative and patriotic periods under Beatrix Miller's strong editorship. An equivalent, nationally orientated editorial approach coloured the pages of American *Vogue* under Diana Vreeland in the late sixties.

None the less London was not the only source of fashion. Clare Rendlesham, who worked on the Young Ideas pages of British *Vogue* until 1961, believes that the origins of change can be traced to a handful of designers in London – Quant, Tuffin and Foale, and Jean Muir at Jane & Jane – and Paris – Michelle Rosier, Christian Bailley at V de V and Emanuelle Khanh. As they gained strength through national recognition, these designers began to export their ideas. Quant's first trip to New York in 1959 led the way. Within a fortnight of her unannounced arrival she had been taken up by the doyens of New York fashion: Sally Kirkland, Eugenia Shepard, Rosemary McMerture and the women of the Tobé agency. *Life* magazine featured 'the Quants' in a six-page welcome to America.

American interest in fashion and music trends in Europe, especially in Britain, escalated during the early sixties. It was the Beatles who made Quant; for the first time a style of dress could be identified with a style of music, a style of life. The mini and the Beatles made their impact on America simultaneously in 1964 and were inextricably linked. The Beatles, their 'birds' and what they wore were big news and big business. To Plunket-Greene it seemed that within weeks American youth had embraced London as the world's fashion capital and Quant as its best-known designer.

J. C. Penney, an American chainstore with 1,600 outlets, was first to offer the London mode to American youth. Englishman Paul Young, a manager there, decided in 1963 that an up-to-the-minute promotion of European youth fashion would revamp the store's image. Having met Quant, he decided to concentrate on her work and signed a licensing agreement that was to last ten years. Initially the chain found it difficult to tune into the English Mod look. Betsey Johnson, one of the few rebellious, untrained young American designers who determined fashion during this period, recalls with amusement that when the mini was first marketed in J. C. Penney's, the manufacturers, fearing that American customers were too conservative to accept the mini, had dropped the hem by 8 inches!

The fashion was to look as childlike as possible – coltish, long legs, flat torso and attention focused on a big baby-eyed head. Bobby socks, footballers' socks and novelty stockings accentuated legs, armholes were cut high to make the torso appear long and skinny and shoulders were deeply inset to give an angular silhouette. At its briefest the mini skirt could no longer be worn with stockings, as suspenders and garters would be revealed, so tights were introduced. They paraded every form of contemporary decoration – from op art to clocks – and the introduction of Lurex and Trilobal

Scene from Antonioni's Blow Up, *a film which recorded the London fashion scene through the eyes of a jaded fashion photographer, 1966.*

Lady Clare Rendlesham, the British Vogue *fashion editor.*

The Beatles.

The team at Paraphernalia: foreground, left, Betsey Johnson, centre, Diana Dew, right, Paul Young.

The Beat face, 1962.

The Space Girl face, 1966.

The Biba face.

Still from the film The Knack; *a queue of girls in the 1966 fashion essentials – skinny rib jumpers and hipster skirts.*

nylon gave a shimmer from ankle to thigh. Underwear changed; girdles and corselettes were replaced by the mini brief and Gernreich's 'no-bra' bra. Eventually the brassière was discarded altogether. Every fashion tenet was challenged and broken.

The 'total look' was dependent not only on clothes but also accessories: jewellery, shoes, boots, wigs and make-up. The face was the key to the fashionable look: be it the kohl-black eyes, pale complexion and beehive hairstyle of the Beat woman, or the false eyelashes, silver metallic wig and frosted pink lips of Courrèges's or Ungaro's space girl, or the plum-coloured lipstick, putty-coloured foundation and Pre-Raphaelite locks of the Biba girl. Accessory designers became important: Roger Vivier and Charles Jourdan for shoes, Corocraft for throwaway jewellery, Oliver Goldsmith for spectacles, Alexandre and Vidal Sassoon for hairstyles and wigs, James Wedge for hats.

James Wedge's and Pat Booth's two shops Top Gear and Countdown on the King's Road were among the boutiques that sold the total look – clothes from Tuffin and Foale, Laura Ashley, Dorothée Bis and Emanuelle Khanh, and James Wedge's jewellery and millinery, which included John Lennon's memorable leather cap. The latest fads would sell out or go out of fashion within a matter of hours; Wedge recalls being stuck with 5,000 black 'skinny-ribs' only twenty-four hours after they had been all the rage. One of Wedge's most amusing successes was his chorister mini dress. He saw a choirboy walking into a church and asked the vicar if he could buy a smock. The vicar was taken aback but accepted two pounds for it and within a couple of hours Wedge had sold it for three in the shop. He returned and ordered a hundred and for the next month girls were spotted on the King's Road wearing white starched choristers' smocks as mini dresses.

Top Gear's windows were blacked out like a target and the clothes swung from scaffolding; at Countdown, sheet-aluminium walls and rocket-shaped changing rooms evoked space travel. At Biba, the fashion emporium of Barbara Hulanicki, the clothes were presented amidst a profusion of peacock feathers, tassels and beads. Gone were the days when one studied the quality of the merchandise under strip lighting; the dark, mysterious store had arrived. Biba kept one pace ahead of the mood on the streets. Its strength lay in colouring and accessories and it was popular for its dyed T-shirts, minuscule bikinis, cloche hats, beads, satin day wear, sultry make-up and berry colours. Trendsetters squeezed their way into these crammed, joss-stick scented caverns, where they couldn't even push in front of a mirror to try on the clothes; they simply bought and left.

In sharp contrast, the fashion scene in America was very conservative. Tuffin and Foale, amongst the first fashionable young London designers to visit America, were amused to learn that American fashion buyers could be seen wearing their 'hip London gear' during working hours but would discard it for more conservative styles in the evening.

Jacqueline Kennedy, as First Lady of the United States from 1961 to 1963, was instrumental in portraying and defining an emergent American style. A young and attractive fashion-plate, she took great care to promote American designers, notably Oleg Cassini, her official dress designer, and Halston, her milliner. Although her look was quintessentially French, in that it was a pastiche of Balenciaga's and Chanel's besuited chic, she made it an American one in the eyes of the public. Her appealing, fashionable style was brought to a wider audience than ever before by television, inspiring many American women to follow her sartorial example.

In 1962 the Council of Fashion Designers of America was founded, with Norman Norell as president. An honorary, non-profit-making society, its purpose is to further fashion design as an expression of American culture, to establish codes of professional practice, to improve public and trade relations, and to promote international appreciation of the American fashion arts.

Bonnie Cashin was one of the few American designers to contribute to the changes in fashion in the early sixties. She created advanced sportswear such as leather separates and hooded dresses, and promoted the layered look.

In 1965 Paul Young opened Paraphernalia in New York, the first 'Mod' shop in the country. A close friend of Emanuelle Khanh, Paco Rabanne and Daniel Hechter in Paris and Mary Quant in London, Young imported the best young European fashions. He also employed American designers such as Betsey Johnson and Diana Dew to create home-grown interpretations. These included disposable paper dresses, dresses that grew when watered at night (the material was paper embedded with bean-sprouts), and kinetic light dresses that lit up when the wearer moved. 'People really thought of their clothes as a statement of where they were at,' says Johnson, who was inspired by Andy Warhol, London Rockers and Californian Hell's Angels motorcycle gangs. She designed tight, sexy bike gear with big zips and studs, shifts with contemporary art dancing across them, T-shirt dresses and Quant- and Muir-inspired English schoolgirl clothes.

It was a time of unrestrained creativity in which the pre-eminence of youth and its preoccupation with itself and 'now' were constantly reiterated. Social realism and the media were influencing painters, film producers, musicians and fashion designers alike. The motifs and expressions captured in the art of Peter Blake, Richard Hamilton, Roy Lichtenstein, Jasper John and Robert Rauschenberg, the *nouvelle vague* films of François Truffaut and Jean-Luc Godard, the writings of Colin Wilson, John Braine, Colin McInnes, James Baldwin and Jacqueline Susann, the music of the Beatles, Rolling Stones and James Brown, the frocks of Mary Quant, Ossie Clark, Emanuelle Khanh and Betsey Johnson – all were born of a similar youthful interest in the popular, the uncomplicated, the immediate. Popular art met popular culture on the clothes of the young 'Mod' dresser. The exhibition of Bridget Riley's op art pictures at the Museum of Modern Art in New York in 1965 was, much to her fury, pre-empted by boutique dresses printed with copies of her pictures, while Duggie Field's pop art was emblazoned on Zandra Rhodes's materials.

The couture was inevitably affected. At first the traditional houses chose to ignore the emerging influence of youth, although some gave the young a chance to express their talent. During Dior's final illness in 1957 Yves Saint Laurent's hand was evident on the 'Spindle', or loose chemise, collection. Yves Saint Laurent became head of the house in 1958, at the age of twenty-one, and continued to experiment with loose, geometric shapes in his 'Trapeze' collection that year and the 'Puff Ball' collection in 1960. In 1961 some of Saint Laurent's associates thought he was straying too far from the exclusive environs of the couture when he presented Brando-inspired bikers' jackets in crocodile and mink. Saint Laurent knew that high fashion needed popular youth culture to inject new verve into the stale atmosphere of the couture, but his associates did not recognize this. By 1962 he had left Dior and opened Yves Saint Laurent, which was to be one of the greatest couture houses of the following decades. Saint Laurent frequently visited London during the sixties to find inspiration in the boutiques on King's Road.

Barbara Hulanicki of Biba.

Edie Sedgwick, the Warhol girl.

Yves Saint Laurent, victorious on the balcony of the Maison Dior, following his début collection for them in 1958.

André Courrèges, 1968.

Emanuel Ungaro.

Lady Annabel Birley, wearing a Wallis copy of Chanel, and her daughter, India Jane.

Inspired by the innovations and success of the young British designers, many couturiers in Paris, New York, London and Rome concentrated on the simple, childlike lines of the 'chemmy', collarless, cuffless and naïvely decorated with a large bow across a high waist, similar to the Quant schoolgirl fashions. Pierre Cardin experimented with geometric clothes in his Eve boutique, perfecting his fluid line and acidic colours by the mid-sixties, while Balenciaga, who trained Courrèges and Ungaro, offered the most daring and severe shapes of all.

Throughout this 'youthquake' Chanel continued to impress her classic mark on popular fashion. From about 1958 her clothes, or their ready-to-wear copies, became a part of every fashionable woman's wardrobe. Chanel had an original way of making suits. Rather than using canvas interfacing between the mohair or tweed and the silk lining to hold the shape of the jacket, she quilted both layers together with horizontal and vertical rows of stitching, one and a half inches apart. Consequently, the jacket would be as soft as a cardigan and easy to move in, but the quilting maintained the silhouette. She also inserted gilt chains along the hem of the jacket, which kept it down.

One of Chanel's most successful emulators was Jeffrey Wallis, who copied her models in precise detail and identical materials and sold them through his Wallis shops in England within ten days of the couture release date, at one-tenth of the couture price. In the late fifties, when Wallis's copies had been appearing for several seasons, Chanel acknowledged that the worldwide sales of his excellent replicas had stimulated her scent and boutique sales, and offered him twelve garments a season to copy rather than the usual two.

The first couture minis were presented simultaneously in 1961 by Marc Bohan at Dior and André Courrèges. Financially stable houses such as these could afford opulent staging and accessory back-up to accentuate a mode. Courrèges's 'Space Age' collection of 1964 combined the Parisian traditions of perfect cut, the best and latest materials, a powerful publicity machine and show-stopping thematic presentations with London's daring young styles. Using ice pinks and blues against stark white, his garments were cut into simple shapes outlined by welted seams. Though childlike in their short, shift-shape simplicity and worn with baby bonnets and flat toddler sandals, they were worn by the most sophisticated women.

Christian Bailley at V de V and Emanuelle Khanh were the mainstays of the French avant-garde, and made Saint-Germain the Chelsea of Paris fashion. Bailley changed the look of skiwear to black ciré body clothes in 1962 and introduced coats in 'cigarette paper' and silver plastic in the mid-sixties. In 1963 Khanh made the dramatic leap from being a model at Balenciaga and Givenchy to designing clothes for the embryonic French prêt-à-porter market, represented by firms such as Belletête and Cacharel and boutiques like Dorothée Bis and Laura. She also introduced the Italian ready-to-wear of Missoni, Krizia, Max Mara and Bistro du Tricot to Paris.

In Milan Tai and Rosita Missoni were extending the possibilities of knitwear. Tai Missoni's career in fashion began when he designed the ski clothes for the Italian Olympic ski team, of which he was a member. In 1958, influenced by the American stocking dresses, they designed their first knitted dresses. In the early sixties, having found some abandoned 1920s knitting machines that could knit twenty different coloured yarns a row, they revived decorative knitting. Tai Missoni experimented with dyeing and knitting techniques, while Rosita Missoni developed the fashion shapes, and thus the

'Italian knit' made its entrance on the fashion stage. Between 1964 and 1966 they collaborated with Emanuelle Khanh on four collections that were international successes.

Textile designers and fabric houses felt a strong sense of collaboration in a couturier's creations, as their materials often stimulated a designer's imagination and suggested themes. Nattier (a name adopted by the Italian firm of Azzario to overcome the prejudice of the Parisian couture against foreign manufacturers) was the first fabric house to promote the black-and-white houndstooth pattern that became a hallmark of the period. Their triple gabardine, which could be moulded like plasticine, was directly responsible for the type of clothes designed: because of its weight, the clothes had to be short and close to the body; without it, Courrèges could not have achieved his space-age look.

Textiles also influenced the work of Ossie Clark and Celia Birtwell. Using her romantic painted chiffons, voiles and satins Clark created slinky, romantic, thirties-style lines and reintroduced Hollywood glamour and nostalgia to fashion. He owed much to Bernard Nevill's fine tuition at the Royal College of Art.

In 1966 *Time*'s article extolling 'Swinging London' coincided with the year of the mini, yet by 1967 the hemline had dropped dramatically and fashion seemed to have abandoned the future for the romantic past. The midi appeared consecutively in Paris and London. Marit Allen styled its arrival in London 'Ossie Clark's New Proportions'. Clark believed that the midi failed in Paris because the couturiers had not changed the silhouette but simply dropped the hem of the shift by two and a half feet. He raised and cinched the waist and widened the skirt, creating a flowing, thirties-inspired line. He credits its initial success partly to the film *Bonnie and Clyde* (1967), which brought the fashion of the thirties to a new audience.

However, the midi was never a commercial success. It was often styled in slinky, slippery materials and cut on the bias, and therefore was not as easy to copy as the straight, simply cut mini. Furthermore, the public found it difficult to accept such a radical change in hemline. But change was in the air. By 1966 Regency waistcoats, Victorian petticoats and Cavalier hats were making their appearance. They belonged as much to the foppish heritage of the English aristocracy, as worn by Jane Ormsby-Gore and Catherine Tennant, as to the hippy generation of Haight-Ashbury in San Francisco.

Optimism fell with the hemline. 'The early sixties were about a few people, who weren't from middle-class backgrounds, being given the opportunity to be young,' recalls Bailey. But disillusion set in. Quant and her husband had intended to break fashion's dictatorship, 'We wanted to get rid of fashion rules but, to our horror, we had developed new ones. We had wanted to liberate people.' Every fashion-conscious girl was wearing the mini, flat pumps and the Vidal Sassoon haircut and pale lipstick. Hulanicki agreed that the young did not want to be dictated to but they *did* want to be led.

The sixties generation talked hopefully of sexual liberation but donned the most sexually stereotyped clothing of the century. The mini and little-girl styling typecast women as sex symbols. Felicity Green, as fashion editor on the *Daily Mirror*, recalled that her allocated space was in direct proportion to reader interest – mostly men. Lady-like fashion styling had been of little appeal to them. But suddenly, when the mini arrived, there was great interest in the women's page. 'You see, the mini was light porn; in many ways it was the precursor of the page-three girl.'

Tai and Rossita Missoni.

Ossie Clarke.

Jane Ormsby-Gore, British Vogue's *Shophound.*

1957

The fashionable line this year combined flowing softness with simplicity from hat to shoe. Inventive seaming and cut returned as decorative devices on simple dresses and, apart from Dior's short, tight Saharienne jacket, which cinched the waist, there was hardly a taut line in Paris. Dior and Lanvin–Castillo chose an Oriental theme for day and evening wear in the spring, showing sarong dresses wrapped high to one side. Chanel continued to show cardigan-jacket suits for day, now with soft blouses that matched the linings, and ankle length, bias-cut gowns for evening. Cocktail dresses in London and Paris favoured close-cut curvaceous black lace, highlighting deep décolletés.

Femininity was accentuated in summer evening wear as chiffon reappeared after years of banishment. Griffe draped pale chiffon in Empire-line gowns, as did Howard Greer and Samuel Winston in America, and Balmain offered floral chiffon sheaths with pleated trains. Evening capes were a distinctive feature at Givenchy and Balenciaga, billowing from the shoulders or incorporated into the cut of the dress. Shades of coral through jonquil yellow were prominent, with colours toning. Chanel even matched the shoe with the stocking to lengthen the leg.

1. Lanvin-Castillo's black layered point d'esprit cocktail hat.   2. Chanel adds a crocheted edging to the small, wavy collar, gauntlet cuffs and flap pockets of her almond-green rough tweed suit. Lion's head brass buttons and a loose-necked, tie overblouse complete the outfit.   3. Dior's straight leopardskin jacket with scooped-out neckline, oatmeal tweed skirt and natural straw sou'wester.   4. Castillo's blue-and-black checked mohair sheath under a jacket, and black velours cap.   5. Dior's natural-coloured shantung 'Saharienne' jacket with matching two-piece dress, and Simone Mirman's pancake bamboo straw hat.

Autumn sparkled with innovations. Zika Ascher combined mohair, previously used only for scarves, with nylon, which improved its durability and shape retention and provided the couture with a new material. Being loosely woven, it could not be neatly tailored, but demanded enormous enveloping shapes. The mohair blend was seen first in London, in Roland Paterson's collection, and shortly afterwards Castillo featured it in huge, soft, soufflé coats.

Dior's 'Spindle', or chemise, line took the stage. Slim and loose like a nightshirt, the dress bypassed the waist and narrowed towards the hem, neither clinging to nor restricting the body. Although Balenciaga had been developing the line for some years, it was Dior who refined the basic sheath and made it popular.

The London collections demonstrated a clarity and authority of design that owed little to outside influences. The big story was coats, with lengths varying

6. Dior's Young Collection: a pale frost-blue poult-de-soie dinner dress with ribbon streamers at the waist and a flowered bow. 7. Givenchy's black point d'esprit mantilla and fan. 8. Dior's full-skirted black wool dress with moulded torso and hips and a nipped-in waist. 9. Dior's ivory-coloured shan-tung, Chinese-style dress for late day and evening, split at the side and worn over a shorter underskirt.

10

11

12

13

14

from thigh-level to just above the skirt hemline; it was difficult to distinguish between cropped topcoats and long jackets. As in Paris, suits were unfitted, creating a silhouette of controlled ease.

Americans preferred fitted shapes, showing the waisted suit for day and the short-at-the-front, high-waisted sheath based on Balenciaga's work for evening. Flowered prints appeared in many col-

lections, and were used beautifully for evening wear. American *Vogue* showed particular interest in a new venture from Dior: his Young Collection. These luxurious casual and sports clothes were made up under licence by David Crystal in America.

Youth was becoming the centre of attention everywhere. British *Vogue* was consistently reporting on fashions for

younger readers, who demanded colourful, amusing clothes. In Paris the young Yves Saint Laurent was making an impression at Dior, and Givenchy and Laroche were rising stars. Laroche, working at Fath, created his first boutique collection, which received more attention than the couture collection.

Balenciaga and Givenchy decided to emphasize their exclusivity by showing their collections between a fortnight and a month after all the other couturiers. From now on, therefore, the press had to return to Paris to see these important shows.

In Paris Jean-Louis Scherrer opened his couture house, Pierre Cardin launched his 'Adam' boutique and Ken Scott opened in Paris. Sybil Connolly opened her shop in Dublin, having worked for Richard Allen.

15

16

17

18

VOGUE

1958

Paris rejoiced as the newspaper boys shouted 'Saint Laurent has saved France'. For the nation's third largest industry, the well-being of its most prominent couture house was of great social and economic importance. Dior had died at the end of 1957, entrusting his fashion empire to his much-loved and very talented twenty-one-year-old protégé. Saint Laurent's first collection introduced a new silhouette, the wedge-shaped 'Trapeze' and was a resounding success. The dress sloped down from the shoulders to a widened hem just below the knees, maintaining a definite geometric line through precise tailoring. It had a minimum of decorative detail: a simple, childlike collar, no cuffs and just one bow above the high waist. Spring suits at Dior showed a double wedge line: a simple middy top flaring slightly and stiffly to the hem and an equally geometrically flaring skirt.

The other notable silhouette in Paris was Pierre Cardin's 'puff-ball' skirt. Yves Saint Laurent took up this shape in his famous collection of 1960. (Balenciaga had experimented with a full-length version in 1950, as had Chéruit in the early twenties.)

1. Estrava's version of the Trapeze line: light-grey tweed coat with loose back belt and widening flare. 2. McCardell's black, white and red gingham dress. 3. Saint Laurent (at Dior) grey-tweed Trapeze dress. 4. Dior's single-wedge line, in black-and-white printed silk, held into the waist at the front by a slotted drawstring, leaving the back to billow out.

With the demise of the constricting fashions promoted by French couture houses in the past, international fashion seemed to have caught up with the natural, casual approach promoted by McCardell in America for so many years. Lines curved and moved gently against the figure in Paris and London. Most dresses and jackets were collarless, with the narrowest of inset shoulders, narrow and uncuffed sleeves and bow details, all accentuating the feeling of dressmaker ease. Waistlines, cut high to counteract the abbreviated skirt length, were skilfully indented at the front and hung loose at the back. Jackets followed the same line and tended to end just on the hipbone. One of the most popular casual looks combined tight black ski trousers with a loose mohair or jersey top and brightly coloured costume jewellery. It was not a new style, but one that only now was accepted as mainstream fashion.

Evening wear remained formal and elegant. In Paris avalanches of diaphanous chiffon and organza were sharply abbreviated below the knee, and classically embroidered organza and tulle were used for high-bodiced shifts. Americans continued to promote the high-waisted Récamier line introduced last year.

5. Cardin's brightly coloured Hurel wool coat with high waist, wide, slit neck tied with a cravat and simple, straight sleeves. Wig-like hat of bright red roses. 6. Castillo's wrapped coat tied beneath a shirred band, and matching fur-trimmed turban. 7. Givenchy's funnel-collared, reversible coat – one side of which is black wool, the other red. The large armholes are cut in the shape of a hexagon. 8. Cardin's beige wool coat with a large strawberry-coloured collar and castor toque. 9. American three-quarter-length coat in flamingo-pink and white tweed fastened with three large black passementerie buttons.

5   6   7   8   9

By the autumn Saint Laurent's 'Trapeze' line dresses and suits had become the vogue, and were enthusiastically adopted by the young. British *Vogue*'s 'Young Ideas' feature reported that 'its outgoing shape is a favourite in most unreactionary wardrobes'. The idea of shorter skirts caught on in America; as American *Vogue* pointed out, 'What the Greek nose is to the Greeks, what the English complexion is to the English ... well, that's what legs are in America!'

Coats were generally big and bulky, following Castillo's lead last year. Bulky wools and the mohair blend were the most fashionable materials. Distinctive details were a high waist, a wide slit neck, simple set-in sleeves and a knee-grazing length. The cocoon shape, with a big cape collar, loose top and kimono sleeves, created a top-heavy look. Givenchy showed a reversible coat with a large 'funnel' collar that required perfect cut to prevent it looking awkward. Such experimental cutting, which challenged accepted lines and silhouettes, became more widespread as the fifties moved towards their end.

In America there were high-waisted coats, tent coats, and bubble coats as well as the traditional trench coat. The most innovative line came from Traina–Norell: a smock greatcoat, its fullness falling from a prominent high yoke. The cut-away bubble coat, a Capucci invention, was offered by David Furs in Russian broadtail. Capucci's dramatic new architectural cut was the 'Box' line. It was a flop in Europe, but the Americans raved about it and gave him the Boston Award.

Vogue suggested beauty tips to

10. *Ann Fogarty's black silk crêpe Recamier dress.*
11. *Chanel's sable-banded white crêpe evening tunic is sleeveless and gently bloused.* 12. *Castillo's billowing white organdie and black lace skirt, pushed flat at the front and out at the sides, with a shoulder-wide bow.*
13. *Griffe's mass of tulle falls freely over a black silk shift dress.*
14. *Simonetta's bloused-back, black-and-white striped chiffon evening dress, halo coif of black tulle, and black gloves.*

10

accompany the new lines. Out went the French twist and the bob, and in came wildly coloured, bouffant hair, false eyelashes and pale tones of foundation. The 'vamp band' had a passing success, especially in America, creating a twenties-cum-getting-into-the-bath look.

The ISLFD now decided to time its shows after, instead of before, those in

Paris, in order to attract a larger international clientele to the British couture. The British ready-to-wear houses of Susan Small, Dorville, Harry B. Popper and Frederick Starke, which had no problems attracting buyers, formed the Model House Group.

Mila Schön and Michael Goma opened this year.

15. *Balmain's Prince of Wales check cardigan suit with slim, short-sleeved dress.* 16. *Michael's navy-blue and white duster checked suit with bolero jacket, loosely flaring at the back. The knife pleats of the skirt fall from the hips rather than the waist.*
17. *Pierre Cardin's short, puff-ball line in black-and-white checked wool.*
18. *Dior's double-wedge suit in Garique's grey wool, lightly veiled, caramel coloured boater and Vivier shoes.*

15   16   17   18

11

12

13

14

19

20

19. *Boutique fashions.*
Left: Givenchy's red
mohair skirt and rose-
coloured stockings. Right:
from Porter-Bennett-
Gaucherand, black,
burgundy and green
checked wool skirt.
20. *Delphinium, apricot*
and cherry-coloured
mohair sweater over black
needlecord trousers and
Italian black velvet
slippers.

1959

Italian designers made a dramatic contribution to international fashion this year. They prided themselves on sumptuousness and splendid exaggeration. If a collar was to be big, it was colossal; if a skirt was to be short, it barely grazed the top of the kneecap. The most daring Italian couturier was Patrick de Barentzen, who opened this year. His spring collection was full of dash and fun, with eye-high collars, heroic cuffs and severe, enormously wide skirts held out by padding and crinolines. Simonetta was the other prominent Italian success. Her strongly structured silhouettes, with rounded, padded skirts and shoulder-hugging collars, caused one

1

2   3

American buyer to remark, 'They look rather hard to move in', to which Simonetta retorted, 'In my dresses you're not supposed to move – you're supposed to look smart!'

In Paris, too, the shape was emphatic and confident: necklines were wide, shoulders were broad, bosoms rounded, and décolletés deep. Wide belts cinching the waist were a prominent feature. At Dior Saint Laurent showed belted jackets over belted pleated dresses with bertha collars. Balenciaga placed loose belts and bands near the natural waistline, although he continued to develop the high waist and the sack dress. He introduced the shield-shaped cape

1. Atirma's simple silk sheath covered with delicate black lace. 2. Gloria Vanderbilt models Mainbocher's black silk crêpe dress and sableskin circlet. 3. Saks's copy of Jules François Crahay at Ricci's black organdie bell-shaped dress with a seventeenth-century-style décolleté. 4. Patrick de Barentzen's black faille dress with a fichu collar and white organdie over-collar pulled mysteriously over the eyes. Two pockets on the collar – 'For carrying false eyelashes!' supposed Vogue. 5. Dior's taffeta dress, ruffled with lace to the knees and wrapped with a lace-edged stole. 6. Susan Small's copy of Simonetta's white silk shantung puff-skirted evening dress with cape-like, ladybird sleeves enfolding the shoulders.

4

5

6

7. *Dior's two-piece, grey and black pied-de-poule dress with a tunic top creating a bloused second hemline further up the leg.* 8. *Alexandre for Dior: high-dressed coiffure focusing attention on the head and compensating for the shortness of skirt. It is worn with ornate crystal-bead jewellery.* 9. *Roger Vivier (for Dior) black-and-white houndstooth check pump with a new heel and oval-shaped instep.*

10. *Dior's chalk-striped navy-blue flannel suit with furled belt and stand-away neckline, accessorized with a veiled hat and a long umbrella.* 11. *Cardin's creamy wicker-weave wool suit features his new tucked sleeves and extended shoulderline.* 12. *Balenciaga's shield-shaped, cape-bolero in men's-weight tussore, buttoned at the waist and worn over a slim, sleeveless, round-necked dress.* 13. *Givenchy's beige bolting cloth tunic dress with double-wrapping leather belt.*

bolero, which he kept short, like his unfitted jackets, to reveal the dress's sash.

The most exciting suit this spring came from Cardin and featured tucked sleeves attached to an extended shoulderline. At Nina Ricci the latest talent was Jules François Crahay, a Belgian, who contributed the bell-shaped silhouette. His evening wear, like Simonetta's, sported wide collars that turned into scarves flowing down the front of the dresses. The basic spring colours in Paris included navy blue, beige and grey.

The London couture's designs were generally conservative and derivative. Hartnell, for example, presented pailletted sheaths, as

he had done for most of the decade. It was not surprising, therefore, that international trade buyers found the inspiration for their ready-to-wear ranges in the French and Italian, rather than British, couture collections. American fashion-store buyers were the first to exploit the design talents of the emerging Italian designers. They bought original models and held 'line by line' shows, displaying the original and the American copy side by side on double catwalks.

America's own couture collections flaunted lavishness – 'the luxury of generosity', acclaimed *Vogue*. Coats and jackets were lined with expensive fur and worn with fur hats. Greatcoats were cut from entire bolts of material, and cape coats were immersed in folds. The American classic, the trench coat, was the basis of the popular 'Brigand' coat.

In the autumn Jessica Daves of American *Vogue* reported, 'The most French collection in Paris was, to my eye, the Dior collection.' Saint Laurent popularized Dietrich's thirties, chalk-striped suits and showed a memorable bright red wool suit blousing over a narrow knee-length black fur band. His evening collection featured glittering high chokers, printed, bejewelled shoes and masses of satin.

Balenciaga's autumn offerings were youthful in their simplicity. He showed evening dresses that were loose-bodied and uncluttered, and coats seamed at integral points to regulate the slightly narrowing shape, with deep armholes.

Chanel was unaffected by the apparent changes, as freedom of movement and youthfulness had been her fashion philosophy for years. She was consistent in her designs and remained the most popular influence in fashion.

Valentino opened in Rome and Cardin showed his first prêt-à-porter collection.

15

14

14. *Balenciaga's beige wool kimono coat with hip seams.* 15. *March and Mendl's beige Creslan and Sea Island cotton brigand coat lined with pink-flowered cotton.* 16. *Dior's pale-blue silk shantung pleated dress with bertha collar and waist-defining belt.* 17. *Simonetta's black wool, egg-shaped dress with belted skirt and cape doubling as collar jacket. The lining stands out with the aid of a new stiffener by Keybak.* 18. *Patou's boat neckline, with tucks to emphasize the Infanta bodice, narrowing to the waist of the brilliant-red wool dress with a round-hipped skirt, and deep-crowned boater.* 19. *Trigère's collarless, narrow-sleeved black wool cape-coat and hair-sheathing leopardskin pillbox.* 20. *Patrick de Barentzen's black-and-white, 'Lollobrigida-style' tweed coat and Gillies's matching tweed slouch hat.* 21. *Cavanagh uses Ascher's mohair for a black skunk-edged coat, reversed to dark-grey and cinnamon tweed, with a wide belled hem.* 22. *Princess Odile de Croy wears Chanel's traditional braid-edged, cardigan-style coat. The nubbly beige wool is piped and lined with navy-blue silk.*

1960

The Paris spring collections were perfectly copiable; pull-over suits, and smock and bloused dresses were available in New York and London shops within weeks. Eleven couture houses — Carven, Claude Rivière, Laroche, Grès, Griffe, Heim, Dessès, Lanvin–Castillo, de Rauch, Rouff and Ricci — formed a group to show their prêt-à-porter

collections. This became the Association des Maisons Françaises de Couture-en-Gros and included most of the major ready-to-wear houses. French *Vogue* allocated greater editorial space to prêt-à-porter and boutique collections in Paris, acknowledging the growing tendency for even the wealthiest private couture clients to buy casual day clothes from these sources.

While the international ready-to-wear market seemed to be inspired by the Paris couture, many of the younger Paris couturiers were being influenced by young British designers, who ignored the couture and were making London the fashion capital of the world. Mary Quant

1. Saint Laurent (for Dior) Marlon Brando-style mink and black crocodileskin windbreaker and mink 'crash helmet'.   2. Cardin's black-and-white diagonal tweed suit with scalloped hem. The black velvet overblouse is tied with a tweed string.   3. Chanel's white wool two-piece suit with navy-blue braid and gold buttons.   4. Paul Blanche's African violet leather suit: sleeveless top, slim skirt, simple sweater and stiletto-heeled shoes.   5. Galanos's peppery, black-and-white tweed suit with braised black straw side-tilted cartwheel.   6. Hermès's peasant-shaped black goatskin blouse coat.   7. Dereta's lime-and-yellow tweed tough country coat with half belt and large patch pockets.   8. Laroche's check ratine reversible coat with high collar.   9. Saint Laurent's American mink coat, edged in fox.   10. Saint Laurent's sleeveless, nine-tenths, beige linen coat.

was seen as the leader of this movement. She did not have collections, but her cheap, uncomplicated, youthful, versatile clothes were covered enthusiastically in British *Vogue*. This year Quant featured the simple streamlined sleeveless pinafore, typically in striped grey worsted, which could be worn with a plain pullover and flat pumps by day and with high-heeled court shoes for evening. Kiki Byrne, who had worked for Quant, featured lean black leather suits in Glass & Black, her boutique on the King's Road.

Saint Laurent's decision to interpret this youthful street fashion in expensive materials caused a furore at Dior this autumn. His Left Bank 'Beat Look' included black leather suits and coats, knitted caps, high turtleneck collars, and biker-style jackets in mink and crocodile skin. He also showed the puff-ball silhouette, shortened and accentuated to create a bubble shape around the thighs, and the full-skirted Infanta line. American *Vogue* was shocked, and complained that Saint Laurent's collection for Dior was 'designed for the very young women ... who expect to change the line with frequency and rapidity, and who are possessed of superb legs and slim, young, goddess figures'. Unlike the more experienced masters such as Balenciaga and

16

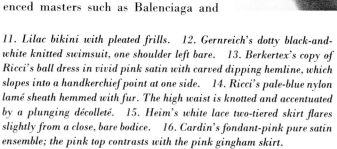

11

12

11. Lilac bikini with pleated frills. 12. Gernreich's dotty black-and-white knitted swimsuit, one shoulder left bare. 13. Berkertex's copy of Ricci's ball dress in vivid pink satin with carved dipping hemline, which slopes into a handkerchief point at one side. 14. Ricci's pale-blue nylon lamé sheath hemmed with fur. The high waist is knotted and accentuated by a plunging décolleté. 15. Heim's white lace two-tiered skirt flares slightly from a close, bare bodice. 16. Cardin's fondant-pink pure satin ensemble; the pink top contrasts with the pink gingham skirt.

13   14   15

17. *Elsa Martinelli models Heims's black leather ensemble.* 18. *Swallow's shower-proof dress, tailored like a man's shirt and worn with just-over-the-knee bright checked socks and a black, huge-collared jersey. The boots are by Dolcis.* 19. *Kiki Byrne's red flannel dress with a plush printed fur hat, pigskin shoes, an outsized bag and a clatter of gilt bracelets.* 20. *Pat Woodward's green-and-white cotton gingham dress and Mr John parasol hat.* 21. *Quant's black-and-grey tartan wool, sleeveless, box-pleated dress is waisted across the hipbone and marked there with a narrow belt.*

Dior, Saint Laurent had failed to court the buyers and press by gently evolving a line collection by collection, offering them a taste of styles to come while maintaining a popular silhouette for a few seasons. His unbridled imagination ricocheted from idea to idea, leaving the critics several steps behind.

Other collections attracted more favourable comment. Narrow-sided, wrapped coats with snug fur collars and head-hugging cloches from Cardin were the autumn sensation. Multicoloured, reversible coats, and particularly houndstooth and diamond checks, were also popular. Pleats and a version of the princess line were seen in virtually every collection, and Castillo gave the straight line a mid-twenties interpretation through accessories such as period headbands and long strings of beads. Magnificent brocades were cut into luxurious evening sheaths and coats, and the quirk of the year was to wear a long evening coat over a short evening dress.

The collections from Rome and Florence made fashion news headlines. Simonetta focused interest on sleeves, introducing a short, square sleeve chopped off at the elbow, and a widened, stiffened, curved version that arched away from the body. Her greatest success was a selection of coats with batwing sleeves, which were greeted with exuberant cheers.

Patrick de Barentzen showed skirts above the knee, skirts so full that all others seemed like tight sheaths, and rounded cape coats with giant wings. He featured leather as supple as velvet and employed blindingly bright colours, as did Capucci in shiny ciré, and Pucci in vivid silks.

There was a lack of direction in the American collections, which showed various silhouettes; American *Vogue* claimed that the American woman refused to be pigeon-holed into a single look. Rudi Gernreich, a former Hollywood dancer, introduced dancers' leotards, tights and work-out clothing on to the fashion stage, and Norman Norell contributed the culottes suit, as did Emanuelle Khanh, who started designing in Paris. She was to become the cult designer among French teenagers who modelled themselves on stars such as Jean-Paul Belmondo in Godard's *A Bout de Souffle*.

263

1961

A riot of colours and prints distinguished the Paris spring collections, from the glorious Oriental garden prints at Cardin to the red-and-black printed evening gowns at Patou. Balmain concentrated on floor-length chiffon teamed with little jumper tops in matching embroidered chiffon. Marc Bohan took over from Saint Laurent as chief designer at Dior and won the approval of the established clientele with his first collection, carefully steering a course between a desire to create modern clothing and the need to cater for the essentially conservative taste of the customers. He showed a variety of bejewelled peach, pale jade, moonstone, and pink evening gowns, garden party chiffons and dresses that bloused sinuously over the natural waistline.

The Italian collections, too, continued to concentrate on bright colours. Princess Galitzine featured a series of jewel-coloured maharaja-style trouser suits worn with jewel-encrusted mules. Emilio Pucci presented a collection of simple evening dresses with a deep V-shaped panel inset into bias cut, unpatterned material.

The European influence was evident in America, where Galanos, Bill Blass, Ben Zuckerman and Harvey Berin tailored boldly printed chiffon and crêpe into summer suits cut on Chanel or Balenciaga lines. Scassi, Cecil Chapman, Sarmi and Talmark presented flowing evening wear in the classical Greek style in jewel-coloured chiffons. Stretch fabrics, such as stretch jersey and terry towelling, added ease and comfort, and were especially good for clothing that

2

3 *4* *5*

1. Courrèges's grey-and-white dogtooth check suit, black buckskin blouse and tie.   2. Quant's pale-grey flannel jumper suit.   3. Simonetta's dark-grey wool jersey suit.   4. One of the shortest skirts in Paris: Bohan (at Dior) black-and-white Besson tweed suit.   5. Burke-Amey's grape-pink wild silk (with a tweedy face) sleeveless dress and jacket tied with a brown satin sash. The neckline is swirled in brown point d'esprit.

6. Cardin's white Arabian crêpe pleated dress.   7. Salen's white and chestnut-brown striped dress.   8. Quant's low-slung moss crêpe party shift with tiered bodice.   9. Left: Kiki Byrne's beige tweed dress and red kid boots from Gamba. Right: Young Jaeger's supple black suede Princess line dress.

6 *7* *8* *9*

10. *Dior's hooded cloak.*   11. *Berghaus's grey wool coat, lined with mock sheepskin.*   12. *Balenciaga's mango-coloured fleece coat constructed of curves. High-domed black velvet hat.*   13. *Dior's leopardskin-lined cape with camel-hair hood and head-hugging Dutch bonnet.*

10

11

12

13

14. *Pucci's red jersey loose trousers, falling from a hip yoke, and simple, straight matching top.* 15. *Pucci's chequerboard-print, pink-and-white foulard silk two-piece dress.* 16. *Lanvin-Castillo's high-waisted dress has a short shield of jewels in a bolero slanting over a creamy evening dress.* 17. *Galitizine's white silk palazzo pyjamas encrusted with beads.* 18. *Lanvin-Castillo's short Ducharne silk organdie evening dress bordered with a double-pleated ruff across the knees, repeated across the bodice.* 19. *White lace and elastic underwear.*

was not individually fitted. The bold textile design, particularly on printed cottons, that was gaining popularity on both sides of the Atlantic was attributed directly to the work of the Scandinavian textile designer Marimekko.

For the autumn Ben Zuckerman designed a series of fitted coats in black-and-white wool that were similar in line to Bohan's collection. Most American coats, however, were simple, straight, short and double-breasted, in light-coloured wools or animal-skin prints. The most artful controller of the daytime silhouette was Galanos, who showed sleeveless wool and mohair coat-dresses that moulded the figure through bias cutting rather than seams and darts, while Geoffrey Beene was an early promoter of the wide-belted, high-waisted look. John Fredericks, Greta Plattery, Sloat, Goldworm, Richard Cole, Kimberley and Mr John provided mainstream fashion with fairly short, straight, knitted jumper suits and pinafore dresses.

The Paris couture also decided to expose the legs. Bohan and Courrèges were the first couturiers to show mini skirts. Courrèges had broken away from Balenciaga, but his style echoed Balenciaga's clean lines. Although skirts were decidedly short, the width varied from the skin-tight to full, skating styles. There was an almost fanatical interest in flying panels on coats, dresses and suits and fastenings tended to be left of centre.

Balenciaga decreed that the silhouette should be less bulky this year and showed arching coat-hanger shoulders on tailored coats that closed around the waist without cinching. He also contributed the most perfect little black dresses of the couture – slim, belted, wrapped or drawstring fastened. The daytime curfew on the black dress ended at about six o'clock, after which it emerged in fashionable cafés and restaurants. The most memorable dinner

17

18

19

and theatre suits came from Dior and Chanel, tailored in satin or velvet, edged in fur and worn with blouses intricately embroidered with jet.

Fur abounded as a seasonal trimming. Long fur scarves were wrapped across shoulders and coats were shown with body-wrapping fur jabots. Fur was used for head-coverings too, from turbans to hoods. Dior showed hoods based on an aviator's cap, Patou offered a hooded dinner suit, Laroche a hooded blouse, and Balmain a mink hood under a cloth coat. Grès, who was an old hand at hoods, added mink-lined hoods to bright red wool coats.

John Bates was appointed designer-in-chief at Jean Varon in London.

1962

Vogue saluted the young designers: the new independents Venet and Hechter; the established talents Bohan and Courrèges; and the return of the brilliant Saint Laurent, who was joined by many of the staff from Dior when he opened his own house. He received financial backing

268

from a variety of sources including a businessman from Georgia and the cosmetics company Charles of the Ritz, while Abrahams, the textile house, offered him favourable trading terms.

While most of the couture favoured bright colours for evening, Saint Laurent concentrated on black and white, and launched the brassière dress, an early example of the cut-out theme. The 'beat' look was abandoned in favour of the gamine style popularized by Truffaut's film *Jules et Jim* and the clothes designed by Emanuelle Khanh and Jean Muir a Jane and Jane. None the less there w

5

1. 'Beat look' black-and-white jumpers: two-tone sweater by Korrigan, striped sweater from Galeries Lafayette and sweater with contrasting collar and cuffs by Eos. All worn with straight black jersey pants, trilbys and boots.   2. Levi jeans.
3. Cardin's cross-gartered gillie shoes with little heels.
4. Howard Company's 'Les Snobs': black suede double-breasted trench coat and crisp, clean V-necked black coat. Roll-neck sweater by John Laing.
5. Muir (at Jane and Jane) shorter-length bright-red sweater, muffler and clean-cut, black-and-white check skirt worn with Anello and Davide check gaiters (commissioned by Vogue's Clare Rendlesham) decorated with a row of black buttons.

a dearth of innovation and no definitive line at the Paris shows this spring. Blurred softness characterized many of the 2,600 designs shown, aided by frills, ruffles, veils and shawls, which were a widely adopted substitute for coats. Waists made a comeback under large, tight belts.

In America the emphasis on the waist was so important that *Vogue* featured recent developments in waist-cinching corsetry. Geoffrey Beene, who launched his own label this year, emphasized the waist on his suits and dresses with a wide, soft, black leather belt. Galanos drew the eye to the cinched midriff with a dark jacket cut-away to the navel and worn over a white linen dickey. Plain, brightly coloured dresses with simple seams to emphasize the narrow waist and wide, short skirt were shown by Scassi, while Norell's suits featured full, circular, knee-length skirts, with wide, tight belts and little square-cut jackets. The main contrast came from Adolpho, who preferred straight, pale-coloured tunic coats and tunic suits worn with rich turbans.

Clean-cut, unisex casuals were the ultimate in youthful chic in America. American *Vogue* recommended the Wild West cowboy look, as young, free, easy and mischievous as a tomboy. Denim jeans still epitomized this look, but corduroys were an alternative, both now worn with bright mannish shirts, outlandish hats, and bare feet or simple pumps.

For evening the length of the hemline was no indication of formality, and American dresses were long or short,

6. Saint Laurent's belted basque bodice with.long, close-fitting sleeves embroidered with jet beads; black ciré satin skirt.   7. Trigère's short black peau-de-soie evening dress cloaked with a huge, wing-like panel with dipping hem. 8. Saint Laurent's white impasto satin brassière dress and exotic turban. 9. Saint Laurent's glossy black ciré satin jacket, cuffed in black mink.   10. Harrods' copy of Balenciaga's overblouse suit with flap pockets.

11   12

11. Norell's little black dress belted in calf-skin. 12. Hartnell's simple T-shirt dress in Mexican ocelot with black leather belt. A black wool coat lined with the same fur could be worn over it. Claude St Cyr's black felt policeman's helmet.

coloured wools no matter what the season, and light colours for winter also became hallmarks of the Cardin and Courrèges collections. Dior showed the new rectangular matchbox coats.

Paris seemed to take its cue from London as well as New York this autumn. Following in the wake of Quant's PVC creations, French *Vogue* showed vinyl-covered black cotton raincoats with corduroy collars and turn-back cuffs. Balenciaga stepped out in black patent-leather boots styled like the Life Guards' and zipped up one side. Cardin dropped the hemline of dresses by three inches, but few followed him. The mini was still an international fashion favourite, now in fur: real tiger from Lanvin–Castillo, panther at Galitzine, and ocelot from the normally conservative Hartnell.

13   14   15

The silhouette remained straight and lean, the figure largely ignored. Only a few designers added interest to this plain line. Crahay at Ricci rounded the shoulders and filled out full skirts, and Saint Laurent showed Raj coat-dresses. Khanh presented a *nouveau classique* collection of architectural precision with meticulous seaming, narrow armholes and tailored details. She doted on Harris tweed and Shetland wool, using them for schoolgirl culottes, double-breasted coats and pert little suits.

Colours bordered on the sombre: blacks, greys and browns. Dormeuil's simple black-and-white check was seen everywhere. It was quieter and more subtle than the earlier houndstooth, dogtooth and tattersall checks and lent itself more readily to the lean, precise tailoring that prevailed. Brilliant colour was reserved for evening wear and coats. Saint Laurent showed particularly colourful enormous plaid coats. The most important coat to come out of the couture this year was Saint Laurent's 'pea jacket'. Modelled on the sailor's traditional double-breasted garment and already an American classic, it now gained lasting international popularity.

13. Quant's PVC Collection: black, vinyl-covered cotton raincoat with corduroy collar and turn-back cuffs. 14. Patou's rose-coloured A-line coat with double-waved collar. 15. Gerald McCann's 'affordable fur': a rabbitskin coat. 16. Monté Sano and Pruzan's three-piece white wool suit: collarless jacket, sleeveless overblouse and skirt. 17. Bohan's beige, black, and grey plaid suit: a loose jumper over a wide pleated skirt, and tossed scarf.

narrow and panelled. Jacques Tiffeau showed beautiful evening suits in bright silk matelassé, with yoked, high-waisted, belted jackets. In Paris hair was piled high in a towering chignon for the evening, a coiffure popularized by Saint Laurent.

New York and London were united this autumn in offering long redingote coats, fur hats and muffs, and suede or flat fur boots for evening, and preferring velvet and straight, long-line jackets for daytime. Black leather was very fashionable for coats, suits, dresses and gilets. American suits were tailored in light-

The Camera Nazionale Della Moda Italiana, an organization similar to the French Chambre Syndicale de la Couture, was established in Rome. Diana Vreeland left *Harper's Bazaar* to become editor-in-chief of American *Vogue*. Her individualistic chic boosted the wit, the verve and the visual distinction of the magazine.

16   17

1963

Simplicity continued to guide fashion. Lines were clean and fabric tone and texture paramount. *The* fashionable dress was still the childlike shift, occasionally cut out at the sides or back, or with a high waist for summer. Culottes and pinafores, which could be worn from dawn to dusk with a simple change of hairstyle and accessories, remained very popular with the young. '*N'oubliez pas la femme*', admonished Bohan at Dior amid all the little-girl looks. He made his point by presenting short and long two-piece evening gowns full of ruffles, coquetry, and the return of the décolleté, framed by seductive Chantilly lace.

Suits had a variety of new sleeves and shoulderlines, but emphasis was on cut and master tailoring, rather than complicated trimmings or patterned materials. Khanh, who epitomized this attitude, introduced a new long-petal-shaped collar that was dubbed the 'droop'. Saint Laurent's peasant smock now had bulkier shoulders, cuffed sleeves, a slimmer line and a greater waist indentation. The most willowy

2

1. *Saint Laurent's new winter face: eyes like Christmas daisies, framed with brown suede casque and suede balaclava helmet, which was shown with his boot and jerkin collection.* 2. *Khanh wearing her slightly flared, unwaisted dress with cut-out armholes and a white organdie petal collar around the horseshoe neckline.* 3. *Deliss of London shifts. Left: simple red-and-white polkadot shirt with round collar. Right: pale-grey wool shift with black-and-white silk collar and cuffs. Oliver Goldsmith's glasses.* 4. *Polly Peck's piebald-print shift.* 5. *Donald Davies's camel-coloured Irish linen dress with yoke and peasant scarf tied like a nurse's headdress.* 6. *Tuffin and Foale's near-bare midriff: flag-red cotton dress slipped over a bikini or worn for the evening with Saxone's gold sandals with low, curvy heels.*

3   4   5   6

smocks were seen at Cardin, the squarest at Ricci.

Make-up, accessories and any degree of artifice were used to enhance the simple, basic wardrobe. Vidal Sassoon's innovative geometric bob prompted many French houses to include stylized wigs in their collections. *Vogue* goaded its readers in this direction: 'A little fakery

these days means a whole lot of chic.' Wigs were soon worn with the same nonchalance as lipstick and nail varnish. Paris raved about white kidskin boots from Courrèges and thigh-high alligator boots from Saint Laurent.

In the autumn Quant launched her Ginger Group label – mix-and-match separates based on the college look and cheap enough to collect piece by piece to build up a wardrobe. The actress Françoise Hardy was adopted by *Vogue* as a new model to epitomize the scrubbed college-girl look, showing her in clothes that could be worn by any modern, lithe young woman with a taste for adventure.

The winter materials were a blend of warmth and bulkiness. Double-faced twills, coverts, Meltons and thick strong tweeds were all precisely tailored, with prominent seams, welts, extended sloping shoulders, flap pockets and collars worked like sculptor's clay. Tail-

7. Courrèges's white 'Coconut cake' lace bodice, leggings and black satin skirt. 8. Balenciaga's black crêpe bias-cut, dolman-sleeved dress with a tiny waist and rounded hips.

9. Sloat's synthetic white overblouse and suede pigskin boots. 10. Saint Laurent's mohair tweed tunic and matching short skirt, mannish walking shoes and wool stockings. 11. Norell's cocoa-coloured cavalry twill cape and trousers. 12. Françoise Hardy wears Brett's bush jacket, a brown cashmere turtleneck sweater and wool whipcord trousers. 13. Audrey Hepburn models Givenchy's white felt helmet-shaped hat, white wool suit threaded with black, and black silk twill cowl-necked blouse. 14. Courrèges's Indian-inspired, leather-thonged tunic coat in ribbed wool jersey, scarfed silk overblouse and narrow, prominently creased trousers breaking over white kid boots. 15. Grès's bias-cut kaftan in natural-coloured wool. 16. Givenchy's candy-pink cloqué evening gown. 17. Left: Norell's 'bathrobe' of smoky-pink mohair. Centre: clipped white alpaca dinner dress and jacket. Right: tank-top dress and jacket in heavy, lacquer-red wool jersey. 18. Bohan's Chantilly lace top.

for Chanel-inspired cardigan suits. Monte-Sano Pruzan offered three-piece suits, combining abbreviated greatcoats with loosely tailored waistcoats and straight skirts. Saint Laurent's 1960 beat look was belatedly adapted: Samuel Robery showed simple leather shifts, Scassi presented black alligator trousers, Ellen Brooke used black lacquered alligator for windbreaker jackets, and mock alligator was chosen by Modelia for polo coats and by David Kidd for short coats.

Norell presented one of his greatest collections, styling every suit, coat and dress with well-tailored precision, to follow the lines of the small, round head, long, slender throat, and long, narrow back. His double-thickness rolled collars were cut expertly on the bias or he cut clothes very low on the nape of the neck. Refusing to use inner stiffenings, Norell chose strong, pliable materials. 'I close my eyes, squash a piece of coating round my hands, feel its heft, solidness.... Good fabric has good weight.... It has reason.'

The Italian couture suffered a severe set-back; three of its leading designers – Capucci, Simonetta and Fabiani – decided to show in Paris, where they were greeted by a short-lived wave of interest. However, Pino Lancetti presented his famous 'Military' line at his first show at the Pitti Palace in Florence.

In London Thea Porter and Caroline Charles opened. The latter had worked as an apprentice at the couture house of Michael Sherard and with Mary Quant. Issey Miyake showed his first collection in Tokyo.

ored topcoats, jackets and dresses were worn with tall boots, textured stockings, turbans, wide-brimmed and chin-strapped Anzac hats, helmets, foulards, turtle-necks and pigskin gloves. Saint Laurent chose Anna Karenina as his theme, presenting hooded coats, fur hemlines and frogging. Russian styles were also seen at Dior. Courrèges showed white for his winter collection, another indication of the influence of his maestro, Balenciaga.

In America Altman's, Ben Zuckerman and Julius Garfinckel showed simply tailored suits and coats in pale tweeds and wools, and Trigère used bold checks

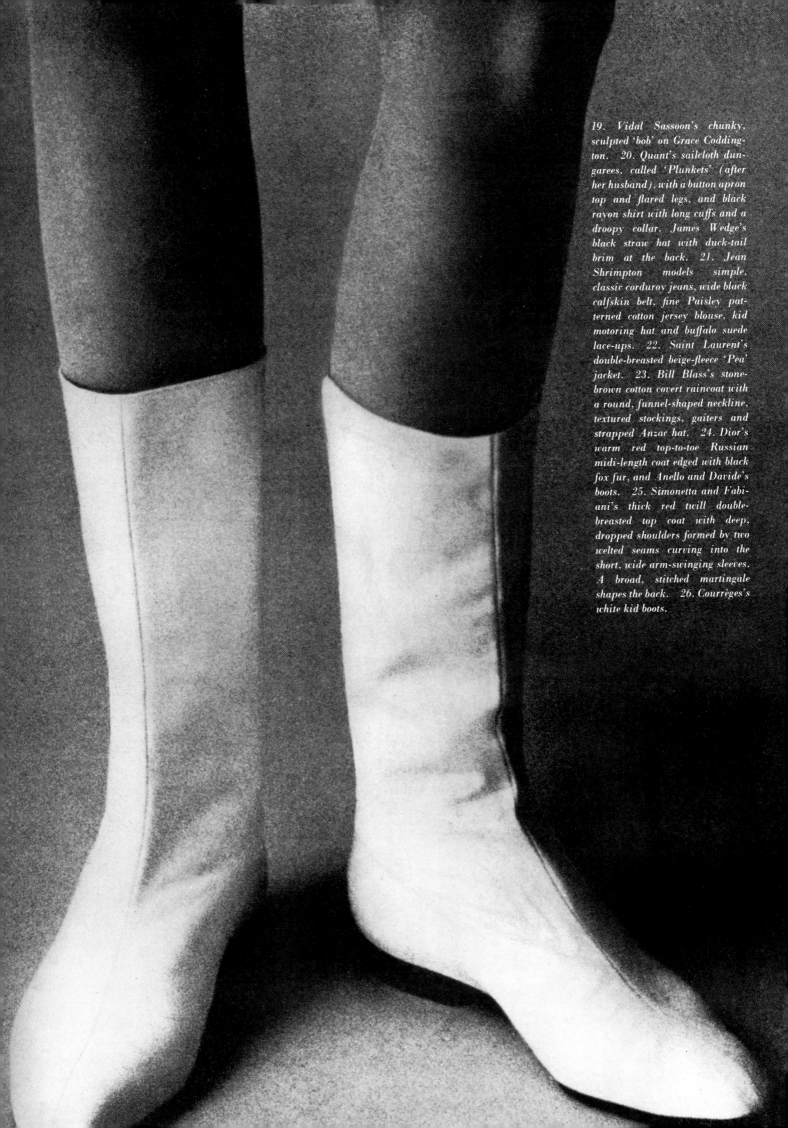

22

19. *Vidal Sassoon's chunky, sculpted 'bob' on Grace Codding-ton.* 20. *Quant's sailcloth dun-garees, called 'Plunkets' (after her husband), with a button apron top and flared legs, and black rayon shirt with long cuffs and a droopy collar. James Wedge's black straw hat with duck-tail brim at the back.* 21. *Jean Shrimpton models simple, classic corduroy jeans, wide black calfskin belt, fine Paisley pat-terned cotton jersey blouse, kid motoring hat and buffalo suede lace-ups.* 22. *Saint Laurent's double-breasted beige-fleece 'Pea' jacket.* 23. *Bill Blass's stone-brown cotton covert raincoat with a round, funnel-shaped neckline, textured stockings, gaiters and strapped Anzac hat.* 24. *Dior's warm red top-to-toe Russian midi-length coat edged with black fox fur, and Anello and Davide's boots.* 25. *Simonetta and Fabi-ani's thick red twill double-breasted top coat with deep, dropped shoulders formed by two welted seams curving into the short, wide arm-swinging sleeves. A broad, stitched martingale shapes the back.* 26. *Courrèges's white kid boots.*

1964

Contrasts punctuated fashion as the coquettish and the shocking triumphed in Paris. At Dior Bohan's suits promoted both the English schoolgirl and the *mondaine* woman. Recalling times past but very much of the present were the modesty vest, the pussycat bow, ruching, the trouser suit, the seven-eighths-length coat, box pleats, cropped jackets and the slender shift.

Saint Laurent showed two evening lines this spring: the long tunic over a silk dress, and long country-style printed skirts. His narrow evening sheaths were seen through a layer of gauze which swung seductively over the hem.

Courrèges hit the headlines with his 'Space Age' collection. His precise, unadorned line was achieved through perfect cut and handling of the fabric. He used the new triple gabardine from Nattier for trousers, suits and dresses that seemed sculpted rather than sewn; *Vogue* commented, 'Courrèges clearly dreams of moon parties.' The pure line of his white trousers, cut straight over the ankles and slashed on the instep of the white kidskin boots, stretched legs to infinity. More controversial was his presentation of a single rectangle of ciré material worn as a coat – attire only for the adventurous, decided *Vogue*.

Despite the great emphasis on line, clothes were also soft and supple. The fine tailoring that persisted was never harsh, tight or angular. The close-to-the-figure fit was pursued, shoulders were still narrow, armholes and waistlines set high, and collars small and rounded.

All the leading designers continued to experiment with the cut-out in various positions around the anatomy, and both Courrèges and Cardin chose the back as a sensual focal point of their dresses. Courrèges showed the shortest skirts and Cardin created a sensation with the lowest plunging necklines.

The leader of the American avant-garde, Rudi Gernreich, went one step further, presenting an eye-catching topless dress, which made headline news but not large sales, and the topless bathing suit, the monokini, which was promptly banned from many beaches. When his clothes had tops, Gernreich achieved a close-to-the-body line with unusual seaming and no darts. Like his Parisian contemporaries, he loved bulky fabrics, such as camel hair backed with thick wool.

6

7

8
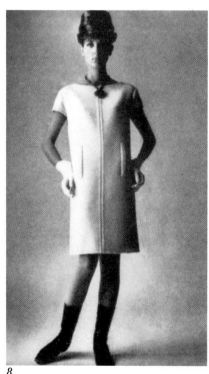

9

1. Courrèges's ciré bathtowel wrap, red felt hood and shiny, red boots. 2. Rudi Gernreich's reversible camel-and-black wool 'nightrider' coat and dress and black felt yashmak helmet. 3. The shorter coat in Paris – Courrèges's cocoa-and-white plaid coat with wide shoulders and short, rounded sleeves and simple linen dress, the hem of which peeps out and balances the proportions. 4. Sybil Zelker's sugar-pink rayon coat and James Wedge's pink sequined bonnet. 5. Maxwell Croft's black Mongolian lamb jacket worn with black stretch ski pants. 6. Polly Peck's seashell-pink rayon dress with graded drawn-threadwork and a Peter Pan collar worn with James Wedge's orange gingham piccaninny hat. 7. Sarah Miles wears Jane and Jane's olive-green homespun tweed smock. 8. Courrèges's clean-cut white twill shift with tiny sleeves, brown snakeskin boots and flattened moonshape beads. 9. Quant's navy-blue and white Provençal print dress cinched widely at the waist, cuffed and collared in white and teamed with a schoolgirl panama.

10

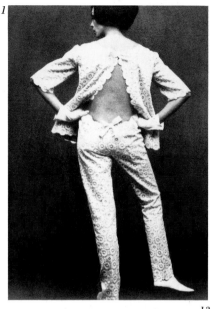

11

12

13

10. Grès's heavy white brocade robe, embroidered with red and dark turquoise motifs.
11. Courrèges's white guipure lace suit with straight trousers lined with cocoa-coloured silk.
12. Ben Zuckerman's peach-coloured worsted wool evening suit, and Herbert Levine's lace boots.
13. Cardin fills the plunging neck-line of his jade-green crêpe dress with a veil of chiffon over the bodice of paper-fan pleats. The naked back is flaunted.
14. Cardin's ice-blue organza blouse with a small polo collar and accordion-frilled sleeves under a simple, pale-blue herringbone gabardine suit.
15. Woollands' pink kid jacket, Jeanne Aymes's matching stretch pants, and Herbert Johnson's helmet.
16. Ricci's thirties-style honey-beige shantung suit.
17. Harry Hall's check pants and matching jacket.
18. Courrèges's brown-and-white ponyskin and Spanish white twill suit.
19. Ben Khan's sleeveless Russian fox top, 'flower-power' tight trousers and jodhpur boots.
20. Left: grey wool flannel skirt with wide front and back pleats and flap pockets. Right: Regency-grey worsted skirt with large inverted pleat at the front.

The more classic American tailoring, perfected by Zuckerman and Norell, favoured the simple two-colour pastel weave suit and coat. Bill Blass and Jacques Tiffeau chose pale pink and blue tweed for simple Balenciaga-style suits worn with matching silk overblouses. The younger woman favoured shifts, tunics, skirts, jackets and trousers in leather and suede from Leathermode, John Weitz, Samuel Robert, Bonnie Cashin and Bety Belmont. Sportswear continued to combine practicality with excitement. Casual skirts adopted the swinging, knee-baring hem, and were worn with firm leather belts, white textured stockings and silver-buckled pilgrim shoes. The full-length skirt, whether brightly coloured and boldly patterned or in black-and-white *cloqué*, was still dominant for evening wear.

Designers were on the move. Castillo left Lanvin to open his own house, but Lagerfeld, bored with the rarefied atmosphere of the couture, left Patou to freelance. Mandelli of Krizia presented her first Pitti Palace show in Florence, and Gina Fratini opened in London. Zandra Rhodes graduated from the Royal College of Art and took the first steps in her career as a great textile and fashion designer. Sonia Rykiel began designing innovative knitwear for Laura, her husband's boutique, in Paris. Despite poor eyesight, Molyneux returned briefly to his couture house in London, which was headed by John Tullis in his absence.

14

15

16

17

18

20

19

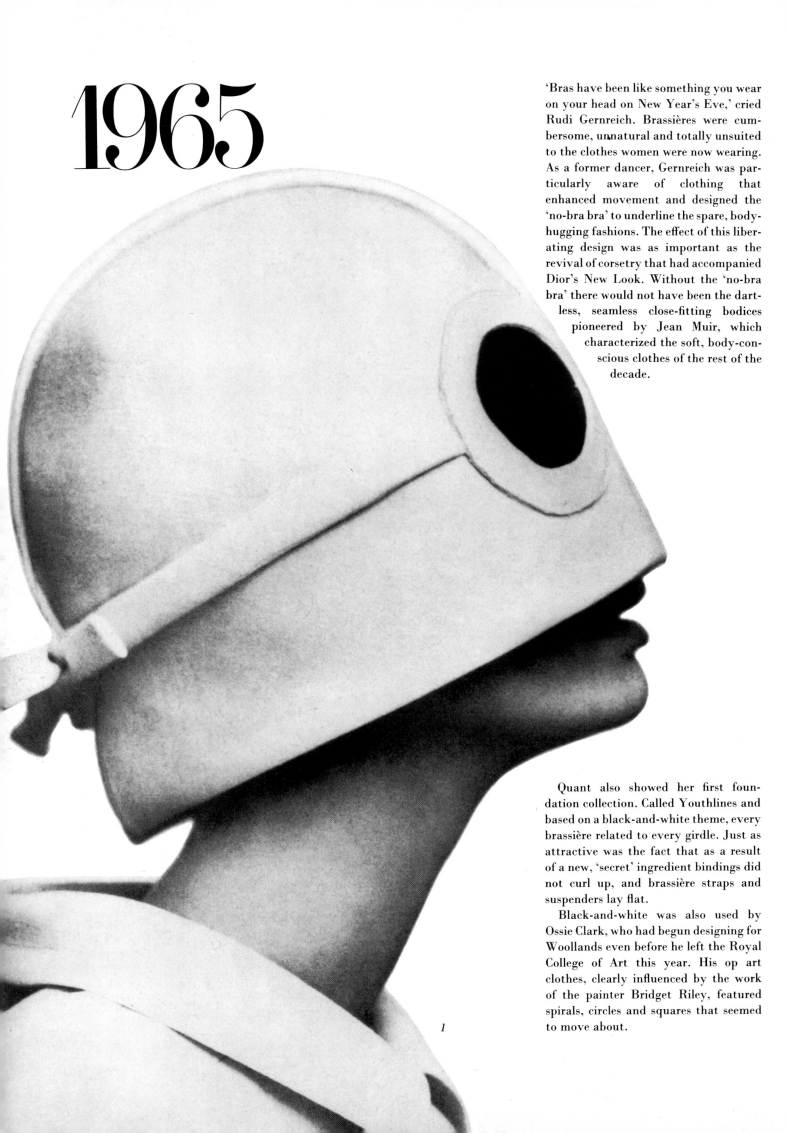

1965

'Bras have been like something you wear on your head on New Year's Eve,' cried Rudi Gernreich. Brassières were cumbersome, unnatural and totally unsuited to the clothes women were now wearing. As a former dancer, Gernreich was particularly aware of clothing that enhanced movement and designed the 'no-bra bra' to underline the spare, body-hugging fashions. The effect of this liberating design was as important as the revival of corsetry that had accompanied Dior's New Look. Without the 'no-bra bra' there would not have been the dartless, seamless close-fitting bodices pioneered by Jean Muir, which characterized the soft, body-conscious clothes of the rest of the decade.

Quant also showed her first foundation collection. Called Youthlines and based on a black-and-white theme, every brassière related to every girdle. Just as attractive was the fact that as a result of a new, 'secret' ingredient bindings did not curl up, and brassière straps and suspenders lay flat.

Black-and-white was also used by Ossie Clark, who had begun designing for Woollands even before he left the Royal College of Art this year. His op art clothes, clearly influenced by the work of the painter Bridget Riley, featured spirals, circles and squares that seemed to move about.

1

2

1. *Antonelli's goggle hat in clear, white Space Age linen and glass.*   2. *Cuddlecoats' black and clear vinyl mac and Mini de N's brass jewellery.*   3. *Black-and-white check vinyl tube dress with rhinestone straps by Joel Schulmacher for Paraphernalia.*   4. *Lanvin-Castillo's black-and-cyclamen wool jersey dress.*   5. *Mondrian's geometric paintings inspired this Saint Laurent dress.*   6. *Ossie Clark's black-and-white Op Art quilted silk coat.*

3

4

5

6

Op art was particularly effective on evening dresses, where the greater expanse of cloth gave more prominence, strength and perspective to the pattern. In a similar vein, the Lanvin–Castillo boutique offered a series of full-length jersey shifts with geometric patterns. Saint Laurent contributed the memorable Mondrian dress – blocks of colour within straight black lines taken straight from the painter's work of the early twenties. The canvases of the great artist danced across simply cut sheaths and men's shirt shapes. Dresses became smaller and smaller, designs bolder and bolder. Some of the boldest patterns continued to come from Marimekko, and were seen on everything from bikinis to bedlinen in Europe and America. Emanuelle Khanh designed a collection based on chevron stripes, which was manufactured by Pierre D'Alby.

Colours ranged from deep navy blue and black through glowing tangerine and orange to delicate pastels laced with ribbons of yellow and white. Matt crêpes and springy wools were favoured materials, but lace was the ultimate in fashion for all times of day and all occasions. The Total Look was consolidated in all the fashion centres. Dresses and coats, skirts and blouses, trousers and boots, ear-rings and bracelets, and even hats and hairstyles were co-ordinated as fashion enjoyed an Indian summer of uniformity. The cut-out scissored its way through every aspect of women's attire and gave impetus to the health and fitness movement, since the maximum skin exposure demanded sleek young bodies.

For evening Americans tended to choose more exotic styles based on brightly woven materials evocative of Arabia and the Orient, and Zemors – deftly wrapped miniature turbans of Indian silk – were the latest accessory (first seen at Saint Laurent). Parties were afloat with the airiest chiffons, and rippling ruffles of lace and organza were wrapped across the back of short evening dresses. Cream, black or white crêpe dresses were a popular alternative. In Paris the avant-garde wore Courrèges's spangled baby bonnet.

Emanuelle Khanh arrived in America, where her clothes were stocked by Paraphernalia; she was considered the top designer of ready-to-wear for the young. She used a narrow, minimal line, swung skirts from the hipbone, and called attention to the collar, wrists and waist.

In Paris the short dress was preferred to the trouser suits that had been so widely acclaimed last year. Coats gently outlined the body, Cardin's new line being dubbed the 'cocoon'.

Emmanuel Ungaro, who had assisted André Courrèges, opened his own house. He worked in collaboration with the textile designer Sonia Knapp and became well known for his rich, colourful prints. Having trained at Balenciaga's house in Spain and at Lanvin–Castillo, Oscar de la Renta set up a company with Jane Derby, named after her, in New York. After her death he renamed it Oscar de la Renta.

As Chairman of the Fashion House Group of London, Frederick Starke took a collection of British fashion from various leading houses to New York on the *Queen Elizabeth*. This grand promotion, entitled 'US 66', was very well received and resulted in many orders from enthusiastic buyers who relished buoyant British chic.

7. Givenchy's raglan-sleeved, single-breasted brocade evening coat. 8. Belinda Belville's bold tweed coat in black-and-white hound's-tooth check and short-sleeved dress with a black wool bodice, and Otto Lucas's zebra-striped, leather-peaked helmet in clipped chapel coney fur. 9. Emmanuelle Khanh's (for Pierre D'Alby) geometrically patterned chapel coney-fur coat. 10. Balenciaga's pink evening dress, opening like a tulip at the back and suspended from jewelled shoulder straps. 11. Baroness Thyssen-Bornemisza wears Maximilian's black broad-tail sheath with a sable hem and sable stole. 12. Rayne's white leather driving moccasins with studded soles, white-striped and black-ribbed stockings by Morley. Dogtooth-checked stockings by Adler. Glove in Prince of Wales check at Army & Navy stores, and Shepherd's check glove. 13. Corocraft daisy earrings and large ring, worn with Susan Small's Orlon crocheted dress with a skimp top, scooped, scalloped neckline and short, flared skirt. 14. John Bates's skirt and bikini top covered with clusters of marguerites and matching daisy bracelet by Corocraft. 15. Marianne Faithfull wears Quant's black trouser suit with bright brass buttons and Quant's flower logo on the pocket. The boots are from Bally.

12

13

14

15

1. *Giorgio di Sant' Angelo's huge black-and-white circles in squares dropped at right angles to each other, with rings to match.*   2. *V de V's black-and-white striped vinyl macintosh, trousers and bonnet.*   3. *Paco Rabanne's plastic square-chips shift.*   4. *Venet's kite-coat: plastic diamonds attached edge-to-edge to thick white full-length coat.*   5. *Ungaro's double-faced wool gabardine cutaway dress.*   6. *Dorothée Bis's clear vinyl trousers worn over coloured tights.*

1966

'Legs are it,' declared *Vogue* as the mini dominated the spring collections in all the fashion centres. The silhouette fell from the neck or shoulders to a free-swinging hem, and stark geometry was still expressed with cut-outs. Modesty was banished. There were bared backs, bared midriffs and even total bareness lightly veiled with transparent material. Saint Laurent presented ultra-short ultra-sheer organza dresses with sequined patterns or peekaboo bare panels across the torso. Such revelations were not always intentional. At Missoni's first prêt-à-porter show at the Pitti Palace the mannequins were told to

5

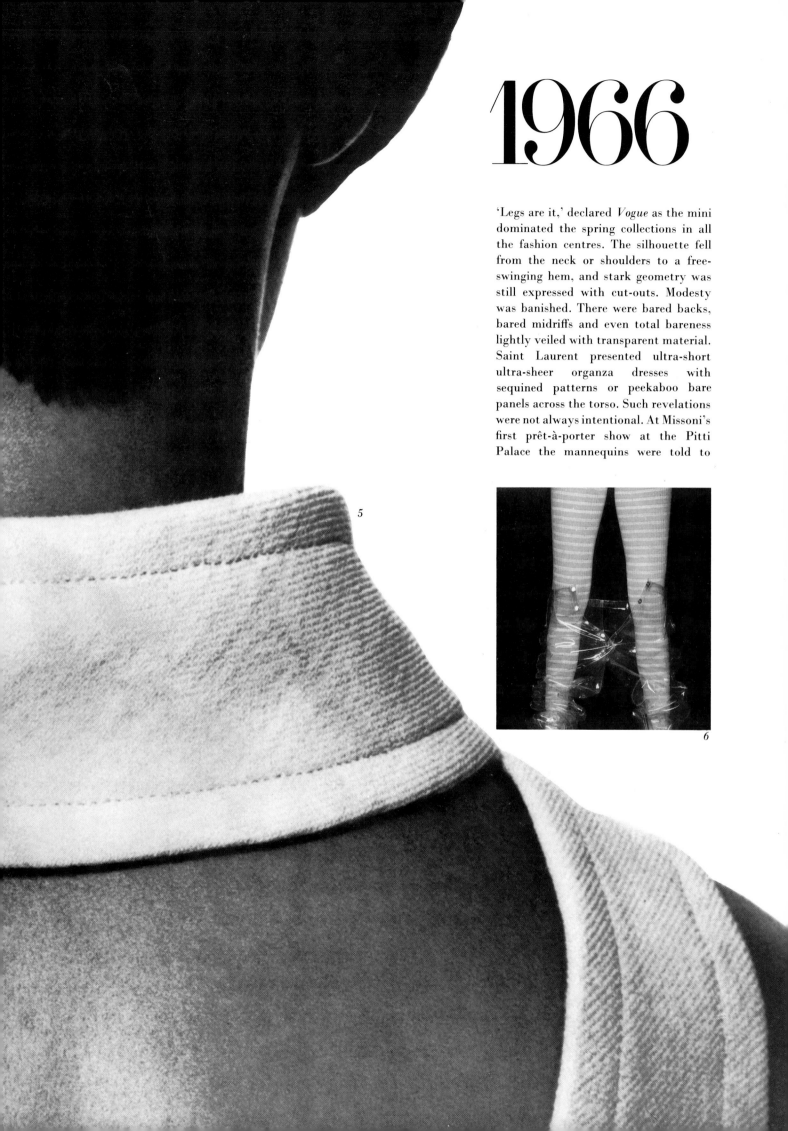

6

7

8

7. *Saint Laurent's pea jacket, tailored trousers and rollnecked sweater.*
8. *Krizia's blue-and-white Pop Art dress and Varese's Greek sandals.*
9. *Saint Laurent's navy-blue pure wool whipcord nautical coat, double-breasted with brass buttons and side-tilted cap. Vivier's buckle shoes.*
10. *Grace Coddington models Bagatel's scarlet-and-ochre coat from the young London chain store, Miss Selfridge.* 11. *Left: Corneyel's black-and-white jersey two piece. Right: Bettina's black-and-white synthetic jersey two piece.*

9

10

11

12

12. *Batman cartoon-strip captioning in British* Vogue. 13. *John Bates's wasp-striped jersey dress, child-like sandals and a Sassoon haircut.* 14. *Françoise Hardy wears Saint Laurent's* Rive Gauche-*knitted tube in navy and yellow wool.* 15. *Twiggy models Betsey Johnson's skin-tight leather jumpsuit with legs zipped from top to toe. The top zips up to a polo neck and back down all along the sleeves.* 16. *Paper dress worn by Wendy Vanderbilt in black-and-white patterned Kleenex paper and nylon.*

remove underwear that was showing through the light lamé blouses. Under the bright lights on the catwalk the clothes became transparent, and they were greeted with applause by buyers and reproaches from the management.

Traditional fashion rules were broken as designers tried to create clothes from unlikely materials – paper, tin cans and even mirrors. Each gimmick had its brief moment before being swept aside by another. In Paris Paco Rabanne featured plastic discs linked like chain-mail. Geometric plastic, perspex and paper jewellery accompanied the simple op art shifts.

In London the *Daily Mail*'s 'Face of

13

14

15

16

289

17. *Dior's two models under Carita's new coiffure. Left: a grey wool coat edged with black braid. Right: a similar wool belted coat. 18. John Bates's full-length, high-waisted pale-pink vinyl coat, with long mirror ear-rings. 19. Tuffin and Foale's white wool coat is double-breasted and tailored with a wide collar. 20. Daniel Hechter, for Bagatel, designed the camel wool Regency suit, and the boots are by Anello and Davide, the theatrical cobblers. 21. Bergdorf Goodman brown tweed midi suit with a tie leather belt. 22. Cos Cob's Dandy Pants suit in burgundy-red and beige windowpane check. It is worn with a ruffled lace shirt, buckled pumps and a sailor hat.*

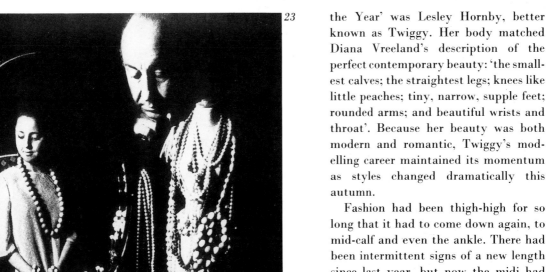

23. *Teresa Topolski models Biba's primrose-spotted voile dress, shaped like a triangle, with half sleeves and a bow tied at the back of the neck.* 24. *Twiggy models Gina Fratini's flared and fluted dress of Ascher's Giselle material.* 25. *Emmanuelle Khanh working with the Missonis: knitted silk jersey tube and Paco Rabanne's jewellery.* 26. *Jeanne Do (for Chloé) square pastiche: dress with a short, cutaway top and a skirt falling to the ankles, decorated with silver squares and pearls.*

24   25   26

the Year' was Lesley Hornby, better known as Twiggy. Her body matched Diana Vreeland's description of the perfect contemporary beauty: 'the smallest calves; the straightest legs; knees like little peaches; tiny, narrow, supple feet; rounded arms; and beautiful wrists and throat'. Because her beauty was both modern and romantic, Twiggy's modelling career maintained its momentum as styles changed dramatically this autumn.

Fashion had been thigh-high for so long that it had to come down again, to mid-calf and even the ankle. There had been intermittent signs of a new length since last year, but now the midi had definitely arrived and *Vogue* advised its readers to get accustomed to the new proportions. The hemline was only sixteen inches from the ground and brought back a softer, more elegant look. British *Vogue* referred to it as the Regency Beau style and showed it with fob watches, walking sticks, and dandy accessories. Coats came down inches over knee-high boots, and were often worn over still minuscule dresses and suits. The intention, expressed most clearly at Dior and Saint Laurent, was to train the customer's eye down from the mini to the midi by showing one over the other.

This desire to straddle the two modes was also reflected in evening wear. For dances and formal parties Paris collections showed glorified nightdresses with a Regency air, as well as brassière tops, asymmetric and halter necklines and layers of chiffon, while the Italians preferred the magnificence of formal ballgowns. Despite the couture's direction, most young women still wore their daytime minis right through the night, simply changing their accessories.

Boutique fashion continued to thrive and in London eclipsed the couture salons, which began to fade from the pages of *Vogue*. Quant sold well in New York, Tuffin & Foale was stocked in Paraphernalia, Betsey Johnson was available in Bazaar. In London Barbara Hulanicki opened a new boutique called Biba, a treasure chest of the new romanticism. In Paris Khanh was designing for the ready-to-wear house Cacharel, and the nautical theme launched by Saint Laurent in the spring — reefer coats, more pea jackets, bell-bottom trousers, and T-shirt dresses — was copied for the ready-to-wear by Bagatel.

1967

The hippy movement, which originated in the Haight-Ashbury district of San Francisco, made its own contribution to the romantic fashion of the day. Its symbol of peace, the flower, adorned buttonholes, sandals, headbands and hairpieces, and the brightly coloured, irregular, abstract, psychedelic patterns associated with its drug culture paraded across clothes that had little to do with modernity or practicality.

An air of impracticality or otherworldliness pervaded boutique and couture fashions alike and romance was a unifying theme that took its inspiration from a wide variety of often contrasting sources. The Beau Brummel style was masculine – berets, waistcoats, walking canes, finely tailored trousers and suits. The trouser suit eclipsed skirt suits and Saint Laurent turned to men's tailoring techniques and men's stiff suiting materials. There was the feminine style – women could look like Hollywood film stars, sixteenth-century heroines swathed in velvet and sables, or the *dolce vita* girls in seductive tiger-printed lamé. For evening Saint Laurent showed Camelot dresses and brown velvet medieval page-boy suits worn with high, high boots. Styles were mixed with abandon: knickerbockers in tweed or velvet were worn with long jackets, turtleneck sweaters, felt d'Artagnan hats with trailing

1. Susan Small's Regency velvet trouser suit, quilted paisley waistcoat, silk satin shirt with pearl buttons from Turnbull and Asser. 2. Halston's black and white broadcloth shirts, white stitching outlining the seams of the black shirt, and vice versa. 3. Forquets' black wool coat and catsuit and Caressa's wide-brimmed hat. 4. Ossie Clark's long black coat in Vistram (a new textured fabric) with outsized collar and belt, pilot helmet and Russell and Bromley boots imitating shoes with leggings. 5. Ricci's Dr Zhivago-style wool coat edged with white fur. 6. Navy-blue velour, circular-seamed cape over matching culottes, six foot muffler from Wallis.

2

feathers, long door-catching scarves and full-length motoring coats.

Couture clothes had a new largesse this autumn. Dresses and trousers widened towards the hem, and double-faced materials swung from small, tailored, feminine shoulders into wide capes and full coats. Fur coats were especially popular, ranging from the tie-belted

minks of the jet-setters to fun furs dyed outrageous colours. Many women improvised and made old coats fashionable by adding fur hems and big buckle belts.

Big zips up the front of dresses were prominent and chains were the ubiquitous detail: chain belts across the hips, big chain necklaces worn over high-necked jumpers, snaffle-chained shoes,

3

4

5

6

7. *Norell's simple wool evening dress, split up one side.*
8. *Balenciaga's ivory-coloured Gazar, shoulder-encircling headdress and wedding-dress.* 9. *Jantzen's psychedelic swimsuit.* 10. *Saint Laurent's African beaded dress with matching 'necklace' sandals.* 11. *Saint Laurent's navy-blue shantung silk shirt-dress.*

and little chain martingales across the front and back of jackets. Autumn colours were either rampantly vivid or pale: lacquer red and deadly-nightshade purple, or tender pink and silver, seen night and day.

The alternative fashion story belonged to those designers, led by Courrèges, Paco Rabanne and Ungaro, who refused to give up the long-legged, short-skirted mode. Their 'bare as you dare' styles prompted Coty to introduce a new line of cosmetics – body paint. Courrèges launched his Couture Future boutique range in order to profit at least as much as other manufacturers did from copies of his couture collections.

With the emphasis on the leg, be it under long or short clothes, shoes assumed greater importance. Dior models wore perspex heels, Charles Jourdan introduced the doubled-up rounded heel, and Vivier revived the forties' platform shoe. A Parisian novelty was the U-shaped shoe in brown patent leather, with its U throat, U toe and square stacked heel. Square-toed black crocodile-skin boots were also popular. Black or white 'wet-look' leggings were worn with patent or wet-look shoes as an alternative to boots. The leather look-alike, Corfam, produced by Du Pont, was considered healthier than other synthetics because it allowed the foot to breathe and was widely used by French shoe manufacturers. Matt gold slippers were worn for the evening with ankle-to-wrist dresses in black velvet.

Fashion's dictatorship had at last been overthrown. From day to day, from one occasion to the next, women could choose between the amusing, the mobile and the sporty, the shocking, the romantic and the classic.

12

13   *14*

15

12. Quant's dandy: long jacket and straight-legged trousers and a Sassoon bob.
13. Saint Laurent's double-breasted, striped wool gabardine trouser suit with black 'kipper' tie – as wide as a smoked herring. 14. Roger Nelson's blue-red-and-coffee check Madras cotton shorts–vest dress.

This summer British *Vogue* launched a regular feature entitled 'More Dash than Cash', while American *Vogue* promoted Penelope Tree as the epitome late sixties romantic beauty. Large-eyed, small-faced, wan and precious, she shared the fragile, child-like looks of Twiggy and Mia Farrow.

Pinky and Dianne started their own business in New York this year, offering colourful pop clothes.

16   *17*   *18*

15. The Big Zip.
16. Dorothée Bis's dress: white cotton organdie skirt and crocheted cotton bodice, worn with lace party tights.
17. Ungaro's red, navy-blue and white striped leotard with poppy-red Nattier pure wool gabardine pinafore.
18. Gina Fratini's butterfly-and-flower bestrewn, pastel-coloured smock.

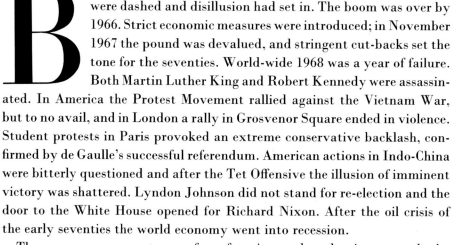

Catherine Deneuve in a Saint Laurent classic, the black smoking suit.

1968-1975

Saint Laurent designs for women with double lives. His day clothes help a woman confront the world of strangers. They permit her to go everywhere without drawing unwelcome attention and, with their somewhat masculine quality, they give her a certain force, prepare her for encounters that may become a conflict of wills. In the evening when a woman chooses to be with those she is fond of, he makes her seductive.

Catherine Deneuve

Karl Lagerfeld.

Bill Gibb.

By the end of the decade the sixties had turned sour; hopes were dashed and disillusion had set in. The boom was over by 1966. Strict economic measures were introduced; in November 1967 the pound was devalued, and stringent cut-backs set the tone for the seventies. World-wide 1968 was a year of failure. Both Martin Luther King and Robert Kennedy were assassinated. In America the Protest Movement rallied against the Vietnam War, but to no avail, and in London a rally in Grosvenor Square ended in violence. Student protests in Paris provoked an extreme conservative backlash, confirmed by de Gaulle's successful referendum. American actions in Indo-China were bitterly questioned and after the Tet Offensive the illusion of imminent victory was shattered. Lyndon Johnson did not stand for re-election and the door to the White House opened for Richard Nixon. After the oil crisis of the early seventies the world economy went into recession.

There was a movement away from futurism and modernism towards the past and the cultures of the East. 'We' gave way to 'me' as the communal ethic was replaced by narcissism. Hallucinogenic and 'mind expanding' drugs accelerated the trend towards introspection and by 1966 were widely used by hippies, who came to embody the search for an 'alternative' society. The use of LSD was popularized by pop stars and was even intellectually 'justified' by acid expert Dr Timothy Leary of Harvard University, who encouraged free-thinking youth to 'Turn on, tune in, drop out'.

The alternative hippy style was the most memorable expression of the turmoil in fashion. The philosophy of self-expression and inner freedom led to an abandonment of social convention. Interest in the Orient and mysticism was reflected in hippy clothes, which tended to be home-made and decorated with pseudo-political symbols, notably flowers, a symbol of peace. Typical hippies wore beads, leather, suede and commune-made, ethnic jewellery. Making clothes and jewellery was also a source of income for them.

There was a general movement away from the 'metropolitan dream' in favour of a rural ideal. The young wanted to put down roots, whether by setting up communes or decorating their urban 'crash pads'. In Britain Terence Conran anticipated this, opening Habitat in 1966, which offered cheap, well-designed, mass-produced household goods.

Hand crafts such as knitting, embroidery, natural dyeing and leather tanning enjoyed a revival as a result of the interest in ecology. The clothes of Laura Ashley and Ralph Lauren evoked the simple joys of the past. Opening her first shop in 1967 in London, Laura Ashley offered the Victorian milkmaid look – dresses in sprigged cottons and white high-necked blouses – at affordable prices. Having tapped the nostalgic mood, she enjoyed rapid success. Her clothes coincided with a strong anti-fashion movement and also reflected the prevailing confusion about women's roles.

The simple, 'honest' lifestyle of the artisan was idealized and emulated by small workshops such as Pablo and Delia, Kaffe Fassett, Bill Gibb and Missoni. Gibb combined his Celtic background with a love for the historic, especially the Renaissance, and the American hippy culture introduced to him by Fassett. Together in 1970 they produced an exotic collection of hand-dyed tartan and handknits, for which Gibb was elected Designer of the Year by British *Vogue*. Specializing in fantasy, embroidery and appliqué, he presented huge, doll-like smocks, often adorned with his bee motif.

Zandra Rhodes wanted to raise the status of textile art. Having graduated from the Royal College of Art in 1964, she opened a studio producing materials based on American pop art, comic strips and neon signs. She decided to go into partnership with Sylvia Ayton in 1967 but as her work became more figurative (motifs included lipsticks, teddy bears and hands, for she was 'tired of good taste'), they parted company.

Her first solo collection in 1969 strongly reflected the prevailing nostalgic and rural interest. Having studied historic knits in the Victoria and Albert Museum, she designed dresses printed with motifs of classic knitting stitches. Her clothes were taken up by American *Vogue* and Bendels, and after an introduction by British *Vogue* she was stocked exclusively by Fortnum & Mason. Through the early seventies each Rhodes collection was based on a definite theme, often inspired by travel: the chevron-striped Ukraine shawl and the North American Indian in 1970 – the first collection in which she used feathers; Elizabethan slashed doublets, Boucher frills and button flowers (1971); Japanese flowers, calligraphy and shells (1972). She evolved new textile techniques such as intercutting and reverse printing and became a greatly respected designer of fantasy evening gowns.

The revival of art nouveau and art deco was another borrowing from the past that affected mainstream and off-beat design. There were art deco exhibitions in Minneapolis and Paris in 1966 and Bernard Nevill produced a series of popular Vorticist-inspired textiles for Liberty. His 1966 Jazz Age collection consisted of smoking jackets, Nijinsky shirts and silk pyjamas. Between 1969 and 1972 Karl Lagerfeld's work for Chloé was clearly influenced by the art deco collection he was amassing.

High fashion was confused. The mini, midi and maxi in space age, Hollywood 'glam' and gypsy styles were shown side by side on the catwalks. The fashion industry had attempted to oust the mini with the midi, but to no avail. The rejection in 1968 of the midi was hailed on both sides of the Atlantic as an indication of the contemporary woman's raised consciousness – ironically so, since the mini was one of the most sexist fashions of all times.

Richard Nixon.

'Let the world know how groovy you can be,' recommended Vogue. *Picnicking at Woodstock peace concert in 1969.*

The cast of Hair, 1969.

Zandra Rhodes.

Germaine Greer, feminist author of The Female Eunuch, *1971.*

Pablo and Delia.

Faye Dunaway, *heroine of the film* Network, *1974.*

Midis were split up to the thigh and cut in slinky or diaphanous materials to make them more overtly sexy, but few would accept this confidence trick. The fashion establishment tried again; 'hot pants' (christened by *Women's Wear Daily* in 1971) appeared in 1969 under a split midi. Women simply discarded the skirt and paraded yet more flesh in one of fashion's most amusing and vulgar fads.

Many women were tired of high-fashion gimmicks. Indeed to be fashion-conscious was deemed ill-informed by the early seventies. 'The seventies were just O D-ing. How can you maintain that frenzy, that amount of invention? By the seventies everyone wanted to trash the sixties,' recalls Betsey Johnson. Fashion was now interpreted in two relatively new ways. Some chose to find alternative, anti-fashion styles such as denim, army fatigue and nostalgic, junkshop chic. 'Clothes are just not important,' Rudi Gernreich told *Time* magazine in 1967; 'they're not status symbols any longer. They're for fun.' Battalions of denim-clad women hit the streets, for the material had become an anti-fashion statement, supposedly representing freedom and a reaction to the frivolity of a biannual change. However, designers seized this 'underground' material and made it high fashion. French prêt-à-porter houses styled second-hand or 'fatigued' denim into skirts, jackets, waistcoats and midi coats, richly embroidered in peasant styles or adorned with studs and chains, flooding America, 'the home of denim', with European 'designer' versions, and turning workers' clothing into a fad. The next move was the enormous commercial success of designer jeans.

However, working or older women reacted against fads by demanding classics and many designers focused on this market. Although glam-rock clothes in colourful satin, velvet and suede, hot pants and platform shoes – typically found at Mr Freedom in London, Paraphernalia and Etcetera in New York and Orbit and Miranda's Boutique in San Francisco – are the most easily recalled styles of the early seventies, in fact it was these understated classics that became the mainstay of the fashion industry.

Some of the most outstanding designers of working clothes were women, who approached the problem with intelligence, artistic flare and business acumen, while understanding what was comfortable and alluring. What distinguished their collections was a profound evolution of style rather than random changes. Jean Muir, Sonia Rykiel, Laura Biagiotti and the Fendi sisters were acclaimed as style adjusters, following the traditions of Chanel, Schiaparelli, Grès and McCardell. Perhaps an intelligent, intuitive woman will always have an edge over her male counterpart when producing clothes that women really feel comfortable in.

Muir did not regard fashion as a political platform and disapproved of being referred to as a 'feminist' designer: 'I design *feminine* not feminist clothes.' Her greatest contribution was the elimination of darts, for she hated harsh lines, creating snug, easy, close-fitting bodices. She was indebted to lessons learnt at Jaeger designing knitwear, where she discovered how to achieve an effect with simple means. She paid more attention than most to pattern cutting and specialized in knitted rather than woven materials.

In contrast to Grès, who draped jersey, Muir cut the material to exact proportions on the basis of the 'square grain'. Thinking of the figure as an elongated cube, all the shaping is done within this cube, be it a straight cut or a bias cut. 'The whole balance of the garment is closely related to the female anatomy. The art of good cutting is to understand this balance,' insisted Muir.

From 1969 Muir concentrated on matt jersey, which was lightweight and clinging, like her silk crêpes and chiffons. Pockets were placed at the hip seam, a Chanel touch enhancing an elegant and relaxed poise, and decorative top-stitching became a distinctive trademark. Her idea of a modern woman was 'loose-limbed, open-minded and not afraid of her body'. Grace and sense characterized her timeless, perfect clothes rather than obvious glamour. Evolving rather than revolutionizing clothes, she considered that to be in fashion was to be out of style. Her top-stitching, elasticated waists and key-hole collars were copied world-wide. An American survey in 1975, when the popularity of jersey was at its height, reported that Muir and Saint Laurent were the most widely copied designers in the world.

Jean Muir.

Sonia Rykiel, like Muir, had little regard for fashion in the sense of fitting into a contemporary mould. Challenging the established rule of specific clothes for specific occasions, she developed co-ordinated layers of separates, which, with accessories, could be added or removed to create a different look. She also evolved her own system of sizing, which was totally unrelated to standard sizes. She created a layered, body-hugging look in rabbit hair, angora and cashmere. Her hemless skirts and trousers could have a double life by turning them inside out. Having designed for her husband's boutique, Laura, in the mid-sixties, she opened her own in 1968 on the Left Bank, which had become the centre of Parisian prêt-à-porter. In 1970 she was voted one of the fifteen most sensuous women in the world on the strength of her knitwear, and in 1973 was appointed vice-president of the Chambre Syndicale du Prêt-à-porter des Couturiers et des Créateurs de Mode.

Rykiel does not think that only women can understand what women need in terms of dress. She compares the designer to a writer. One only has to look at Flaubert's *Madame Bovary* to see that some men can explain exactly what a woman feels, and the same is true in fashion. It is interesting that the French feminist movement is sympathetic to Rykiel's ideas and work. Maison des Femmes, a feminist bookshop in Paris, devoted an entire window to her book and posters of her collections in 1985.

Sonia Rykiel.

Laura Biagiotti, like Muir and Rykiel, realized that there was a need for a simple 'capsule' wardrobe for the working woman who had to wear the same clothes from nine in the morning to the late evening. However, the working woman had to feel feminine, not a surrogate man; she had to travel frequently and longed for quality and comfort. Biagiotti satisfied all these needs in her clothes. She was interested in selling dresses not to the very rich, who buy twenty dresses a season, typically from Saint Laurent and Valentino, but to ordinary women. She rejected the sexual typecasting that masculine designers imposed on women, believing that politeness makes it inappropriate for women to look sexy at work. Because knitted clothes are easy to wear and travel well, she began designing in cashmere and, having bought a cashmere factory in Pisa, became known as the 'Queen of cashmere', with an extensive colour card of eighty tones.

Biagiotti was one of those who promoted seasonless, sizeless fashion. Central heating and air conditioning made climate less important. Designing clothes for all shapes, never forgetting the reality of life – a large pasta lunch or early pregnancy – her clothes had elasticated waistbands. 'A well-designed dress is the best diet,' she assured her clients. Her clothing philosophy was encapsulated in the 'Bambola' dress, a large tent shape, which was her greatest success. Presented annually from 1974, it was a practical, feminine, seasonless dress.

Laura Biagiotti.

The long-established fur and leather firm of Fendi in Rome was run by five sisters, who decided to confront the international market. While admiring the work of Gucci and Hermès, they realized that the classic luxury handbag – a stiff envelope that held very little – was inappropriate for working women. They concentrated on top-quality, big, soft, unstructured bags. The Fendi sisters employed Karl Lagerfeld to design their fur range and he changed the whole silhouette of modern furs. Classic furs were made from pelts with the hide intact, so they had to be lined and were very heavy. Lagerfeld insisted that the underside of the pelts be stripped down to the very thinnest layer needed to support the pile, and by softening and treating the underside, made it unnecessary to line the garment.

In America the most successful modernists were Calvin Klein, Ralph Lauren, Geoffrey Beene and Roy Halston, all working in ready-to-wear. They evolved an American chic based on classic tailored separates combined with knitwear, in mix-and-match tones. Their aim was to capture the increasingly wealthy market of working women, who wanted easy, comfortable, co-ordinated clothing, which could be added to season by season to create a capsule wardrobe. Accessories and hairstyles denoted the latest fashion, rather than dramatic changes in the silhouette.

The difference between these large American ready-to-wear houses and the traditional French houses was the process of designing. While many of the French designers could be accused of a myopic, almost dictatorial attitude to dress, which was invariably based on an aesthetic notion rather than a practical need, the Americans prided themselves on being completely client-orientated. Seeking to fill gaps in the market and designing for a specific, modern lifestyle that the chic set in Paris had not yet acknowledged, they acted upon the responses of their customers. Bill Blass spent most of the year on the road, visiting the women he dressed and listening to their needs; Norma Kamali insisted on controlling her retail outlet so that she could instantly gauge her clients' reaction to a garment the day it was put in stock – the boutique was her laboratory; Calvin Klein made his debut in fashion to fill a specific gap in the market – coats for the young.

Halston, the father of minimalism, purged clothing of zips, reduced the number of seams and buttons, and avoided collars and cuffs. He also minimalized the number of clothes in a wardrobe, for he believed that the modern woman did not want the burden of a capacious wardrobe but rather a compact, integrated and carefree range. The quintessential Halston was a narrow shirtwaister in 'ultra-suede', tied easily at the waist.

Geoffrey Beene combined virtual couture quality with modern, easy sportswear lines. 'I have never liked rigid clothes. I like freedom. I am an American; I love sweatshirts, skirts and loafers, and I have never deviated from the premise of freedom and effortlessness.' Having been fired from a Seventh Avenue house for designing a collection that was too avant-garde – he regarded it as one of his best – he eventually launched his own label in 1963. His clothes were easy, flirty and showed legs, legs, legs.

One of his most significant contributions was making synthetics more acceptable. In the early sixties he was one of ten leading international designers approached by Du Pont to promote a new synthetic, Qiana, intended for the mass market. Du Pont offered to have the yarn made up into any material by the factory of their choice. Beene chose satin velour decoupé. 'Working with this material proved to me that synthetics could be perfected, for it was exactly like a pure silk velour, only it did not crease.'

Gloria Vanderbilt and her mirrored reflection flank Geoffrey Beene.

Beene believed that the future of fashion lay with perfected synthetics.

Calvin Klein's clothes, a leading contribution to fashion in the seventies, were distinguished by their sensuous body-consciousness. The body was implied under the best-quality materials (never American – he engaged in a running battle with the American textile industry over their lack of quality and innovation), typically linen, suede, cashmere, flannel and tweed. Klein believed that 'If you're really interested in clothes, then your body should be in shape'. He made modern clothes for modern women and refused to look back to the thirties or forties. The clothes were easy, pure and simple – which is far from simple to achieve. The image of Faye Dunaway in *Network* – sexy and modern – immediately springs to mind when describing Klein's clothes (he would have loved to design the clothes for this film).

The essence of his modernism was a total disregard for the European couture tradition, yet at this time Europe was becoming increasingly interested in American style. Pioneers such as André Putman in Paris and Grace Coddington in London, following a Japanese lead around 1974, adopted the American, and specifically Klein's, mode of dress. Klein admitted that 'When I was at school I wouldn't have believed that the European press would ever be here, especially the French, but now they recognize a strong American style.' The existence of American style was not new, and over the past two decades many European designers had borrowed from American traditions, Saint Laurent's pea jacket being a notable example. However, in such a big, wealthy country designers had not needed to try to export to Europe.

Though Klein evolved a distinctly avant-garde style, he was happy to acknowledge the influence of Claire McCardell. She was the first American designer to totally disregard Europeanism and created the sportswear for which America became famous. 'They are the only clothes from the late forties and fifties that could still be worn today beautifully,' claimed Klein. Other sources of inspiration included Luis Barrogan's buildings and the terrain of south-west America; his neutral palette was indebted to the paintings of Andrew Wyeth – the stones, sands, buffs and earth tones – and of Georgia O'Keefe – the azures, violets, whites and oysters.

Designer ownership changed the American fashion industry in the late sixties. Until then designers had been employed by large manufacturers who controlled their creative output and submerged their identity. John Fairchild of *Women's Wear Daily* and Nicolas de Gunzburg of American *Vogue* consistently promoted the designer names in these publications, ensuring that their identity was brought to the attention of the retailer and the consumer.

Bill Blass, who started his career as a sketch artist at David Crystal before the war, joined Anna Miller, which merged with Maurice Rentner in 1959. He set about securing ownership of the company, becoming vice-president and then sole owner in 1970, the first ready-to-wear designer to buy out his bosses and own his label on Seventh Avenue. Blass knew his market: status-conscious, rich American women, who demanded glitter and glamour for the evening and comfortable, simple sportswear by day. His travels round the country led him to believe that, with the expansion of inter-city communications, styles differed very little between the East and West Coasts. Blass, like his contemporaries, loved highly tailored, simple clothes and regretted that he did not have a chance to study in Paris, the top place for cutting. When asked whether he regarded fashion-designing as an art, he replied: 'No. It's a craft – sometimes a creative one, sometimes a technical one. It only becomes an art in the hands of Mme Grès or Balenciaga.'

Calvin Klein.

Grace Coddington, ex-model and British Vogue *fashion editor.*

Oscar de la Renta with his spaniels.

James Galanos.

Oscar de la Renta offered opulent exclusivity. His luxury gypsy and peasant clothes of the late sixties brought couture chic to hippy styles. He found a niche in American fashion by combining Mediterranean notions of romance, elegance and above all femininity in his evening wear with American demands for casual day clothes.

James Galanos, who trained at Piguet, was specializing in clothes of the utmost luxury, distinguished by fastidious cut, thereby bringing the status of top American ready-to-wear close to that of couture. Stephen Burrows and John Kloss were promoted through boutique operations in Henri Bendels, New York, in the early seventies. Both experimented with the gaucho look, appliqué and quilted hippy styles. Kloss then developed understated American classic sportswear in rich, brilliant colours.

Grooming and fitness had become key requirements of the fashionable look, particularly in the United States, where they became a veritable obsession. Designers abandoned the architectural shapes in heavy materials that had distinguished mid-sixties fashion in favour of an easier, softer silhouette in light materials that gently contoured the body. As a reaction to the gimmicky fashions and doll-like, heavy make-up of the previous period, fashion and cosmetics were now relatively understated. Women were advised to concentrate on natural beauty combined with a personal clothes style that would enhance them, rather than following the vagaries of the mode. The body had to be trim and supple, since controlling corsetry had been abandoned. It was now as important for a woman to attend a gymnasium or dance class as a hairdressing salon or beauty parlour. Beauty tips based on greater scientific knowledge were suggested in *Vogue*, such as exercise routines and health foods, and diet and health were allotted more editorial space. With high medical costs and an increase in the number of working women, many felt that they could not afford to be ill and took determined precautions. Though this interest in health and exercise was beneficial on a large scale, in some cases it turned into an obsession. The desperation to appear young and nubile perhaps reflected the marital instability in the West, where divorce figures soared.

The French fashion industry developed in two distinct directions. The couture still concentrated on exclusive luxury, especially evening gowns and formal day wear, largely abandoning the youthful, novelty-consciousness of the sixties, while the prêt-à-porter now determined the course of mainstream fashion, as important designers chose to work in this medium.

In 1968 Balenciaga closed his house, stating that the era of the couture was over. Mrs Paul Mellon, a faithful client, was devastated and asked Balenciaga, 'But where shall I go?' By way of answer, he took her by the hand across the street to Givenchy, where she remained. Givenchy inherited many of Balenciaga's customers, many of whom were Americans who had both the purses and the figures to afford his simple French luxury.

Throughout the seventies and eighties the couture had to struggle, for it now existed solely as a flagship for the profitable ready-to-wear industry. The tradition of selling toiles to manufacturers had waned as ready-to-wear fashion no longer copied the couture. Marc Bohan at Dior revealed that each couture outfit was a 'gift' to his customers: the real price of a couture dress was now so high (because of labour, premises and materials) that many garments were under-priced in order to sell them. Couture gowns became advertisements for the house; socialites and actresses became virtual house mannequins, notably Paloma Picasso and Catherine Deneuve for Saint

Laurent and Princess Caroline of Monaco for Dior. The *vendeuse mondaine*, who was lent clothes to wear at the 'right' parties, was another method of promoting a designer's work that had prevailed since couture began.

Yves Saint Laurent's assistant, Loulou de la Falaise, played a vital role in inspiring and encouraging him. His close companion and dedicated supporter, her witty chic became an essential ingredient in his creative life. Such an association between couturier and assistant was not without precedent: Dior worked closely with Victoire, Givenchy with Bettina (both house models); Calvin Klein's inspiration was Frances Stein and Karl Lagerfeld's Anna Piaggi of Italian *Vogue*.

Saint Laurent was the most successful and influential designer to combine the art of the couture with the economic realities of the prêt-à-porter. In the mid-sixties he perceived that the couture was waning and decided to launch a boutique range, Rive Gauche – the name reflected his interest in Left Bank activities. He also experimented with numerous contemporary influences including pop art, often after other designers but somehow with a more show-stopping effect. By the early seventies he found his *métier*: casual, masculine clothes for the day and unrivalled fantasy for the evening. By the mid-seventies he had settled into the role of supreme ready-to-wear designer. Having evolved his classics – the blazer, smoking jacket, pea jacket, bolero, tailored trousers and short, straight skirt – he now simply changed colours and accessories each season; accessories, he believed, had become the essence of high fashion, which is why he and Loulou de la Falaise spent so much time designing costume jewellery. Each collection had an historical or theatrical theme – Dr Zhivago, Little Lord Fauntleroy, African art, Carmen, chinoiserie or forties tarts – but he no longer offered novelty of cut, revolutionary dress theories or the show-stopping techniques that had once been the wonder of the fashion world. His distinctive style was the product of his firm belief in a basic wardrobe of classics, which would give a woman confidence, in the same way that a man had the security of sartorial traditions.

By 1972 Saint Laurent considered that change was old-fashioned. 'Once we needed to have changes in fashion. New looks and new guises. But it is ridiculous to think that clothes must change, that hemlines must change, that women want pants this season and not the next. Women will change their clothes but always within the ideas that we have now developed.'

His exotic fantasy was unrivalled. As Anthony Burgess once said of his collection, 'Nobody had to swallow the whole rich draught, nobody could. But you can sip, you can make your own mild cocktail of the ingredients.' His clothes enhanced the gestures of women and made perfection seem both easy and inevitable, though these clothes were born of artistic trauma. The distressed and hyper-sensitive Saint Laurent was to suffer from the demands of his career – the need to create several collections a year.

The Japanese influence on European style was led by Kenzo Takada and Issey Miyake, who brought a radically different approach to silhouette and a peculiar sensitivity to texture and colour. A completely different attitude to the body and clothing was introduced to the West: the Eastern tradition of covering the body in loose layers rather than outlining it by close cut.

Before the war traditional styles of dress dominated Japanese clothing; fashions certainly did not change twice a year. The East was gradually flooded with Western ideas and styles, but none of the Japanese designers had the confidence to challenge the centre of high fashion, Paris, until Kenzo arrived there in 1969.

Marc Bohan, designer-in-chief at Dior.

Paloma Picasso.

Yves Saint Laurent and Loulou de la Falaise.

Kenzo.

One source of Kenzo's inspirations, traditional Japanese dress.

A Kenzo interpretation.

The Bunka school of fashion in Tokyo, headed by Chie Koike, who was in the same year as Saint Laurent and a year above Karl Lagerfeld at the Ecole de la Chambre Syndicale, was an important influence in developing the talents of Japanese designers. Unlike their British counterparts, the students on this course had to study all aspects of clothing production for two or three years before being admitted on to the design course. This system was successful in producing designers with technical expertise. Kenzo, one of the first to study fashion at the Bunka school, had always dreamed of visiting Paris, but rejected the old, untouchable image of Parisian couture. His young, easy style gave a feeling of independence from the past. His models were lively and informal, in contrast to the cold, elegant couture girls.

He made his début with a collection presented in the spring of 1970, which was an acclaimed success. Like Givenchy's, it was presented in economical cotton. The October collection that year offered a range of square-cut jumpers influenced by the rectangular looseness and versatility of the kimono, which was echoed in his dresses and jackets. Kenzo's unstructured clothes had a delicate sensuousness. On being asked recently why he did not design close-fitted, 'sexy' clothes, he winced and coyly replied, 'I couldn't, I'm too shy'. He designed for an energetic, informal thirty-year-old woman, offering the colourful richness of his travels: the folklore of the Orient, Peru or India. Constantly referring to the folkloric mixture and layering of patterns on prints, he played with bright, happy colours and his clothes, mostly daywear, contrasted boldly with the glamorous, self-conscious couture garments.

In many ways Kenzo's designs became more international after he settled in Paris. Miyake offered the East to the West in a much more undiluted form; he maintained a base in Japan and an unmistakably Japanese feel to his clothes. Concentrating on fluidity and textures, he combined these with the professional technique he had learned at the Ecole de la Chambre Syndicale. Having designed for Geoffrey Beene, he returned to Tokyo in 1970 and established his own studio. After winning recognition and success in Japan and America, he returned to Paris in 1973 and presented his first collection. Miyake allied traditional Eastern styles, materials, colours and skills, such as *sashiko* quilting, with ultra-modern techniques of manufacture, to create loose, comfortable, fluid clothes.

By the mid-seventies Milan had become an essential stop on the international fashion circuit, as Italian ready-to-wear was now based there. The top firms included Basile, Byblos, Cadette, Genny, Krizia and Maxmara; they employed freelance designers particularly from the French and the English art schools, many of whom remained anonymous.

FTM, a partnership between Ferrante, Tositti and Monti, was founded in 1967 to distribute prêt-à-porter labels – de Parisini, Missoni, Montedoro, Caumont, Cerruti, Callaghan, and some French houses – and in 1967 set up the ready-to-wear house of Basile. In 1970 the designing was co-ordinated by the young stylist Walter Albini, who was later joined by Muriel Grateau. Walter Albini also designed for Cadette, founded by Enzo Clocchiatti and Christine Tidmarsh, Billy Ballo and Mariuccia Mandelli's Krizia. One of Krizia's most distinctive and recurring themes was animals; from 1968 she chose an animal as a motif for each collection – sheep, bears and foxes were intricately knitted or appliquéd on her clothes.

Walter Albini was acclaimed as a formative and inspirational talent. Working in association with avant-garde editors such as Anna Piaggi of Italian *Vogue*, he was hailed as a master of casual, colourful ease. By 1971 he was presenting collections for five different houses each season.

Though the classics prevailed during the early and mid-seventies, a more daring, creative look was evident on the outskirts of mainstream fashion. Anarchic chic from the streets was gradually given high fashion status. Vivienne Westwood, John Krevine and Steph Rayner of Acme Attractions, Esme Young, Willie Walters, Judy Dewsbury and Melanie Harberfield of Swanky Modes in London, and Pinky and Dianne in New York were the most vibrant examples of downbeat chic.

Westwood offered ageless, classless fashion, using clothes as an eloquent vocabulary of rebellion. Influenced by her partner, McLaren, who was interested in reviving rock 'n' roll, she opened Let It Rock in 1971 in the King's Road and visited the East End of London to buy old record singles and clothes. She began designing mock-fifties dress based on Teddy-boy styles. Mr Freedom, Swanky Modes (established in 1972) and Acme Attractions were also offering nostalgic clothes based on pop music.

Issey Miyake.

Eighteen months later Westwood and McLaren renamed their shop Too Fast to Live, Too Young to Die; they regularly closed their boutique to redecorate and 're-image'. Westwood sold bikers' jackets and leather mini skirts decorated with chains, slogans, hair and tyre tubing. Having researched gang cults among the young, Westwood enjoyed creating authentic-looking and shocking gear. T-shirts became an anchor for the shop. They were printed with the prevailing cult message, which gradually became increasingly pornographic. Police raids and court cases inevitably secured a youth following and, with startling frankness, the shop was renamed Sex in 1975. Punk Fashion had arrived. Westwood mischievously designed 'rubber for the street, rubber for the office and rubber for the esoteric types who've always been into it. We're interested in anything rebellious and we see that in terms of all youth cults.'

Acme Attractions rejected the glam-rock and teeny-bopper clothes associated with the Glitter Band, Roxy Music, Abba and Showaddywaddy, offering American punk band looks and updating the teenage styles of the forties and fifties. Mr Freedom, opened by Tommy Roberts, Jimmy O'Connor and Pamela Harvey in 1969, stocked fast fad fashion, including Mickey Mouse T-shirts, satin hot pants, fatigue denim and stack-soled, glam-rock boots.

Mariuccia Mandelli of Krizia.

Fiorucci opened in Milan in 1967. Like these London boutiques it sold clothing inspired by elements of mass culture such as disco and glam-rock music and cartoon and pop art. Initially aimed at teenagers, the image soon appealed to a non-age related market. Elio Fiorucci's windowless shop, lit by quartz-iodine lamps – the first to be seen in Milan – imported Ossie Clark and Zandra Rhodes clothes, and in 1970 he launched the 'status symbols' Fiorucci jeans, for which he hired a top pattern cutter from Valentino. They prompted a flood of 'designer' jeans over the next decade. Fiorucci is associated with the *Saturday Night Fever* disco clothes of the seventies and throw-away gimmicks, for he believed that luxury fashion was irrelevant. He commissioned house designers who reinterpreted American youth cults, returning it to the Americans with the magic of Italian styling.

Designers and public alike grew tired of 'good taste' classics and the 'big look' was introduced in the mid-seventies – loose, baggy, layered capes, smocks, tent dresses, leg-warmers and balaclavas – combined with the ethnic look. The more moderate classics, though never abandoned, were overshadowed by a bolder style in which London's youth, Japan's novelty and the couture's glamour were to play a more dramatic role.

A London punk.

1968

Balenciaga retired from the couture this year. His parting remark was, 'The life that supported the couture is finished. Real couture is a luxury which is just impossible to do any more.' The couture had lost its greatest artist.

There were now two veins of fashion: the romantic look and the soft, classic line. Couture, boutique and home-made clothes all reflected the romance of hippy styles – Balkan, gypsy, Oriental and theatrical influences: Isadora Duncan scarves, pantomime-like outfits with full sleeves, tassels and gold appliqué.

The alternative was the functional classic. The explosions were over. High fashion changed course towards clothes to work in, not parade in; tweed, camel-hair and wool predominated, as did a cleaner, trimmer cut. Clothes suitable for working women of all ages were now fashion's chief concern. The baby-doll look was out, the cult of youth over, leaving women freer to dress as they chose.

The softer classic look for autumn was epitomized by soft jersey dresses with high necklines, long, narrow sleeves and skirts that spun out in a graceful circle or fell into flutes or pleats. Printed jersey had flowered or formal patterns and plain colours were lifted with a dash of white. Jean Muir's meticulously cut dresses in plum-coloured jersey were the epitome of this mood. Plum was *the* colour – adaptable, subtle, muted – from Paris couture to Biba and American do-it-yourself tie-dye.

The Paris collections were softly seductive. The body-conscious, swinging dresses were worn with hair rolled up under alluring, floppy hats. Make-up, too, was muted: pale skin rouged with baby pink, shiny plum-coloured lips and smoky eyes. Quant's 'Sex Pot' and 'Ink Pot' make-up range painted this magnolia face. Hair was styled flat and close to the head, with any fullness centred at the nape of the neck. In came the smooth, shaped, 'page-boy' cut.

The prettiest dresses defined the waist and had tabs, pockets and flashes of appliqué in a contrasting colour. Appliqué, revived by hippy clothes, was borrowed by all. Zandra Rhodes artfully applied it to hand-painted felts and silks.

Marc Bohan's collection for Dior immortalized the Sloane Ranger, or preppy, look: velvet jackets teamed with tailored, pleated skirts, pussy-cat-bow blouses, shoulder bags with gilt chains and matching snaffle-chain shoes. French separates from the boutique and prêt-à-porter collections were unrivalled for quality, style and wearability. Tan Giudicelli for Mic Mac embodied this classic French sporty approach, with easy cardigans worn over tailored trou-

1. Dior's red, white and blue daisy-printed, side-wrapped dress, floppy hat and rolled hair. 2. Muir's grey checked Harris tweed waistcoat, short flared skirt with a blue and pale-grey flowered silk shirt. 3. Bernshaw's Hollywood-style navy-blue soft jersey dressing-gown dress, and an emerald-green knitted border. 4. Quant's dotty voile dress, ruffled at the collar and hem. 5. Gina Fratini's white Vamp Dicel jersey, multi-buttoned trouser ensemble and forties-style turban. 6. Valentino's evening dress patterned with Delft-blue flowers and foliage. 7. Galanos' trouser and bikini ensemble in black flowered lace under transparent lace tunic. 8. Ossie Clark's scarlet crêpe dressing-gown jacket, fluid trousers and voile scarf wrapped into a headband. 9. Goma's (at Patou) storm of feathers gathered up to a polo collar and tied with a wide sash at the waist. The feathers are backed with chiffon.

306

sers, great tweeds, knits and flannels in *11* misty brown, blue, grey, plum and red.

Trouser suits dominated the couture, though they had been available in boutiques for some seasons, for both day and evening wear. The fashion for trousers caused some consternation at more formal venues: the Ritz claimed that one could dine in their restaurant if they couldn't tell whether you were wearing trousers, so many baggy culottes fooled doormen, while the Savoy stated that they would 'use their discretion', but Claridges said emphatically 'No'. But who cared?

The tunic-top fastened with a tab at the front replaced the conventional jacket worn with trousers. Saint Laurent showed tailored suits in black wool and tweeds, while Valentino's carved suits were worn with dashing maxi coats.

By the autumn the maxi coat had arrived in London, worn with two-yard long mufflers. In Rome the unisex suit was presented by Cerruti in his début collection and a mildly androgenous theme evolved. Men's tailoring was hijacked for women's clothes following the release of *Bonnie and Clyde* in 1967, in which Faye Dunaway wore tailored flannel trousers, berets and trench coats.

American women had not accepted the midi or maxi hemlines, preferring the leggy mini, which appeared in various guises – the Hiawatha, Grecian-slave or school-girl look, worn with the mini wrap coat, the Regency coat or the cape.

Coats, whether tailored or romantic, were fashionable everywhere. Perfect redingotes in plain wools with precise small collars or prominent lapels and decorative buttons, romantic capes or long, double-breasted highwayman's coats dominated outer wear.

By the autumn romance characterized evening styling; waists were tightly belted over full, rich skirts of moiré, taffeta or velvet. Plum velvet was the ultimate in contemporary chic, teamed with champagne-coloured satin and turquoise or peach trimmings. Mid-calf was the latest length, drawing attention to luxurious buckled and braid-decorated shoes. In Paris Roger Vivier introduced lower heels at Saint Laurent – $2\frac{1}{2}$ inches at the instep, which give the body a new stance.

In America brilliantly coloured berbers (based on North African tribal costume) took over from the kaftan.

10

12

308

Alternatives were richly embroidered floral skirts with waistcoats or boleros worn over full-sleeved, peasant blouses, with suede boots.

Saint Laurent, the master of evening allure, laced bodices. 'First of all, I think one should want to undo something that a woman is wearing. From the point of view of seduction, it can be a dress that's laced up the front or something knotted on one shoulder so that one thinks: if I pull there, the whole dress will fall down. The laced corset is, of course, the very emblem of sexuality.'

In America Ben Zuckerman retired this year, while Calvin Klein and Barry Schwartz founded their coat company. In Madrid Manuel Pertegaz opened his boutique, specializing in dramatic, boldly cut clothes. Grace Coddington, an ex-model, joined British *Vogue*, to become an internationally respected fashion editor.

Norma Kamali opened her shop in New York, importing wacky British fashion from Biba and Carnaby Street, supplemented by her own designs. Roy Halston, having trained as a milliner with Lilly D'Aché and then with Charles James, opened in New York. He became the father of minimalism. Belinda Belville opened in London, while in Paris Sonia Rykiel opened her own boutique, offering gentle, unstructured jersey co-ordinates, which James Wedge imported for Top Gear in London.

10. *Roger Vivier's 2½-inch heel.*   11. *Saint Laurent's black wool, tailored culottes suit and transparent chiffon blouse.*   12. *Muir's black trousers, white crêpe blouse and crêpe coat.*   13. *Dior's double-breasted, slim black jacket and striped, pleated culottes.*   14. *Mic Mac chevron-printed knit trousers and cardigan.*   15. *Zandra Rhodes and Sylvia Ayton's outfit modelled by Vanessa Redgrave, their financial backer.*   16. *Verushka swathed by Giorgio di Sant'Angelo in exotic silks and tasselled cords.*   17. *Leslie's beige doeskin jacket.*   18. *Norell's narrow, double-breasted coat.*   19. *Ossie Clark's mist-pink tweed coat.*   20. *Saint Laurent's shiny rubber trench coat.*   21. *Cashin's storm-cape circled in leather.*

1969

2   3   4

The hemline was irrelevant; the length of a woman's skirt now depended on personal taste. The international collections endorsed variety, showing minis, midis, maxis and trousers.

However, fashion's followers were confused by the juxtaposition of floor-length hemlines and revealing fashions – skirts slit thigh-high and fringed dresses with deep décolletés were all the rage in Paris this spring; Cardin's white, pailetted 'Merveilleuse' dress was the most extreme example: it was cut so low that the nipples peeped out over a rounded *directoire* neck-line. Karl Lagerfeld at Chloé and Harry Algo also favoured deep necklines.

Midi and maxi dresses followed a softly tailored, body-conscious and sophisticated line across the bodice, capitalizing on the freedom gained from Gernreich's 'no-bra bra'.

There were dominant themes amidst the variety: unisex, art deco, African styles, hand-made and fun clothing. With the opening of the hit musical *Hair*, *Vogue* announced the arrival of 'Afro-dizzyaction': vibrant colours, beadwork, brave, bold prints and accessories. Celia Birtwell, Ossie Clark's partner, explored African themes. Ken Scott's splendid prints in rare colours with velvet patches were inspired by the Cubist work of Robert Delaunay.

Hand crafts such as knitting, painting, tie-dying and patchwork enjoyed popularity as a reaction against 'the age of computers' and the hard, artificial fashions of recent years. A layered, hippy style and the romantic look were seen in Italy: leather bodices and demi-long tiered skirts in wool or organdie, golden bells worn on bare feet, and waists wound with ropes of coral. Feet and legs were still the focus of high fashion; by the autumn the platform shoe prevailed. *Vogue* commented: 'Clunk, clunk, sschump, sschump, bump ... No more clickety, click, tippy, tap, tap – it's the new sound of soles we're talking about – the soles of shoes and sandals are now lifted, thickened, platformed.'

The American collections veered towards the British-inspired classics of mix-and-match separates: tweed hacking jackets, kilts, velvet breeches and pig-skin suede separates. This look was epitomized by Anne Klein and Halston. John Anthony showed the long, belted coat, Henry Fredericks the Edwardian jacket, Aldrich the long Regency coat, and Rizkallah the long-

1. Pattie Harrison and Twiggy model Ken Scott's Robert Delaunay-inspired Cubist patched-velvet evening coats, in combinations of lavender, grey, dusty-blue and brown.   2. Grès's cinnamon-coloured shiny leather short raincoat and crinkly wading boots, both lined with muskrat, and cinnamon-coloured knit jumpsuit.   3. Trigère's brown-and-cream plaid wool short, full coat with a skunk-lined brown jersey hood and Latina boots. 4. Howard's brown and beige herringbone tweed coat lined with borg.   5. Muir's Liberty coin-and-wave-patterned black-and-grey wool crêpe dress with quilted collar and cuffs.   6. Lee Bender's (at Bus Stop) long skinny-rib-knit acrylic bouclé cardigan, buttoned nearly all the way down, and Ravel's 'wet-look' skin-tight plastic boots.   7. Marimekko's red-and-white cotton tent dress with a high yoke.   8. Dorville's pale and dark slate-grey checked wool pinafore worn with two pewter belts and a white crêpe shirt.   9. Leslie Poole's silk 'Flapper' dress.

5   6   7   8   9

10. *Dior's loose lamé dress over matching trousers.* 11. *Cardin's double-faced satin evening dress with simple bow bodice.* 12. *Mademoiselle red-beaded clogs strapped over glitter-gold stockings and Giorgio di Sant'Angelo's glittering gold chain-mail pants with a matching fringed vest.* 13. *Gina Fratini's marigold crêpe jersey dress.* 14. *Quant's seamless silver Lurex body stocking.* 15. *Bonnie Cashin's wheat-coloured suede coat, cut to show the mushroom-coloured wool jersey dress.*

line tunic. Hide fringes were popular on both day and evening wear, worn with knee-length boots. The wide-skirted coat or classic cape with tailored trousers of tweed or jersey were presented at Bill Blass and Oscar de la Renta.

Discretion was the key note of American evening fashion: modest, long dresses or two-piece pyjama ensembles in vivid colours and patterns. Sari colours were combined with mulberry shades and cloudy blues.

The Paris collections could be divided into two schools. At many houses the mini refused to die. It was shown in flimsy, diaphanous materials in exotic colours to highlight and reveal young, tanned, healthy skin. The second school, led by Saint Laurent, showed dark, often black, body-hugging clothes in crêpe, georgette and jersey. This tailored, body-conscious style was softened by a nonchalant, casual, sophisticated air. Harsh lines were unfashionable. Dresses were soft and pretty, and hems, lapels and pocket flaps were rounded. The long body line was emphasized by a low-slung, thin belt and pockets were set low on the hips. Saint Laurent showed gypsy dresses in patchwork prints, with pleated and tiered skirts falling gently against the body. The models wore handkerchiefs tied at the throat.

Brown was a prominent colour for both day and evening wear. Brown linen was popular for summer, worn with white shoes with a contrasting black heel. Where shape was strict, colours and materials were extravagant – damson, prune, amber and black-cherry were the shades for the autumn; for the summer clear, precise colours – white, coral red

16. *Afrodizzyaction: Pourelle's black ciré catsuit, Leonard 'Afro-frizz' wig, African earrings and intricate, multicoloured Nigerian bead necklace and belt.* 17. *Saint Laurent's 'Sloane Ranger' jacket, Ban-Lon blouse, pleated check skirt, gilt chains and neck scarf.* 18. *Cerruti's white wool long-line pullover and pants, worn with navy-blue scarf, low-slung leather belt and stetson hat.*

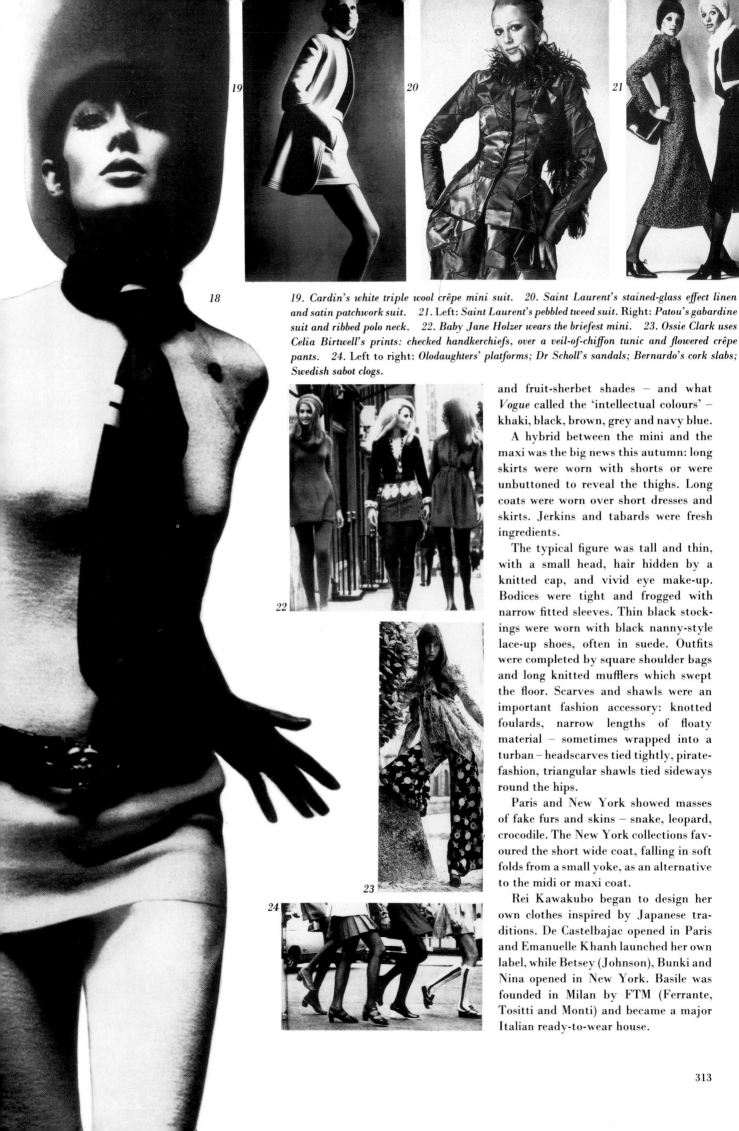

19. *Cardin's white triple wool crêpe mini suit.*   20. *Saint Laurent's stained-glass effect linen and satin patchwork suit.*   21. Left: *Saint Laurent's pebbled tweed suit.* Right: *Patou's gabardine suit and ribbed polo neck.*   22. *Baby Jane Holzer wears the briefest mini.*   23. *Ossie Clark uses Celia Birtwell's prints: checked handkerchiefs, over a veil-of-chiffon tunic and flowered crêpe pants.*   24. *Left to right: Olodaughters' platforms; Dr Scholl's sandals; Bernardo's cork slabs; Swedish sabot clogs.*

and fruit-sherbet shades – and what *Vogue* called the 'intellectual colours' – khaki, black, brown, grey and navy blue.

A hybrid between the mini and the maxi was the big news this autumn: long skirts were worn with shorts or were unbuttoned to reveal the thighs. Long coats were worn over short dresses and skirts. Jerkins and tabards were fresh ingredients.

The typical figure was tall and thin, with a small head, hair hidden by a knitted cap, and vivid eye make-up. Bodices were tight and frogged with narrow fitted sleeves. Thin black stockings were worn with black nanny-style lace-up shoes, often in suede. Outfits were completed by square shoulder bags and long knitted mufflers which swept the floor. Scarves and shawls were an important fashion accessory: knotted foulards, narrow lengths of floaty material – sometimes wrapped into a turban – headscarves tied tightly, pirate-fashion, triangular shawls tied sideways round the hips.

Paris and New York showed masses of fake furs and skins – snake, leopard, crocodile. The New York collections favoured the short wide coat, falling in soft folds from a small yoke, as an alternative to the midi or maxi coat.

Rei Kawakubo began to design her own clothes inspired by Japanese traditions. De Castelbajac opened in Paris and Emanuelle Khanh launched her own label, while Betsey (Johnson), Bunki and Nina opened in New York. Basile was founded in Milan by FTM (Ferrante, Tositti and Monti) and became a major Italian ready-to-wear house.

1970

The 'me decade', as it was christened by Tom Wolfe, commenced. Choice had become so wide that women could dress exactly as they wanted, with no need for consistency in self image. There was no *one* look. Fashion magazines encouraged the gypsy look, which flourished among the young attending pop festivals: calico, big leather belts, beads, shawls, handkerchiefs and leather thongs tied round the neck, canvas boots or rope-soled espadrilles were *de rigueur*. Prints abounded – everything from imitations of Lichtenstein paintings to dots and spots with multi-coloured borders, which were a sensation at Chloé. Fake fur, silk head-dresses, tapestry coats and boots, zouave pants bloused out over suede boots that were laced up the leg like a corset – everything was patterned.

America welcomed 'a great Tartar invasion, coming in on a fusillade of brilliant colour'. A Far East shop opened in New York, an Aladdin's cave of fabulously tie-dyed silk and cotton scarves, sarongs and lengths of material.

British *Vogue* featured the hand crafts of Zandra Rhodes, Pablo and Delia,

Ossie Clark, Celia Birtwell and Kaffe Fassett, and Barbara Hulanicki's range of appliqué work in her new, larger Biba emporium in Kensington High Street. Bill Gibb, renowned for his leather work, appliqué and elaborate knits, was chosen by British *Vogue* as Designer of the Year. The emphasis on do-it-yourself fashion was also found in San Francisco, where

numerous boutiques offered hippy clothing. Pablo and Delia, from Buenos Aires, were a personification of the alternative, self-expressive, artistic fashion talent of the early seventies. They made clothes reminiscent of a Bavarian fantasy, belts and bags decorated with imaginary landscapes and rainbow-coloured shoes.

Romance inevitably led to retro,

1. Dorothée Bis's pastel-coloured fur jackets in chèvre-de-Chine closed by frogged loops, printed velvet trousers and long-sleeved wool T-shirts. The buckskin hats are banded with plaited hair. 2. Remoma's patchwork leather blouson biker's jacket. 3. Guy Laroche's blue, fuchsia and beige chamois-leather laced tunic, New Man's velvet jeans and a panther-print pouch bag. 4. Oscar de la Renta's patterned and painted black leather midi coat, with black fox-fur borders, over a zouave jumpsuit and painted boots. 5. Willi Althof's floor-length wool drap coat printed like snakeskin, worn with thonged snakeskin shoulderbag. 6. Chloé's panne velvet coat with raglan sleeves and narrow collar is hand-painted with clouds and a snow scene. Ostrich-trimmed panne velvet hat. 7. Dolores Guinness wears Givenchy's greige buckskin coat and white trouser suit.

4

5

6

7

8. Trigère's taupe silk poncho dress and small-headed coiffure.

9. Twiggy models Pablo & Delia's sky-blue two-tiered leather dress and Ravel's platform shoes, threaded through with ribbons.

10. Renaissance splendour. Left: Thea Porter's furred, gold/brown panne velvet, sleeves slashed with gold, frilled at cuffs and finished with trefoils of gold. High waist, skirt falling into drapes on either side of a green velvet panel. Right: Belville Sassoon long bois de rose flowering wool, slashes opening on royal-blue velvet sleeves gathered into a long, tight cuff.

11

notable in the work of Thea Porter and Belville. *Vogue* covered the work of Piero Tosi, the Italian film costumier and recluse, famed for his wardrobes for *The Damned* (1969), *Death in Venice* (1970) and *Medea* (1970).

The alternative to the anarchic, romantic style was the mix-and-match capsule wardrobe. The chief American promoters of this were Anne Klein and Calvin Klein, who produced tailored classics for modern working women, as did Jean Muir in London and Laura Biagiotti in Italy.

Saint Laurent incorporated both influences, showing gypsy clothes along-side conservative, masculine classics.

Although there was not a single short skirt in British *Vogue* by the end of the

year, legs were still the focal point in Paris and London, revealed through split and slashed skirts. Muir considered that the new length made one look leggier and thinner. 'The point about the bodice is it fits. The point about the skirt is it's not just long, it's shaped. The longer the more shape.' She advised wearing a 'no-bra bra', a body stocking, or nothing at all, under her clinging tops.

In almost every Paris collection the suit for the autumn was a waist-length jacket over a seven-eighths or nine-tenths skirt or culottes, invariably worn with boots. Leather and suede were the most fashionable materials, either for sports coats and jackets or used in strips and panels to trim tweed or woollen dresses and coats. British *Vogue* featured the rustic look: country girls wearing natural-fibre, Provençal prints, long, easy skirts, and low-necked dresses trimmed with brilliant suede ribbons. Gaucho pants, tweed knickerbockers and breeches were teamed with waistcoats and gathered silk open-necked blouses, worn bra-less; ruffled skirts were worn with gardeners' straw hats or velvet, paisley headscarves, laced boots or clogs. Ecology-consciousness was in.

The evening wear from Paris borrowed from Edwardian styling: strong, feminine, black velvet dresses with huge sleeves or long, close-fitting black crêpe dresses with ruffled hems, wrists and necklines, worn with silver polished plaques on dog collars. Everything was discreet and demure.

Valentino opened a new boutique in New York and Mainbocher retired. Chanel died, though her house continued. Fiorucci introduced his famous jeans and Georgio Armani presented his first collection with Sergio Gateotti at the Pitti Palace. David Sassoon joined Belinda Belville and the company changed its name to Belville Sassoon. Jacques Tiffeau opened his own house in New York, having designed for Monte-Sano since 1952. Bill Blass's company took his own name, and the young Stephen Burrows became house designer at Bendels. Tan Giudicelli, who had worked for Mic Mac since 1968, launched his own company.

Kenzo Takada presented his first collection for his boutique Jungle Jap. He used plain and quilted cotton, a traditional Japanese fabric, for both summer and winter clothes.

12

13

17   *18*

11. Rhodes's quilted printed satin dress in bright parrot colours, opening, fold on fold, from a small yoke, and green snakeskin choker hung with knotted suede by Pablo & Delia. 12. Bill Gibb's honey-coloured pigskin dress printed in a black and chocolate pattern. Jersey and tweed check skirt and suede 'La Goulue' boots by Chelsea Cobbler. 13. Ossie Clark's tiny smoky Prussian-blue velvet cropped jacket and long skirt split from ankle to thigh. The Celia Birtwell print is black trelliswork and flowers and is worn with a painted leather beret. 14. Cerruti's black satin asymmetrical sheath edged with white silk ruffles and closed with a rose. 15. Saint Laurent's black silk crêpe gown, with Chantilly lace set into the cut-out. 16. Valentino's printed silk evening dresses worn with complementary printed silk chiffon blouses, turbans and floating scarves. 17. Dior's crêpe-de-Chine dress with long georgette sleeves that match the floor-length screen over it. The cashmere turban and pheasant-feather fan complete the Eastern theme. 18. Saint Laurent's gold-and-black lamé dress.

1971

The classic wardrobe superseded the short-lived impact of fun clothing. The most notable examples of minimalist separates came from the Americans Roy Halston, Calvin Klein, Ralph Lauren, who launched his womenswear label this year, and John Anthony, who opened in New York backed by the manufacturer Robert Levine. Their mix-and-match classics made things simple for their busy clients and gradually the world press took note of their realistic, very wearable clothes.

Paris, too, veered away from theatrical gimmicks. Clothes were luxurious, witty and flirtatious, but the wearer's needs were paramount: Jap's kicky fashions, Givenchy's tailored luxury, the sexy swing of Chloé's skirts, sporty rich jersey and sweater dresses at Sonia Rykiel, the practical dash of Emanuelle Khanh and classics at Saint Laurent.

Paris couture gave a humorous twist to the functional classics in comparison to the Americans. Tight trousers of every length were included in the collections; some were rolled up and worn with thick ribbed coloured stockings and heavy-soled lace-up shoes. The beret was popular with casual ensembles,

1. Chloé's two silk semicircles: one acts as a wrap-over skirt, the other as a shawl and black jersey halterneck top.   2. Dior's crêpe-de-Chine flowers magnified towards the hem.   3. Patou's scarlet crêpe tucked dress.   4. Thierry Mugler (for Karim) velvet jersey, bias-cut skirt and blouse. 5. Halston's wool dress and Goldwater's cotton 'hot pants'.   6. Bill Gibb (for Baccarat) puffed-sleeved white linen tunic, gaucho pants and Chelsea Cobbler boots.   7. Stirling Cooper's single-breasted tailored suit.   8. Left: Biba's plum-and-oatmeal wool suit and crêpe shirt. Right: green, black and white Prince of Wales check suit from Bus Stop.   9. Tuffin and Foale's red quilt trousers, and red-and-blue checkerboard dress.

10   11

12   13

10. Status symbol clothing: Dior's insignia-printed brown-and-white canvas and leather jacket and big zipper shoulderbag. 11. Saint Laurent's loosely cut double-breasted vanilla twill trench coat. 12. Left: Way In's ink-blue wool coat with scarlet sleeves and straight scarlet skirt. Right: D.J. Girl's bulky-shouldered scarlet jacket over brilliant blazer and striped skirt. 13. Biba's brown, peach and beige check swagger coat, pulled close at the front like a peignoir, and hat. 14. Cardin. Left: cerise taffeta flower-shaped evening dress. The face-hiding petal could be peeled off. Right: black dress with minuscule pailletted bodice suspended from spaghetti straps. 15. Kansai Yamamoto's Kabuki-theatre-style loose-sleeved and loose-legged playsuit, striped tights and striking cape, which unzips at the front from the chin to the toes and at the back from the nape of the neck to the heels of the high white patent boots. 16. Thea Porter's misty-beige silk chiffon frilled and tiered dress (influenced by Death in Venice) and beige straw hat piled high with ostrich feathers.

especially trousers and cropped jackets. Layers were important: sweaters, shirts, fitted vests and tank tops.

Parisian designers refused to abandon bare legs, revealed this year in the shortest shorts. 'Hot pants' were worn either on their own or peeping through slit dresses and skirts or transparent chiffon and georgette. Saint Laurent showed forties-style tarts in hot pants and wide-lapelled blazers or fun-fur boleros, while Krizia offered tight hot pants in patterned jersey.

The flippy little dress, worn with flesh-coloured stockings, also revealed the legs. The most popular hemline was now slightly above the knee and was set off by ankle-strapped shoes and the small, neat head. Hair was cropped, worn in a chignon or hidden completely under a small cap or cloche. Shoulders were slightly widened, sometimes padded, with a very high, small armhole or dolman sleeves.

Extravagant evening wear off-set practical classics by day: hats, chiffons, romantic taffeta and organza all conjured up Boldini portraits. Saint Laurent presented clinging, ruched and flounced taffeta ball gowns, cut short to reveal the ankle. Sleek, classic, sophisticated black gowns were also shown.

Separates dressing was extended to evening attire: black spangled sweaters and flounced organza skirts from Givenchy, black velvet from Patou, black chiffon inset with black Chantilly lace from Tan Giudicelli and black silk jersey from Kitty Foyle. Saint Laurent showed clinging, ribbed, black catsuits, with sheer black stockings and high-heeled black shoes.

An Oriental influence was evident in evening wear shown in most fashion capitals: simple lines were combined with exotic materials and white-faced models wore theatrical make-up. Tuffin & Foale's autumn collection was a glorious mixture of Liberty prints with an Oriental cut: smocks, wide-legged, simple trousers and quilted jackets that could be combined and added to.

This autumn Saint Laurent presented his new wide-shouldered, waisted and shirty smock coat and the blouson coat, which was full but controlled, in velvety wool or velvet, worn over a dress or a ribbed catsuit.

London's finest designer during the early 1970s was the internationally

14

15

16

acclaimed Jean Muir, whose clothes were now stocked in Paris boutiques. This autumn she showed a series of sexy brown jersey dresses with *petit pois* buttons and fitted sleeves. She also continued to use jewel colours such as brilliant cyclamen, terracotta and lacquer red, and masses of black.

The most wearable dress this year was the gaily coloured smock with full sleeves in cotton peasant prints or plain calico for the summer and matt jersey or wool for the winter; Kenzo was its greatest exponent. Decorative emphasis was placed on the inset front bodice panel.

Paris prêt-à-porter was stealing the economic importance, if not the limelight, from the couture, particularly in terms of separates. The most successful names included Daniel Hechter, MacDouglas and Jap (Kenzo).

Thierry Mugler showed his first collection in Paris, which concentrated on an angular, wide-shouldered cut reminiscent of the forties. Margaret Howell launched her own label for accessories this year and Donna Karan, a graduate of the Parsons School of Design in New York, joined the full-time staff of Anne Klein. Kansai Yamamoto started his own firm in Japan this year, and Issey Miyake opened his own boutique in Bloomingdales.

17

17. *Valentino's red wool front-fastened skirt over cream wool shorts, worn with knitted red stockings and red-and-white lace-ups.* 18. *Alistair Cowin's red jersey bibbed 'hot pants' with yellow pockets, black-and-cream domino-print blouse by Geoff Banks, Tifter's electric satin cap and green plastic parrot.* 19. *Hans Metzen's cotton satin jacket with snap fastening and trousers with horseshoe-shaped seam. Diane Logan's pink silky Tricel hat.* 20. *Brosseau's large felt hat with gold and haematite chip, worn with an orange 'skinny-rib' jumper.* 21. *Dorothée Bis's pink, grey and plum knitted cotton shorts and halter top, and Jourdan's peach suede platforms.* 22. *Paint-your-own platform shoes.*

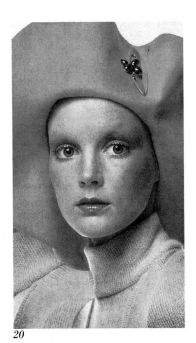

18 19 20 21

1972

Casual, soft, textured styles in neutral
colourings accentuated easy separates
dressing. Those suits that were presented
tended to be styled to look like separates;
what was *not* fashionable was the strictly
tailored suit. Figure-revealing details
distinguished the essentially classic separates, such as loose, batwing or dolman
sleeves, ribbing at the waist and wrists,
back-buckling waspies and loose, heavy
Oxford bags, combining the fullest of
gathered fronts with the tightest of
bottoms.

Keep-fit and the 'body beautiful' were
essential elements in this new spirit. The
firm, tanned midriff, for instance, was
the new erogenous zone, and fashion
emphasized it. Jumpers were cut short,
with tight ribbing across the midriff, and
shirts and halter-neck blouses were tied
up under the bust. *Vogue* encouraged

1

fitness and exercise rather than artifice as a means to beauty. Fashion shoots featured beaches, 'work-out' classes, bicycles and tennis courts, and numerous articles appeared on diet and exercise programmes.

Skirts were short and full (circular or pleated) and always kicky and leg-conscious. Summer dresses in organza, chiffon and crêpe with tiered skirts were designed to reveal the legs with the slightest movement or breeze. High-heeled platform sling-back sandals, small hats, short white gloves and ankle socks completed the little-girl air, which originated in Paris. The blazer, a separate essential, continued its reign. The shirt dress, another classic, could be smart and businesslike or flippy and sexy, depending on the wearer's personal style. 'Don't copy: create,' *Vogue* told women in its advice on putting outfits together.

Missoni knitwear from Italy epitomized casual separates dressing. The Missonis, who worked with Bill Gibb and Kaffe Fassett, were influential in promoting the 'put-together' look.

The American collections concentrated on clean-cut classics worn with a silk shirt and Shetland sweater, the status-symbol watch, junk beads and pearl or gold stud earrings. Drawers full of shirts and sweaters in every shade

were recommended by *Vogue*. Halston showed knee-length jersey shirt dresses that could be unbuttoned to reveal brown, slender legs.

Haute couture had rediscovered its role of dressing a certain type of privileged woman, who had abandoned outrageous street fashion, if indeed she had ever accepted it, in favour of exclusivity. Such women were dressed by Givenchy, Grès, Balmain, Oscar de la Renta, Valen-

1. *Mario Valentino's 5-inch-high shoes worn with Chloé's pleated dresses.   2. Halston's T-shirt dresses, shirtwaisters, jumpers and skirts.   3. Muir's bottle-green leather halterneck dress, and Graham Smith's green jersey stitched hat and clutch bag.   4. Ossie Clark uses Celia Birtwell's floral chiffon for a tiered dress tied at each shoulder.   5. Left: Chloé's sprigged crêpe-de-Chine skirt and shirt, pink straw petal-brimmed hat and shiny, high red leather shoes. Right: Quant's black Crimplene suit, puff-sleeved jacket buttoned to the waist in red, with whirling skirt. 6. Kenzo of Jap. Left to right: small-print, puff-sleeved top and matching dirndl shorts; little print dress in black and white with white collar; similar blouse.*

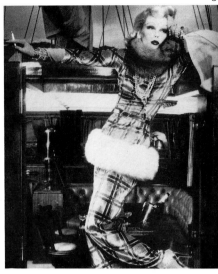

7. Zandra Rhodes's circularly cut felt evening coat with an undulating, ribboned-edged collar.   8. Walter Albini's Prince-of-Wales-check-stamped velvet suit bordered in cream swan feathers.   9. Saint Laurent's beaded cable-knit cardigan, navy-blue sequinned blouse, belted in silver, and knife-pleated navy-blue skirt.   10. Chanel's black sequinned trouser suit, white organdie blouse and blouson made entirely of black satin ribbons.   11. Cole of California's black jersey top and short polkadot skating skirt, and Gianfranco Ferre's jewellery.   12. Bill Gibb's marble-patterned silk smocked dress worn over matador trousers and striped socks. Platform sandals by Chelsea Cobbler.

11

tino and Galanos. The couture provided exclusive, made-to-measure clothes for the very few, beautifully cut from the most expensive materials, with hand-sewn hems and details. It took three or four fittings to complete each garment, at a cost of up to £1,000.

The exotic, limited-edition, couture collections were a kind of beacon for the more profitable, commercial ready-to-wear collections, some of which almost parodied the glamorous look. Biba in London offered Hollywood-style glamour clothes: fur and feather jackets, turbans, fluffy coats, slinky dresses and all manner of decorative, filmstar-like accessories, such as cigarette holders, clutch bags and feather boas, worn with sultry, plum-coloured make-up. Hulanicki was enchanted by white, which she believed was the important new colour.

Hats made a comeback: huge-brimmed at Saint Laurent, chipper corn straw at Dior, sou'westers or white leghorns, or flip-up bretons. Louis Féraud showed little boaters, Jap black or white bowlers, berets, tam-o'-shanters trimmed with ribbons and berries or cherries, or the simple silk or crêpe turban for the day and the evening.

In Paris, last year's smocked blouse evolved into the blanket wool jacket in deck-chair stripes, with a little collar over the yoke. It was worn with dirndl skirts or pleated Oxford bags and halter-neck tops or in some cases a simple bra

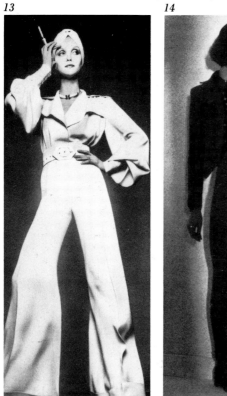

13. *Donna Mitchell's Garbo-inspired cream silk blouse with wide revers, fluid, wide-legged trousers and turban.*   14. *Walter Albini's check jodhpur suit: bell-hop jacket with large buttons, tartan waistcoat, check shirt, jodhpurs and lace-up shoes.*   15. *Ann Buck and Katherine Hamnett (for Tuttabankem) soft-brown bird's-eye-patterned tweed jodhpur suit with suede patches, Walter Albini check shirt and felt school hat.*   16. *A selection of red-and-white striped Oxford bags by St Clair, Avid and Real.*

top or 'boob tube'. City jodhpurs, shown in Paris, London and Rome by Cerruti, Albini, Ungaro, Biba and others were an alternative to Oxford bags. They were to become a fashion stalwart for the rest of the decade, being comfortable and versatile. The narrow-legged trousers of the previous year were outmoded. Christian Aujard and Timwear created ready-to-wear separates based on the tailored jacket and trousers.

Formal evening gowns featured deep décolletés at the back or front, or split sides, revealing a tanned body. Figure-revealing fabrics such as slinky silk jersey, silk crêpe or chiffon were used.

Wrap-around, dressing-gown coats were shown in all the fashion capitals, by Saint Laurent, Ossie Clark and others. Valentino designed a pioneering poncho coat, which was square and loose. The short jacket or blazer was preferred for informal occasions, while the full-skirted raincoat with an inverted pleat was an essential part of any wardrobe. Saint Laurent, Jap, Cacharel and others showed a series of wide-shouldered, blouson jackets with pockets placed high.

Wendy Dagworthy, Norma Kamali and Yuki all showed their first collections and Biagiotti held her first show at the Pitti Palace.

17. *Kenzo's knitted halterneck top and Chevalier sunglasses.* 18. *Krizia's Twenties pastiche: champagne-coloured mohair jacket with huge, horseshoe collar, matching skirt, silk shirt and small knitted mohair gilet.* 19. *Biagotti's navy-blue double-breasted, wide-lapelled flannel coat worn with a geometrically printed scarf and turban.* 20. *Judy Hornby's navy-blue wrap-over wool coat, cut like a dressing-gown, with patch pockets and large collar, white Oxford bags, blue-and-white striped cashmere sweater and navy-blue felt beret.*

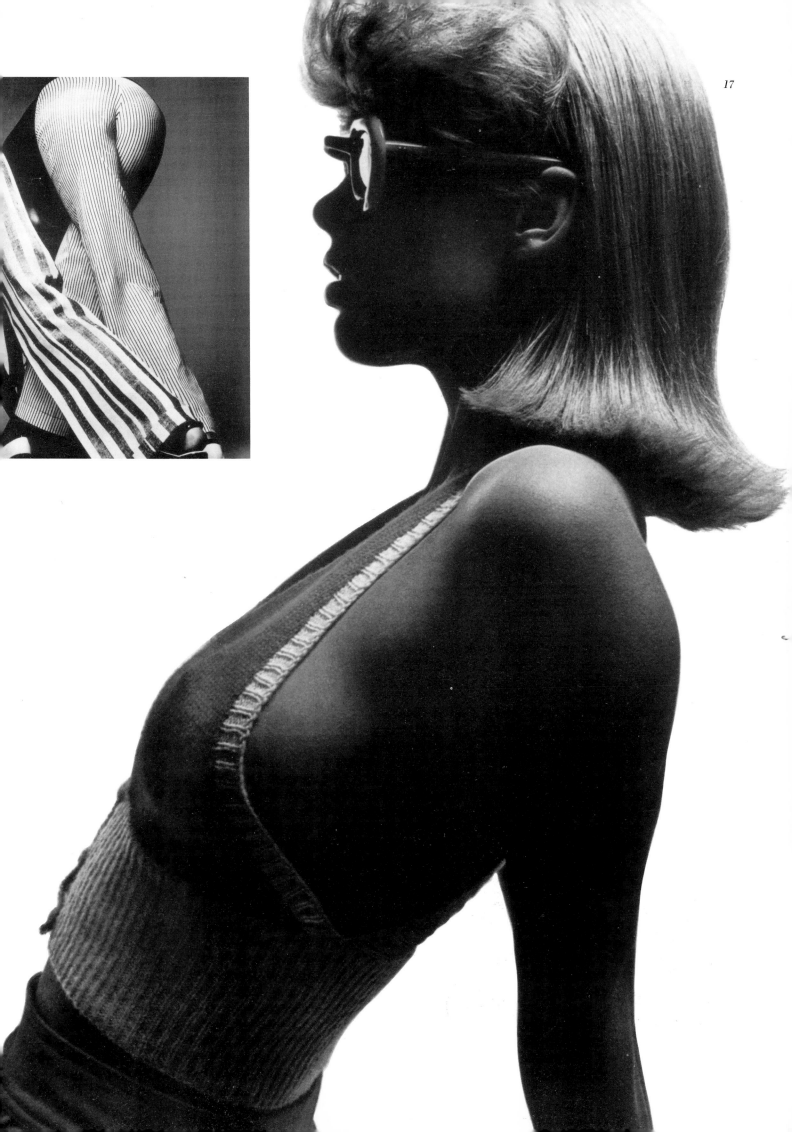

1973

1

1. *Saint Laurent's wool and chenille velvet cardigan bedecked with ostrich feathers, wool crêpe skirt, 'see-thru' mousseline de soie blouse and veiled hat.   2. Sonia Rykiel's short, loose trousers and slinky tops.   3. Chloé's tweed cardigan coat and jumper, crêpe-de-Chine shirt and straight flannel skirt.   4. Lapidus's wool finger-length paletôt jacket and bell-bottom trousers.   5. Missoni's ribbed sweater, cardigan, skirt and hat.*

'We are in an era of under-dressing,' declared *Vogue*. The layered look that had been so fashionable in recent years was now completely *démodé*. Simple, body-conscious and, most important of all, unconstructed clothes were in. The revival of the interchangeable, investment classic was well timed, in view of the economic climate.

The American designers consolidated the body-conscious, simple style, borrowing many English classics – cashmere, tweed, twin-sets and trench coats – and restyling them with modern panache. Opposed to the constantly changing dictates of fashion, Ralph Lauren revitalized the classics, creating witty, colourful clothes that did not date. Stephen Burrows won the Coty Award, the annual accolade of the American fashion industry, while Oscar de la Renta was elected to the 'Coty Hall of Fame' to join Galanos, Norell, Gernreich, Anne Klein, Trigère, Cashin and Blass. His easy clothes varied in length from above the knee to just above the ankle. His 'unconstructed' mid-calf-length cashmere coats were unlined and cut close to the body, sometimes trimmed with fur at the collar and cuffs, and were worn with tailored, straight trousers, typically in grey flannel.

Calvin Klein won his first Winnie Award, having designed a full and interchangeable wardrobe. He understood that women wanted clothes that worked for them, not clothes that they had to work at. His daytime classics were tailored in grey flannel, camel-hair and

tweed; many of his jackets were styled like a loose shirt, which was easy to wear both with trousers and skirts.

Anne Klein's collections were based on body-conscious sportswear, such as blouson jackets teamed with dead straight skirts that touched the knee – the fashionable length, for, according to *Vogue*, 'a covered knee is dowdy'.

The influence of American fashion

across the Atlantic was crystallized at Le Grand Divertissement in Versailles in November, where five leading French couturiers (Bohan, Cardin, Givenchy, Saint Laurent and Ungaro) showed collections alongside five Americans (Blass, Burrows, de la Renta, Halston and Anne Klein).

Colours were muted this season and the wispy, limp chiffons were replaced

6. Ted Lapidus's white wool paletôt-jacketed suit, cut on the bias, with raglan sleeves. White hat by Jean-Charles Brosseau.
7. Saint Laurent's flowered pink silk ensemble and turban.
8. Missoni's sea-green thick-knit cardigan, styled like a shawl, and long, slinky Lurex dress, shaded from pink to sea-green, with matching scull-cap.
9. Copy of Saint Laurent's long, pale-grey cable-knit, belted wool cardigan with dyed grey fox-fur collar and cuffs. Saint Laurent's Rive Gauche grey flannel pleated skirt and Brosseau's plumed felt hat.

331

by fabrics that highlighted the body's line, such as charmeuse, georgette, pongee, crêpe de Chine, cashmere and satin.

Much of London's fashion was also based on the restyled classics: tweed and checked coats, trench coats, coats as full as capes with details concentrated on the back, such as inverted pleats falling from a yoke. Jackets, often in checked materials, were piped and worn with pleated skirts or tailored trousers. The fake sheepskin, ocelot and fox fur were fashion gimmicks this winter.

Spring coats in Paris ranged from the over-sized jacket to the simple straight coat cut close to the body. For the autumn Saint Laurent showed capes for both day and evening wear and Lagerfeld designed a series of very roomy coats with raglan sleeves and tie belts.

The latest shoes and hosiery reflected the waning of gimmicks in favour of the classic fashions: pale stockings and slim shoes – light sling-backs for evening and pumps or lace-ups for the day. *Vogue* proclaimed that the exaggerated stack-

heeled platform shoe was out: 'the era of Minnie Mouse feet is officially over'. However, although fashion editors suggested that the flat-heeled shoe was right with knee-length skirts, they were not immediately adopted by readers. Manolo Blahnik of Zapata in London was designing shoes that were sheer flights of fantasy.

The paring down of layers resulted in the 'tailored' jumper, with a V or oval neck rather than a turtle-neck, while the cardigan took on the role of a jacket or a coat. Saint Laurent showed fur-trimmed tie-belted cardigans instead of coats for the autumn.

Missoni offered the shawl as an alternative to the cardigan, with over-sized ribbed shawl collars that rolled down to hip level, and hidden split pockets at the sides. Jacqueline Jacobson designed sexy, skinny knits knitted on giant needles. They caught on fast, as even the most inexperienced knitter could run up a simple jumper in a few hours.

Paris showed many big cricket sweaters or striped nautical sweaters with white Oxford bags. Fair Isles with skinny ribbed waists were worn over white breeches and boots. Long loose sweaters, styled like T-shirt dresses, were worn with high strappy sandals. Very wide shin-length trousers, sometimes turned up at the hem, were the new alternative to Oxford bags, worn with matching sweaters.

Kenzo of Jap designed colourful, unconstructed, outsized clothes that he felt were flattering to all women. His enormous sweaters, skirts and trousers in classic tweeds and cable-knits, with Tibetan-style costumes and bright peasant-style floral prints, heralded an era of unsized clothes based on classic Japanese dress.

The easy day dress was important in all the fashion capitals, for it could be worn in any number of ways. The shirty, small-bodied dress, with a pleated skirt swinging to the knee was the typical style. *Vogue* suggested leaving the neck unbuttoned quite low, and that it should be worn with armloads of bangles.

Evening clothes were very varied this year, ranging from slinky black satin pyjamas and black jersey knee-length wrap-around dresses at Saint Laurent, to halter-necked creamy dresses and thirties-style chiffon tea gowns in London. Thea Porter concentrated on

10. *Saint Laurent's town dress in navy-blue gabardine, buttoned in gilt and collared in white piqué, navy-blue straw hat and slender lizard skin belt.* 11. *Muir's honeycomb wool dress, framed and sashed in suede.* 12. *Saint Laurent's Rive Gauche white crêpe-de-Chine shirt, pleated crêpe skirt and silk scarf.* 13. *Saint Laurent's plaid, full-skirted dress.*

10

11

12

13

ultra-glamorous, theatrical clothes. The most important American contribution was the T-shirt dress or shirtwaister in luxurious materials for the evening. French *Vogue* believed that drapery should return for the evening. Madame Grès had been the master of this line and *Vogue* emphasized her influence since the thirties, but the relatively amateur handling of drapery by young designers was hardly comparable.

Rei Kawakubo opened her boutiques, Commes des Garçons, this year and the ingenious Issey Miyake presented his first show in Paris. Gianni Versace began designing for Genny and later Callaghan, two important Italian ready-to-wear labels, while Enrico Coveri started to design for a knitwear company.

14. Bill Gibb's jersey evening coat with gathered yoke and sleeves cut in one, embroidered with seed pearls and sequins, with matching turban. 15. Alice Pollock's hand-embroidered cream French lace and silk chiffon halterneck dress and matching chiffon square headscarf. 16. Walter Albini's thin violet silk jersey petticoat and inky-coloured ruffled chiffon overdress. 17. Roland Klein's black silky jersey gown with tiny covered buttons down the front. 18. Biba's gold satin shirt dress, slit to the thighs and buttoned from there up, with matching bandeau. 19. Ungaro's low-slung blouson jacket and contrasting check shirt dress. 20. Wallis's brown-and-blue checked dogtooth tweed coat.

19

1974

In comparison with the sixties, mainstream fashion had lost its excitement. *Vogue* responded to the economic repercussions of the oil crisis and to readers' demands for functional yet alluring clothes. Advice was given on how to enhance one's figure. The 'most slimming skirt', for instance, was flat and fitted around the hips, with pleats or fullness giving movement lower down. Trousers should enhance a long, lean line, but women with short legs were warned against trousers with turn-ups. Jackets were longer this year, but again *Vogue* warned its readers, 'Unless you're tall, a jacket which comes well below the hip can make you look as if you're standing in a hole!'

Gradually the more ostentatious signs of wealth – large jewels, lavish furs and showy, extravagant clothes were cast aside. With a growing awareness of the threat to endangered species, fur became less of a status symbol. Its warmth was still valued, but it was mainly used to line coats and jackets. In 1973, following the Convention on the International Trade in Endangered Species of Flora and Fauna in Washington, an agreement had been signed by a number of countries to protect wild-animal products. It came into force in 1975 and was ratified by the UK in 1976. The agreement listed animals such as the tiger, cheetah, leopard, lion and Grevy's zebra that were now strictly protected and could not be

traded under any circumstances; it also listed vulnerable species that could only be traded with a permit from the country of origin. The effect of the agreement has been dramatic. For example, the tiger population in India has doubled over the last ten years and the international market in tiger skins has been virtually eradicated. It quickly became socially unacceptable to wear rare pelts and artificial furs and 'fun' furs were promoted as an alternative.

Seasonless dressing emerged: the addition of a cardigan or jacket meant that summer clothes could be worn in the spring or autumn. The seasonless coat, generally styled like a macintosh, was unlined and relatively light; in cold

1. Left: Cacharel's printed crêpe dress. Right: Tan Giudicelli (for MicMac) 'two-piece' crêpe dress. 2. Dorothée Bis's navy-blue and white spotted dress. 3. Chloé's loose shirt with Peter Pan collar and wide cuffs and long, flaring skirt. 4. Dior's black velvet dinner dress with white georgette crêpe and lace collar. 5. John Bates's black worsted crêpe dress, decorated with rust, mustard and slate-blue birds and diamonds, and red-dyed opossum muff. 6. Kenzo's long, circular cotton and linen skirt and short spencer jacket. 7. Serena Shaffer's straight culottes in grey-green and natural check tweed, with short jacket. 8. Left: Louis Féraud's white safari jacket over chevron-patterned, pleated skirt. Right: Gaston Jaunet's red-and-cream linen jacket and flared skirt. 9. Adolfo's knitted wool and silk cardigan, tank-top and skirt. 10. Beene's wool two-piece.

11

12

13

14

weather one- simply wore a heavier jumper and muffler with it. Colours, too, were less stereotyped. For example, Laura Biagiotti designed a series of white winter collections.

Grey flannel, camel-hair and traditional tweeds were the most popular coat materials, although knitted outer garments, such as ponchos and shawls, were also worn, creating what British *Vogue* dubbed a 'waste not, want not' image. Capes or shawls were shown in all the fashion capitals, often with Cossack or toggle styling.

The latest dress material was the slinky knit, which clung to the body. Sonia Rykiel popularized it in Paris. Colour, she claimed, was the most important feature of her collections, which she would base on only four or five colours. This spring she chose green, almond, sea blue and navy blue, and for the autumn a harmonious palette of dove and slate greys.

American designers revived the chemise as an alternative to the shirt-waister. It was seen at Mollie Parnis and Oscar de la Renta, crêpe de Chine being the most popular fabric.

Kenzo anticipated a major change this winter by creating a full, circular skirt, easily caught by the wind, often worn with cotton or linen braces. A close-fitting corsage contrasted with the full skirt. He also designed a series of loose, silky kimono trousers and loosely wrapped tops, which gave great freedom of movement. The replacement of the short, kicky skirt by the longer, fuller style was the most important change in the silhouette this autumn. The new coat and cape shapes were also looser, fuller and longer – the hemline was anywhere from 3 inches below the knee to the ankle. This voluminous, unconstructed style was christened the 'Big Look'.

Ready-to-wear collections from France and Italy showed dirndl skirts, full skirts with perfectly placed gathers, unpressed pleats falling from a wide waistband or pressed pleats that lay flat over the stomach and hips.

Glamour was the keynote of evening wear: either floating romance or sexy sophistication. Zandra Rhodes, John Bates and Bill Gibb all designed fantastic, romantic dresses with intricate appliqué, while diaphanous chiffons, crêpes de Chine and bias-cut satins glittering with sequins and beading,

15

16

11. Saint Laurent's black velvet suit with shiny feathers on the collar. 12. Laug's pleated gold lamé top over black pleated crêpe georgette skirt. 13. Pablo & Delia's peach silk chiffon gown decorated with organza and tinsel flowers.

17

18

especially at Scherrer, floated from ballrooom to ballroom. Original Edwardian lace trimmings were used by London's Belville Sassoon and Thea Porter. Guipure lace, night dresses and petticoat dresses created an enchanting little-girl look, contrasting with bare, *mondaine* dresses in slinky materials with daring décolletés, spaghetti straps or halter necks. Ribbons, lace, flowers, ostrich feathers, ruffles and frills *à la* Carmen adorned the slender silhouette.

American evening wear catered for every type of occasion: a soft blouse, fashion cardigan and mid-calf skirt for the casual dinner or trip to the cinema; slinky, seductive pyjamas for a 'don't dress' dinner party; ankle-length, low-cut crêpe de Chine gowns worn with jewelled gold chains for more formal occasions. The little black dress was a linchpin in most wardrobes. Bill Blass showed several this year. Stephen Burrows showed sexy, matt jersey dresses and chiffon gowns with layered tops and skirts that created a ruffled *mille feuilles* effect. He also combined floral chiffon bed-jackets with slinky jersey midi dresses.

Norma Kamali opened her shop in New York this year and Yohji Yamamoto presented his first show in Tokyo. Janice Wainwright, who had been working for the Simon Massey Company, with Sheridan Barnett, launched her own label in London, as did Benny Ong.

14. Loris Azzare's 'Gatsby Look': rose-coloured mousseline de soie gown and crêpe undersheath, pailletted in pearls and strass.   15. Ungaro's beige-and-white knitted Jacquard vest-cardigan.   16. Missoni's long, diamond-patterned pleated skirt and cardigan.   17. Rykiel's grey jersey flannel cape, grey wool and angora jumper, loose, easy skirt and hat.   18. Miyake's simple vest, with stitching details across the straps, and back-tied turban.   19. Pierre D'Alby's verdigris wool velour cape, beige wool skirt and Maud Frizon boots.   20. Muir's soft, dusty-blue coat and mustard jersey dress. The hat is by Graham Smith.   21. Unlined Fendi fur: glossy black summer ermine, swinging like silk over matching fur waistcoat, and long, soft black wool jersey gathered skirt. The boots are by Valentino.   22. Valentino's brown-and-beige tweed coat, collared and cuffed in fur.

19   *20*   *21*   *22*

1975

There were no major stylistic changes evident in the spring collections but a consolidation of economy-conscious separates, which drove one exasperated reporter to remark that this 'general move to economy must have involved an economy of ideas!' Designers were responding to the needs of their clients. Bill Blass, for instance, discovered when travelling around America that women wanted a dress that they could wear to a cocktail party and then on to dinner at a restaurant, so this spring he presented the 'cocktail dress' – full-sleeved, edged in lace, with a simple neckline, the hemline reaching just below the knees. It was a modern interpretation of the 'little black dress'.

The Big Look, which had been introduced in Paris last autumn, had not been widely adopted as yet; in fact American women rejected it, for their figure-consciousness demanded body-revealing

1

The Far East and Middle East were important sources of inspiration. Saint Laurent was influenced by Morocco, Kenzo by the Middle and Far East and Patou by the Arab nations. Black dominated the autumn collections, enhanced by grey, loden green, mulberry and brilliant reds, greens and blues. Necklines were either close to the throat or open, showing a straight, simple camisole underneath. Loose, straight kimono sleeves predominated – there was hardly a tailored cuff to be found on casual clothes. The alternative was a shorter, wider sleeve, falling just below the elbow, perhaps with a longer, narrower sleeve worn under it.

2 *3* *4*

lines, not layers. However, it was an indication that bold fashion statements were making a return, existing alongside the widely accepted classics. Saint Laurent presented a pared-down silhouette based on the strictly tailored masculine suit, with wide revers and square shoulders over straight, tailored trousers or a skirt. The nautical and school-girl looks were alternative themes. The 'tube' dress was seen at various houses and Dior offered the 'tube' coat. Narrow tunics and simple T-shaped tops were worn over slender skirts and under loose coats. Chinese styling emphasized the narrow line – cheongsams, kimonos, quilted jackets and pyjamas.

Sweater dressing (combinations of sweaters, cardigans, knitted skirts, dresses and accessories) was presented in every fashion capital but most memorably by Jacobson at Dorothée Bis, who opened this year, by Missoni and Sonia Rykiel.

By the autumn the Big Look had gained wider acceptance and the small, controlled silhouette waned. Miyake and Kenzo concentrated on the new line. 'Much too big is the right size,' as Kenzo put it. He produced larger-than-life, loose, casual clothes – smocks, tent dresses and huge striped dungarees with elephant legs, worn with pouch bags and thick-soled sandals. The loose smock dress was also found at Rykiel, Muir, Saint Laurent, Burrows and Calvin Klein. Layers were the essence of the Big Look; soft, unstructured fabrics fell straight to the hips or were eased in by drawstrings; cowl necks completed the loose look.

1. Missoni's white-and-coffee short tent-like jacket, turban and long, fine cotton skirt. 2. Army Surplus dressing. 3. Missoni's tapestry flowers printed on silk, sleeveless overblouse and knitted beret. 4. Ralph Lauren's white cable-knit cashmere pullover and classic covert trousers. 5. Biagotti's multi-purpose angora 'Bambola' dress. 6. Alice Pollock's wide-sleeved grey wool dress with red, green and jet nylon knit bands. 7. Laura Ashley's blue cotton pinafore and white cotton, pin-tucked skirt. 8. Anne Tyrrell's spruce-green angora dress. 9. Muir's white jersey chemise. 10. Khanh's striped cotton button-through skirt, sun top and matching shoes.

5 *6* *7*

8 *9* *10*

339

11. Jacqueline Jacobson's (for Dorothée Bis) apricot, pistachio, hydrangea-red and grey striped tank tops and bouclé knit skirts. 12. Galanos's silver-white beaded top over narrow brown and cream striped crêpe skirt. 13. Saint Laurent's hound's-tooth check wool suit and crêpe georgette blouse. 14. Bill Gibb's pearl-grey, peach and pale-green striped smock dress with short raglan sleeves. 15. Ungaro's strict poudre-lacque suit with wrap-over skirt. 16. Stephen Burrows's loose, short-sleeved smock top and easy skirt, printed in 'Road Runner' turquoise on red challis. 17. Lagerfeld (for Chloé) black jersey sarong dress. 18. Muir's leafy chiffon evening dress gathered from a narrow garland of sequins.

Cost-consciousness and a refusal to slavishly follow fashion meant that alternative dressing continued to be popular and *Vogue* featured layers of clothes from junk shops or industrial clothing from army-surplus stores. *Vogue* believed that these tough, cheap, comfortable, oversized clothes could enhance the underlying femininity of the wearer.

The dominant colours for evening were the 'natural' hues of cashmere, alpaca and mohair: grey, beige and black created a clean, sophisticated look, lifted with white or red. Hair was short, clearing the nape of the neck, or swept back into a chignon, and enhanced the seductive, revealing necklines. John Anthony's roomy evening bodice falling

from an elasticated, off-the-shoulder smocked band was popular.

American evening gowns tended to be simple, concentrating on fabric, colour and easy lines that highlighted the body underneath. Galanos was the undisputed master of this understated mode. Halston offered the 'skimp', a short evening dress with spaghetti straps, for, 'What's more enticing than a pair of beautiful legs on the dance floor?'

Dior showed camisole-top dresses, while Galitzine bared the shoulders with Grecian-style dresses draped from one shoulder. Saint Laurent showed gowns with straps criss-crossed at the back or chiffons and voiles falling from halter necks. Givenchy favoured deep V necks at the back and front and emphasized

the nape of the neck with a small chignon wrapped in a dazzling ribbon.

Valentino and Laug showed light, subtle gowns in pleated georgettes that were almost transparent against the skin. Valentino wanted allure; he was 'tired of sad-looking women, of drab suffragettes, of dull and unbecoming colours'.

Annette Worsley Taylor founded the London Designer Collections. She ran a small manufacturing company with three designers, one of whom was Bruce Oldfield, and had found that there was no exclusive venue to present the best British designers. Having approached the Clothing Export Council, she held a small exhibition entitled 'The New Wave' at the Ritz in 1974. Joining forces

19. Saint Laurent's garnet-coloured panne velvet robe, cut to black rose at the front and rippling from buttoned cuffs. 20. Courrèges. Left: Long wool crêpe sheath with a halterneck bodice encrusted with pailletted roses. Right: shocking rose-coloured wool sheath with a décolleté crossed with straps. 21. André Peters's winter-grass-coloured wool and angora cape and short over-cape with scarf ties, and Wendy Dagworthy's plum-coloured check tweed trousers. 22. Walter Albini's blue, brown, russet and beige striped wool coat, fishnet knit wool tunic dress and gunmetal knit T-shirt. 23. John Bates's full-skirted navy-blue and white chevron-striped duster coat with dolman sleeves, over a navy-blue dirndl.

with some mass-market clothing companies this year, the LDC was set up to show top British fashion designers. It evolved as a non-profit-making concern, providing similar services to its French, Italian and American counterparts.

Perry Ellis and Pinky and Dianne launched their own labels in New York. Benny Ong and Bruce Oldfield, both graduates of St Martin's College of Art, set up their own businesses in London. Luciano Soprani, who had designed for Maxmara and Sportsmax, and Georgio Armani founded their own companies in Milan. The expert tailoring and professionalism of Armani and Gianfranco Ferre, who had launched his own label in 1974, led to the Milanese being recognized as a major fashion force.

1976-1986

Yesterday I saw a young woman down in that street. She looked very chic in her Chanel suit *and* the buttons and the bag *and* the belt *and* the shoes. And yet twenty years ago her mother was dressed *exactly* the same, and her grandmother forty years before. That's incredible. You see, Chanel understood what attraction was all about.

Marc Bohan, Paris 1984

'Gender-bending, Huh! It's a game. Young people understand that to dress like a tart doesn't reflect one's moral stance – perhaps those *jolies madames* in little Chanel suits are the real tarts? I'm offering equality of sex appeal.'

Jean-Paul Gaultier, Paris 1984

Jean-Paul Gaultier's two cornetti, orange velvet corset dress, 1984.

Fashion during this period reflected a constant search for novelty. Style became more mercurial. Consumers had two options: to identify with the look or, more importantly, the reasoning of a chosen designer – conceptual dressing – or to play a frivolous image game – a reaction to the sobriety of the early seventies.

Though the classics were by no means abandoned, by 1976 the Big Look – large, layered, peasant-inspired dressing – dominated *Vogue* (meanwhile, punk stalked the London streets). Since the silhouette was entirely figure-concealing, some heralded these comfortable clothes as a triumph of feminist dressing. In the wake of International Women's Year (1975) was fashion at last in tune with feminism? Even the uniform of the committed 'sister', the baggy boiler suit, was glamorized by the fashion industry.

However, the Big Look failed in America, where the efficient working woman wanted a neat, unobtrusive, co-ordinated look. It was not considered sexy and coincided with the tremendous body-conscious boom; if American women had exercised and dieted their way down to a size eight, they wanted to show it off. In France the Secretary for the Condition of Women, appointed by President Giscard d'Estaing in 1976, criticized the Big Look as a waste of material and a pointless novelty. She had clearly disregarded the lessons learnt from the New Look, for her strictures were ineffectual. As women everywhere became more confident in their roles and careers many abandoned the pseudo-masculine image adopted for professional credibility.

The French Socialist Government elected in 1981 actively encouraged the fashion industry, which generated 1 billion francs a year, 60 per cent of which was export income, and which employed 100,000 people in the couture and ready-to-wear. For example, the government allowed the prêt-à-porter designers to show their collections in the Louvre.

The bastions of French fashion had faced a two-pronged attack from the London streets and the Japanese designers, but they welcomed and absorbed these influences to their own advantage. Jacques Mouclier, President Elect of the Chambre Syndical de la Couture, encouraged the Japanese to show in Paris, believing that the French could bask in their reflected glory and benefit financially from the inevitable spin-offs. By 1982 twelve major Japanese designers were showing in Paris.

Kenzo and Miyake, who had commenced the Japanese influx in the early seventies, were followed by Yohji Yamamoto, Rei Kawakubo, Matsuda and Hiroko Koshino in the early eighties. Their style, based on traditional loose Japanese dress, radical textiles and sombre colour tones, was nick-named 'bag lady chic' by the popular American press and had traceable roots in London street fashion. Controversy greeted them. They defied established methods of dressmaking, eliminated colour and played games with androgyny and garment details, for example, by cutting an extra armhole to gape across a torso, tearing and shredding materials, using tops as bottoms, or cutting one trouser leg at the knee and the other at the ankle. Their initial presentation in Paris was uncompromising and bold, though they undoubtedly became affected by exaggerated Parisian catwalk-styling and showmanship, perhaps to their loss. Nevertheless the appeal of Japanese clothes prevailed; buyers soon learnt that they did not have to buy the whole Japanese look and could select the 'wearable' items. Many American designers were particularly indebted to the Japanese ideas on texture, colour and inventive construction. They carefully extracted innovative elements and reinterpreted them in their own more sober, more accessible collections.

Inès de la Fressange wears post-modernist Chanel; a princess-line dress in blue silk and gilt buttons, 1984.

Rei Kawakubo of Commes des Garçons was amongst the most uncompromising and daring of Japanese designers. Unappreciative Western journalists dubbed her clothes 'post-holocaust attire', a label she rejected. Usually based on sombre shades of black, navy blue and neutral, attention was focused on a dramatic silhouette. Natural materials, which were largely hand-woven and hand-dyed in Japan, were used, as the tactile quality of her clothes was important. Mirrors were confined to changing rooms in her boutiques so that women could walk about the shop and enjoy the feel of the garments before worrying about their visual effect.

Yohji Yamamoto also emphasized fabric and loose fit rather than colour, claiming that 'For me the body is nothing'. Issey Miyake's clothes were based on irregularly shaped pieces of cloth. During the late seventies his use of texture and volume became more controlled; he often cut fabric on the bias and arranged it in folds of statuesque drapery.

The second main influence on French fashion was the imagination and anarchic style of London youth. Street chic was synthesized into high fashion, most obviously by Jean-Paul Gaultier and the Japanese, but also by some of the exclusive couture salons.

The heyday of punk was 1976–8. Its bitter criticism of faddish, commercially controlled glam-rock clothes and music was succeeded by the foppish New Romantic look (1978–81). These were the two most widely publicized and emulated street styles of this period.

Coco Chanel was similarly dressed in 1937.

Bryan Ferry, lead singer of Roxy Music.

David Bowie.

The Sex Pistols, 1978.

Punk T-shirt from Westwood and McLaren's shop, Sex.

The original punks were called 'plastic peculiars' because they wore plastic, rubber or leather clothes. All codes of decency were broken by them; under the transparent stiffness of plastic macs teenage girls wore provocative black underwear, and panels of PVC were inserted into the rear of trousers. Plastic beach sandals and plastic glasses completed the look.

Vivienne Westwood and partner Malcolm McLaren articulated this youth culture, whose roots lay in music. McLaren managed the New York Dolls and later the Sex Pistols; Westwood designed clothes for the groups and sold her creations in Sex, their shop on the King's Road, which was later renamed Seditionaries. 'We were interested in anything rebellious, in anything that had a heartbeat.' Seducing the public into revolt was their aim. Anti-establishment and sexual slogans, such as 'Anarchy in the UK' or 'God Save the Queen and the Fascist Regime', were emblazoned on T-shirts. The police prosecuted them for obscenity.

Though punk's roots lay in the fifties, the 'second wave' started in 1971. Punk music hit the top of the pop charts and violence accompanied the concerts. 'God Save the Queen' was the title of the Sex Pistols' single released in 1977, which, despite having been banned from television and radio, went to number one in time for the Queen's Silver Jubilee. Punk was now seen and heard. Punk dress was invariably home-made, rather than bought in boutiques (Westwood approved of that), and for this reason was not widely covered by *Vogue*. Punk was not class-based; the working-class kid and the privileged rebel walked down the King's Road in mini tartan kilts, leggings and torn PVC, rubber, leather and dustbin-liners.

Why did punk emerge with such force in the mid-seventies? One explanation is that the young were largely unemployed, unfulfilled and wanted to kick against the establishment. Another is that it was simply an apolitical pose promoted by their heroes, David Bowie and Roxy Music. In retrospect it was perhaps just one great music and fashion fraud, for McLaren's aptly-named film, *The Great Rock 'n' Roll Swindle*, ended with Johnnie Rotten yelling to the audience, 'Ever get the feeling you've been had? Ha, ha, ha.'

Since the war, style wars had traditionally been fought amongst urban British youth. Punk and New Romanticism were cravings for both individualism and group identity. The sensuousness of early New Romanticism was tainted by sado-masochism by the late seventies; there was a dramatic shift from Millais-inspired frilled and laundered white blouses, worn with flat, bowed pumps and velvet breeches, to sinister, black rubber dresses, oversized crosses, Nazi memorabilia, spike-heeled shoes, black leather corsetry, death-symbolist accessories and white, caked make-up. Decadent youth flirted with the occult and affected moral or sexual ambiguity. Gradually, in response, black dominated the international collections.

Helen Robinson of PX, Stephen Jones, Steve Linard, Christopher and Susan Brick of Demob, Melissa Caplan, and Stevie Stewart and David Holah of Body Map all emerged as innovative designers between 1978 and 1983. Most of them were involved in the pop-music scene, designing clothes for such stars as Steve Strange of Visage, Helen Terry and Boy George of Culture Club, Adam Ant, Haysi Fantayzee and Annie Lennox of the Eurythmics. In many cases the image was more important than the music; mass coverage in the press, whether scandalized or appreciative, was far more effective than any advertising campaign and their sub-culture styles quickly became mainstream fashion, as uninspired official designers looked to these young innovators for leads.

Videos were an essential medium in communicating alternative London fashion and went hand in hand with the promotion of British pop music. Stephen Jones's club style reached the Parisian catwalks partly as a result of the video *Do You Really Want to Hurt Me*, in which Boy George wore a fez he had designed. Jean-Paul Gaultier saw the video and invited Jones to design the hats. The appeal of Stephen Jones's hats was that they were more French than the French, quirkily and arrestingly stylish in their perfected irreverence, following the witty tradition of Schiaparelli.

David Holah and Stevie Stewart of Body Map.

Jones combined a thorough, classical training with the camp wit of street fashion. His international success was due to his professional expertise and determination, not just his ideas. Jones created custom-made extravagances for London club and pop heroes and for royalty; by 1980 he had a stall at the back of P X's shop. Millinery was fashionable again and the almost extinct skills of fine hat-making were revived with gusto.

Similarly, Jean-Paul Gaultier fused the showmanship of a couture training (at Cardin and Patou) with the design anarchy borrowed from London's streets, which he visited regularly. Gaultier's affinity with the young and unorthodox led him to create cult rather than status clothing, for he scorned the couture, which he believed was too conservative and humourless. He became the favoured mischief-maker of Paris and dabbled in the fetishist and androgynous clothes that had been pioneered by Westwood. Not only did he question the current feminist reaction against women dressing as coquettes but he also sought to present men as sex objects – for fun.

Stephen Jones behind one of his hats.

Gaultier's women were dressed like fetishistic whores in bondage, corsetry and dishevelled clothing. Gaultier played with the parodies and contradictions of dress, such as adding romantic velvet collars and Dickensian hats to aggressive street clothes.

Underground art also surfaced as high fashion; Jean-Charles de Castelbajac commissioned a number of avant-garde artists to decorate his simple, canvaslike shifts, while Vivienne Westwood used the graffiti and occult symbolism of New York artist Keith Haring to their mutual advantage.

Some French designers such as Lagerfeld, Mugler, Montana and Alaïa reacted against the Japanese and street-fashion influences by making their clothes even more Parisian, combating the sombre Oriental styles with Gallic colour and sex appeal. Like Gaultier and Montana, Mugler married couture traditions with cult dressing (a union that Saint Laurent had explored in the early sixties), presenting plastic breastplates, space suits, three-foot-wide shoulders, moulded nipples, cinched torsos and tottering high heels.

The overt sexuality of Mugler's clothes was upstaged by his close friend Azzedine Alaïa, who virtually carved Paris's latest sex symbol, the outline was so strong. He arrived in Paris in 1960 and worked at Dior (one week), Mugler and Guy Laroche (two seasons). He then left the couture and perfected his cutting and dressmaking skills working for private clients from his Left Bank flat. From 1981 Alaïa presented official collections. He celebrated the female anatomy, stripping off detail to reveal the raw line of the body. It was a well-timed reaction against the veiled, asexual clothes of the Japanese. His belief that the body is fundamental to fashion was emphasized by unpatterned, dark, 'mouldable' materials, predominantly wool jersey and leather, though he also enjoyed working with synthetics, especially rayon. Inspired by a close study of Vionnet's work, he used bias cut and simple seaming for decorative detail. However, in comparison with thirties clothes, he presented a crude, almost vicious picture of feminine sex appeal,

Jean-Paul Gaultier, left, with his models.

Thierry Mugler.

Azzedine Alaïa.

at times lacking sensuousness. He designed clothes that reincarnated his screen idols, Marilyn Monroe and Ava Gardner, bestowing a feeling of sexual stardom on his clients.

Ladicòrbic Zoran, working in New York, purged clothing of unnecessary detail, for example, collars, cuffs and lapels but for very different reasons. His minimalism was not intended to highlight the female form but was an expression of undistracted functionalism. He did not have womanhood in mind when he designed, but a being of incidental gender.

Zoran was a fashion 'rinser'. He cleaned clothes of their decorative devices, which he discounted as the trappings of seasonal commerce. He was by no means the originator of minimalism – pioneered by Halston – but he was more extreme in his defence of its beauty. Sexual type-casting, colour and pattern were all redundant complications that modern women should jettison in favour of seasonless, multi-occasion, label-less, size-less dressing.

Having trained as an architect in Yugoslavia, his first collection, shown in 1976, consisted of five interchangeable black and ivory tops, trousers and skirts. His clothes changed very little from that point and were made of the finest materials, such as satin, linen, cashmere, cotton and flannel. They were simply cut in square shapes, with as few seams as possible, for he refused to cut beautiful cloth into 'purposeless' pieces.

The fashion world was attracted by Zoran's easy clothes and his belief in efficient, unobtrusive dress. Perhaps reflecting his puritanical and socialist upbringing, he considered that it was only the unintelligent and unoccupied women who indulged in faddish dressing up. Ironically, these simple, easily copied clothes were amongst the most expensive American ready-to-wear. The quintessential Zoran was a ten-piece collection of clothes that would fit into a small bag. Jewellery and accessories were abolished. Zoran claimed that his look complemented American health consciousness, but for many the style was too stark and his outrageously priced cashmere jogging suits prompted cynical criticism. Thorstein Veblen's long-held notion that fashion paraded women's conspicuous leisure had been turned on its head; even the leisured class sought to look like working women.

Norma Kamali's clothes encapsulated the energy, wit and glamour of urban New York. After graduating from the Fashion Institute of Technology she opened a shop in New York, importing gear from Biba and Carnaby Street. The demise of London's style in the seventies proved to be her catalyst; she started to design hip clothes in snakeskin, patchwork, appliqué and rhinestones for pop stars such as Sonny and Cher and Alice Cooper.

Kamali designed a number of firsts, which Paris followed in the mid-seventies: the 'eiderdown' or 'duvet' coat (1975); parachute-material separates (1976), which were granted the accolade 'true originals' by Diana Vreeland at the Metropolitan Museum; the high-cut bikini (1976) and 'sweats' – cotton-fleece co-ordinates (1980). By 1978 she had launched a company up town, OMO (On My Own), her 'own grown, own store ... I need a retail store to keep in touch with the street, remain independent of third-party pressure and survive creatively'. She was the most successful exponent of the dance and exercise clothing adopted for everyday wear as a result of the exercise fad.

Stephen Sprouse, like Jones and Gaultier, had experience of the couture, having worked for three years as a tailoring assistant to Halston. Moving into pop-music circles in New York, he began photographing rock bands and designing clothes for Blondie's lead singer Debbie Harry. Competent tailoring and the music culture of the sixties were clearly reflected in his début collection in April 1983. His chic, urban hobo style combined simple sixties shifts in vivid, day-glow colours, printed with blown-up photographs, with black leather, white lipstick and fluorescent Mod wigs. Despite the patronage of American *Vogue*, Sprouse's business naïvety dogged his early career.

During this period Americans became the most alert and knowledgeable fashion critics and customers. Having always been enthusiastic shoppers and label-buyers, they were spurred on by increasing affluence and the inauguration of President Reagan. Calvin Klein recalls that 'We all guessed on Seventh Avenue that glamour would be back and we'd be doing glam evening dresses to show it off. Because the Reagans are Californian and California is pretty showy. It was a great change from the Carter administration, which was very much, you sewed your own dress!'

A style-conscious First Lady who enjoyed being in the public eye was a tremendous boost for American fashion. Nancy Reagan invited American designers to dress her and being a perfect size 8, she was Seventh Avenue's dream. She preferred the very fitted, linear dress, without fussy detail; for the evenings she favoured flamboyant James Galanos sheath dresses.

During the late seventies the top American designers abandoned synthetics, which had given American fashion such a bad reputation. The American public responded with interest. Trade papers such as *Women's Wear Daily* were read not only by those in the industry but also by the general public, who wanted to know about the theories and activities of their leading designers and European counterparts. American *Vogue* was quick to respond to the growth in the American fashion market, giving its readers advice on how to create a coherent wardrobe by making ingenious additions each season, rather than totally restocking it. 'No matter how wealthy, our reader is very conscious of the dollar. She will have a debit and credit attitude to dress,' noted Polly Allen Mellen, American *Vogue*'s fashion editor.

Grace Coddington, senior fashion editor on British *Vogue*, was arguably the most important co-ordinator, editor and inspirer of modern dressing throughout this period. From the disparate, contradictory looks that prevailed season by season she put together a wearable, new and modern look for her readership. She was instrumental in communicating the ideas of leading American designers, notably Calvin Klein and Zoran, to Europe. She nurtured many new talents, and photographers, designers and models alike – Azzedine Alaïa, Bruce Weber, Sheridan Barnett, Sloane, to name but a few – readily acknowledged her outstanding creativity. She alone could take a simple white shirt, pencil skirt and cashmere sweater and, with a modern haircut, accessories or just in the way that they were worn, create a new look. With deceptive abandon she combined the old and the new, the tattered and the tailored, to memorable, and more importantly, influential effect.

Ralph Lauren, who regarded himself as a clothing stylist rather than a fashion designer, launched a look that endowed American and European utility and sports garments with nostalgic appeal. 'I paint dreams. These clothes have a heritage, they're not frivolous, but things to treasure, even when they get old.' His work touched a nerve in many Americans who loved clothes but were not fashion-conscious, and was a great success.

Similarly Perry Ellis was determined not to be associated with trends, with fashion. He felt that his greatest contribution was to point out alternatives, 'to keep the doors open, reiterate that there are no rights and wrongs in fashion anymore. I fight for that.' Unlike other American designers he did

Norma Kamali.

Stephen Sprouse.

As clothes became simpler the human, narrative element of fashion photography was highlighted by Bruce Weber who was inspired by the pioneering qualities of Edward Weston's early photographs.

Ralph Lauren.

Mary McFadden.

not seek to fill a gap in the market but rather designed what he loved – American sportswear interpreted in painterly colours and prints inspired by an artist that had touched him at the moment, such as Sonia Delaunay.

Oscar de la Renta, Halston and Bill Blass dressed the Reagan 'court' in feminine luxury. De la Renta's de luxe suits and brilliantly embroidered evening gowns allied a Latin love of luxury and voluptuousness with the chic demanded by a certain type of very wealthy American woman.

By contrast Geoffrey Beene believed that the ball gown was an archaic form of dress. He only designed easy, short evening dresses and concentrated on daywear separates in various price ranges. However, with the arrival of the Reagans he did include a more formal evening wear line.

One of Beene's greatest contributions to fashion was gaining European respectability for American clothes. In 1976 with $140,000 raised by a private bank loan, he took a Beene fashion show to Milan – the first American show there. 'What happened in that room was much more than fashion – it was a reawakening, a penetration of American style into Europe,' recalled Beene. He presented an indisputably American show. The collection was based on the Beene Bag range of young, sporty co-ordinates in relatively inexpensive materials, such as mattress ticking. By the end of the show the audience was convinced that the Americans could design more than jeans.

Mary McFadden, who had worked for American *Vogue*, offered the American public a cocktail of cultural influences: quilted silk fencing jackets, tunics and trousers from China, pleated silk gowns reminiscent of Fortuny dresses; the colours of Africa. Like Armani, she believed her work to be a synthesis of technology and cultural exchange.

The American soap operas, such as *Dallas* and *Dynasty*, fuelled the trend towards lavish exhibitionism. In 1985 the *Dynasty* costumier Nolan Miller launched a commercial collection of the ridiculously extravagant clothes coveted by women on both sides of the Atlantic.

From 1979 there was a renewed interest in haute couture as a result of the prevailing conservatism in America and Britain, the new custom from the Middle East and a concern to preserve the craftsmanship of the fashion industry. The press extensively covered the sparkling 'petro-dollar chic' typified by the ball gowns of Saint Laurent, Valentino, Lagerfeld, de la Renta, Galanos, Scherrer, Dior, Lancetti and Barocco, who tried to outshine each other with sequins, beadwork and extravagant embroidery.

By 1982 it was estimated that there were about 3,000 women in the world who regularly bought Parisian couture: 50 per cent were American, 20 per cent Gulf Arabs and 10 per cent French, amounting to a turnover of 800 million francs a year. *Vogue* patterns were the biggest commercial customer, far exceeding the manufacturers and small boutiques. The couture, France's eighth-largest industry, was essentially a loss-making flagship for mass-market ready-to-wear and accessories. In 1982 the *Financial Times* broke down the costs for a £2,500 dress: 39 per cent would be labour, 4 per cent workshop charges, 25 per cent overheads, 24.5 per cent materials and 5 per cent commission, leaving only 2.5 per cent profit. This precarious business was fought over by about twenty-three houses, all members of the Chambre Syndicale de la Couture. There were those who continued to decry the couture as an anachronism but the art of the improbable, the fantastic, was surviving against impossible odds as the ready-to-wear's loss leader. One of Scherrer's dresses, for example, was studded with 400,000 pearls.

In 1983, after a dispute over perfume sale rights, Karl Lagerfeld left the ready-to-wear company Chloé to launch his own label, KL, and to become designer-in-chief of Chanel couture. He aimed to modernize Chanel's internationally recognized style rather than revere the clothes of a bygone age. By 1984 Chanel had become the most expensive couture house and even though one of the jackets in the 1984 collection was priced at $75,000, the house could not make them fast enough. Many were very critical of what they saw as Lagerfeld's brash, showy reinterpretation of Chanel, the most obvious examples being his use of prominent shoulder pads and heavy gilt jewellery – a parody of Chanel's earlier, understated style. Others acknowledged that he restored the commercial strength of the house and brought Chanel's style to those under twenty-five. Lagerfeld believed that a fashion designer must be an opportunist and avoid becoming a prisoner of his own, or anyone else's, image. For this reason he enjoyed working for his own label and Fendi as well as Chanel.

Design 'moonlighting' was particularly prominent in the Italian ready-to-wear, which was dominated by anonymous, conglomerate producers such as GFT (Gruppo Finanziario Tessile) and Genny, which employed numerous French and British designers, such as Claude Montana, Thierry Mugler, Keith Varty and Vivienne Westwood. However, several individual Italian designers achieved world-wide recognition, the most talented being Giorgio Armani, Gianfranco Ferre and Gianni Versace.

Armani, like Zoran and others, elected to return to pure, simple basics; he swept away layers of disguise to reveal a bold, contemporary, elegant silhouette. In 1970 he had set up a studio with Sergio Galeotti and launched his own label in 1975. He felt that too much high fashion was aimed at fad-seeking teenagers, so he concentrated on clothes for the mature, affluent woman, who, he believed, should be offered elegant and appropriate clothing, not gimmicks. He mastered the blazer, making it soft, unstructured and as 'wearable' as a casual jumper. His tailoring was very simple and precise, but he disliked the notion of unisex clothes or 'suit slavery'. He combined various co-ordinating tweeds in one ensemble to break up the rigidity of a single tweed or wool suit, creating an elegantly 'dressed down' look.

Giorgio Armani fitting Lauren Hutton.

Versace combined the classicism and experimentation of the Renaissance craftsman. His style, an amalgamation of functionalism and beauty, was achieved through a restyling of basic sports clothes in luxurious materials such as leather and silk. Like Armani, he explored contrasting textures and patterns. Experimentation was a vital part of his work, for he believed that to break new ground was the only justification for design. His bias-cutting produced some of the most daring asymmetrical effects since Vionnet, whose work he admired. In 1982 he introduced a lightweight aluminium-mesh cloth; the following autumn, having studied the use of lasers in Japan, Versace used them to seam rubber and leather, creating a relief effect. This synthesis of the old and the new, of craftsmanship and technology, was a striking expression of the neo-couture.

Gianfranco Ferre had studied architecture before presenting his first collection in 1976, in which clean-lined discipline was immediately apparent. 'Planning for a building and making a collection are a similar exercise. The linear approach is exactly the same.' Many other Italian designers were trapped by the old-fashioned concern with ostentation and sexually stereotyped clothes that allowed little room for eccentricity. Valentino was the Italian master of conservative luxury. 'I love femininity. I've always designed glamorous, flattering and becoming dresses that appeal to women

Gianni Versace.

Versace's designs for the ballet Lieb und Leid *at La Scala in Milan, 1983.*

Gianfranco Ferre, architect turned fashion designer.

and their husbands.'

While the artistic talent of Italian, French and American designers was backed by industrial and governmental support, the British were hampered by a lack of government interest, narrow fashion training and a lack of communication between the textile mills and factories of the north and the style creators based in the metropolitan south. In France and Italy there was no such divide; the mills of Lyons, Como and Prato and the couture and ready-to-wear houses of Paris, Rome and Florence were closely linked, as textile producers and fashion designers worked hand in hand.

Disorganization further hampered London fashion, as separate and unconnected groups showed at various venues throughout the capital; the Clothing Export Council showed at the Grosvenor House Hotel and other designers at the Earls Court Exhibition Centre. There was no concerted attack on foreign markets. The London Designer Collection was set up by Annette Worsley Taylor in 1975 to co-ordinate a selection of Britain's top ready-to-wear for foreign buyers, but the organization received little government aid or promotion. In 1977 Britain exported £598 million and imported £766 million of fashion garments.

British talent was driven abroad. On graduating, many designers refused to work for unexciting British mass-production companies and rejected the idea of training in one of the few fashionable British couture houses or of working abroad: they attempted to present their own collections with inadequate investment. Their inspired ideas were often snatched by French, Japanese or Italian firms. Vivienne Westwood, like the Japanese, decided that she would only get international recognition if she showed in Paris. She was mistaken, for the Parisian press and industry found her clothes irrelevant, rooted as they were in the culture of British urban youth, while some in Britain found her self-imposed exile unpatriotic.

There were few backers or retail outlets for avant-garde British designers in London. Browns and Joseph were two exceptions. Joan Bernstein's Browns introduced young London designers such as John Galliano (later backed by Butelsen) and Body Map, as well as Missoni, Armani, Versace, Basile, Kamali, Calvin Klein, Ralph Lauren, Perry Ellis and Rei Kawakubo from abroad. Joseph Ettedgui was a tireless promoter of new talent, who oversaw the careers of Kenzo, Katherine Hamnett, Stevie Stewart and David Holah of Body Map, Sue Clowes and many others. His power as a buyer was such that he could lift designers into the highest circles by presenting a convincing display of their work; however, he realized that it was fatal to buy everything from one collection. Joseph mastered the game of promotion, combining slick advertising campaigns with stylized shops, which were usually sympathetic to the look of the clothes and accessories on sale.

One of the most dedicated promoters of young British talent was Suzanne Bartsch in New York. She backed Stevie Stewart and David Holah of Body Map, Sue Clowes and Stephen Jones, and in 1983 organized a very successful visit of twenty young British designers to New York. British photographers, models and stylists also sought fortune and fame in New York, for the American fashion industry was thriving.

The British government finally took an interest in the fashion industry in the early eighties, when Norman Lamont, parliamentary undersecretary at the Department of Trade and Industry, commissioned a 'fashion think tank' and the British Fashion Council was formed. The B F C was chaired by Edward Rayne and its members included the most prestigious people in the business, such as Beatrix Miller, editor of British *Vogue*, Jean Muir and Sir Terence Conran. It set out to co-ordinate the fragmented industry and present a united front to overseas buyers and press. Government receptions hosted by Margaret Thatcher were held during fashion week.

Katherine Hamnett in London used fashion to communicate her ideas on ecology, politics and survival. For example, her 1983/4 collection featured T-shirts printed with '58% against Pershing'. By mass-producing practical, durable, classless clothes such as boiler suits, T-shirts and rough-wear trousers, she brought environmental awareness directly to the fashionable public – 'If people think they can't make a stand, then at least they can wear one.'

Though the international press focused on London as the provider of wacky amateurism, it did have a hard core of professional designers of long standing. In the eighties Jean Muir and Zandra Rhodes were joined by Sheridan Barnett, Jasper Conran, Arabella Pollen and Benny Ong, who married sensitive creativity with business acumen.

Victor Edelstein opened in London in 1982, specializing in evening wear and injected verve into the stagnant London couture, becoming its most talented exponent. Reacting against the limitations of ready-to-wear, such as the inevitable disappointment of standardizing gowns and dealing with quality control, he turned to couture for greater freedom of expression and stricter precision. 'There's more direction coming from [Continental] couture than from ready-to-wear these days.' Inspired by Dior and Balenciaga, he provided a contemporary twist to the luxurious elegance of fifties dressing, working in the finest satins, velvets and wools. He also mastered the wardrobe essential – the little black evening dress.

Barnett offered imaginative, modern and wearable clothes. Producing collections of thirty or forty pieces each season for Reldan, which he joined in 1980, gave his creative work a commercial edge. Delighting in the work of Calvin Klein, Alaïa and Armani, he presented simple, slick co-ordinates, which could be worn by any age and would not date quickly. Barnett concentrated on day clothes, whereas Benny Ong focused on late day and evening clothes of consistently alluring simplicity.

As the choice available to women became wider and wider, the fashion industry became more competitive. To succeed designers had to know their clients and anticipate their needs. Donna Karan, a good example of a modern designer, set out to design *exactly* what was missing from her wardrobe. Like Biagiotti and Rykiel before her, she designed the clothes that women needed and felt comfortable in; she rejected any garments or accessories that were impractical or peripheral. 'When I travel, the dream would be to move around with no bags. So I've come up with something almost as good. One bag ... The clothes are totally packable.'

Norman Kamali, working in commercial and cut-throat New York, summed up: 'Almost anyone can design clothes, but to succeed you have to be obsessed. We're at the sharp edge of competition and if a designer does not satisfy his client's clothing demands he will lose her, and probably for good.'

'There's too much similarity and not enough homework,' insists Polly Mellen. 'Designers should ask themselves: Am I *designing* or am I just refabricating last season's silhouette. If the answer is yes, it's just not good enough.'

Dance and action, the spirit of eighties clothing, by Norma Komali and Liza Bruce.

Didier Malige's version of the 'buzz' cut.

Katherine Hamnett's protest clothing dedicated to the CND women of Greenham Common.

1976

2

3

4

While the West's attention was focused on the political and economic moves of the OPEC countries, traditional Middle Eastern dress was reinterpreted on the European catwalks. Djellabahs, harem trousers, tunics and turbans in striped, simple cottons were worn with flat sandals for the summer, while many winter collections of capes, hoods, layered tunics, sweaters and straight-legged trousers revealed a Tyrolean and Russian influence.

Layering distinguished this ethnic style: a rectangular, unlined tunic or kimono was worn over a straight or bias-cut long supple skirt, or over harem trousers, with a waistcoat or a loose, unlined, blazer.

Accessories emphasized an outdoor, rustic look – for the head, bandeaux,

balaclavas, hoods, enveloping shawls or Peruvian-style hats worn over a peasant scarf. Leg warmers, arm warmers and heavy boots were popular. Quilted boots and wrapped leggings were seen at Kansai Yamamoto; Mugler showed theatrical gold gathered boots; Ungaro presented après-ski boots.

The punk image began to be covered in Italian *Vogue*, which featured page after page of black clothing worn with aggressive accessories: low-slung, studded belts, leather knuckle-dusters, dog chains, and wrap-around sunglasses. Hair was dishevelled and tied with black lace ribbons.

The waistline had dropped to the hip and was typically swathed with jersey or emphasized by a low-slung belt. Kenzo was the instigator of this change, which

was more figure-revealing than the balloon-like smock of previous seasons. The rectangular shape dominated the silhouette: waistless, straight, un-structured shifts with few dress-making details, such as tabs and tucks. Shoulders were undefined, the sleeves large and straight and often worn casually rolled up. Miyake combined layers of Japanese prints and presented a series of nomad's tunics and hooded dresses, as did Basile.

This was Saint Laurent's *annus mirabilis*. In a feast of theatrics and colour he showed his first famous Carmen dresses. His Moroccan-style prêt-à-porter collection for the spring offered harem trousers, vivid silk belts, tunics in bright purple and orange striped cottons and even brighter jewels. This year the

1. Fiorucci's black bermuda shorts, T-shirt and leather cap. 2. Rykiel's long wool-angora vest in pink and cream stripes, jersey skirt and cardigan. 3. Hamilton's black silk skirt and jersey camisole. 4. Chloé's embroidered cream silk and lace dress and pantaloons. 5. Saint Laurent's dark-brown knitted cardigan banded in violet, mohair and acrylic striped polo-neck and violet wool crêpe skirt. 6. Kenzo's wrapped cotton blouson and wrapped hipster skirt. 7. Kenzo's Tyrolean wool jacket, cotton shirt, waistcoat, printed-cotton pleated skirt and wool pantaloons. 8. Lauren's brown wool tweed jacket over tan twill trousers.

5

6

7

8

9

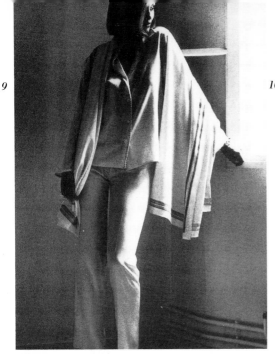

10

9. *Jacqueline Jacobson's (for Dorothée Bis) striped wool coat/cardigan and trousers.*
10. *Kenzo's sage-green cotton chintz cowl-necked blouse, green and black striped canvas waistcoat, heavy black cord skirt, black cord gown with sleeves drawn up on to the shoulders and trilby.*
11. *Scherrer's white flannel blouson top and straight skirt with navy-blue trimming.*
12. *Miyake's seaweed-coloured fluid linen jumpsuit with harem trousers and scarf.*
13. *Saint Laurent's candy-striped souk robe, bright silk rope tie, cream canvas turban and flat sandals. 14. Biagotti's long, buttoned white linen, tunic-coat over trousers. 15. Yuki's cream-coloured silk jersey tube, the hem of which doubles back as a hood. 16. Saint Laurent. Left: quilted gold lamé coat, bordered with black mink, black-and-gold mousseline de soie blouse, huge black velvet skirt hemmed in gold, fur cape, fur toque and gold leather boots. Centre: black velvet jacket bordered with sequins, gold and black blouse, wide claret velvet skirt, gold lamé turban and passementerie belt. Right: long, sleeveless bolero in purple shot silk, green silk faille skirt and burgundy taffeta underskirt.*

11

12

house launched the profitable scent 'Opium' and 'designer' furs.

Saint Laurent's autumn collection burst forth with romantic fantasy. For the day, he showed a collarless, slightly square jacket with Tyrolean fastenings, either plain or with a subtle stripe, worn over a dirndl skirt and Russian blouse, lying flat on the collar bone and simply tied. A dramatic shawl, Russian-style fur-trimmed hat and a hooded, velvet cape completed the look. Trousers were very narrow and everything was worn with Cossack-style, baggy boots. His waisted, wide-sleeved coat was invariably braid-bound. Ungaro also presented the ethnic look, showing Tyrolean, Rumanian and Balkan-inspired

13

14

lines in brilliant colours, with a profusion of patterns and contrasting textures.

The American designers were relatively untouched by the ethnic romanticism or street chic of Europe – the classics prevailed. The versatile sports jacket, parka and blouson were more prevalent than the coat, though Norma Kamali's duvet coat was widely adopted. Cut in quilted, showerproof poplin, filled with down, it was practical but never flattering.

Simplicity was a key note of the evening collections. Calvin Klein's evening wear was cut on T-shirt or chemise lines, from luxury fabrics. Geoffrey Beene presented a new Beene Bag range of cheaper, soft, easy sports clothes that could be rolled up and put into a tote bag and formalized with a tailored jacket.

Vibrant evening clothes were worn with high-heeled gold sandals. Long, sleek, gold lamé or black satin sheaths, narrow-legged satin trousers, pantaloons with gathered ankles, with matching track-suit-style tops in fantastic colours were shown. Harem pants combined with the side-slit tunic or kimono top appeared for day and evening wear.

Fantasy and exotica dominated the autumn collections in Paris. Women were dressed in taffeta with finger-deep embroidery. These gowns were highly labour-intensive: Saint Laurent's evening suit and dresses took between eighty-five and a hundred hours to make, and Givenchy's deceptively simple black velvet and taffeta sheaths took forty hours.

The anarchic and witty Jean-Paul Gaultier launched his first independent show. Having limited funds, he used old upholstery materials, tapestry and canvas from markets. The second show was chaotic; the small theatre where it was presented had no lights backstage so the models lost their shoes and had to appear in socks. The press were amused by what they thought was a calculated, 'darling' idea.

Jean-Claude de Luca, Givenchy-trained, and Chantal Thomass launched their own labels. Patricia Roberts opened a shop in London, having been helped by British *Vogue* to sell her knitwear wholesale, while Zoran and Mary McFadden opened in New York, with, respectively, minimalism and colourful exotica from her travels.

15

16

17   18   19

17. Saint Laurent's violet-and-white silk jersey evening dress with a smocked bodice and elasticated hips.   18. Saint Laurent's braided black velvet corset, laced with silk rope, and vast, ruffled peacock-blue taffeta skirt over black taffeta knife-pleated underskirt. 19. Dior's white silk chiffon tube dress printed with pale terracotta brown and leaf-green flowers, under a thigh-high split tabard with kimono sleeves.

1977

'The year hair stood on end with fluorescent dyes, the year of the war paint.' Punk went public, reaching the pages of *Vogue* and the couture catwalks with ferocious, provocative self-adornment. Youth, more controversial and colourful than ever, made the mature, 'good-taste', 'good-sense', conservative classics pale into insignificance.

During the Queen's Silver Jubilee royalist London jostled with punk London. The controversial creativity of punk provided rich pickings for the fashion and music industries. Leading fashion designers such as Zandra Rhodes, Thierry Mugler, Claude Montana and Jean-Paul Gaultier applied the street art to their own collections. Rhodes presented a 'punk' collection of ripped, zipped and safety-pinned jersey evening dresses, which *Vogue* aptly entitled 'What a rip-off'.

Moderation was démodé. Alongside punk, period dressing was revived. Rhodes used the crinoline and similar stiff Winterhalter-style evening dresses appeared at Valentino. Flounced, 'dressing-up box' fashions appeared at Chloé; Lagerfeld styled women as Jacobean mistresses in white lace and fur-trimmed, deep décolleté gowns with silk and velvet bows. Saint Laurent's evening gowns revived the mock-bustles of the 1880s and leg-of-mutton sleeves. The low-heeled pump was deemed more romantic than the more popular high-heeled, crossed-strapped sandal.

Day clothes were generally soft, loose and wide, although the waist was definitely back. Voluminous dresses were pulled in over other layers with a large, decorative belt, a sash or strip of leather, suede or self-fabric. Halston tailored his sashes, Lagerfeld designed little vest ends which wrapped about the waist, Dior revived the cummerbund and many Italians used sarongs and pareus (rectangular, figured cotton skirts or loin cloths worn by the natives of the Pacific Islands).

American designers continued to offer slender, body-conscious dresses as well as the smock. Stephen Burrows cut soft, sinuous dresses in chamois, cashmere and fine cotton, casually belted. Ropes of yarn twisted with bronze threads were Calvin Klein's signature. The easy, co-

3

1. *Quintessential punk: Jordan, Vivienne Westwood's shop assistant, as 'Amyl Nitrate' in Derek Jarman's film* Jubilee. *2. The broken doll: beige chintz double skirt and bodice belted and bowed in black by Vincent Grenon for Didier Hagler. 3. Fernando Martinez (for Balenciaga) black silk shantung long skirt and matching cowl-necked, backless top edged with rhinestones. 4. Rhodes' punk 'rip-off' dress in black jersey with blue cotton stitching, and Manolo Blahnik's high gold sandals.*

ordinated ensemble was more fashionable than the strict suit in America, with designers presenting a total look. Beene showed a fur vest over a knitted sweater, a foulard blouse and a contrasting velveteen skirt. Perry Ellis presented big, slouchy, unlined tweed jackets, worn with the sleeves rolled up, over brushed-cotton dirndl skirts. Ralph Lauren, who had favoured the very tailored suit, now showed short tweed blazers worn with soft ruffled blouses and challis dirndls. In the film *Annie Hall* Diane Keaton wore his memorable interpretation of casual, layered chic.

Muted, harmonious tones of brown complimented the softer silhouette, as did the use of lace, fleece and leather and silk and satin trimmings.

The blouson jacket was the alternative to the baggy, double-breasted jacket. Valentino showed them for day and evening wear in sporty checks, in black georgette with a lace collar and cuffs, in loden-green suede. One was even worn over another. Big, easy coats with raised shoulders and neat buttoned cuffs, or coats with smocked or quilted bodices over soft, full skirts were also shown.

Baccarat's Monte Black designed the new British Airways hostess uniforms. He moved away from strict tailoring to easier, more relaxed suits and coats. The

6

hostesses could put together their own version of the uniform from twelve co-ordinated items.

Cardin promoted a new idea this autumn, the 'prêt-couture', a collection of hand-made clothes made in standard sizes. Potential customers had to pay to see them, but alterations, within reason, were on the house.

Scherrer presented capes, tweeds, jerkins, corduroys, boots and panther-print slips for the evening. The jungle and Raquel Welch were his inspiration, and howls from *The Hound of the Baskervilles* accompanied the show.

Per Spook showed his first collection, having studied at the Ecole des Beaux Arts and the Ecole de la Chambre Syndicale and freelanced for Saint Laurent and Louis Féraud. Rocco Barocco, having worked in an atelier in Rome since 1965, set up his own house.

5. *Chloé's 'Jacobean mistress' in fine cream Chantilly lace ruffles and mink ruffs, dusty beige stitched with gold sequins and gilt thread, tied with bows. 6. Dior's Elizabethan: enormous black-and-fuchsia shirred faille cape and satin dress. 7. Balestra's beige silk chiffon and gold lamé Directoire-style evening dress. 8. Montana for Ferrer y Sentice's pleated black silk taffeta top, banded in beige, and black silk taffeta skirt. Headdress by Brosseau. 9. Saint Laurent's violet cloqué silk and black Chantilly lace dress with puffed shoulders. The black velvet saucer hat has two mauve and silver sequinned butterflies on the ends of two-foot antennae. 10. Chloé's flower-printed wool dress, hitched up into boots, and brown felt Cavalier hat trimmed with an indigo feather. 11. Rhodes's crinoline in yellow and green silk organza over net and viscose petti-coats. 12. Bill Gibb's quilted orange silk jacket with ballooning sleeves appliquéd with butterflies, flowers and hundreds of glass buttons. The long, pleated gold lamé skirt is sashed around the hips.*

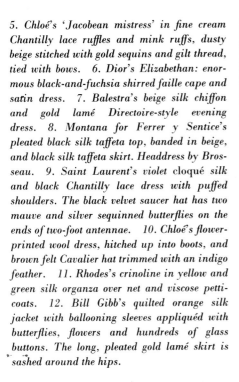

1978

The silhouette gradually became tighter and more controlled. With the exception of the Japanese, designers abandoned layers in favour of precise lines and emphatic colour. 'The body is back. Waists exist. There's a legginess that hasn't been seen for years – ankles are suddenly sexy,' reported *Vogue*. It was essentially Saint Laurent who masterminded this return to the sexy *mondaine*.

Mugler, Montana, Versace and Complice all showed broad-shouldered suits and belted, military trench coats in leather or gabardine. Kenzo's models were dressed as tin soldiers in sleek pants and tunics bedecked with military braid and sashes. Montana, influenced by Piero Tosi's costumes for the film *The Damned*, designed aggressive sailor suits in crisp white cotton gabardine, combining spencer jackets with jodhpurs or sailor trousers and sailor hats.

New Romanticism hit London's streets. Like punk fashion, it was adapted for the mass market, which was flooded with white ruffled blouses, cavalier boots and related accessories.

Romance in America took the form of

1. Calvin Klein's sand-rose cotton lisle slipdress. 2. Courregès's chevron-patterned cotton jacket trimmed with black velvet, pullover and black cotton satin trousers. Grey-and-white chevron tweed jacket, pink-and-white pullover and pink crêpe blouse over beige corded velvet trousers. 3. Oscar de la Renta's soft, narrow black velvet dress with full sleeves, and Tess Shalom's hammered-brass belt. 4. Lauren's pale-blue embroidered camisole, full greige linen skirt and pale-pink velvet jacket. 5. Kenzo's giant pyjama-striped cotton jodhpurs, cummerbund and Sam Browne-style beads. 6. Dior's pencil-slim black wool coat over a Bordeaux gingham silk taffeta vest, pinstriped cream silk shirt and grey flannel trousers. 7. Tatters' second-hand thick white cotton nightshirt belted over Dorothy Perkins's triple-tiered, flounced skirt, strap sandals and a straw panama.

3

4

5

6

7

8

Ralph Lauren's cowgirl, dressed in a full ruffled linen, cotton or denim skirt, ruffled shirt, ten-gallon hat, cowboy boots, and Navaho-Indian belt. However, most American designers preferred figure-revealing clothes to character dressing. T-shirts were worn with stringy, knitted vests (a very refined version of the punk prototype). Sweaters in chenille, suede and lace knits were more fashionable than traditional wool. Some had shawl collars or gently ruffled necklines.

Calvin Klein's simple printed camisole and square-cut collarless suede blouse/jacket worn with unstructured loose suede or leather trousers were the acme of American simplicity. 'All-year-round suedes' in clean, clear, natural colours were a modern status symbol, for they were expensive both to buy and clean. Herringbone tweed trousers with over-sized jackets were an alternative.

Black dominated the winter collections, but there was a profusion of white summer casuals. The great 'white' designers were Kenzo, Genny, Saint Laurent and Chloé. Kenzo showed white Nehru suits (tunics and narrow-legged trousers) and pirate clothes, while Lagerfeld designed dreamy white and cream lace dresses with camisoles and thick cream stockings.

Textures and the grain of modern fabrics became more and more noticeable, largely as a result of the Japanese influence. Amongst the most popular summer choices were open-weave marquisettes in silk or cotton, nubbly *bourrette de soie*, thin cotton damasks, silk damask and a whole range of linen and new linen blends. Italian fabrics were highly acclaimed for their quality and exciting design.

Bold, obvious accessories were still the essence of fashion: enormous glittery paste jewellery, popularized by Chloé and Saint Laurent, huge bows, gilets, black leather belts and various hats. Punk accessories, such as leather and chains, were worn on even the mildest fashion ensemble.

The autumn couture collections in Rome and Paris concentrated on black or grey with flashes of brilliant red, yellow and blue. Cropped jackets, wide shoulders and tapered trousers abbreviated above the ankle bone were the new suit proportions.

Fur and leather triumphed this

8. De Castelbajac's quilted leather 'duvet' coat. 9. Deni Cler's long, Bordeaux-dotted grey flannel tunic, pleated over the bodice and worn with Rival's clerical hat. 10. Mugler's vast, rib-shouldered gold/khaki leather greatcoat with stud fastenings and leather helmet. The brooch is by Chloé. 11. Margaret Howell's thick brown Harris tweed single-breasted coat, tan leather, wool-lined jerkin, oatmeal-coloured Irish tweed skirt buttoned up one side, and double-collared apricot cotton shirt. Heavy, flat tan lace-ups complete the outfit.

9

10

11

winter: de la Renta showed big leather jackets with shawls and capes, de Castelbajac presented quilted leather duvet coats, Montana pseudo-military black leathers, Ralph Lauren shaggy fur jackets and the great American fur overcoat with cowboy boots and belt. Jean Muir controlled skins perfectly, cutting them into neat little jackets, breeches and soft, body-conscious dresses.

Margaret Howell and Ralph Lauren showed the country gentry and 'preppy' images, which were regularly covered in *Vogue*. Not all the revivals of British classics were amusing or stylish, however, particularly the drab Miss Brodie tweed skirts and twin-sets. *Women's Wear Daily* was driven to rechristen them 'British drizzle'.

There was little change in high-fashion evening wear. Black silks and taffetas were threaded with gold; sleek satins were sliced, split and wrapped on the bias, sashed easily at the waist, or fell in lean, simple lines. Beige, peach, soft dove grey and gunmetal were the seductive alternatives to the dominant sexy black diamanté trimmed clothes.

Norma Kamali presented a range of 'bodywear' at O M O based on the leotard and exercise leggings. Bruce Oldfield set up his private clientele service, concentrating on couture evening and wedding gowns. Jasper Conran, having worked for Bendels in New York and Wallis in London, launched his own label, characterized by practical simplicity, and Monica Chong opened in London.

12

13

12. *Enea Gabrielli's cardigan in black and chocolate-brown wool and black shirtwaister.* 13. *Halston's seven-eighths-length flannel coat, matching straight skirt and silver fox fur boa.* 14. *Montana's white cotton gabardine jacket, jodhpurs and cap.* 15. *Gaultier's chevron-striped pure wool jacket.* 16. *Simonnot Goddard's white cotton piqué damask jacket belted with passementerie, over black satin trousers.* 17. *Saint Laurent. Left: caramel-coloured suede jacket, embroidered in satin-edged black velvet. Right: thin black broadcloth jacket with Oriental velvet embroidery outlined in white felt.* 18. *Grès's white viscose jersey dress.* 19. *Saint Laurent's black wool and satin 'smoking' suit.*

14

15

16

17

18

19

1979

The French couture had become a theatre of melodramatic glamour. A hard, constructed, uncompromising silhouette prevailed: padded shoulders, sometimes three feet wide, cinched waists, staggering heels, gripped hips and magpie glitter. Montana's leather greatcoat was the butchest silhouette. These clothes had little relevance to most women's lives; they looked to America and Italy for wearable clothing.

Lagerfeld at Chloé was the new darling of Paris. He insisted that 'Fashion without wit is disastrous', but wit took the form of a cruel parody of womanhood, particularly by night. Short slashed skirts, sarongs and wrap-around skirts focused attention on the thighs. For the evening Bohan at Dior showed sarong-style dresses split at the front under brightly sequinned waist-length jackets, and Ungaro pulled the drapes of the sarong right up to the upper thigh.

Rich reds, deep purples, electric blues and shimmering gold and bronze predominated, inspired by Diana Vreeland's spectacular exhibition of costumes from the Ballets Russes at the Metropolitan Museum in New York in 1978.

1. Thierry Mugler's white cotton gabardine jumpsuit. 2. Valentino's brown Gandini wool jacket with a velvet strip that gives the effect of a shadow across the diagonally closed bodice. 3. Umberto Ginocchietti's terracotta wool and linen Jacquard suit based on 1950s styling. 4. Saint Laurent's spencer, Bermuda shorts and wool jersey T-shirt. 5. Halston's cream double-faced silk-wool suit.

2

3

4

5

6. *Saint Laurent: Rive Gauche's sporty wool jacket and velvet breeches.* 7. *Adrian Cartmell's vivid fifties-inspired crêpe-de-Chine T-shirts, skirts and wide tie belts.* 8. *Missoni's coats. Left: cobalt-blue mohair coat, reversing to quilted navy nylon, with alpaca wool dress. Centre: multi-coloured cardigan-coat in mohair and gold Lurex, with silk jersey dress. Right: two-piece dress in rust stripes with matching mohair-ribbed seven-eighths coat.* 9. *Miyake's leather-piped overall under a wide-shouldered brown wool jacket, cinched with a plastic belt.* 10. *Norma Kamali's tight spandex vest.* 11. *Claude Montana's wide-shouldered gabardine trench coat.* 12. *Versace's double silk gabardine umbrella-skirted coat.* 13. *Ferre's double-faced mac over knitted pea jacket, white wool blouse and black skirt.* 14. *Perry Ellis's wool-mohair jacket and tweed skirt.*

15. Jean Muir's short, shaped black leather jacket over a slender V-necked black jersey dress. Small-brimmed black jersey pull-on hat by Graham Smith for Jean Muir.

American designers and fashion magazines were keen to emphasize that 'real' clothes did not have to be dull. Calvin Klein, the 'king of unclutter', Giorgio Armani and Gianni Versace provided the most successful compromise between ease and allure. Klein's co-ordinated wardrobe of neutral-coloured leather, suede, silk and linen featured kimono wraps, skirt wraps, strapless camisoles and narrow pants.

Halston, Klein's mentor, showed strong and simple coat-dresses, swirling skirts belted over cashmere T-shirts and slightly gathered skirts. In a similar vein Beene offered easy silk T-shirts and silk-knit sweaters over bias-cut skirts. Armani's hallmark was the asymmetric jacket buttoned on one shoulder in fine muted tweed or Prince of Wales check over a narrow wrapped skirt. Versace showed black and rose-red sheepskins or padded suede jackets over diagonally fastened black satin or suede trousers.

The flip side of American classics was fun clothes, such as Norma Kamali's stretch spandex disco fashions in bright colours, inspired by the disco film *Saturday Night Fever* (1978). She and Perry Ellis introduced the short rah-rah skirt, worn with short-sleeved jumpers, knee-high socks and pedal pushers.

Italian and American evening wear favoured simplicity. Basile's asymmetric, lustrous satins, Genny's metallic-coloured satins with spaghetti straps worn with little spencer jackets, and Calvin Klein's strapless wrapped dresses in gold and bronze lamé all emphasized a natural, easy glamour.

Paris evening dresses were far from simple: the bell or bouffant ball dress was high fashion at Saint Laurent and Ricci, while Givenchy and Lancetti showed bustles. Saint Laurent's autumn collection was a homage to Picasso, coinciding with an exhibition at the Grand Palais in Paris. Lustrous jackets recalled Picasso's harlequins and pailletted evening dresses were embroidered to depict a Picasso face. Nostalgia and romance led many designers to costume themes. Saint Laurent also presented Highland tartans over velvet knickerbockers, and embroidered matador jackets and breeches, while in Rome Lancetti presented rich brocade suits in beautiful colours and New Romantic-style hats.

The dressing-gown appeared on the Ralph Lauren catwalk for evening wear, in fine wool and belted with braided cord, conjuring up days of Noël Coward.

Katharine Hamnett launched her own label in London, concentrating on pre-washed, cotton casuals.

16

16. *Saint Laurent's tribute to Picasso: black silk dress embroidered by Lesage.* 17. *Capucci's sculptural black-and-white silk dress with wave-pleated shoulders gathered into the décolleté bodice.* 18. *Scherrer's fitted moiré jacket inset with black velvet bands, ruffled blouse in crisp white linen and black velvet beret.* 19. *Giancarlo Ripa's white ermine corselette, with fur belt and white silk jodhpurs.* 20. *Mugler's body-hugging gown of iridescent silk with a Medici collar, pleated train, padded shoulders and skin-tight sleeves.* 21. *Capucci's Grecian peach-and-lilac silk jersey togas.* 22. *Montana's angora jersey dress bordered in gold, with diagonal rows of paillettes.* 23. *Victor Edelstein's spiral-patterned, waisted crêpe-de-Chine dress with spaghetti straps under a tie-waisted jacket, worn with a straw hat by Graham Smith.* 24. *Calvin Klein's simple, 'nothing extra' dress in silky suede, wrapped like a coat and held with a leather sash.* 25. *Di Ugo Correari's yellow tafetta strapless dress, with a wrapped, heart-shaped bodice.* 26. *Valentino's short-sleeved Jacquard linen dress with side-buttoned bodice.*

1980

Skirts grew shorter and shorter, varying from flouncy rah-rahs to tight sheaths. Kenzo, Chloé and others now showed pretty, floral printed-cotton versions of the rah-rah introduced by Kamali and Ellis in 1979. It was teamed with big novelty-pattern jumpers and coloured woollen tights, ankle socks or leg warmers and short flat boots for the winter. Trousers of all lengths were the alternative to the mini – short, rolled-up shorts, Bermuda shorts, pedal pushers or trousers cropped to reveal the ankle (a style introduced by Sonia Rykiel in the early seventies). Flat shoes, narrow shoulders and the long-legged teenage look created a neat, sporty silhouette.

Sportswear was seen on every city street this year – leotards, running shorts, track suits, exercise shoes, dance pumps and trainers. There was a transport strike in New York and many walked to work in neat gabardine suits with, literally, training shoes, Adidas, Nike, Etonic, Saucony and New Balance being the most popular. The fitness craze had become a fashion craze. Norma Kamali launched her 'sweats' collection: rah-rah skirts, leggings and jogging suits cut in grey and brightly coloured cotton sweatshirting. The tops often had huge, American-footballer shoulder pads. These low-priced co-ordinates were copied worldwide.

American *Vogue* criticized the recent

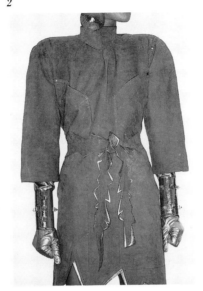

1. Montana's taupe knitted wool dresses and 'orbital' hats. 2. Mugler's sand-coloured suede dress, gold-edged suede tie belt, gold lamé gloves and gilt armbands. 3. Givenchy's white wool spencer and black polkadotted crêpe-de-Chine dress. 4. John Bates's pleated silk dress with touches of brilliant colour. 5. Valentino's camel coat with maroon velvet collar and pleated shoulders. 6. Montana's high-collared loden capes and hats. 7. Fendi's spruce-green wool coat and Paul Smith's large tartan scarf. 8. Koos van den Akker's seven-eighths-length wool coat with a black-and-white collage, cowl-neck jersey and black wool trousers.

extremes and exaggerations: the retrospective and the over-done – shoulders were too square, skirts too brief, jackets too tight. An easy, in-between attitude to dressing was felt to be more relevant than the drama of Paris novelties.

Cotton knits in soft, smudged pastels added colour and contrast texture to tweed jackets or skirts, full, easy linen

trousers or *femme fatale* leathers. Edina and Lena in London presented the most luxurious novelty jumpers, plain cotton knits and Fair Isles.

Asymmetry slanted through the international collections, with one-shouldered dresses at Saint Laurent, Chloé, Stephen Burrows and John Bates, handkerchief hemlines from Rhodes and diagonally

closed coats and jackets at Armani. Wrapped bodices from Versace, double wrapped skirts and blouses at Calvin Klein and diagonal fan pleats at Bruce Oldfield reiterated this theme.

The fashionable coat was cut in leather or boldly checked wool with tiered cape details, which added width to shoulders. The alternative was the light, unlined, seasonless coat or mackintosh, cut like a trench coat or a duster coat. Many jackets, particularly from the American designers, were short and styled like a bolero or sometimes closed simply with a soft, wrapped belt of leather, suede or fabric. By contrast Mugler showed tight-fitting leather jackets stud-fastened along the spine.

Azzedine Alaïa was taken up by the fashion press after a feature appeared on his gauntlet gloves. His début collection of body-clinging, provocatively seamed garments established his signature.

In America the short dress dominated evening wear. Zoran's evening separates – black cashmere sweater tops and satin or jersey trousers – were in fact day clothes, since he believed that evening wear was obsolete. However, he did present gold lamé shorts and a two-yard-long lamé scarf that could be worn as a sarong. By contrast, the Paris spring collections revelled in full-scale evening magnificence. Ruffles, dipped flounces and tiers adorned skirts and sleeves. Alternatively, delicate floral organzas and chiffons floated down the Parisian and Roman catwalks.

Montana's surrealist clothes, particularly for the evening, verged on the macabre and the grotesque. They were essentially Spanish. His baroque kitsch appealed to the theatrical customer. In contrast, Kenzo's gentler, active clothes tended to appeal to young, out-going women. His easy crisp white cottons for the summer featured slash or boat necks, square-cut sailor tops and drawstring trousers, worn with baggy berets and flat espadrilles. Kenzo was not interested in designing evening clothes, for he felt that they were irrelevant to the type of woman who bought his clothes.

Both Saint Laurent and Valentino used a Spanish theme: ruffled jackets and skirts decorated with braid and flouncy blouses with detachable Pierrot collars. Saint Laurent and Chloé showed a basic bold black-and-white theme outlined with braid and buttons.

9

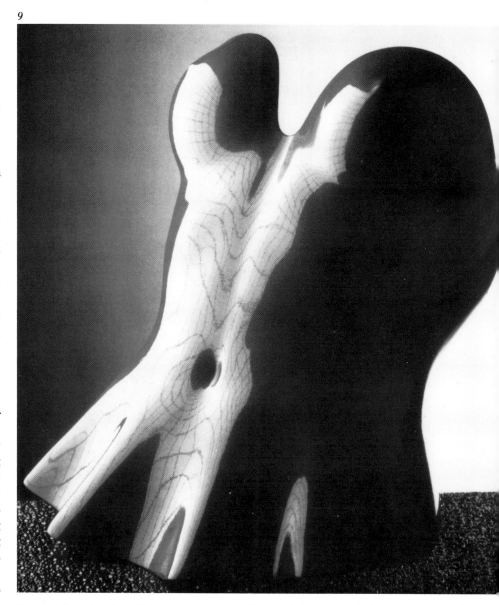

9. Issey Miyake's red moulded-plastic bustier. 10. Krizia's leopard-motif, buff-coloured knitted jumper, culottes and tights. The wrists and ankles are circled with leopard-print bands. 11. Edina and Lena's Fair Isle slipovers, one worn with Genny's tan leather jodhpurs with buttoned calves, the other with Complice's dark-brown leather trousers. 12. Issey Miyake's squaw-like knitted minis trimmed with leather.

10   11   12

372

Margaret Howell reinterpreted classic English clothes in modern colours with modern accessories, an approach similar to Ralph Lauren's in New York. Her clothes changed only very subtly, season by season. Also in London, Katharine Hamnett added pre-washed silks to her successful pre-washed cotton co-ordinates of 1979.

Op art returned to London's streets, coinciding with a musical revival led by The Specials and Madness (who wore only black and white clothing). Cubist prints, Mondrian patterns, geometrics, triangles, harlequin and radio-wave prints decorated summer shifts, T-shirts and jackets.

The most dramatic Italian silhouette emphasized the waist with full double skirts, graduated in tiers, and stiffened peplums at Valentino; sleeves were puffed and ruffled to balance tight bodices. Versace's dramatic leather jodhpurs were worn under waist-cinching tweed jackets. Valentino produced a baroque collection, which played with the contrast of thick black braid or frothy creamy-white lace against jewel-coloured tailored clothes by day and luscious satins and silks by night. Lancetti combined his interest in novel prints with a revival of fifties styling.

Miyake presented moulded plastic bodices that even had indented tummy buttons and prominent nipples.

13. Saint Laurent's suit manqué: *a soft mohair plaid jacket, cashmere jumper and flannel wrap-over skirt. 14. Coreri's sports clothes for the city in loden and flannel: voluminous cape and jodhpur suit trimmed in velvet. 15. Saint Laurent's Viennese-style suits: velvet skirts and hats and wool jackets with passementerie. 16. Jap's crisp white sailor shirt, baggy trousers and beret. 17. Capucci's evening dress with stiff, cyclamen-coloured collar. 18. Valentino's black velvet dress with peplum and black point d'esprit veil. 19. Bruce Oldfield's smoke-and-bronze taffeta, puffed-sleeved shirt, matching trousers and bow-tied overskirt. 20. Kamali's jersey dress with tucked and padded shoulders and a diving décolleté, with bronze shoes by Charles Jourdan.*

13 14 15 16

1981

2

3

4

The wedding of Lady Diana Spencer and Charles, Prince of Wales, and Ronald and Nancy Reagan's inauguration to the White House provided fashion with two colourful excuses to pursue luxury and romance.

The spring silhouette was either emphatically short, body-skimming and sexy, or blousy and romantic. Montana, Chloé, Saint Laurent, Rykiel and Beene chose a navy-blue and white sailor theme for their neat, small silhouette. In contrast Lauren, Westwood and Perry Ellis showed voluminous styles that cast women as pioneers, swashbuckling pirates or demure, Sunday-school children in lace collars and Victorian-style clothing. Delicate lawn and lace, 'pioneer' cottons and Madras checks,

nonchalantly layered, and tousled hair tied with silk and lace 'rags' all enhanced the romantic look.

London's New Romanticism and its new Princess sported velvet bloomers, breeches and cavalier clothes. Helen Robinson at P X and Vivienne Westwood at World's End created the most spectacular fops and pirates. This fancy-dress look could be both escapist and cheap, as the young and brave raided charity shops and second-hand stores. However, it pervaded all the fashion ranks.

Wendy Dagworthy showed the romantic simplicity of farmers' smocks and breeches, and Tyrolean embroidery on skirts, jackets and waistcoats. Ralph Lauren's Santa Fe look, rustic and Vic-

torian in mood, tapped American nostalgia. His big bulky knit sweaters, cotton blouses, calf-length blanket skirts and boots presented a layered combination of rough-wear classics. Perry Ellis's Burren-tweed winter trousers were wide, long and oversized, like Chaplinesque bags, and worn with oversized jackets. He chose a romantic Edwardian theme for the summer: tightly waisted jackets in thick cotton over long full skirts in muted, broad vertical stripes. Fellow American designers, such as Klein and Beene, presented versatile, classic khaki co-ordinates and easy sportswear. Hand-made, hand-knit and hand-embroidered clothes were still cherished, especially in America.

McCardell, the pioneer of American

5

6

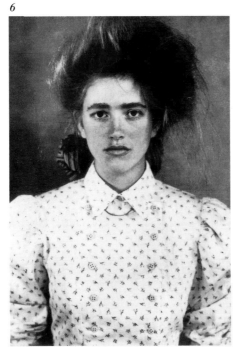

7

1. Westwood. Left: club-print cotton scarf, broderie anglaise culottes, muslin stockings and Flip's Arctic-style sweater. Right: cotton petticoat-drawers and Indian sweater from Flip. 2. Kamali's brushed cotton jacket, check trousers and black vest. 3. Perry Ellis's tweed suit. 4. Perry Ellis's fitted coat over Cossack trousers. 5. Ralph Lauren's hand-knitted Fair Isle wool cardigan, cotton chambray blouse and suede skirt. 6. Perry Ellis's 'pioneer' look: cotton piqué jacket. 7. White linen shift, with cotton trousers from Pukka Pants.

sportswear, was rediscovered. Lord & Taylor stocked updated versions of her 'popover', wrap-around dress, bias top, dirndl skirt and diaper swimsuit.

While most fashion capitals concentrated on the skirt, the Milanese designers favoured trousers. Byblos showed the simplest jodhpurs, gracefully tapering to the ankle, in cord, suede or flannel. Armani focused on two lengths: jodhpurs to the ankle and breeches to the knee. The Paris collection included Dior's shorter, wider trousers with drawstring waists, Givenchy's animal print trousers and an abundance of black and

white classic trousers. Lagerfeld presented a compromise between the skirt and trouser, the 'twin step': slim pants worn under a light wool full-skirted dress, which was split and buttoned.

The couture line was short and body-skimming or voluminous and layered: for example, blossom-printed chemises, tunics and smocks were worn over short skirts or trousers. Saint Laurent accessorized his loose summer tunics and smocks with bold costume jewellery. Norma Kamali followed up the success of her sweat-shirting collections with a thirty-five-piece co-ordinated wardrobe,

all in cotton sweatshirting. No piece cost more than $80.

Bigger, bolder and richer were the fashion adjectives used in the autumn; voluminous skirts flowed from tiny waists to the lower calf and boldly printed and striped shawls and ponchos encircled fashionable shoulders. The soft, oversized, unstructured, unlined overcoat was the most fashionable coat. Calvin Klein's, cut in plain, plaid or striped blanket wools with shawl collars and wrapped leather belts, were particularly distinctive. Basile showed hooded, monk-like habits in fine soft

8. Ferragamo's check mohair poncho, socks and gillie shoes. 9. Rykiel's palest-beige wool jersey coat over matching, loose-cuffed, mid-calf-length trousers. 10. Calvin Klein's new, long proportions: a pink 'Molletone' (brushed) wool coat with a huge shawl collar and tight leather belt and burnt-sienna suede boots. 11. Hanae Mori's panther-print silk mousseline dress with a deep décolleté, paillette edgings and handkerchief sleeves. 12. Mila Schön's violet-and-black check taffeta blouse, violet-and-black spotted taffeta skirt and pied-de-poule net 'throw'. 13. Ungaro's silk Jacquard shawl, tunic and pantaloons. 14. Saint Laurent's rich ruby velvet jacket, embroidered with solid gold thread and studded with turquoises and rubies, with a sable collar, a chiffon camisole beaded with jet, and a heavy satin skirt with fish-tail hem.

11   12   13   14

wools, belted and loosely bloused over a low waist. Navy-blue melton coats with exaggerated lapels and full, caped collars were seen at Fendi and Montana. Kenzo's oversized tent shapes were belted and bloused. By contrast, Chloé's swirling coats in embroidered grey flannel had defined waists and full skirts.

The new cropped jacket, similar to those from Ellis, fitted neatly at the waist or was cut long and lean with a mandarin collar.

Saint Laurent and Valentino preferred the knee-length hemline to the lower-calf length; it was more *mondaine*. Saint Laurent showed short sexy outfits, dapper, tailored city suits, impeccably cut tuxedos in black or cream wool, and a pretty range of fur-trimmed velvet coats.

The contrasting textures of silks, wools and leather and various patterns – plaids, stripes and polka dots – were tossed together, apparently with gay abandon, in all the fashion capitals.

The Irishman Paul Costelloe, who had trained at the Ecole de la Chambre Syndicale, showed his first collection of easy, comfortable clothes. He exported 80 per cent of his merchandise to the United States. Like Margaret Howell, his clothes hardly altered from season to season and he tried to concentrate on classic Irish materials – tweeds, linens and woollens. He told *Vogue* that he found it very difficult to do evening wear, 'That takes a different mentality; it's got to do with fantasy. I don't believe in fantasy … well, not in clothes.'

Eastern promise, the Renaissance, deep colours, velvet, beads, braid and piles of fur, tapestried flowers of Persian-carpet richness appeared on the couture catwalks. Scherrer and Givenchy used lavishly trimmed Mongolian furs and the silks and braids of mandarin China.

In Rome there was no place for business suits or attitudes. The couturiers concentrated on fantastic fabrics cut on clean, classic lines. Three hundred women worked in Valentino's ateliers, taking fifty-six hours to make a coat, or 200 for a ball gown.

Betty Jackson, having worked with Wendy Dagworthy, Quorum and Notre Dame X, launched her own label in London this year. At the degree show at St Martin's School of Art Steve Linnard's menswear collection received a standing ovation. In Paris Yohji Yamamoto opened a boutique in Les Halles.

15

16

17

18

15. Saint Laurent's off-the-shoulder evening smock in silk satin damask crêpe. 16. Montana's high-collared, knitted dress with sleeves banded in primary colours. 17. Lagerfeld's black and white silk culottes, blouse, skirt and dress. 18. Ferre's pleated silk djellaba. 19. Saint Laurent's black grain de poudre oversized smoking jacket, short, narrow skirt and satin crêpe T-shirt. 20. Versace's checked silk sleeveless vest braided with gold at the neck and armholes over checked silk trousers gathered onto a wide leather waistband. 21. Kenzo's short, belted jacket with bias-cut basque over a mini skirt with undulating hem.

19

20

21

1982

The new Japanese designers dominated the Paris collections and received international acclaim. The twelve ready-to-wear designers included Rei Kawakubo of Comme des Garçons and Yohji Yamamoto. They offered an uncompromisingly Oriental style – a far more radical alternative to occidental notions of dress than predecessors such as Kenzo. They experimented with the traditional kimono and Eastern work wear, abstracting the form with refined anarchy. The comfort, novel textiles and sizelessness of their clothes attracted Western women. Most leading Japanese designers concentrated on experimenting with new textiles and dyes or reviving old ones, considering textile design to be as fundamental as the silhouette. They used neutral tints – black, off-white, grey and inky blue.

The dual theme presented by Western designers last year – short and lean or long and full – continued. The former was seen at Saint Laurent, Valentino, Chloé, Mugler and Montana, in deep, poster-paint colours and was worn with high heels, dramatic millinery and loud paste jewellery. The latter, promoted by Ralph Lauren, Margaret Howell and others, was a softer, folkloric style in muted, neutral tones of berry, grey, oatmeal and khaki, accessorized by flat, simple shoes and natural suede or leather bags and belts. *Vogue* suggested a wardrobe of unstructured pieces: plain linen or satin shifts with light, unpressed pleats, simple chemises, smocks, dirndls, sarongs and shorts. Deep armholes, raglan sleeves, softer and slightly fuller shoulders made for easy clothes.

The New York collections promoted pioneer prettiness this summer in linens, suedes and silks in fine and broad stripes. Camisoles, embroidery, patchwork belts, leather-thonged shoes, cotton knits and curved hip belts created a softened elegance. Perry Ellis showed an interpretation of twenties sportswear: pleated, straight linen skirts, loose linen jackets and jumpers with puffed sleeves, all in white, cream or pastel colours.

1. Comme des Garçons's cotton ensembles: oversized coats, loose trousers and massive wraps.
2. Miyake's waisted, double-breasted black polyester ciré dress-coat. 3. Comme des Garçons's one-piece dress, fine cotton apron, cotton cap, woollen tights and cow-hide shoes. 4. Miyake's pleated black ciré cape/coat, long matching skirt and black-lacquered bamboo breastplate.
5. Comme des Garçons's hand-woven, crinkled white muslin shirt in three layers over undyed muslin trousers with attached hip sash.

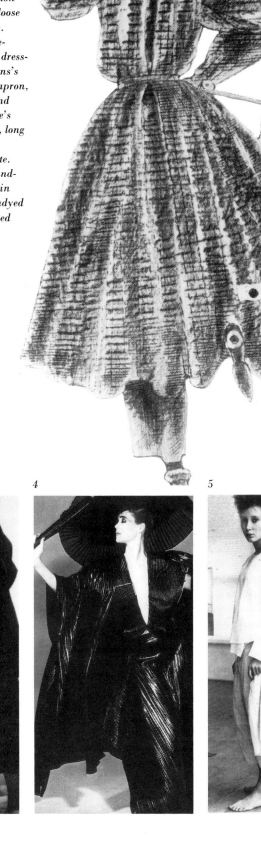

6   7   8

9

Calvin Klein offered flowing suedes and linens in sugar-almond colours, the long, full skirts worn with petticoats and laced, patchwork belts.

However, by the autumn these two American designers decided to follow the Parisian road to high chic, showing stylized, 'old world' elegance. Many were disappointed by this volte-face, having come to expect the more 'modern', sporty look from them.

Armani was equally controversial this season, abandoning the catwalk presentation for a while. Instead he showed his collection on still-life displays backed up by videos of his clothes being worn, because he believed that the expense and drama of the twice-yearly show with fifty models was an anachronism that led to theatrical, irrelevant self-indulgence. Armani considered that fashion needed to return to simplicity and basic concepts. His broad-shouldered jackets and shorter skirts, sashed and knotted at the hip, were very popular.

Though much of the foreign press focused on London's young anarchic chic, British *Vogue* considered that the modern classics were just as newsworthy and more wearable. However, the magazine regularly covered the degree shows of the British schools of fashion. The collections tended to be rich in ideas, but the plethora of accessories and fancy-dress tricks often detracted from the silhouettes.

Jasper Conran used a range of deep

6. Perry Ellis's long, single-breasted linen jacket, pleated grey and white striped linen skirt and pull-on hat.
7. Calvin Klein's pinstripe wool jacket over ivory ruffled blouse. 8. Arabella Pollen's check tweed suit with full gathered skirt and pinch-pleat jacket. 9. Perry Ellis's deep-cuffed scarlet wool greatcoat, waisted wool jacket and pencil-slim skirt; astrakhan-collared wool coat over nipped-in flannel suit. 10. Ralph Lauren's white linen blouse, patchwork sash under tan leather belt, and full, pink pinstripe skirt. 11. Chloé's grey flannel skirt, charcoal-grey and dove-grey cardigan, cream silk blouse and grey leather stomacher.
12. Armani's pine-green suede tunic with short, royal-blue suede under-sleeves and tan leather over-sleeves caught up at the shoulder with a band. 13. Krizia's printed cotton bloomers. 14. Fendi's leather shirtdress, with deep dolman sleeves, wrapped and tied with a rouleau belt and worn with Ferragamo's cuffed suede boots. 15. Kenzo's mohair coat, Joia's plumed felt hat, Manolo Blahnik's leather boots and carpet bag by Naturally British.

10

11

12

13

14

15

16

colours set off by matt black wool-crêpe for his collection. His classic culottes and trousers, full calf-length skirts, blazers, tailored wool suits, silk-damask evening blouses and hand-knitted wool sweaters gave an interchangeable, controlled and elegant look. Conran was indebted to his mentor, Jean Muir.

Muir and Rhodes remained the two great British professionals of international repute. Muir showed short peplumed jackets in punched suede that owed something to the New Romantic influence, worn with angora, silk moiré or lamé. Her long bias-cut skirts, fluid, draped jersey dresses, puff-sleeved coats and easy, unbelted, collarless jackets were international sellers.

Nigel Preston at Maxfield Parrish was cutting suede into long coat-dresses and lean skirts, while Sheridan Barnett used neutral colours – charcoal, oyster, beige and dark navy – for loose, unstructured garments based on almost masculine matrix shapes, in mohair, cashmere, leather, tweed, suede and white silk-damask.

Vivienne Westwood presented a savage winter collection – models were dressed as ethnic hobos in asymmetrically cut and ripped bulky clothes – while for her summer collection buffalo girls wore bras outside their dresses. In

22. Chlóe's boat-necked silk jersey dress with straight, above-the-knee skirt and slashed silver chameleon frills, elbow-length kid gloves and high-heeled kid boots. 23. Lanvin's printed mohair piped jacket and godet skirt. 24. Norma Kamali's grey flannel dress worn with a white cotton dance T-shirt, linen belt and wool beret. Walter Steiger's court shoes.

22

23

24

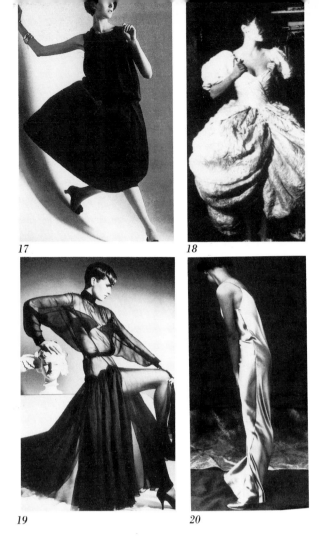

17

18

19

20

16. *Saint Laurent's tight, black velvet evening dress with oyster-coloured satin knotted corsage and puffed sleeves.*
17. *Chelsea Design Company's satin gym slip and Charles Jourdan's rosette-decorated pumps.* 18. *Jean Claude de Lucci's white-lacquered crushed crêpe pannier dress.*
19. *Alaïa's panel-cut silk chiffon evening dress.*
20. *Anne Klein's silver-grey satin bias-cut slip dress and silver-grey satin high-heeled courts.* 21. *Saint Laurent's black velvet body dress with ruby-red satin flounces, suede gloves, net and feathers.*

21

a similar vein Sonia Rykiel revealed decorative black bras under jackets.

Waists were in at Chloé this summer – Lagerfeld's tight, bright wide belts and corselettes were a highlight of the collection, worn over long and short nautical-style dresses. For the autumn his ritzy tarts wore short jewel-coloured swagger coats accessorized with bright gauntlet gloves, black sombreros and black patent high-heeled boots. It was a powerful, coquettish, Gallic retort to the austere androgeny popularized by the Japanese 'invaders'.

The oversized coat was the most fashionable winter outer garment, worn over both the short, lean look and the long, full silhouette.

Winter evenings were aglow with fireside reds, contrasted with black, for ballgowns and slinky cocktail dresses. Chequered red at Perry Ellis, racing-silk red at Chloé, ripe red satin from Ferre and Calvin Klein all competed with the black and shocking pink of Saint Laurent and others.

Roland Klein, who had worked at Patou, and Marcel Fenez established their own labels this year.

1983

The British and Japanese avant-garde consolidated the androgynous look. Some girls adopted neuter poses and the male models flirted down the catwalks in skirts, 'feminine' accessories and obvious make-up. Rules of construction, fit and sexual message were broken down still further. Rei Kawakubo turned clothes inside out (this was not new, for Sonia Rykiel had been showing double-sided clothes since the early seventies). The art of the unexpected and misplaced was explored: bandaged limbs, mismatched swatches and the calculated disarray of knotted, torn and slashed garments.

In reaction, houses in Paris, Italy and America offered high vamp, high-price chic, flaunting the sexual marketability of women. Mugler, Montana, Alaïa and others depicted women as a wicked, Hollywood murderess, a bondaged retailer of illicit sex or a Mae West clone. Narrow, girded loins, tight skirts, wide, aggressive shoulders, camp, revealing corsetry worn

like armour plating, and blank, harshly made-up or bruised faces amounted to a travesty of womanhood. 'The current fantasy woman of high fashion appears like a giant, a bulwark, a citadel that cannot be stormed, because that's what the crisis-ridden West longs itself to be,' observed Marina Warner in British Vogue.

Karl Lagerfeld added to his freelance commitments by becoming designer-in-chief of Chanel couture. He had spent several years researching her work and chose to restyle her 1939 collection – a professional and bold updating of the couture range. The old guard had always loved her look, but now the under-twenty-fives wanted to wear Chanel. Marc Bohan at Dior rejoiced in the Chanel revival. 'Chanel had a feeling, not only for design, but also for life, for attraction. You see, the cut and technique are for the trade, backstage. Chanel understood this and designed to make that woman look attractive to that man she meets down on that street, in real life.'

The opulence of Lagerfeld's Chanel was echoed in evening magnificence at Chloé, Oscar de la Renta, Ungaro and Galanos. Silver and gilt embroidery, bugle beading, embossed lace and lurex, chain mail and fantastic jewellery added

2

1. *Vivienne Westwood (for* World's End), *with Malcolm McLaren models her own grey flannel suit and,* centre, *a fuchsia/deep-green Keith Haring wool-knit body suit, worn with a 'Smurf' hat.* 2. *White gel coiffure.* 3. *Comme des Garçons's black-blue cotton, wool and nylon double-wrapped coat.* 4. *Comme des Garçons's V-neck T-shirt dress in two layers and slashed.* 5. *Comme des Garçons's knotted wool jersey dress.*

3

4

5

6   7

up to what Hebé Dorsay of the *International Herald Tribune* described as 'the big bucks look'. Kamali showed slender draped dresses twisted under the bust like a Greek goddess's gown; Beene showed beige satin slips and many offered the little black dress. Alluring accessories accentuated the glamorous mode: fur-trimmed gauntlets or elbow-high gloves, veils, fur trims on every conceivable edge, sequins, net and lace. Make up was deep-coloured, heavy-lidded and provocative.

Trompe-l'oeil provided fashion with a witty twist this year, conjuring up the surrealist tricks of the thirties. Stephen Jones's hats, Didier Malige's hairstyles and Paolo Roversi's photography for Grace Coddington of British *Vogue* reflected the renewed interest in surrealism. Tribute was paid to fashion's greatest surrealist, Schiaparelli, in an exhibition in 1984 at the Musée de la Mode et du Costume in Paris. Geoffrey Beene was inspired by the eighteenth-century *trompe-l'oeil* paintings he had recently acquired, while Perry Ellis created pictorial effects with knits. By far the most dramatic popularist of *trompe-l'oeil* in Paris was Lagerfeld, who embroidered a sequinned guitar on the back of dresses and a silver-sequinned shower attachment gushing down the back of tricolour crêpe evening dresses for Chloé. His neat tailored day clothes were fastened with costume jewellery shaped like spanners and hammers –

6. Westwood's black cotton-knit tube. 7. Alaïa's 'no escape' shape: belted skin-tight swimsuit dress in black knitted viscose.
8. Gaultier's black satin bra and black velvet and satin corset with a long lace skirt attached.
9. Yamamoto's beige-and-black oversized jacket with asymmetrical hem and tie ends.
10. Chloé's Prince of Wales check wool blouse, skirt and seven-eighths coat over a black under-skirt. 11. Norma Komali's yellow slicker jacket with a black-and-white flannel check trumpet skirt. 12. Kenzo's fuchsia wool jersey back-wrapping dress with scarf and red wool jersey front-wrapping coat. 13. Mugler's yellow wool velvet coat with padded shoulders and bias-cut skirt, and red wool jersey 'cocotte' suit. 14. Alaïa's wool jersey dress with asymmetrical décolleté and hood. 15. Norma Komali's pearl-studded jersey gown and 'winged' jersey top.

9   10   11   12   13

useless tools emphasizing the conspicuous leisure of their wearers. The ultimate in conspicuous extravagance from the couture was Valentino's full-skirted, black-and-white check coat worn with high black court shoes, the soles of which matched the check of the coat!

Italy offered a sporty classicism in luxurious materials. Versace's latest innovation was the use of lasers to fuse the seams of his rubber and leather wear. Ferre's most distinctive theme was wide, oblong, beaver fur revers on numerous jackets and coats.

Despite the variety of hemlines offered in all the fashion capitals for daywear, the knee-length version prevailed. Ungaro favoured the shortest skirts – 3 inches above the knee. Sharp, daytime tailoring, typically in black or navy-blue whipcord or gabardine distinguished the collections of Saint Laurent, Givenchy, Valentino and Ungaro. Suits were styled with wide revers and shoulders above tiny, cinched waists. In general the blouse was abandoned under these suits, as the spencer, matador and bolero jackets focused attention above the indented waistline.

A swathed, figure-hugging silhouette appeared at Gaultier, Alaïa and Westwood, amongst others. Gaultier accentuated the sexy, bondage look with corsets and bustiers worn outside garments. Kenzo laced bare backs; Beretta wrapped and crossed backs with strips of material; Westwood strapped and slashed knitted tube dresses up the side, an idea first seen at Swanky Modes in London. Westwood's 'Witches' collection was produced in collaboration with graffiti artist Keith Haring, emphasizing her belief that street culture and fashion were intertwined.

The Americans favoured the big silhouette for the winter. Blass showed double-faced balmacaans (raglan-sleeved, loose, flared overcoats with small collars) in menswear plaids and checks over contrasting jackets and trousers, while Calvin Klein offered trench coats and roomy shawl-collared overcoats. Perry Ellis's sweeping officers' coats were cut in navy and trimmed with brass buttons, and Ralph Lauren showed navy reefers in luxurious cashmere. Kamali's were the biggest coats – in *Vogue* models wore one over another.

There were fewer skirts than trousers in the American collections, but amongst the most memorable were Kamali's midi-length trumpet skirts and Ellis's narrow tubes, which flared out slightly at the hem. One novelty that caught on this year, following its introduction in 1982 in Paris, was Calvin Klein's boxer shorts for women.

The sensational *arrivistes* of 1983 were Stevie Stewart and David Holah, young graduates from St Martin's School of Art in London, who formed Body Map. Romeo Gigli, an architect by training, showed his first collection in Milan.

14   15

1984

1. *Vivienne Westwood's sports collection: fluorescent body suit, anorak and triple-tongued baseball shoes.* 2. *Wendy Riggs's cropped, boat-necked top with long sleeves worn over dress with cut away waist.* 3. *Body Map's black-and-white 'wit knits' using Hilde Smith's starfish prints: starfish and stripe loose cotton/Lycra top, tight skirt with extra panel, striped socks, square hat bag.* 4. *Helen Robinson of P X's part-padded cotton sweats: violet-red long-sleeved cotton jersey polo-neck, wide-cropped trousers and silk-lined acrylic fur coat.* 5. *Charlotte Faber's velvet and piped tartan bonnets and paisley dressing gowns from Blax, Hacketts and Cornucopia (second-hand); Lewis Gould's cream silk wing-collar shirt.*

London sub-culture cornered the international market. The young avant-garde designers invited women to play charades: be a neon acrobat (Body Map and Westwood), padded Nehru figure (Crolla), a French Revolutionary or Afghan banker (Galliano), a nursery child or cowgirl (P X), an Edie Sedgwick meteor (Sprouse), or a tartan urchin (Gaultier). International buyers rushed to London to place their orders. It was estimated that three-quarters of London's anarchic cult dressing was exported across the Atlantic; behind the naïve, mischievous grins of these designers was a precocious and determined commercialism.

Androgyny, which had prevailed for some seasons, was given another twist this year: Gaultier presented *l'homme fatal*, Body Map sent beskirted and made-up boys down the catwalk, while Galliano's fops outdid *directoire* beaux.

Galliano, St Martin's School of Art's latest protégé, sought to capture the innocence and creativity of children. Watching toddlers dress – putting legs through armholes, arms through necks – led him to reconsider forms, for example, puckering waistcoats by misbuttoning the fronts. The accessories too were naïvely innovative, for example, corks and coins were used as buttons. His 'Les Incroyables' degree show, based on French Revolutionaries, received a standing ovation and an exclusive window in Joan Burstein's Browns. Sheridan Barnett, Galliano's mentor at the college, marvelled at his trickery.

2

3

4

5

The 'Afghan Bankers' collection was inspired by an account of the king of Afghanistan visiting the British royal family and being so impressed by British dress that on his return to his country he banned national costume and demanded that Western suits be worn. Galliano's imagination conjured up fat Afghans in ill-fitting pin-stripes.

Stephen Sprouse combined graffiti, xeroxes and video silk-screen prints. The ghost of Edie Sedgwick, the Warhol starlet of the sixties, stalked his runway dressed in day-glow TV cut-out dresses, hipster minis, tubes and protest jewellery.

The most sophisticated synthesis of masculine and feminine dress came from Saint Laurent and Armani. Saint Laurent's check tailoring, functional classicism and easy smoking jackets were offered with his unrivalled sense of colour. Armani had mastered the discreet charm of bourgeois dressing: proud, active, modern tailoring. His clothes were entirely contemporary, free of historicism or cult analogy. His multimillion-pound empire dressed many professional women in tailored separates of alluring precision. He softened the ultimate respectable garment, the suit, providing the wearer with the confidence inherent in men's clothes without the butchness of Schwarzenegger shoulders.

By contrast, historicism was taken to romanticized extremes in the style for dressing-gowns, reminiscent of Oscar Wilde: printed bath-robes at Gaultier, Chloé, Chanel and Calvin Klein, cream silk dressing-gowns at Krizia, metal mesh at Versace and, most evocative of all, Ralph Lauren's velvet and fur. British *Vogue*'s Lucinda Chambers communicated this Edwardian eclecticism with charm.

In general New York stuck to modernism. Patricia Field dressed vintage Barbie dolls in replicas of her stock; in the windows of her boutique she juxtaposed the best of the European and home-grown avant-garde, as Paraphernalia and Suzanne Bartsch had before her. Here art, popular culture and fashion were truly integrated: one could

6. *Sheridan Barnett's red, shawl-collared linen coat and button-through circular skirt.*
7. *Norma Kamali's chestnut towelling and sooty fake-fur wrap-coat, black fake-fur hat and fake-fur boots.*
8. *Coveri's mushroom-coloured wool coat fastened on one shoulder through a loop.*

6

7

8

buy a T-shirt painted by Jean-Michele Basquiat (New York's hottest graffiti artist after Keith Haring), Demob jeans from London and street savvy clothes. Norma Kamali remained the Big Apple's greatest wit, filling her windows with concrete figures depicting the three graces and breeze blocks supporting banks of videos screening her latest collection. Pampered New Yorkers patronized Diane von Fürstenberg's up-town neo-classical store designed by Michael Graves.

Prints in strong colours were a feature of many collections. Montana acknowledged the influence of Cocteau, Perry Ellis's jumpers were knitted with Delaunay patterns, Picasso and Cocteau-esque faces were sketched on Timney and Fowler's materials and the work of Milan's Memphis Studio was parodied. Accessories inspired by Calder mobiles accompanied black and jewel-coloured clothes at many houses.

Comme des Garçons' textiles this summer were innovative: using cottons, wools and acrylics Rei Kawakubo spun cobwebs of fine pleats and drapery. The acrylic was needed because natural fibres would not hold the fine pleats. Acrylics were enjoying a revival: Sprouse, Liza Bruce, Kamali, Versace, Westwood and Body Map used them in high-voltage, fluorescent colours for baseball and cycling clothes – T-shirts, shorts and head bands – in racy stripes. Liza Bruce had begun designing swimwear for body-builder Lisa Lyons, who was projected as the ideal modern woman.

The tight, body-hugging silhouette tended to prevail amidst the mayhem, particularly for the evening, when the sheath dominated. No matter what the hemline (whether elongated tunic, to-the-knee skirt or calf-length tube), full skirts were out. Even the Japanese, for so long the promoters of loose clothes, complied. Azzedine Alaïa was the chief exponent of the body-revealing look, his models sirens in leather, rayon and chiffon, but there were also clinging summer knits and T-shirt dresses from Joseph and Joan Vass, and Gaultier's knitted tubes strapped provocatively with six-foot belts evoked bondage – or the Sunday roast!

Soap operas were a new fashion influence. Just as the cinema-goers of the thirties and forties had mimicked the wardrobes of Greta Garbo and Joan Crawford,

9. *Crolla's damask jacket with pearl buttons over tapestry trousers.*
10. *Stephen Sprouse's electric-orange mini-dress suspended from an asymmetrical shoulder strap and covered in paillettes.* 11. *Mugler's cotton jersey tunic dress.*
12. *Alaïa's snuff-coloured jersey 'body'/leotard and fitted jersey skirt.*

13. *Gaultier's wool drap jacket with black velvet collar, wool pullover and cotton velours skirt.* 14. *Chanel couture: Inès de la Fresanges models long cotton ecru cardigan buttoned in gilt.* 15. *Montana's black velvet sheath dress, collared and trained in cerise satin.* 16. *Dior's Klimt-beaded silk chiffon tunic in silver, white and gold.* 17. *Ungaro's silver lamé velvet evening dress and satin jacket with ostrich feathers.*

9

10

so Joan Collins/Alexis and Linda Gray/ Sue-Ellen became a source of inspiration. The soap stars wore the clothes of Saint Laurent, Ferre, Oscar de la Renta and Calvin Klein. 'The clothes have to be believable as well as enviable,' Erica Phillips, the women's costume supervisor of *Emerald Point* told American *Vogue*; the viewers' definition of glamour was to be dressed up at all times, through suicide, divorce and murder.

Bernard Perris was promoted at Bloomingdales; like Cardin's *Prêt-couture*, he offered the best mix of couture and ready-to-wear, coming over to the store twice a year to oversee fittings and offer advice.

Amidst the scramble for show-stopping novelty some fashion immutables stood their ground: Zoran's minimalism, Muir's precision, Klein's clean-line charm. Zoran had decided to show in Washington rather than New York, forcing the press and buyers to visit yet one more city on their whistle-stop tour. Like Armani before him, he whittled the 'show' down to a minimum: 'Clothes are to be sold, to be worn, not to be fantasized about. If I wanted to do theatre, I'd work for a movie company.'

Karl Lagerfeld presented his last collection for Chloé this summer before launching his own label, K L. His work at Chanel was personified by Inès de la Fressange: 'the image of everything Chanel liked: the bones, the attitude, the elegance, the movement'.

Georgina Godley presented her first women's collection for Crolla.

11

13

12

14

15

16

17

1985

The silhouette took a soft turn; emphasis on full uplifted breasts, bustle-rounded bottoms and bias-seamed waists created a voluptuous yet sinuous profile. Swathing across the hips, bust and waist drew attention to this curvaceous figure. Bigger models at last ousted the shapeless gamine and pre-Raphaelite locks replaced the short 'Buzz' cut. Woman was cast as a Fortuny maiden at Mary McFadden and Patricia Lester, a neohippy at Pam Hogg, a curvaceous huntswoman at Ferre, Lauren and McIntyre, and a bead-encrusted queen at Givenchy and Chanel.

However, shape and comfort were not at odds. The corsets and girdles of the New Look were not reimposed; a trim body was enhanced by ingenious cut and well-chosen materials – chiffons, organzas, cottons and velvets printed with moody blooms. Technique rather than artifice was the strength of modern dressing, particularly at Alaïa and the newly launched Donna Karan.

This autumn Karan presented her capsule wardrobe based on her body suit. Owing much to the dress theories of Alaïa, Zoran and Claire McCardell, she offered sexy wearability with minimum fuss – clothes that would 'travel, interchange and impress'. With the addition of her high-impact gold jewellery, designed by Robert Lee Morris of Artwear, they took the wearer from morning through to late evening.

2

1. Kristin Woodward's Surrealist millinery for Lagerfeld: turquoise velvet and pink satin armchair.   2. John Galliano's Afghan wool jacket with sleeves to the knees worn pushed up; backless waistcoat with reversed mother-of-pearl buttons that button up oddly; striped cotton shirt.   3. English Eccentrics's cream-and-grey print organza and Tom Binns's duck pin.   4. Betty Jackson's blue, ivory and buff striped silk seersucker coat over ice-blue satin waistcoat from S. Fisher, Armani's organza shirt and Comme des Garçons's paperbag turban.   5. Dean Bright's printed and embossed velvet jacket with occasional bronze-centred daisies.   6. Hamnett's linen trousers, circular linen skirt and linen jacket.

3   4   5   6

7

10

8

9

7. *Jean-Paul Gaultier's printed cotton trousers and fringed wrap-over bodice.* 8. *Soprani's striped tweed: slightly shaped gabardine jacket and greige gabardine bags with turnups.* 9. *Genny's floral brocade ensemble, printed on velvet, recalling the grandeur of eighteenth-century textiles. A knee-length overcoat with kimono sleeves and turn-back collar in greige and blue tones over an orange/hyacinth jacket and straight wool skirt.* 10. *Versace's aluminium chainmail evening dress.* 11. *Galanos's black wool jersey knit with diagonal cream band at the hips.* 12. *Edelstein's cotton jersey dress with gold-braided elasticated bodice.*

In contrast to this minimalism, some designers relied upon the tricks of Surrealism, period dress and *objets trouvés*. Surrealism turned somersaults through the collections and the pages of *Vogue*: Kirsten Woodward's millinery for Lagerfeld, Stephen Jones's hats, Didier Malige's coiffures smeared with mud and plaster of Paris, Culture Shock's bits and bones.

Amidst these games the French and Italian couture took evening wear very seriously. Embroidery firms such as Lesage and Brocard were commissioned to add a Midas touch to luxurious velvets, lamés and crêpes de Chine. Despite the prices – for example, a jacket cost $30,000 – these evening gems were in constant demand among wealthy Arabs, Germans and Americans. Metallics prevailed for the evening at Versace, Armani, Beene, Valentino and Karan. Saint Laurent laid melon, lavender and peach hues side by side. The brightest colourists of all were Hamnett, Kenzo, Ferre and Gaultier, who chose clashing reds and oranges.

The body was revealed for the summer in short, sharp suits in linen, cotton and gabardine. Bustles (most memorably at Hamnett and Edelstein), cut-outs and deep décolletés emphasized the figure. Ungaro tailored and swathed prints and Paisleys into baroque suits and dresses. Oversized mannish jackets and shirts were replaced by feminine, fitted poloneck jerseys or gilt-buttoned cardigans worn over peg-top turn-up trousers, which succeeded the over-played leg-

11   12   13   14

gings and ski pants. Even the Japanese, notably Rei Kawakubo, Kenzo and Yohji Yamamoto, used crisp, abstract tailoring. Softly body-hugging leather was favoured at Chanel, Lauren, Muir, Montana and Saint Laurent.

Alaïa believed that hoods 'create a certain feminine mystery' and presented coats in sable-dyed marten with huge, detachable, circular hoods; Valentino knitted hoods into his cashmere cardigan-jackets and Saint Laurent featured velvet-hooded coats. Long and lean was the latest coat line, dispelling the oversized shoulder pads of recent seasons and illustrating the softening of the mode. Shawl collars and kimono sleeves appeared at Valentino and Gaultier, while Chanel and Alaïa showed the shapely redingote.

The precisionists Alaïa, Zoran and Karan concentrated on neutral tones, such as Alaïa's sombre and provocative prune, grape and black, while the exhibitionists, romantics and Surrealists flaunted high colour and high drama. Jewelled reds, purples and oranges were seen in London at Patricia Lester, Dean Bright, Crolla, Richard Ostell and Ellis Flyte, fondant brocades at Culture Shock, watery silks at Commes des Garçons, and Klimt-inspired, psychedelic colours at Pam Hogg.

The long-forgotten house of Patou was revived by Christian Lacroix. Having worked as a freelance designer for some years, he joined the house in 1982, creating collections influenced by *Dallas* and *Dynasty*. This year's Carmen and *toreador* theme won universal acclaim.

Mme Grès, the greatest living couturier, offered her draped, Grecian-style gowns to the Americans in a prêt-à-porter range. For the first time many of her admirers could afford her expert cut and gentle femininity.

Rifat Ozbek, an architect by training, opened in London.

15   16   17

13. *Alaïa's white silk crêpe body dress, bias-cut and seamed to fall in descending pleats, with Cobra & Bellamy's silver jewellery. 14. Oscar de la Renta's quilted silk jacket with gold paisley-patterned embroidery and worn with gold-fringed gloves. 15. Comme des Garçons's tomato/rose rayon dress with looping panel dividing the legs, and Butler and Wilson's silver spiralled pearl earrings. Liberty's silver armlet. 16. Kamali's stretch jersey wrapped and tied about the body to make a dress. 17. Hamnett's white cotton bustle skirt ruched into a zip.*

1986

Flaunt was the message from the collections, be it your figure or your money. Body-skimming T-shirt dresses in plain matt materials emphasized a well-toned body. Nothing was to detract from its curves. Georgina Godley used gossamer-thin, clinging, white cotton-jersey inset with organza panels for maximum body revelation.

High heels drew attention to legs, which were flaunted under puff-ball and tutu hemlines by night at Ungaro, Chanel and Anthony Price. Christian Lacroix at Patou placed taffeta bustles

on strapless velvet evening gowns and showed short umbrella-shaped skirts with wired hems held out by a *mille-feuilles* of net petticoats. Empire waist-lines, A-line silhouettes and baby-doll sophistication were all promoted by this designer. Similarly at Chanel, Lagerfeld showed what he called 'powder-puff' skirts held out with net petticoats, and knee-length crinolines swinging like bells – inspired by Vivienne Westwoods's revival of the crinoline in 1985.

The most important source of inspiration for this year's silhouettes was Cristobal Balenciaga. The first major posthumous exhibition of his work, at the Musée des Tissus in Lyons, resulted in revivals of his short sack dress, billowing faille cape, puff-ball skirt, all proclaiming majestic drapery and architectural proportion. Ungaro, his pupil, was the chief exponent, and

3   **4**

1. Chanel's tutu: black silk organza pleats over frilly tulle petticoats.
2. Georgina Godley's soft, white cotton body dress with a sheer organdie panel running from the nape to the small of the back. Stillettos by Alaïa. 3. Romeo Gigli's simple separates: long black silk skirt, gathered at the waistband, and off-the-shoulder cotton jersey T-shirt with elongated sleeves. 4. John Rocha's black silk looped shift and mortarboard.

2

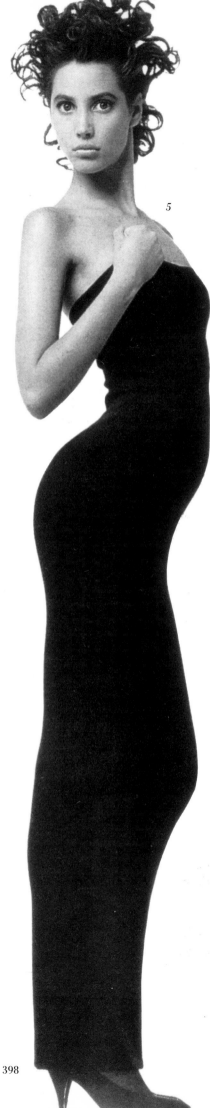

5

entitled his collection *'Hommage à Balenciaga'*. This revival complemented the mood for couture grandeur.

A new wealth and conservatism led to status dressing and hence a boom for the *grandes maisons*: sales, attendance and coverage continued to rise. As the ready-to-wear became more expensive, haute couture seemed more accessible to younger women – the average age of the clientele was between twenty-five and thirty-five, and almost half were Americans. Christian Lacroix at Patou, Eric Bergère at Hermès, and Karl Lagerfeld at Chanel particularly appealed to this market.

Chanel almost parodied status dressing, but many took it seriously, sporting quilted leather Chanel handbags (or Prada copies), large gilt *CC* (the insignia of the house) ear-rings and mini-skirts hung with chains and quilted like the handbags. Fifth Avenue, Bond Street and the Fauborg Saint Honoré clanked with women working the gilt-chain gang.

Hermès benefited from the revival of status dressing. Grace Kelly twinsets, silk snaffle scarves and over-sized Kelly bags, at £1,000 a time (only a few years before Hermès could not sell a single one), were endorsed by American *Vogue*, which sang the praises of the 'sensitively coloured', good-quality cashmere twinset. 'Why this pastoral armour-plating for the city looks so right now is because it works quietly against the

6

chaos, implying an implacable sense of style and giving a new establishment class values and securities against neurotic label dressing.' Ralph Lauren, Calvin Klein and Donna Karan were the chief propagandists of this look in New York, while Hacketts in London offered second-hand top-quality clothes for the 'young fogies'.

In contrast to the bold, structured grandeur by night and the short, tight, tailored look by day of most houses, Romeo Gigli in Milan and Rifat Ozbek in London based their collections on sensuous, gentle dance clothes. Gigli offered unstructured clothes in

5. *Saint Laurent's bare black silk jersey strapless tube, split thigh to ankle, and black satin court shoes.* 6. *Balenciaga retrospective in Lyon inspired many collections featuring his* bulle *shape of winter 1956.* 7. *Galliano's empire-line cheesecloth evening dress.* 8. *Mary McFadden's Fortuny-inspired evening dress.* 9. *Edelstein's silk shantung jacket with deep jeplum over silk fan-tailed skirt.*

7   8   9

10

12

11

10. *Ungaro's homage to Balenciaga: double-layered bouffant black silk moiré cape billowing over a classic white silk satin sheath.* 11. *West-wood's black satin and white organza crinoline skirt and blouse.* 12. *Martine Sitbon's crêpe satin bulle dress.*

diaphanous or plain, matt fabrics, which skimmed the figure. He chose the Empire waistline, bare shoulders, a neat, sometimes wrapped corsage, and long slim sleeves reaching over the fingertips. Grace Coddington of British *Vogue* admired his work: 'Gigli has dispensed with shoulder pads and still made the proportions work. His clothes are about the body ... a younger body', recalling the classical virtues of a Canova marble. Ozbek used *La Dolce Vita* as the theme of his spring collection and the dance in the autumn. He offered the doublet and hose of the male dancer and Martha Graham-inspired, bias-cut plain dresses; each piece could be worn with any other.

Dance prevailed at Alaïa, who presented rippling little skating skirts, tight principal-boy jackets, leotards and tango dresses, while Kamali showed bias-cut drop-waisted jersey dance skirts and dresses. Karan continued to promote the body suit as the fulcrum of her wardrobe. All these designers were proclaiming the modern, mobile figure.

13 14

David Cameron showed his first collection in New York, which *Vogue* entitled 'tarte nouveau'. Like Ozbek's, it recalled Capri of the fifties, with ankle-length pants and striped T-shirts, and the Bardot of Saint Tropez. Sex and spice were what he wanted to administer to the wardrobe of the young. The predictable inclusions were the black leather mini, hoop ear-rings and the off-the-shoulder top. A similar sexy casualness was offered by Jasper Conran this autumn in his collection of strictly cropped jackets over short, bell skirts and bare-midriff tops inspired by Claire McCardell.

Alastair Blair also showed his first collection in London. It embodied the quality of continental couture. He had trained at Dior, Givenchy and Lagerfeld, and was given financial backing by Peder Bertelsen of Aguecheek. In one stylish blow he countered the notion that British design was only good for 'unwearable' fun clothes. He and Edelstein were the couture arrows that the British could now fire back at the French with confidence. Other young designers continued to present witty yet marketable collections – for example, Culture Shock's classics with a twist, Workers For Freedom's riding clothes, Richmond/Cornejo's flannels and Jean-Paul Gaultier's wrinkled puff balls worn with 'bovver' boots.

13. Rifat Ozbeks's principal boy's dance clothing, velvet doublet and hose.   14. Jasper Conran's white linen wide-legged trousers and shirt. 15. Natural Canadian golden-sable jacket with wide turned-back sleeves over black leggings.   16. Donna Karen's soft modern layer-dressing in greige and dark brown: long sleeves, wrapped cashmere body, short fitted wool jersey skirt and short wool cascade coat, cashmere turban and gloves. Gold-plated silver-clip earrings by Robert Lee Morris/Artwear for Donna Karan.   17. Hermès's classic blue-and-white suit, silk scarf and leather gloves, worn with Dr Martin's.   18. Jean Muir's leopard-printed silk faille suit with a curved jacket and leg-of-mutton sleeves over a straight skirt. 19. Working Women. Left: Hermès's giant-sized Kelly-bag and Jean-Paul Gaultier's balloon/kilt skirt and fitted jacket. Right: Henry's crocodile stamped clutch-bag and black-and-burgundy suit by Jean-Paul Gaultier.

15   16   17   18

CREDITS

In the early years of *Vogue*, illustrators were mainly anonymous. It was only after Condé Nast attracted to work for the magazine well-known photographers from outside, such as de Meyer and Steichen, that the name of the artist or photographer began to appear next to the picture. The process was a gradual one, and this accounts for some unavoidable omissions in this list of credits. In later years the occasional missing credit is the result of editorial oversight.

1909–1918
Introduction: *p. 2 (top)* courtesy of Anouska Hempel and Colnaghi, London; *p. 4 Wassiliev; p. 5 (top)* Augustus John, *(bottom left)* Welch; *p. 6 (top)* Jean Cocteau, *(centre)* Raoul Dufy, *(bottom)* Marcel Duchamp; *p. 7 (bottom)* Culver; *p. 8 (bottom)* de Meyer.
1909
10 Banks; *11* Mulligan; *14, 15* Felix.
1910
1 Tighe; *2* Bailey; *3* Felix; *5* Dryden.
1911
1 Dryden; *7* Manny.
1913
2, 6 Geisler and Baumann; *15* Manny.
1914
15 Davis and Sanford.
1915
1 Hill; *5* Reutlinger; *6* Ortiz; *11* Wanamaker; *12* Dryden; *13* Hill; *16* White.
1916
2, 16 Boissonnas Taponier; *4, 6, 11* Hill; *13* Aries.
1917
1 Fall; *6* Walery; *7* Hill; *11* Calosso.
1918
1 de Meyer; *8* Fairchild; *10, 12* de Meyer; *15* Dryden.

1919–1925
Introduction: *p. 48* Beaton; *p. 49 (top)* Park, *(bottom)* Benito *p. 50* Launx; *p. 14 (bottom)* Fish; *p. 52 (bottom)* Covarrubias; *p. 53 (top)* Fish; *p. 54 (top)* Steichen; *p. 55 (right)* Ronnebeck.
1920
9 Oliver; *11* de Meyer; *13* Dryden; *16* de Meyer.
1921
1 Manuel; *2* Woodruff; *5* Genthe; *6* Reville Studios; *9* Simon; *12* Mackinnon; *16* Pollard; *18* Rehbinder; *19* de Meyer.
1922
1, 4, 5 Rehbinder; *8* Locher; *12, 13, 14* Rehbinder; *15* Muray.
1923
2 Lee Creelman Erickson; *7* Woodruff; *8* Rehbinder; *9* Marty; *10* Pollard; *11* Muray.
1924
1 Francis; *4* Steichen; *8* Rehbinder; *9* Steichen; *10* Lee Creelman Erickson; *11* Pollard; *12* Beck and Macgregor; *13* Steichen; *14* Beck and Macgregor; *15* Lee

Creelman Erickson; *16* Woodruff; *17* Rehbinder.
1925
1 Benito; *2* Steichen; *3* Lin; *5* Lee Creelman Erickson; *6* Brissaud; *7, 8* Steichen; *10* Lee Creelman Erickson; *11* Woodruff; *13* Lee Creelman Erickson; *14* Benito; *15* Steichen; *16* Lee Creelman Erickson; *17* W. E. Murphy.

1926–1933
Introduction: *p. 84 (top)* Beaton, *(bottom)* Steichen; *p. 85 (top)* Hoyningen-Huené, *(centre)* Cameragrams, *(bottom)* Steichen; *p. 86 (bottom)* Hoyningen-Huené; *p. 87* Edward Wolfe; *p. 88 (left)* Hoyningen-Huené; *p. 89 (left)* Eric, *(centre and right)* Cross.
1926
1 Steichen; *2* Sheeler; *3* Man Ray; *5* Woodruff; *6* Beck and Macgregor; *8* Pollard; *9, 10* Steichen; *11* Francis; *15* Pollard; *16* Meserole; *17* Beck and Macgregor; *18* Steichen.
1927
1 Lee Creelman Erickson; *2* Beck and Macgregor; *3* Hoyningen-Huené; *4* Cecil; *5* Steichen; *11, 13* Beck and Macgregor.
1928
1 Hoyningen-Huené; *2* Steichen; *3* Hoyningen-Huené; *4* Lee Creelman Erickson; *5* Hoyningen-Huené; *6* Pollard; *7, 8* Hoyningen-Huené; *9* Pollard; *10, 11, 12* Steichen; *13, 14, 15* Hoyningen-Huené; *16* Steichen; *17* Francis.
1929
1 Hoyningen-Huené; *2, 3* Eric; *4, 5* Steichen; *6* Beaton; *7* Hoyningen-Huené; *8* Steichen; *9* Pollard; *10* Steichen; *11* Hoyningen-Huené; *12* Steichen; *13, 14* Hoyningen-Huené; *15* Steichen; *16* Beaton; *17* Steichen; *18* Hoyningen-Huené.
1930
1 Beaton; *2* Steichen; *3* Hoedt Studios; *4, 5* Steichen; *6, 8, 10, 11, 12, 14, 15, 17, 18* Hoyningen-Huené.
1931
1, 2, 3 Hoyningen-Huené; *4* Pollard; *5* Beaton; *6* Wildman; *7* Bolin; *8* Eric; *9* Beaton; *10* Steichen; *12*

Hoyningen-Huené; *14* Beaton; *15* Hoyningen-Huené; *16* Steichen; *17* Pollard; *18* Benito.
1932
2 Pollard; *3* Mourgue; *4* Hoyningen-Huené; *5* Steichen; *7* Hoyningen-Huené; *8* Tabard; *9* Beaton; *10* Studio Sun; *11* Beaton; *12* Steichen; *13* Hoyningen-Huené; *14* Beaton; *15, 16* Hoyningen-Huené.
1933
1, 2 Hoyningen-Huené; *3* Eric; *5, 6, 7, 9, 10* Hoyningen-Huené; *12* Eric; *14* Hoyningen-Huené; *15* Eric; *16, 17* Steichen; *18* Hoyningen-Huené.

1934–1945
Introduction: *p. 122 (top)* Salvador Dali, *(centre)* Fischer, *(bottom)* Horst; *p. 123 (top)* Musée de l'Homme, *(centre)* William Roberts, *(bottom)* Melisse; *p. 124 (left)* Miller, *(right)* Gray; *p. 125 (bottom right)* Brassaï; *p. 126 (top)* Steichen, *(bottom)* Frissell; *p. 127 (top)* Miller, *(centre)* Hofman; *p. 128 (top)* Rawlings, *(centre and bottom)* Frissell; *p. 129 (bottom)* Selberger.
1934
1 Eric; *2* Hoyningen-Huené; *3* Mourgue; *4* Willaumez; *5* Hoyningen-Huené; *6, 7* Eric; *8* Willaumez; *9* Hoyningen-Huené; *10* Horst; *11* Eric; *12* Steichen; *13, 14* Hoyningen-Huené; *17* Willaumez; *18* Steichen; *19* Hoyningen-Huené.
1935
1 Eric; *2* Horst; *3* Horst; *4* Vogue Studio; *5* Horst; *6* Schall; *7* Eric; *8* Schall; *9* Kitrosser; *10, 11* Schall; *12* Horst; *13* Eric; *14* Horst; *15* Hoyningen-Huené; *16* Eric; *17* Horst; *18* Willaumez; *19* Horst.
1936
1 Beaton; *2* Durst; *3* Horst; *4* Durst; *5* Beaton; *6* Bérard; *7* Eric; *8* Schall; *9* Vogue Studio; *10* Durst; *11* Beaton; *12* Horst; *13* Eric; *15* Horst; *16* Mourgue; *17* Horst; *18* Beaton.
1937
1 Beaton; *2* Durst; *3* Molyneux; *4* Grafstrom; *5* Parkinson; *6, 7* Nelson; *9, 10* Horst; *11* Willaumez; *13* Beaton; *14* Horst; *15* Nelson; *16* Horst; *17* Frissell.
1938
1 Bérard; *2* Horst; *3* Beaton;

4 Horst; *5* Durst; *6* Horst; *7* Rawlings; *8* Eric; *9, 10, 11* Horst; *12* Durst; *13* Willaumez; *14* Vogue Studio; *15* Rawlings; *16* Brassai; *17* Vogue Studio.
1939
1 Nepo; *2* Rawlings; *4* Horst; *5* de Dienes; *6* Horst; *7* Frissell; *8, 9* Horst; *11* Willaumez; *12* Eric; *13* Nepo; *15* Schall; *16* Rawlings; *17* Schall.
1940
1 Willaumez; *3, 4* Durst; *5* Miller; *6* Karger-Pix; *7* Miller; *8* Lemus; *10* Rawlings; *11* Horst; *12* Durst; *13, 14* Horst; *15, 16* Rawlings.
1941
1 Rawlings; *2, 3* Miller; *4* Frissell; *5* Beaton; *6* Horst; *7* Willaumez; *8* Rawlings; *9* Beaton; *10* Horst; *11* Miller; *12* Rawlings; *13* Eric; *14* Rawlings; *15, 16* Beaton; *17* Rawlings.
1942
1 Beaton; *2* Frissell; *4, 5* Horst; *6* Frissell; *7* Leen; *8* Beaton; *9* Rawlings; *10* Frissell; *11, 12* Miller; *13* Rawlings; *14* Miller; *15, 17* Rawlings; *18* Glass; *19* Rawlings.
1943
1 Frissell; *2* Willaumez; *4* Miller; *5* Rawlings; *6* Parkinson; *7* Rawlings; *8* Horst; *9* Parkinson; *10* Balkin; *11* Horst; *12* Eric; *13, 14* Rawlings; *15* Balkin; *16* Horst; *17* Willaumez; *18* Miller; *19* Parkinson.
1944
1 Bell; *2* Frissell; *3* Blossac; *4* Parkinson; *5* Bérard; *6* Beaton; *7* Blossac; *8* Penn; *9* Parkinson; *10* Blossac; *11* Miller; *12* Penn; *13* Rawlings; *14* Miller; *15* Bérard; *16* Willaumez; *17, 18* Rawlings.
1945
1 Bell; *2* Rawlings; *3* Balkin; *4* Bell; *5* Descombes; *6* Blossac; *7* Paschkoff; *8* Blumenfeld; *9* Bouché; *10* Beaton; *11* Miller; *12* Blumenfeld; *13* Beaton; *14* Rawlings; *15, 16, 17* Beaton.

1946–1956
Introduction: *p. 180 (top)* Lilla de Nobili, *(bottom)* Beaton; *p. 181 (top)* Erwitt, *(centre)* Coffin, *(bottom)* Beaton; *p. 182 (top)* Eric, *(bottom)* courtesy of **Paris Match**; *p. 183 (top)* Rutledge, *(bottom)* Beaton; *p. 184 (top)*

Beaton, *(bottom)* courtesy of **Paris Match**; *p. 185 (top)* Cunningham, *(bottom)* Beaton; *p. 186 (top)* Horst, *(centre)* Coffin, *(bottom)* Leombruno-Bodi; *p. 187 (top)* Vernier, *(centre)* courtesy of the Prado, Madrid, *(bottom)* courtesy of the Musée des Beaux-Arts, Lyon; *p. 188 (top)* Parkinson, *(centre)* Cartier-Bresson, *(bottom)* Horst; *p. 189* Horst.
1947
1 Balkin; *2* Blumenfeld; *3* Balkin; *4* Coffin; *5, 6, 7* Balkin; *8* Penn; *9* Rutledge; *10* Horst; *11* Balkin; *12, 13* Coffin; *14* Beaton; *15* Balkin; *16* Platt-Lynes; *17, 18* Eric; *19* Rutledge; *20* Horst; *21* Rutledge.
1948
1, 2, 3 Coffin; *4* Nepo; *5* Coffin; *6* Parkinson; *7, 8* Coffin; *9* Parkinson; *10, 11* Beaton; *12, 13, 14* Coffin; *15* Eric; *16, 17* Beaton; *18* Coffin.
1949
1 Dali; *2* Horst; *3* Rutledge; *4* Horst; *6* Bouché; *8* Horst; *9* Munkacsi; *10* Horst; *11* Bouché; *12* Penn; *13* Parkinson; *14* Nepo; *15* Rawlings; *16* Bouché; *17* McLaughlin-Gill.
1950
1 Penn; *2* Rawlings; *3* Parkinson; *4* Horst; *5, 6* Penn; *7* Parkinson; *8* Blumenfeld; *9, 10* Penn; *11* Bouché; *12* Horst; *13* Parkinson; *14* Honeyman; *15, 16* Penn; *17* Honeyman; *18* Bouché; *19, 20* Penn; *21* Parkinson.
1951
1, 2 Rawlings; *3* Penn; *4* Rawlings; *5* Coffin; *6* Beaton; *7* Rawlings; *8* McLaughlin-Gill; *9* Penn; *10* Honeyman; *11* Clarke; *12, 13* Rawlings; *14* Clarke; *15* McLaughlin-Gill; *16* Clarke; *17* McLaughlin-Gill; *18, 19* Clarke; *20* Rawlings.
1952
1 Parkinson; *2, 3* Horst; *4* McLaughlin-Gill; *5* Coffin; *6* McLaughlin-Gill; *7* Clarke; *8* Horst; *9* McLaughlin-Gill; *10* Horst; *11* Clarke; *12* Blumenfeld; *13* Parkinson; *14, 15* Clarke; *16* Croner; *17* Deakin; *18* McLaughlin-Gill; *19* Denney.
1953
1 Rawlings; *2, 3, 4* Clarke; *5* McLaughlin-Gill; *6* Clarke; *7* Randall; *8* Deakin; *9* Parkinson; *10* Rawlings; *11*

Matthews; *12* Rawlings; *13* Parkinson; *14* Rawlings; *15* Clarke; *16, 17, 18* Rawlings; *19* Deakin; *20* Randall; *21* Parkinson; *22* Randall.
1954
1 Clarke; *2* Vernier; *3* Clarke; *4* McLaughlin-Gill; *5* Clarke; *6* Eric; *7* Parkinson; *8* Stemp; *9* Rutledge; *10* Radkai; *11, 12, 13* Clarke; *14* Coffin; *15* Clarke; *16* Sadovy; *17* Rutledge; *18* Clarke; *19* Rutledge.
1955
1 Gruau; *2* Clarke; *3* Weiss; *4* Clarke; *5* Prigent; *6* Clarke; *7* Parkinson; *8* Clarke; *9* Parkinson; *10* Penn; *11* Clarke; *12* Bouché; *13* Clarke; *14* Penn; *15* Vernier; *16, 17* Radkai; *18* Gruau; *19* Rawlings; *20* Gruau.
1956
1 Klein; *2* Clarke; *3* McLaughlin-Gill; *4* Parkinson; *5* Vernier; *6* Clarke; *7* Bouret; *8* Horst; *9* Silverstein; *10* Vernier; *11* Silverstein; *12* Hammarskiöld; *13* Clarke; *14* McLaughlin-Gill; *15* Rutledge; *16* Hammarskiöld; *17* Stemp; *18, 19, 20* Clarke; *21* Bourdin; *22* Clarke.

1957–1967
Introduction: *p. 238 (top)* Roy Lichtenstein, courtesy of the Tate Gallery, London, *(centre)* Mayne; *p. 239 (bottom)* Bailey; *p. 240 (top)* Bridget Riley, *(bottom)* Laurie; *p. 241 (top)* Cowan, *(centre, upper and lower)* Laurie; *p. 242 (top)* Duffy, *(centre, upper)* Penn, *(centre lower)* Moon; *p. 243 (top)* Fresson, *(centre)* Sellerio, *(bottom)* Kammermann-Delmas; *p. 244 (top)* Donovan; *p. 245 (top)* Pagnini, *(bottom)* Traeger.
1957
1 Klein; *2, 3* Clarke; *4* Klein; *5* Clarke; *6* Rutledge; *7* Clarke; *8* Klein; *9* Clarke; *10* Klein; *11* Clarke; *12* Bouché; *13* Penn; *14* Bouret; *15* Parkinson; *16* Klein; *17* Penn; *18* Weiss; *19* Klein.
1958
1 Parkinson; *2, 3* Klein; *4* Bouret; *5* Klein; *6, 7* Schatzberg; *8, 9* Clarke; *10* Penn; *11* Forlano; *12, 13* Clarke; *14* Klein; *15* Parkinson; *16* Clarke; *17* Vernier; *18, 19* Clarke; *20* Bourdin.
1959
1 Armstrong-Jones; *2* Horst;

3 Forlano; *4* Gawronska; *5* Penn; *6* Clarke; *7* Penn; *8, 9* Clarke; *10* Rizzo; *11* Stemp; *12* Penn; *13* Ostier; *14* Stemp; *15* Palumbo; *16* Horst; *17* Gawronska; *18* Parkinson; *19, 20* Clarke; *21* Gawronska; *22* Clarke.
1960
1, 2 Penn; *3* Klein; *4* Virgin; *5* Leombruno-Bodi; *6* Klein; *7* Horvat; *8* Rizzo; *9, 10* Clarke; *11* Duffy; *12* Stern; *13* Duffy; *14* Penn; *15* Rizzo; *16* Penn; *17* Rizzo; *18* Duffy; *19* McLaughlin-Gill; *20* Leombruno-Bodi; *21* Duffy.
1961
1 Penn; *2* Clarke; *3* Duffy; *4, 5* Penn; *6* Klein; *7* Horvat; *8* Bailey; *9* Vernier; *10* Penn; *11* Honeyman; *12* Draz; *13* Penn; *14* Puhlmann; *15* Klein; *16* Penn; *17* Klein; *19* Pascal.
1962
2, 3 Penn; *4, 5* Duffy; *6* Penn; *7* Faurer; *8* Klein; *9* Penn; *10* Klein; *11* Faurer; *12* Penn; *13* Radkai; *14* Bailey; *15* Clarke; *17* Rand.
1963
1 Penn; *2* Bailey; *3* Rand; *4* Pascal; *5* Bailey; *6* Carapetian; *7* Klein; *8* Radkai; *9* Penn; *10, 11* Stern; *12* Penn; *13* Laurents; *14* Penn; *15* Stern; *16* Klein; *17* Stern; *18* Penn; *19* Rand; *20* Donovan; *21* Bailey; *22* Klein; *23* Penn; *24* Duffy; *25, 26* Penn.
1964
1, 2 Bailey; *3* Klein; *4, 5, 6, 7* Bailey; *8* Penn; *9* Bailey; *10* Penn; *11* Klein; *12* Bailey; *13* Klein; *14* Bailey; *15* Newton; *16, 17* Bailey; *18* Penn; *19* Stern; *20* Penn.
1965
1 Stern; *2, 3, 4* Penn; *5* Clarke; *6* Bailey; *7* Penn; *8* Bailey; *9* Moser; *10, 11* Penn; *12, 13, 14, 15* Bailey; *16* Parkinson; *17, 18* Penn.
1966
1 Traeger; *2* Rubartelli; *4* Montgomery; *5* Bailey; *6, 7* Bourdin; *8* Penn; *9, 10* Bourdin; *11* Bailey; *12, 13* Traeger; *15* Bailey; *16* Milinaire; *17* Penn; *18* Leiter; *19* Montgomery; *20* Sieff; *21* Bourdin; *22* Parkinson; *24* Bailey; *25* Hispard; *26* Newton.
1967
1 Bailey; *2* Waldeck; *4* Parkinson; *5* Sieff; *6* Jaeckin; *7* Stern; *8* Bailey; *9* Bourdin; *10, 11* Stern; *12* Clarke; *13* Bailey; *14* Traeger; *15* Newton; *16*

Stern; *17* Traeger; *18* Penn.

1968–1975
Introduction: *p. 296 (top)* Bailey, *(centre)* Horst, *(bottom)* Parkinson; *p. 297 (centre, upper)* Freer, *(centre, lower)* Sieff; *p. 298 (top)* Snowdon, *(centre)* Lategan; *p. 299 (top)* Bailey, *(centre)* Turbeville, *(bottom)* Catalano; *p. 300* Turbeville; *p. 301 (top)* Viviani, *(bottom)* Bailey; *p. 302 (top)* Penn; *p. 303 (centre)* Newton, *(bottom)* Parkinson; *p. 304 (top)* Grignaschi; *p. 305 (centre)* Grignaschi, *(bottom)* Arnaud.
1968
1, 2 Bailey; *3* Jaeckin; *4* Feurer; *5* Newton; *6* Clarke; *7* Stern; *8* Newton; *9* Bailey; *10* Penn; *11* Bailey; *12* Lategan; *13* Bailey; *14* Sieff; *15* Green; *16* Rubartelli; *17* Traeger; *18* Stern; *19* Montgomery; *20* Sieff; *21* Peccinotti.
1969
1 de Villeneuve; *2, 3* Penn; *4* Norvick; *5* Montgomery; *6* Lategan; *7* Cowan; *8, 9* Lategan; *10* Bailey; *11* Bourdin; *12* Parkinson; *13* Clarke; *14* Arrowsmith; *15* Penati; *16* Arrowsmith; *17* Bourdin; *18* Stern; *19* Bourdin; *20, 21* Bailey; *23* Lichfield; *24* Robinson.
1970
1 Bugat; *2, 3* Bourdin; *4* Penn; *6* Lategan; *7* Clarke; *8* Penati; *9, 10* Lategan; *11, 12, 13* Arrowsmith; *14* Lategan; *15, 16* Sieff; *17* Lategan; *18* Arrowsmith; *19* Bourdin.
1971
1 Arrowsmith; *2, 3* Lategan; *4* Bourdin; *5* Stern; *6, 7* Arrowsmith; *8* Jonvelle; *9* Carrara; *10, 11* Lategan; *12* Elgort; *13* Lichfield; *14* Knapp; *15, 16* Arrowsmith; *17* Toscani; *18* Arrowsmith; *19* Maxwell; *20* Rizzo; *21* Bourdin; *22* Bailey.
1972
1 Bourdin; *2* Michals; *3* Arrowsmith; *4* Chatelain; *5* Sacha; *6* Elgort; *7* Arrowsmith; *8* Barbieri; *9* Bailey; *10* Bourdin; *11* Bugat; *12* Penati; *13* Barbieri; *14* Bourdin; *16, 17* Bourdin; *18* Lategan; *19* Toscani; *20* Clarke; *21* Lategan.
1973
1 Barbieri; *2* Cunningham; *4* Toscani; *5* Bailey; *6* Kent; *7* Imrie; *8, 9,* Bailey; *10* Barbieri; *11* Norvick; *12*

Parkinson; *13* Cunningham; *14* Montgomery; *15* Laurence; *16* Montgomery; *17* Laurence; *18* de Villeneuve; *19* Antonio; *20* Toscani.
1974
1 Lartigue; *2* Bourdin; *3* Bourdin; *4* Stupakoff; *5* Parkinson; *6* Bourdin; *7* Elgort; *8* Parkinson; *9* von Wangenheim; *10* Elgort; *11* Scavullo; *12* Barbieri; *13* Bourdin; *14* Clarke; *15* Knapp; *16* Lategan; *17* Chatelain; *18* Barbieri; *19* von Wangenheim; *20* Bailey; *21* Scavullo; *22* Barbieri.
1975
1 Lamy; *3* Bailey; *4* Michals; *6* Toscani; *7* Elgort; *8* Donovan; *9* Bournell; *10* Parkinson; *11* Turbeville; *12* von Wangenheim; *13* Newton; *14* Lategan; *15* Newton; *16* Turbeville; *17* Newton; *18* Montgomery; *19* Parkinson; *20* Rose; *21* Bailey; *22, 23* Toscani.

1976–1986
Introduction: *p. 342* Lindbergh; *p. 343 (top)* Jouanneau, *(bottom)* Beaton; *p. 344 (top)* Mouse, *(centre, upper)* Knight, *(bottom)* Elgort; *p. 346 (top)* Bensimon, *(bottom)* Leibowitz; *p. 347 (bottom)* Lowit; *p. 348 (top, and centre)* Weber, *(bottom)* Post; *p. 349* Warwick; *p. 350 (top)* Stern, *(centre)* Versace, *(bottom)* Pagnini; *p. 351 (top)* Demarchelier, *(centre)* Feurer.
1976
1 Feurer; *2* Bailey; *3* Feurer; *4* Bailey; *5* Boman; *7* Reinhardt; *8* Elgort; *9* Dorrance; *10* Lategan; *11* Reinhardt; *12* Bailey; *13* Duc; *14, 15* Lategan; *16* Bourdin; *17* Barbieri; *18, 19* Lategan.
1977
1 Rozsa; *2* Bourdin; *3* Clarke; *4* Schmid; *5* Boman; *6* Moon; *8* Bourdin; *9* Schmid; *10* Boman; *11* Bailey; *12* Boman.
1978
1 Elgort; *2* Boyd; *3* Elgort; *4* Horst; *6* Elgort; *7* Reinhardt; *8* Bourdin; *9* Bersell; *10, 11* Watson; *12* Grignaschi; *13* Elgort; *14* Bourdin; *15* Reinhardt; *16* Horst; *17* Elgort; *18, 19* Horvat.
1979
1 Watson; *2* Elgort; *3* Bailey;

4 Horst; *5* Piel; *6* Carrara; *7* Reinhardt; *8, 9, 10* Elgort; *11* Gray; *12* Gaffney; *13* Horst; *14* Elgort; *15* Boman; *16* Bailey; *17* Lategan; *18* Chatelain; *19* Wickrath; *20* Bourdin; *21* Lategan; *22* Reinhardt; *23* Boman; *24* Elgort; *25* Feurer; *26* Clarke.
1980
1 Grignaschi; *2* Lategan; *3, 4* Demarchelier; *5* Elgort; *6* Carrara; *7* Lategan; *8* Penn; *9* Jouanneau; *10* Elgort; *11* Weber; *12* Grignaschi; *13* Watson; *14, 15* Carrara; *16* Chatelain; *17* Lategan; *18* Elgort; *19* Piel; *20* Elgort.
1981
1 Weber; *2* Antonio; *3, 4* Ellis; *5* Piel; *6, 7* Lategan; *8* Elgort; *9* von Wangenheim; *10* Horst; *11* Hurrell; *12* Weber; *13* Grignaschi; *14* Lategan; *15* Scavullo; *16* Arnaud; *17* Lindbergh; *18* Elgort; *19* Piel; *20, 21* Elgort.
1982
1 Lindbergh; *2* Zoltan; *3* Weber; *4* Lamy; *5* Moyse; *6* Arnaud; *7* Lategan; *8* Donovan; *9* Lategan; *10, 11, 12* Arnaud; *13* Watson; *14* Elgort; *15* Weber; *16* Jouanneau; *17* Meisel; *18* Bourdin; *19* Horst; *20, 21* Weber; *22* Donovan; *23* Parkinson; *24* Bourdin.
1983
1 Meisel; *2* Lowit; *3* Meisel; *4* Penn; *5* Arnaud; *6* Weber; *7* Demarchelier; *8* Viramontes; *9* Donovan; *10* Hurrell; *11* Turbeville; *12* Demarchelier; *13, 14* Hurrell; *15* Newton.
1984
1 Meisel; *2* Salvatore; *3, 4* Watson; *5* Elgort; *6* Chatelain; *7* Lange; *8* Grignaschi; *9* Donovan; *10* Meisel; *11* Horst; *12* Demarchelier; *13* Watson; *14* Hurrell; *15* Lange; *16* Bourdin; *17* Jouanneau.
1985
1 Roversi; *2* Knott; *3* Lindbergh; *4* Roversi; *5, 6* Knott; *7* Watson; *8* Ritts; *9* Vallhonrat; *10* Chatelain; *11* Metzner; *12* Chatelain; *13* Demarchelier; *14* Metzner; *15* Demarchelier; *16* Varriale; *17* Feurer.
1986
1 Feurer; *2* Chatelain; *3* Puhlmann; *4* Chatelain; *5* Meisel; *6* Anderson; *7* Feurer; *8* Meisel; *9* Roversi; *10* Chatelain; *11* Roversi; *12* Meisel; *13* Kohli; *14* Piel; *15* Maser; *16* King; *17* Watson; *18* Demarchelier; *19* Kirk.

INDEX

References in *italics* denote illustrations.

ACKNOWLEDGEMENTS

The back issues of international *Vogue* have been supplemented by many people's valuable memories. I am especially indebted to dedicated, knowledgeable and generous *Vogue* staff, both past and present, particularly Beatrix Miller, Sheila Wetton, Grace Coddington, Drusilla Beyfus, Madge Garland (Lady Ashton), Audrey Withers, Elizabeth Tilberis, Anna Harvey, Christina Probert, Georgina Howell, Marit Allen, Anne Matthews and the late Clare Rendlesham in London; Diana Vreeland, Polly Allen Mellen, Diana Edkins and Cindy Cathcart in New York; Anna Piaggi and Anna Zavka in Milan; and Gabriella Rodriguez and Andrea Aurelli in Rome. Without Susan Train and her assistant Angela Purdon, few of the doors of the Paris couture would have opened so easily.

Everyone I interviewed must be thanked. There are too many to mention by name (over five hundred), but I would like to single out for special acknowledgement Hardy Amies, Zika Ascher, David Bailey, Peter Blake, Roberto Capucci, Denise Dubois, Robert Elms, Jean-Paul Gaultier, Madame Grès, Hubert de Givenchy, Felicity Green, Vere French, Stephen Jones, Calvin Klein, Karl Lagerfeld, Ralph Lauren, Dr David Mellor, Jean Muir, Mary Quant, Percy Savage, Christopher Sweet, Gianni Versace, Vivienne Westwood and Lesley White.

For off-beat questions and a constant information service I must thank my dear friends Ian Irvine, James Birch and David Thomas. I was welcomed time and time again as a house guest by Bernadino Branca and Suzannah Zevi-Visconti in Milan, Lucca Fabbri in Rome and Aroldo Zevi and Anna Acworth in New York.

The Condé Nast library staff – Bunny Cantor, Jane Meekin, Jane Ross, Fiona Shearer and Max Steiger – have been a constant help, as have Lillie Davies, Robin Muir and Elaine Shaw. Relentless support has been given by my assistants, Sara Longworth, Caroline McGivern and Timothy Hyde.

Valerie Mendes's role in this book has been essential; her expertise, selflessness and friendship were invaluable.

Alex Kroll, editor of Condé Nast Books, has contributed the most. His guidance, experience and patience have steered me through this project. Thank you.

Thank you also to Eleo Gordon at Viking, Michael Shaw, my agent, and Neil McKendrick of Gonville and Caius College, Cambridge, who set me on this path.

Finally I would like to thank my family and Christine Blackwell, who have patiently kept me together, body and soul.

J. M.
June 1988